PRIVATE PRACTICES

"HORRIDLY FASCINATING."
—*The Washington Post*

"SENSUAL AND SUSPENSEFUL . . . KEPT ME READING FROM PAGE TO PAGE."
—Gay Talese, author of *Thy Neighbor's Wife*

"AS A NOVEL ABOUT BROTHERS, *PRIVATE PRACTICES* IS THE SORT OF NIGHTMARE ALL BROTHERS HAVE AND WILL DENY. . . . AS A NOVEL ABOUT MEDICINE, IT IS AN ASSAULT ON THE EMOTIONS . . . [WOLFE] IS A SUPERB REPORTER REPORTING EXACTLY WHAT WE DON'T WANT TO HEAR. AS A NOVEL ABOUT SADO-MASOCHISM, IT IS MORE AMBITIOUS . . . AND MORE DISTURBING: IT IS AN ESSAY ON DOMINATION, ON THE EXERCISE AND ABUSE OF POWER. . . . *PRIVATE PRACTICES* HAS . . . RAW NARRATIVE POWER, AN UNFLINCHING EYE, AND AN APPETITE FOR COMPLICATED IDEAS."
—John Leonard, *The New York Times*

"FOR ONCE, A GOOSE-PIMPLY THRILLER THAT DOEN'T RELY ON THE SUPERNATURAL."
—Susan Brownmiller, author of *Against Our Will*

ALSO BY LINDA WOLFE

Playing Around

PRIVATE PRACTICES

Linda Wolfe

A DELL BOOK

Published by
Dell Publishing Co., Inc.
1 Dag Hammarskjold Plaza
New York, New York 10017

Copyright © 1979 by Linda Wolfe

Dell ® TM 681510, Dell Publishing Co., Inc.

ISBN: 0-440-17185-7

Reprinted by arrangement with Simon and Schuster,
a division of Gulf + Western Corporation.

Printed in the United States of America

First Dell printing—April 1981

To Jessica Wolfe and Max Pollack

A brother offended is harder to be won than a strong city: and their contentions are like the bars of a castle.

OLD TESTAMENT, PROVERBS XVIII:19

PRIVATE PRACTICES

CHAPTER ONE

JANUARY

Emily Harper had given up smoking but during her first appointment with Dr. Ben Zauber she couldn't help asking her husband to give her a cigarette. Philip looked reluctant, but he handed her his pack anyway. He knew that new situations made her nervous and that this one was particularly anxiety laden. He knew she didn't want the baby quite as much as he did.

The doctor, leaning forward in his swivel chair, observed in a quiet voice, "Smoking's not a very good idea when you're pregnant," and Emily nodded.

"I know. I'm just going to have this one."

"Good. And now let's talk about your weight. You're a little overweight, aren't you? It would be best for both you and the baby if you changed your eating habits, cut down now, right from the start."

Emily blushed. She had always wanted to be thin and was ashamed of her plumpness. "Of course," she said uncomfortably to Dr. Zauber. "I'll try my best."

Philip, hearing the strain in her voice, put his arm around the back of her chair and his gesture alleviated her embarrassment. Grateful, she reached out and stroked the nape of his neck and felt, as she often did when she touched him, a physical recollection of their lovemaking that leaped like a current from her fingertips to her genitals. She wished she weren't frightened of bearing his child.

Her fears had nothing to do with Philip. He was as loyal, as supportive, a husband and father-to-be as she could have hoped to find. But ever since her internist had reported that her pregnancy test was positive, she had begun dreaming of producing monsters, had awakened sweating from visions of a two-headed kitten wailing to be let out of a refrigerator, and a mascara-lashed infant lying in its pram and rubbing at its eyes with scaly thumbs.

Her dreams had so disconcerted her that she had delayed calling her gynecologist, old Harry Mulenberg, for several agonizing weeks during which she kept wavering between wanting to ask him to give her an abortion and wanting him to act as her obstetrician. And then, when at last she made up her mind to keep the baby, she learned from Mulenberg's office that he had had a stroke and was no longer practicing.

The doctor his office had recommended, Ben Zauber, seemed nice enough, Emily thought, but she couldn't make up her mind if she would ever like him sufficiently to confide in him, to tell him her fears, to seek his help in overcoming them. With Mulenberg, she would have had no trouble. Bombastic yet benign, he had always been able to relax her, brushing aside anxieties with an antiquated joke or a torrent of grandfatherly advice. The new doctor looked straitlaced and reserved.

"Any questions?" he was saying now, his voice so restrained that she had to lean forward to hear him.

Philip said, "Well, there's the main one," and put a comforting hand over Emily's. "Emily wants natural childbirth. Will you honor her wishes? Deliver the baby without anesthesia?"

The obstetrician smiled for the first time since they had been in his office. His smile was tentative, shy. "So that's the main one, is it?" Then he added in his soft-spoken manner, "Yes, of course, provided everything goes naturally."

"Meaning?" Philip asked him.

"Meaning there are no complications. No dangers."

Emily puffed deeply on her cigarette and joined the interrogation. Something even more important than natural childbirth had flashed through her mind. "Well, suppose there were dangers. I mean, for both me and the baby." And then she paused, unable to proceed. She couldn't bring herself to articulate her thought and yet it seemed to her that she had stumbled upon the crux of what worried her most about having a child.

"Yes, Mrs. Harper?" Dr. Zauber asked.

But she felt tongue-tied, superstitious, and afraid that if she asked her question the doctor would consider her an alarmist. Uneasy, she looked away from him, studying his small office, the walls bare except for a meager handful of framed degrees and a single Van Gogh sunflower print.

"You're worried about which one of you I'd choose," he said gently. "Is that it?" he prodded her.

Suddenly Emily turned and met his heavy-lidded greenish brown eyes. "Yes, which would it be?" she blurted out, relieved that he had phrased the question for her.

Dr. Zauber opened his sleepy-looking eyes wide and spoke more emphatically. "It rarely comes to that. But if it did, there'd be no question. You and Mr. Harper here can always make another baby. Harper-to-be can't make another mother."

Reassured, Emily smiled and stubbed out her cigarette. "Thank you," she murmured. Then she added self-consciously, "I guess it was a dumb question."

"Don't be so hard on yourself." Dr. Zauber's

voice had grown quiet again but Emily found that she no longer disliked its monotonic softness. "Obstetricians almost never have to make a choice between a mother and a baby anymore," he went on, "but women always think it's something that happens regularly. You'd be amazed at how often I'm asked that question."

"I guess I'm commonplace then," Emily teased, beginning to feel more relaxed. "I guess I'm just a statistic."

"Not at all. Every pregnant woman is different, presents different challenges. It's just the questions that are the same. Come, let's see your differences." Dr. Zauber had gotten up and Emily noticed how awkward his posture was. Pointing the way to the examining room, he stood with his back hunched, his shoulders stooped.

A nurse was already waiting for Emily inside the examining room and she directed her to the changing cubicle. Emily slipped out of her clothes and into the paper robe left neatly folded on a shelf. Like at the hairdresser's, she thought, and tried to concentrate on the prosaic, for despite herself she was once again tense. She had always disliked being examined.

The nurse didn't help. "Hurry up, Mother," she called out. "The doctor hasn't got all day."

But Dr. Zauber didn't seem at all rushed when he came in and joined them. He took his time, thoughtfully prodding her belly, probing inside her vagina and rectum, exploring her breasts. His touch was gentle and all the while he examined her, he talked to her of trivia, asking her how she liked the heavy snows they'd been having all month and whether she'd seen any good movies lately. He seemed tired, she thought once, and was reminded of how Philip often said nonsense words to her late at night just to keep a connection of sound between them until he drifted off to sleep.

Finally Dr. Zauber told her to sit up. "You're fine," he said. "A little small, but fine."

"How nice to be called small somewhere," she joked.

Dr. Zauber looked puzzled and then a shy smile crossed his lips again. He didn't tell jokes like her old gynecologist, Mulenberg, Emily thought. But he responded to them, seemed to appreciate her efforts at lightness. And he was certainly sensitive. She did like him, she decided, and already some of her fears, now that she had found herself a champion in the lists of childbirth, seemed diminished and defused.

Ben Zauber said goodbye to the Harpers at the door to his office and they left, Philip's arm around Emily's shoulders. Their closeness made him melancholy. As soon as they had disappeared down the corridor toward the waiting room, he shut the door, sat down heavily at his desk, and began toying with the pills he kept always handy in his jacket pocket. Experience had taught him that the acute moods of sadness that so often attacked him could be splendidly vanquished by the pills. At times they made him so deliciously tranquil that he could cease thinking altogether and fall asleep on command.

He adored sleep. Sleep was his seducer, his love. He dreamed about it all day long, planned surprise encounters with it, sudden unexpected meetings, perhaps in the back of a taxicab or in a crowded elevator, or a hasty two-minute grab at it in his office while nurses and patients waited outside, unknowing. Sometimes he felt ashamed of his love affair with sleep; like any secret liaison, it might be judged harshly by the rest of the world. Other people, his colleagues, his patients, his brother Sidney, had more acceptable affairs, had husbands and wives, lovers and mistresses, fiancées, sweethearts, paramours. Ben fondled the pill container, his hand burrowing in his pocket.

And then he caught a glimpse of his watch and felt disappointment invade him. It was only eleven. He had thought it much later. He would have to wait before taking the pill. Just an hour or two, he comforted himself. After lunch he would take his second pill of the day and maybe even have a go at his beloved sleep.

His receptionist Cora was already at the door with his next patient, a woman whose olive-skinned Mediterranean face looked vaguely familiar. "Ben?" the woman said warmly. Cora moved in front of her and handed him her folder. "Ben?" the woman repeated. "Ben Zauber?"

Cora discreetly exited, shutting the office door noiselessly.

"Do I know you?" he asked the new patient, looking up through a haze of drowsiness and seeing plum-colored eyes fixed intently on his. The woman's mouth was wide, her hair an aureole of dark curls. He had seen her before, he was sure, but he couldn't recall who she was.

"It's Naomi," she announced with a shade of disappointment in her voice. "Naomi Golden. From King Street." She sighed and added, "I guess I've changed a lot."

"No, no," he assured her, embarrassed. With the name, he had at last begun to place her. He had known her when he was a teen-ager, back in the days when he and Sidney and their mother had lived in the mock-Tudor apartment house in Brooklyn. Younger than either Sidney or himself, Naomi had nevertheless occasionally attended some of the same parties to which they had been invited, raucous affairs, twenty or thirty boys and girls from the neighborhood crowding into the radio-resonant living room of someone whose parents had unsuspectingly gone out for the evening. He had always felt uncomfortable at these gatherings, particularly when the lights were turned low and the more daring boys and girls withdrew to the far reaches of the apartment, three or four couples to a bedroom. He recalled that Naomi, like his brother, Sidney, had been one of those who frequently braved the bedrooms.

"I'd have known you anywhere," Naomi was saying. He stood, and she came around his desk and embraced him. She was wearing an Indian shirt replete with embroidery and tiny mirrors, and around her shoulders was draped a thickly knitted Mexican sweater. She looked like a walking boutique, he thought critically, and held himself stiffly in her embrace. She had always dressed in a scattered, unconventional fashion, he recalled. In high school, she had been given to leotards and black stockings when all the other girls wore angora sweaters and bobby sox, and once, when he was already in medical school and rarely in the old neighborhood at all, he had run into her getting out of the subway, moccasined and voluminously skirted, her throat ablaze with Navajo turquoise.

Still, he was surprised to see her still dressed in what looked like bohemian garb to him. He had heard from someone, years ago, that Naomi had settled down, become a writer, married a lawyer, had a child.

"I'm proud of you," she was saying now in her husky Brooklyn-accented voice, and waving a hand around his office. "Park Avenue and all."

He had no facility for small talk. Her energy made him feel tired. "I'm proud of you, too," he ventured at last. "I heard you're a writer."

"A journalist," she shrugged. "I work for a news

magazine." Then she plumped herself expansively down in the chair alongside his desk and grinned. "But as Chekhov said, I may be a journalist now, but I don't intend to die one."

He smiled. He appreciated ruefulness and regrets. They were familiar emotions to him.

"Who'd you hear about me from?" Naomi asked, returning his smile. Hers was large and lazy. It spread across her face and lingered long before it faded.

"Charlie Enson. I ran into him once. He's a dentist."

"A dentist! Oh, God." She made a mock-frightened face and clamped her hand over her teeth. Then she giggled. "But I'm glad to hear it. I always wondered what became of him. And whenever I don't hear about someone, I always imagine that something terrible has happened to them. That they've died." She turned and looked around his office, her shoulders twisting, her eyes inquisitive. She seemed to be perpetually in motion, perpetually augmenting her words with gestures and bold glances. "How's your mother?" she asked, fiddling with an antique silver chain that dangled down her chest. "And your brother, Sidney?"

"They're fine. My mother's in Florida. Sidney and I share the practice here."

"I gathered that," she nodded. Then she asked, "You married?"

It was a troubling subject. He shook his head but said nothing in explanation.

"I'm divorced," she offered. "Well, separated. As of a year ago. But the divorce is on its way."

"I'm sorry."

"No need to be sorry," she answered brightly. "It happens to everyone. A sort of reverse initiation."

"I'm doubly innocent then," Ben managed, trying to emulate her bantering tone. "Not divorced. Not even married yet."

She smiled again. "Count your blessings."

"Didn't you like being married?"

"Does anyone?"

To his surprise, he realized that he was enjoying himself. Naomi's patter had a familiar quality, the rhythm of his childhood. His mother and his uncles had often answered questions with questions, praise with ironic deflections of praise. But he couldn't think what to say in reply to Naomi's comment and he found himself wondering whether she had come to see him as a patient or a friend. He needed to know such things. Structure gave him security. Opening Naomi's folder, he asked abruptly, "Well, what can I do for you?"

She looked unhappy, as if she had wanted their exchange of personal information to continue a while longer, but she said, "I need an IUD. A diaphragm's okay when you're married, but when you're separated, it's a little too risky."

He nodded but closed her folder. "Birth control's Sidney's bailiwick. Didn't the nurse tell you when you called for an appointment?"

Naomi twisted her silver chain around her fingers. "Yes, but I said I wanted to see you. I'm afraid I insisted. I remember Sidney from the old days too and I never cared for him. I thought that under the circumstances—"

He shook his head. "You'll have to see Sidney. He handles all the birth control requests. Keeps notes on them for his research."

Naomi's brow furrowed. "I read something in the *Times* about his research. A new birth control pill, wasn't it?"

"It's going to revolutionize birth control as we know it," Ben said proudly. "In its way it's as remarkable a concept as Pincus' pill, Lippes' loop."

"That's exciting. Is it in use anywhere?"

"No. It's still being tested. In the Caribbean."

Naomi shrugged again. "Well, all right. What do I do? Make another appointment?"

He sighed. "I'm afraid so." Then he said hesitantly, wanting to be helpful, "No. Wait a moment. Sidney's here in the office. It's not one of his patient days, but maybe he'll see you anyway."

"I'd be grateful."

"Sit here. I'll step around and see if he's free."

Sidney was poring over a sheaf of typed papers when Ben tapped on his door. His head bent, it looked leonine and massive, aswirl with luxurious light brown waves. Ben's hair, although he was younger than Sidney, had already begun to thin.

In every way there was less of himself than of his brother, he thought wryly. They were the same height, but Sidney weighed a good forty pounds more than he did, and had always been heavier and better built. Sidney had a square face, with a rugged jaw, imposing nose and full, firm lips. He himself had a narrow, elongated face with sculpted hollows in his cheeks, and his nose and lips were thin. Their mother used to call him a tall drink of water.

Comparing himself to Sidney so distracted him that for a moment he forgot why he had sought him out, and when Sidney lifted his eyes from his typescript and said irritably, "What is it?" he couldn't, for a moment, remember. When he did, he hemmed, "Are you very busy? Could you spare a few minutes? Could you do me a favor?" God knew he did enough favors for Sidney to merit a few of his own, he encouraged himself.

"Sure, old buddy," Sidney said, "provided you'll do one for me, too. You remember when I told you about Lippes' tie clasp?"

"Yeah. Gold and shaped like a loop."

Sidney frowned in annoyed remembrance. "He wears it wherever he goes. Everytime I run into him, he's wearing his damn logo."

Ben nodded. He knew Sidney disdained Lippes and nearly all the other leading birth-control men, and often looked for minor personal traits with which to condemn them.

"Well, I think I'd like something like that," Sidney concluded. "Before the next big meeting. Before Houston."

Ben was surprised. He had expected Sidney to denounce Lippes as vain or egotistical. But here he was wanting to emulate him. He tilted his head, puzzled. "You want a tie clasp shaped like a loop!"

"No. Jesus Christ, *think* for a minute." The telephone began ringing just then and Sidney picked it up, whispering loudly, "A ring. An opal. In the shape of a capsule." Holding the phone with one hand, he fanned out the fingers of the other, which already bore the discreet diamond Claudia had given him on their first anniversary. He kept his ringed hand up, an elbow on the desk, and let his fingers jiggle in the air as he began to talk into the phone, saying firmly, "Yeah. Sure I'm sure. Not if Greeley's heading the panel."

In a short while he shrugged, made a bored face at the phone and turned to Ben, sliding the hand that was holding the receiver down across the mouthpiece. "Rockefeller University," he whispered. "Again. But I told them they'd never get me and Greeley on the same platform." A moment later he returned his attention to the phone and lifted his fingers so that he could speak into the mouthpiece. "No. There's nothing to explain. I just won't do it."

Ben waited for Sidney to finish his conversation, busying himself by admiring the graceful room with its carved plaster moldings, French windows, crystal chandelier and tiled fireplace. It had been the parlor once. A turn-of-the-century apartment. But by the time he and Sidney had taken over the lease, it had already been converted into a professional suite. This big front room was the one Ben had always loved. But from the very beginning of their occupancy it had been clear whose room it was. Sidney's. Ben had moved into the small back office.

Just as well, he thought. Sidney needed space. Needed it the way a fish needs water. He had converted one of the suite's two bathrooms into a lab—though he had one at the hospital too—and had taken over the file room for his research notes. The patients waited in line to use the single bathroom. The medical files had been awkwardly squeezed in behind Cora's front desk. And still he complained of lack of space. He was always expanding. He had even run out of room for his elaborate collection of Milton Avery watercolors and Raphael Soyer drawings. They were competing for wall space behind his desk with his numerous diplomas, honorary degrees and testimonial plaques.

"Okay. Got to go," Sidney was saying at last. He signed to Ben that he was about to terminate the call. "You get back to me. If you get him off, I'll be there." Hanging up, he shook his head vigorously. "Damn sycophants. They know Greeley's recent work sucks but they keep inviting him any-

way." Then he shrugged and smiled at Ben.
"Well, no matter. Let's get back to the ring. I'd
like it to be a surprise. I don't want Claudia to
know I thought it up myself."

Ben nodded. Sidney stood. And Ben started to
leave. Naomi had gone out of his mind. Sidney's
affairs, grander than his own, made his own concerns grow indistinct or vanish altogether. But as
he approached the door, he remembered and said,
"Hey, Sid. I wanted you to do *me* a favor. See a
patient of mine who needs an IUD."

Sidney made a groaning sound.

"She's an old friend or I wouldn't bother you on
the spur of the moment," Ben continued. "Naomi
Golden. Remember her from King Street?"

Sidney shook his head.

"Well, anyway," Ben persisted. "How about it?"

"Why the hell didn't you mention it sooner? Jesus. I already gave you ten minutes. I'm due at
Midstate at two."

"I started to," Ben said, "but we got going
about the ring."

"Yeah, well all right," Sidney grunted. "Tell
Cora to get your friend ready and I'll be along in
about fifteen minutes."

"Thanks. See you at dinner."

"Dinner? Oh, Jesus. I meant to speak to you
about that."

Ben began to rub at his palms with his fingers.
Ashamed of his nervous gesture, he thrust his
hands into the pockets of his white jacket where

his right hand made comforting contact with the pill vial. He closed his fingers around it, worrying it the way a Greek worries his beads.

Sidney pushed back his chair and came around his desk. "Maybe we'd better put it off," he said. "I've got to take an early flight to make the NIH meeting tomorrow."

Ben stared at Sidney in dismay. "You might have made up your mind a little earlier," he said, trying not to reveal how hurt he felt. But his voice betrayed him. He stammered a little. "Not—not at the last minute."

"Oh, forget it. We'll have dinner," Sidney said gruffly.

Ben backed down. "No. It's okay. If you've got to get up early, let's skip it."

Sidney's lips opened in a forced smile. He clapped Ben on the shoulder. "I was just kidding. There's no problem, as long as we make it an early night. I was just fooling about calling dinner off."

Ben felt a familiar fury rise within him. Calling the dinner off was one thing; kidding around about it was worse. "It was just a joke, old buddy," Sidney was saying. "I wouldn't call tonight off. Claudia's got something she's dying to tell you." He squeezed Ben's forearm. "Besides, Mulenberg's coming too and I'm counting on you to keep him out of my hair. You're the tactful one, everyone says so."

Ben began to feel beter. What difference did it make whether Sidney had been serious or joking as long as he didn't cancel. "Thanks again," he smiled, relieved. "You can count on me."

Back in his office, he told Naomi that Sidney would see her in fifteen minutes. "You were gone so long," she said. "I thought maybe you were never coming back."

"Would you have minded that?" He felt unexpectedly flirtatious.

She gave him a surprised look and said sincerely, "Yes. I've really enjoyed seeing you again."

He buzzed Cora, asking her to take Naomi over to Sidney's side of the suite, and promised Naomi he'd stop by in a few minutes.

He thought about her all during his examination of his next patient, anxious Mrs. Rogers whose periods had grown annoyingly profuse. He ought to ask Naomi out for dinner. Or a drink, he mused. His life had become a tight, airless circle. The hospital. The office. An occasional tête-à-tête at Sidney and Claudia's. Mrs. Rogers groaned. Withdrawing gloved fingers, he said, "Okay, you can straighten up now," thinking that if only he had someone else to fall back on, he wouldn't be so easily thrown by Sidney's teasing threats of rejection.

"Are the cysts getting bigger?" Mrs. Rogers asked.

"I'm afraid so," he answered quietly.

"You gotta cut them out?" She looked on the verge of tears.

"No. Not yet. We're going to watch them. Wait and see's the best policy. Don't worry, sweetheart." She looked grateful at his information and when he called her sweetheart, she blushed. Not all his patients liked the familiarity of endearments and unlike some of his colleagues, he had learned to tailor his use of affectionate language, suiting it to each individual woman. Mrs. Rogers clearly had enjoyed it. She was smiling at him contentedly, her cheeks pinkening with a surge of nostalgia. It must have been years since anyone had addressed her so intimately. He helped her off the table with a generous hand.

Why was it that he could be so successful, so instinctual, with patients? Yet so uncomfortable and constrained with the women he saw outside the office. Would it be true with Naomi too? Finished with Mrs. Rogers he headed down the corridor to Sidney's side of the office. What would happen if he took Naomi out? He liked her liveliness, her directness. But then he began to think it through. Most likely he'd only fail at getting into bed with her. He always failed at getting into bed with women these days.

Sidney said he was simply picking the wrong women. Middle-class women. What he needed was someone like Sidney's own wife, Claudia. Money was an aphrodisiac, Sidney always argued.

Especially old money. Once, shortly after he'd married Claudia, he'd shown Ben around his new wife's family's summer compound on a rocky Massachusetts coast. In silent, unused bedrooms, he'd opened for Ben carefully polished mahogany armoires and brass-handled chests. He'd pulled out photographs and letter albums. Pictures of Henry James in Italy with Claudia's great-grandmother. Witty greeting cards and thank-you notes of equally revered distant cousins. "Sexy, huh?"

Ben had nodded, understanding this hidden fraternal advice. He hadn't bothered to remind Sidney that he'd had his share of failures with pedigreed as well as plebeian women. Once Sidney offered advice, Ben always gave it fresh consideration.

Sidney and Naomi were still in Sidney's examining room. The door was slightly ajar. Tapping on it lightly, Ben entered the room, saying, "Hi. How're you two getting on?" to Naomi. But she barely acknowledged him. Sidney was standing over her pink-sheeted, spread-eagled body, saying tutorially, "If you wanted an IUD, you should have come directly to me."

Naomi looked tense. Her feet in the stirrups, she no longer displayed any of the garrulous confidence she'd shown in Ben's office. Looking at her, he remembered how often even the most blasé of women had told him that the gynecological position filled them with an almost inexplicable terror.

"Will it take long?" Naomi was asking Sidney as he measured her, her lips set in a wide smile, more propitiatory than sincere. Sidney turned away. "Will it hurt?" she asked, still smiling fixedly.

Sidney slammed a drawer and bent over her, holding in his hand a tiny plastic loop ornamented with minuscule hairs and, before the words were quite out of Naomi's mouth, inserted the loop. Ben saw Naomi blanch and clutch her stomach as if trying to push away the searing cramp the IUD sent twisting through her. Her body jerked for a moment, fishlike. Then at last Sidney answered her, his voice seeming to come from a long distance away. "Who are you to ask for pleasure without pain?"

Naomi went rigid with fury. "Why didn't you warn me? Prepare me?"

Sidney said, "Would it have made any difference? You came in asking for something. You got it."

"But still," she said.

"Lie still," he said.

And then Sidney passed Ben, striding, and was out the door. He was often brusque with patients, but he had been particularly short with Naomi. It was *his* fault, Ben blamed himself. He should have known better than to ask Sidney for a favor. But for a moment he considered catching up with his brother and making him turn to see the alarm still lodged in Naomi's dark eyes.

Then he let Sidney go. After all, Sidney's attitude was probably correct. He'd done all that had been asked of him. Besides, he often said that it was Ben's elaborate coddling of his women that had kept him delivering babies. Instead of delivering research.

Moving toward Naomi, who had straightened out her legs and adjusted the sheet, he decided, as he always did, that most likely Sidney knew best. Yet as he offered Naomi his hand in getting down off the table, he felt melancholy once again, and it was all he could do to stop brooding and speak to her. "How are you feeling now?" he asked in a voice so low he almost couldn't hear it himself.

"Better," she said ruefully. "No thanks to your brother."

He felt sorry for her. Forcing himself to raise his voice, he said, "My brother doesn't bother with the bedside manner, but he's right, in a way. After all it's an inessential ingredient."

Naomi stared at him. "To you," she said. "Not to me." She waited for him to make some reply and when he didn't, went on, "Sidney's just as arrogant as I remember him."

It was hopeless to expect a stranger to grasp that Sidney couldn't be judged by ordinary rules. That he was a brilliant man, perhaps even a genius. Leading Naomi to the pink-striped cubicle where she had left her clothes, he merely held out his hand and said abruptly, "Well, come see me sometime if you ever change your mind and want a baby."

She was hurt and turned away from him, ignoring his hand. When he went back to his own office he knew that once again, as so often, he had said something foolish, inappropriate. Although the two hours he had sworn to wait before taking one of his pills had not yet elapsed, he drew the container from his pocket and, hurrying, poured himself water. Then he pried open the lid of the vial, extracted a pill, and put it on his tongue. He drank it down with a gulp that was more a bite than a swallow.

Claudia Zauber was dressing. She had rushed home from the photography museum where she worked in the afternoons, made the hors d'oeuvres for the dinner, and started the stock for the fish casserole. Mulenberg was coming. And Ben. She had to hurry. She'd asked Sidney to be sure to tell Ben to come early so that she could tell him their news privately.

He was entitled to getting it that way, she thought, toweling herself dry after her quick shower. Of course, Sidney should have been the one to tell him. But it was typical of him to leave such personal concerns to her. He was always too busy. Too bored, really, by the demands of tact. When she had first mentioned to him that they ought to break the news to Ben privately, and gently, Sidney had asked, "Why?" and only this morning he had told her that he had forgotten *why* they were having Ben to dinner tonight.

"To tell him about the baby," she had reminded him. "Otherwise he might guess it. My breasts are getting bigger already."

Sidney had groaned, "I'm too tired for company tonight. Can't we call it off?"

Concerned, she had said, "He's bound to feel jealous, depressed. We've got to tell him about it in a way that won't make him feel left out. You're all he's got, Sid." More than the brothers themselves, Claudia understood Ben's dependency on Sidney.

She felt it too. There was about Sidney, for all his gruffness, his temper tantrums and self-absorption, an excitement that made life lived near him vivid and life lived away from him bland. Even after five years of marriage, Claudia felt an excited anticipation about his coming home and wondered whether they would make love tonight, after their guests had gone.

Eager, she dabbed Givenchy on her throat and between her breasts, and then held the blow-dryer to her blond, glistening hair. She would have to pay special attention to her appearance now that she was pregnant, she thought. It was terrible the way some expectant mothers just let themselves go.

Her own mother had done it, growing overweight while carrying her. Keeping the extra weight afterward. Thickening. Turning matronly. Not edging into motherhood but retreating into it and ceasing to show interest in her husband. Studying her pale-skinned body in the mirror, Claudia promised herself that no matter how child care preoccupied her, she would never let Sidney slip away from her sexually. She had seen the results of her mother's avoidance of her father, his alcoholism, his mistresses, his need, in the end, to degrade both mother and daughter. A shiver ran through her body despite the heated air the dryer was expelling, and she reached for her Japanese kimono, wrapping it tightly around her still-slender waist before beginning to apply her makeup.

She tinted her cheeks and lips a pale pink but eschewed any eye makeup, preferring a natural look. Then she got dressed. But Sidney was late and so was Ben. Restless, she began applying a clear polish to her already shiny nails. When the doorman rang her to announce Dr. Mulenberg, she realized that Sidney must have forgotten to tell Ben to come early.

Ben, his head on his arms and his arms on his desk, awakened slowly, dreamily, and felt content, but a moment later he saw his watch and anxiety flooded his mind. Why hadn't Sidney awakened him? It was seven-thirty. What time were they supposed to go to dinner? He couldn't recall, but surely they were late by now. Pushing into his examining room, he splashed his face with water at the sink. His limbs felt bloodless and numb. He moved heavily down the corridor to Sidney's office. But it was already locked. Sidney must have gone to the hospital. He'd best get himself uptown on his own. Quickly. But his legs still felt weak. He went back to his own office and wrestled his way into his overcoat.

Outside, on the street, he waved listlessly at several cabs. They sped past him despite the fact that their lights indicated they were available, and he grew increasingly nervous. Sidney would be annoyed at his lateness. He'd made a point of saying he wanted an early night. He moved off the sidewalk, out into the gutter, and waved his arm more strenuously. At last a cab stopped for him. Lethargically, through the window, he gave Sidney's address, his words slurred, and sank motionless into the back seat.

"Fifth and where?" the driver asked irritably.

"Ninety-fifth," he managed a little more clearly, realizing he was not yet in full control of his speech. He sat forward and tried to concentrate on gaining the control, flexing his fingers and murmuring to himself. Then he practiced smiling and frowning. By the time he was in the elevator that opened directly into Sidney and Claudia's foyer, he had mastered his lethargy. He stepped briskly out onto their Bokhara carpet, as alert and agile as he ever was.

"Hi, love." Claudia, wearing a sleeveless silvery dress was coming down the hallway to help him off with his coat. Behind her, in the living room, he could see Harry Mulenberg—ensconced in his wheelchair in front of the fireplace. There was no sign of Sidney. "Sid's on the phone," Claudia announced. "And Harry's growing restless. It'll be better now that you're here." Giving him a cool familial kiss on the cheek, she added, "I was hoping you'd get here early. I have some news for you."

"Sidney said you did. What is it?" he asked, his mind abruptly turning to unhappy possibilities. Were she and Sidney going off to Europe as they had done last winter? Were they moving? Were they buying the sprawling suburban house that Sidney had long dreamed of owning? He tried not to chide himself for always anticipating, whenever people told him they had news for him, reports of distance and separation.

"I can't tell you now," Claudia sighed. "It's for your ears alone." She glanced toward the living room. "Can you stay late?"

Could she be pregnant, he wondered as he indicated his availability with a nod. But no, as far as he knew, Sidney didn't want children, not at this busy stage of his career.

"Harry and Marilyn have separated," Claudia said, interrupting his thoughts. She took his coat and hung it in the spacious closet.

"I heard. Poor Marilyn."

Claudia shrugged. "She'll get over it. They should have done it years ago." Then, "Be nice to Harry," she whispered conspiratorially and brushed

her fingers against his hand, her touch so light that
for a moment he thought he had imagined it.

In the living room Mulenberg greeted him and
Ben sat down near him, trying to do Claudia's bidding—though it wasn't *his* behavior Claudia was
worried about, he knew. It was Sidney's. The old
man was the only person in their circle who persisted in treating Sidney as if he were still just a
fledgling doctor. Not the eminent researcher he
had become. And it made Sidney furious. But
Claudia was a meticulously hospitable person.
And because Harry Mulenberg had been her gynecologist before she had met Sidney, and had
been Sidney's mentor back in the days when the
brothers had first come to the hospital, she always
insisted that for old times' sakes, they ought to entertain him. "Didn't you tell me they told you to
go easy on alcohol?" she asked Mulenberg as he
held up his empty wineglass. "Haven't you drunk
enough for one lifetime?" She looked at his drawn
face with concern.

"Claudia, dear," the old man said. "You remind
me of the gynecologist whose patient, an aged
lady, told him she couldn't urinate. 'Ich kennit
pischen,' she says. So he asks her her age and
when she tells him, 'Ochten-seis'—eighty-six—he
says, 'You've pissed enough.' "

Ben glanced at Claudia's face and saw her lips
curved into a smile. He doubted she would have
laughed at Mulenberg's vulgarity if Sidney had

been in the room. Sidney, something of a puritan, despised Mulenberg's coarse humor. Was Claudia genuinely fond of the old man, he wondered. Or was she just being political, manipulating him for Sidney's sake because despite his age and recent stroke he still had important friends at the hospital? He could never quite figure out his elusive, well-bred sister-in-law.

"Harry, you're incorrigible," she said liltingly now. "You may be seventy-two, but inside you're still a nasty-minded nine-year-old. At ninety-two, you'll still be trying to make women blush."

Mulenberg said, "I only hope," and waited while Claudia rose and opened a new bottle of wine. She filled his glass only halfway and then her eyes clouded over. "Excuse me, I've got to put the fish in now or we'll never eat," she said abruptly and left the room.

Mulenberg muttered, "It looks like Sidney plans to spend the whole night on the phone."

Ben tried to distract him. "He'll be along soon, I'm sure. Tell me, Harry. What do you think of all this snow we've been having. Do you think spring'll ever come?"

Mulenberg made a fretful sound. "First of February tomorrow. Spring'll come. It always does."

Ben realized that the old man was bored with him. He considered him a good doctor. He often recommended patients to him. But he was always restless and somehow disapproving in his presence. He decided to talk about work instead of the weather. "Thanks for sending me Mrs. Harper," he began, but Mulenberg interrupted him. "I'm starving. Why don't you go see if you can get Sidney off the phone. Maybe he doesn't realize we're all waiting."

Ben doubted that but he stood up. "Sure. I'll see what I can do."

Sidney was standing next to the bed talking into a salmon-colored princess phone. Across the center of it he had long ago, on the eve of a party, placed a strip of adhesive tape, obliterating his number. Ben had questioned him about it and Sidney had explained, "Just because I invite someone to a party at my house doesn't mean I want them to know my home phone number." Now he was cupping his hand around the mouthpiece as if Ben too had invaded his privacy. Ben backed away, hearing Sidney in an angry tone saying, "No, I don't believe it! No, it's not possible!" but Sidney gestured to him to wait and, resuming his conversation in a lower voice, finally said, "Okay, okay, I'll look into it. I'll send someone down."

"Anything wrong?" Ben asked when Sidney hung up. "You were in here so long."

"It's nothing," Sidney said, but he sounded singularly on edge. "Just one of my researchers kicking up his heels. A real jerk."

"Speaking of kicking, Mulenberg's out there claiming you're starving him to death."

Sidney made a face. "Remember when he used to keep us waiting?"

"Yes, but he's different these days. I feel sorry for him."

"Are you saying I don't?" Sidney asked in a sharp staccato voice.

"Of course not," Ben said, startled. He felt like leaving the room and slamming the door with a thud.

Over dinner, Mulenberg wanted to know about Sidney's new birth control pill. "I understand it eliminates menstruation altogether," he said, chewing.

"That's true," Sidney nodded, but Ben could see that he was still unusually tense.

"Do you actually think women would tolerate that?"

"I wouldn't mind," Claudia said. "Think of the mess. The bother."

"You don't count," Mulenberg said. "You'd go for whatever Sidney tried."

"That's not so."

"Yes, it is, my dear. You and Ben both. But tell me, Sid, what kinds of side effects are you getting?"

Sidney answered slowly, sipping wine. "Mild nausea. Edema in some women."

"I understood," Mulenberg said between bites, "that the animal tests weren't altogether successful."

"There were problems. But they overdosed. They often do with animals."

"Nothing new in that," Mulenberg commented. "Still, are you sure you're really ready to start large-scale domestic testing? I understand you've applied to the Deutsch Foundation to start testing here in the States this summer."

"Of course we're ready." Impatiently, Sidney directed Claudia to fill his glass and swallowed the golden liquid down thirstily. "I wouldn't have asked for the grant otherwise. And it's none too soon. We've got a world teetering on the edge of self-destruction through overpopulation. How long can we afford to wait without finding a solution?"

"Bullshit. We've already got some good solutions."

"But none as effective and easy to use as this one."

Mulenberg squinted at Sidney. "You really believe in it, don't you? You're a man with a mission."

"For God's sake, Harry," Sidney exploded. "Just because you ended up a clinician, you don't have to go around trying to keep me one!"

Claudia said, "Please, Sidney," her pale porcelain skin turning an infinitesimal shade lighter.

"Stay out of it," Sidney warned her. "This is between me and Harry. He keeps needling me."

"Sidney feels you haven't exactly supported him

in this endeavor," Claudia interposed, still trying to make peace.

"I don't need an interpreter!" Sidney shouted.

Mulenberg set down his utensils noisily. "There's no talking to you anymore, Sid. You're so bent on the Nobel Prize you won't even answer questions."

"I don't have to listen to this!" Sidney pushed his chair away from the table and stalked into the kitchen.

"I'm sorry," Claudia apologized to Mulenberg and, rising, hastily followed Sidney.

"He's impossible," Mulenberg growled to Ben as soon as Claudia was gone. "Always was, but he's getting worse."

Ben kept a loyal silence, staring down into his wineglass.

Mulenberg shook his head and drew a packet of cigars out of his pocket. "Want one?" Ben nodded, and the two of them smoked, not talking, but noisily filling the silence by puffing on their cigars. After a while, Ben felt himself growing sleepy again. The stuffy air was oppressive and he had to force himself to stay awake by trying to concentrate on the sounds of his brother and sister-in-law in the kitchen, their voices raised but the words indistinct, muffled by the closed swinging door and the noise of water running hard and plates clinking. And then suddenly, just as Mulenberg emitted a perfect smoke ring, Ben thought he heard a cry from the kitchen, a high-pitched cat-like sound of pain.

He sat forward. Mulenberg too must have heard the sound for he seemed to start to rise from his chair and only then remember his stroke-wounded leg and sink back, scowling. Then the water stopped running and Ben relaxed, convinced that what they had heard was the mechanical shriek of a faucet turned too far.

Sidney and Claudia came in only moments afterward, Sidney with a coffee pot, Claudia carrying a fluted white bowl of chocolate soufflé. "Anyone for dessert?" she said brightly. Ben said, "Great idea," and Mulenberg too nodded enthusiastically, trying to rescue the evening. Claudia came around the table and set the bowl down between her place and Ben's and he saw a small red patch of skin just above her wrist on the inside of her arm. She saw him looking and pulled her hand away.

"Burn?" he asked.

"I had the hot water on too strong."

"She's careless in the kitchen," Sidney said. "Too cocky."

After Mulenberg called his driver and left, Claudia finally told Ben her news. "I'm pregnant," she said quietly, while Sidney busied himself pouring a cognac. "We wanted you to be the first to know."

Ben glanced at Claudia with guarded eyes and

couldn't, at first, trust himself to speak. Jealousy welled up in him like an acid, spreading from his stomach to the back of his throat. He envied not only Claudia and Sidney their child, but the unborn child its parentage. But he was psychologically sophisticated, and used to his despairing jealousies whenever other people's lives seemed richer than his own. "I'm glad," he finally managed to say to them. "How wonderful. How terrific for you."

Once the words were out of his mouth, he was even able to give Claudia a hug and to act, if not feel, as if he were indeed pleased for her and Sidney. Acts were what counted, he reminded himself. Everyone had angry, infantile thoughts, and such thoughts were harmless as long as they were never accompanied by harmful acts or words.

"You needn't feel left out," Claudia rewarded his congratulations by saying. "We'd like you to be the doctor. That is, if you'll take the case."

Ben let go of her and stepped back, amazed. He had thought Sidney, with his penchant for excellence, would have chosen someone far more distinguished than himself. Martin Stearns, perhaps, or even their department chief, Thomas Alithorn. "Surely Stearns would be a better choice," he began, pleased at being offered a role in the birth of his nephew or niece, but puzzled by it nevertheless. "Or Alithorn. Can't you get him, Sid? He still takes some maternity cases, doesn't he?"

Sidney said emphatically, "Cut it out. You're

the man we want." Then he added teasingly, "Besides, your flaws I know. Better the known than the unknown."

Ben grimaced. He wanted to be sure they really wanted him. "What about you, Claudia?" he asked. "How do you feel about having me as the doctor?"

"She feels fine about it," Sidney said gruffly. "Now forget it. It's settled." He stood up, swallowing the last of his cognac, and went to the teak bar in the corner of the room to pour himself another. "The truth is," he added, his back turned, "I like the idea of keeping it in the family."

Claudia pursed her lips, started to say something, and then thought better of it. "You want a brandy?" Sidney asked, turning and gesticulating with the bottle. Both Ben and Claudia shook their heads and Sidney sat back down on the couch, the bottle still in one hand, his brandy snifter in the other. "Come," Claudia said, suddenly taking Ben's arm. "I want to show you something. A present I got."

She held him and began leading him rapidly through the dining room and the kitchen, heading for the unused maid's room in the back of the apartment. "Don't mind Sidney," she said as they passed through the darkened corridor. "He's had a lot to drink tonight. It makes him jumpy."

He felt grateful for her concern and remembered that at the time Sidney had married her he had also gone through a turbulent period, replete with fears of loss and abandonment. But his fears had proved foolish. If anything Claudia, with her meticulous manners, had brought him and Sidney into even greater contact than they had had before the wedding, had ritualized their meetings by organizing a wealth of family dinners and celebrations.

It made him feel better about the baby. He would bring it into the world and would share in its world. All would be as it had been before. Reassured, he said to Claudia, "Thanks. Thanks for worrying about me." Claudia's politeness usually struck him as superficial and automatic rather than sincere. But he had to admit that she was going out of her way to be kind to him tonight.

In the maid's room Claudia switched on a lamp and Ben saw in front of him an elaborate waist-high wrought-iron cradle surrounded with layers of lacy white curtains. "Isn't it marvelous!" Claudia exclaimed. "My friend Bootie got it in Paris. Remember Bootie from the wedding?"

He nodded, remembering her old roommate, and no longer feeling at all out of sorts. He knew all of Sidney's friends, and even Sidney's wife's friends. Clearly he had a place in Sidney's life, even if Sidney was soon to be the father of a proper child, and no longer as his dependent younger brother alone. He said, "It's absolutely wonderful," and shared with Claudia in admiring the cradle's unique ornamentation.

Just then Sidney entered the room, brandy glass

in hand, and seeing Claudia bent over the cradle, slapped her playfully on the buttocks. Claudia straightened up with a start and Sidney, high on cognac, reached unsteadily past her. Grinning, he grabbed a satin pillow from the cradle and shoved it into Claudia's arms. "Smile!" he commanded and stepped back, pretending to take a picture of Claudia and the pillow with the brandy snifter. "Oh, what a good-looking kid," he said, his thumb poised on the edge of the brandy glass. "Spitting image of its dad." Clowning, he pressed down on the glass.

Ben laughed, amused by Sidney's performance. And then Sidney turned toward him and said, "What's so funny?" his voice stentorian, a clown's challenge to an audience. "Who said you could laugh?"

Ben grew suddenly wary. "I guess I ought to be going now. It's getting late."

"Good thinking!" Sidney set his glass down in the middle of the cradle, came up to Ben and, grimacing and clowning still, pinched Ben's cheeks with both his hands. "Good thinking," he repeated, his thumbs and forefingers shaking Ben's skin vigorously. "Whoever said my baby brother was dull-witted?"

Ben pulled away and left the room hurriedly. At the door he turned back for a moment and saw Sidney drawing Claudia close to him, his fingers sliding inside the neckline of her silvery dress. In the elevator he decided that tonight he would allow himself an extra pill or two.

He was already asleep when, around midnight, his phone began to ring. He heard its clamor but he was flying over a green lake, his body suspended between two perfect gossamer wings, and in his mind the phone was a miniature powerful bow releasing piercing arrows. He tried to fly higher, to soar above the danger, and concentrated on escape. Then he felt one of the arrows tear into his wing and his heart began to beat so loudly he thought it too might tear and he felt himself plummeting, plunging toward the brutal bow of the phone. He forced himself higher, his wounded wing flapping painfully. And then at last he was safe again, his wing miraculously healed. The jangling of the phone continued, but he was out of its reach, gliding. Then it grew silent.

A while later it rang again. This time he came awake but his fingers felt thick and numb. When he reached for the receiver he knocked it off the night table and as he struggled to retrieve it from the floor he heard Arnie Diehl, the obstetrical resident on duty at the hospital, begin talking hurriedly. "Dr. Zauber? Diehl. I've been trying and trying to get you."

Grasping the receiver, Ben muttered, "I was asleep," his lips feeling as deadened as his fingers.

"Sounds like you still are," Diehl commented. His voice was as crisp and forceful as that of a radio news announcer. Ben longed to reduce its impact. "What's up?" he asked and, turning onto his side, rested the receiver on the pillow so that he could push the earpiece away from his ear.

"It's Annette Kinney," Diehl said, his voice more tolerable now. Ben's eyes closed and he felt sleep clutch and draw at him as if it were quicksand. "She got here about an hour ago and I've been calling you ever since. She's almost ready to go."

"What's that?" He was in his flying dream again. He was poised at the edge of a broad chasm, about to traverse it with straining, fluttering wings. He forced himself not to take off yet but to talk intelligibly to Diehl. "What do you mean by almost ready?" he managed. "Won't she keep till morning?"

"I don't think so."

"Why not?"

"It's going fast."

The chasm loomed black. He had to soar now or he would fall, crash against cliffs and brittle stones. "Call me when she's ready," he mumbled. "Really ready."

"But I'm telling you it's going to be very soon."

"Right," Ben said, "that's right," and with a swooping gesture thrust out his arm and let the phone receiver descend into the cradle.

CHAPTER TWO

FEBRUARY

"Dr. Zauber? She's ready."

Diehl's words in Ben's ear were meaningless at first. He had come awake as soon as the phone began its imperious ringing, but he had no memory of Diehl's previous call. "Who?" he shot out. "Who's ready?"

"Mrs. Kinney. She's eight centimeters."

"Why the hell didn't you call me earlier?" he said. "Goddamn it, why'd you wait until the last minute?"

"I did call." Diehl was indignant. "You said to get back to you when she was really ready."

Slowly, their previous conversation drifted back into Ben's mind. "Oh, Christ," he sighed. "Yeah. That's right. I did say that."

"I could deliver her," Diehl offered eagerly.

"No. She'd never forgive me." He was wide awake now. "I've known her for seven years. Delivered both her other kids." Standing, he began groping for his shoes. "Just snow her for a few moments. I'll be there faster than you can wheel her into the delivery room."

"Snow her?"

"Delay her. Give her a shot. And have the nurse tell her not to push."

"You sure you don't want me to deliver her?"

But Ben was already hanging up and within seconds he was into his shoes and coat and out the door. Rushing along the windy street that separated his apartment from the hospital, his coat flapping behind him, he was racing as in his dream.

Annette Kinney was in the delivery room wide awake, and Angela Rogers, one of the nurses, was holding her legs together and telling her in her soft Southern drawl not to bear down, not yet. Annette's face was contorted, but when she saw Ben she managed a smile. "I'm so glad you're here," she whispered and then her body heaved.

"Have I ever let you down?" Angela checked the fetal heart while another nurse dried Ben's arms. Water was still running down to his wrists from his double-quick scrubbing. Then he heard Angela say, "Heart rate's gone down to 115" and suddenly he was intensely at work, ordering oxygen for Annette in order to keep the baby's own supply mighty and telling her now to push, push hard, as hard as she could.

He could see the top of the baby's head, its matted hair a mound of black twisted seaweed. But it had stopped its voyage through her vagina. He ordered forceps and began pulling down on the head, directing Diehl to cut the episiotomy while he braced himself against the baby's stubbornness. Then suddenly he had a firm hold on the baby and he maneuvered its head half out, working now with his hands alone. The head was slippery but he held it and at last eased out a shoulder. There was a torrent of fluid and a second later he was grasping the baby by its heels, sucking mucus from its sticky face, and hitting it hard, waiting for the belligerent world-hating cry and the bellicose red color to come. But the baby merely whimpered, made no warrior cry, and although when the cord was clamped his small penis swelled, his color didn't come.

Troubled, but trusting that the infant would soon enough perk up, he handed it to Diehl and directed him to start the required measurements of heart, muscle tone, and breathing. In the meantime, he concentrated on the afterbirth.

It was coming rapidly. He helped Annette deliver it, pushing on her stomach, then quickly checked to see if it had all come out. When he heard Angela at his elbow saying something to him, he asked her to wait a second, and completed his careful examination of the placenta. Then he heard Angela whisper loudly, "It's Apgar three," and knew that Annette's baby had not turned red.

When he had finished with Annette and she was being sponged and dressed, he went over to take a look at the infant. A pediatric resident had been called and the baby placed in an isolette. It was breathing oxygen, its small stomach rising and flattening laboriously. "It's hypoxic," the pediatrician said. "We'll have to hold it here for a while." He sighed and looked uneasy. "Do you want to tell the mother?"

Annette Kinney was lying flat when he got down to her room, but she was already whispering animatedly with a woman in the bed next to hers. Tired but triumphant, she reminded him of a schoolgirl still awake at dawn after a New Year's Eve date. He wished she didn't look quite so joyous. Pulling the curtain around her bed so they could have privacy, he began, "Where's Frank?"

"Home. We thought it would be best for the kids if he stayed with them."

"Have you called him yet?"

"No. I was just about to."

Ben bit on the inside of his cheek. "We're going to have to keep the baby on oxygen for a day or so."

He hadn't expected her to take his report calmly, but he was unprepared for the way her forehead suddenly gashed into great, deap wrinkles. "He'll be fine. You'll see," he went on, trying not to let her see his own anxiety. "He just needs a day or two of special care. He's a little hypoxic, but he'll flourish rapidly on oxygen."

Annette sank down onto the pillow, her gaiety gone. "Really just a day or two?" she asked doubtfully.

"Really. I'm sure of it. I've seen these things often. Have I ever lied to you?"

"No, never," she said, her eyes narrowing. "But there's always a first time."

"Trust me," he said. "And relax. And after you call Frank, try to get some rest. Who knows? You might even get the baby by afternoon."

He felt a power in his voice, saw how she relaxed her forehead, hypnotized by his drawl, and he left right afterward, promising to see her later on in the day. It seemed to satisfy her.

But he himself was beyond consolation. He had been asleep and oblivious and to cover up that first unfortunate error, he had had Annette's labor slowed down. It should have gone all right even so; most of the time a little slowdown produced only a negligible effect on labor. But Annette's baby had responded by getting altogether sluggish. It had tarried in her vagina and been poisoned by inadequate air. He felt monstrous, ashamed.

On his way out of the hospital, he stopped in front of the darkened gift shop, and, peering into the display window, wished the shop were open so that he could buy something for Annette. A plant.

A bottle of perfume. A book. Anything. Then he pushed past the window, abashed, recognizing the irrationality of his urge to buy Annette a gift. It was audacious to imagine that there was anything he or anyone else could give her to make up for what would, most likely, soon be taken from her.

He made his way out into the street and, too angry with himself to permit himself the solace of sleep once again, went over to his office where he read until dawn and called the pediatric intensive care unit several times to check on the Kinney baby's progress. But each time he called, the resident on duty informed him that there had been no improvement yet.

Cora was the first person to arrive in the morning. She saw his light on, tapped on the door, took one look at him and said, "What's the matter? You look terrible."

"It's nothing," he answered, not wanting to talk about the Kinney baby. "When's Sidney expected?" Above all, he wanted to avoid Sidney just now. Seeing Sidney, who had never compromised a birth, would just make him feel worse. If he could feel worse.

"Not till late," Cora said. "He's in Washington."

"Oh. Right! I forgot!" Relieved, he washed and shaved in the office bathroom and prepared himself to start seeing his patients. He was sure that once he was busy he would forget about Annette Kinney for a while. But he couldn't forget about her. As each new patient arrived, he kept seeing Annette's disappointment anew, kept seeing disdain in each woman's face and himself for the failure he had become.

All morning he was regretful and disgusted with himself for having indulged in the extra pills just because Claudia and Sidney had made him feel so left out. If only he could relive last night. If only such second chances were possible. If they were, he thought once, he could have called Naomi instead of taking the extra pills.

When the office emptied out a little he took his lunch break. Cora brought him a hamburger and a milkshake and before unwrapping them he called Pediatric Intensive Care again. But the resident's voice was flat and thin as he said, "Still no change."

"Well, let's give it twenty-four hours," Ben said. "It's still too soon to be sure the oxygen won't make a difference."

"Sure," the resident agreed. But when Ben hung up the phone he couldn't bring himself to eat.

Cora, returning to clear away his lunch, insisted on his having the milkshake at least. Her face was wind-reddened and she looked angry and disapproving as she fussed over him, ripping open the paper bag and forcing a straw into the thick, dark liquid. "You need to get out more," she muttered. "To think about other things besides work."

She came in again when he had seen his last patient. He was sitting at his desk, his head in his hands. Cora reminded him that he had promised her the day after Lincoln's Birthday off because she was going skiing and told him that she had found a good replacement for herself while she was on vacation. But when he simply nodded and seemed uninterested in who it was, she began to grow fiercely maternal. "You should take days off sometimes too," she said. "All work and no play—"

"I know," he said.

"Dull boy," she finished.

When she was gone he put his head and his arms down on the desk, not expecting to sleep but intending merely to rest. He was too upset to sleep, he thought. In a few minutes he would go over to the hospital again, check with his own eyes on the progress of the baby and pay his promised visit to Annette Kinney. But fatigue overwhelmed him. Without any exertion of will, his eyes started to shut, and his ears ceased to register Cora's footsteps in the hallway. Instead, in his mind, he kept hearing the voice of his mother, Sara. She was talking to somebody he couldn't recognize and she was crying and saying, "He's dull. Let's face it. Let's just face up to it."

Poor Sara, Ben mused, and sat with his head buried in his arms. Whenever he thought of his mother, he felt sorry for her. Drowsy, he remembered how she had told him that when she was young, she had always dreamed of marrying a prince. An immigrant, she had learned English late in childhood, read fairy tales well into her teens, and fantasized overlong about princes charming, bewitched and benighted.

The man she had married, Samuel Zauber, Ben and Sidney's father, had clearly been no prince. An accountant for the Mid Hudson Dairy, he spoke with an accent, smoked cigars whose odor Sara detested and left his socks strewn about the living room floor. After his death, Sara complained about him incessantly. But while he was alive, Ben imagined, she must have kept her complaints to herself, for she had made an alteration in her fantasies and Samuel was necessary to that alteration. She had decided that although she had not married royally, she might, instead, produce a prince for herself.

Sara tried, from the first month of her married life. In bed with Samuel she smelled his feet, was aware of the odor even when he had bathed them in the porcelain tub. She herself felt hot, sweaty, sunstruck. He would ride her, straddling her and galloping, a courier who did not know the errand he was on, the reason why she lay so willingly beneath him though he rode and rode her to exhaustion. And she never told Samuel how she felt. Feelings as a matter of display between husbands and wives were invented later, when Sara was already an older woman. In their midnight rides across the bed, physical presence was all.

Then at last Sara became pregnant and rejoiced, never once doubting that the weight within her was a son, a prince. But after six bloodless months she awoke screaming and bleeding in the night and Samuel called their doctor, the only Jewish physician in Poughkeepsie, and he came and took Sara in his black Ford to the hospital and she was assured, when she was sent home several days later, that there was no cause for the miscarriage, that there was nothing wrong with her, that it had just been an idiopathic event. She was urged to try again.

And she did try, and did try, and for the next eight years she was pregnant seven times and seven times Samuel telephoned in the night for the doctor and Sara was taken to the hospital and then returned home to try again. She began to believe that God had forsaken her, and grew depressed and stayed at home, friendless. And then, on her ninth effort God decided in her favor and let her have Sidney. Or so it seemed to her. That he was God-given she never questioned, and, even more than most Jewish women of her age and background, treated her first son as a being at whose feet both she and her husband should worship.

She knitted and embroidered and sewed and fed him, first with her breasts and then with a large, ornate spoon, never a small one. She kissed and bathed and caressed him and put him to sleep, once he reached the age of nightmares, in her own fluffy bed, urging Samuel to settle down on the couch. She taught him to read and recited her fairy tales to him and told him he must be a doctor when he grew up, and help God help poor women like herself, and she sat him on her knees for piano lessons before he was three years old. He was everything she had ever wanted in life.

In a way the second baby, Ben, was superfluous. She had had all her prayers answered by Sidney. Ben was an afterthought, God's postscript.

Still, she had done her best to love them equally. She was indefatigable and exquisitely fair. It was not her fault that Ben was a much more lethargic baby than Sidney, undemanding, absorbed in his own fingers and toes and unimpressed by rattles and colored wooden beads. Not her fault that Sidney, at two, had memorized his picture books, whereas Ben, stubby-fingered, could barely manage to turn pages one at a time. Not her fault that Sidney, at three, could print his name in great wobbly, giant strokes, whereas Ben clutched a pencil in his chubby palm and tried to make the eraser write. Worst of all, Ben did not speak until he was three or at least spoke only nonsense words, meaningless to the entire family. Sara lost interest in Ben.

Not so Samuel. Ben could still remember how his father had spent hours tutoring him, trying to teach him to speak, holding him on his lap and saying over and over, "Mommy. Dadda. Sidney." It was his last memory of his father. Samuel had died when Ben was three and Sidney six, and Ben had learned to speak only after his father's death and only as Sidney's pupil. His mother still told the story of how it had happened with wonder and adoration in her eyes.

She had awakened early one morning shortly after Samuel's death and heard loud sounds from the boys' room. Ben was shouting, "Maddern gail," and Sidney was shouting back, "Sailboat, moron! Say, 'Gimme the sailboat!'"

A moment later Sara heard a loud, thunderous crack and a rain of whimpers and Ben sobbing, "Maddern gail thina rihm!" and she had hurried to the door of the boys' room just in time to see Sidney stomping the wooden sailboat she had just given Ben for his birthday. He was in tears. On his knees. Clutching at slivers of wood. His groping hands were dangerously close to Sidney's still-stomping shoes. Sara had started to rush for her youngest son when, his voice in a howl, his fingers pinioned, he had shrieked, "Gimme sailboat, moron."

Suddenly both Sara and Sidney stood still, and then Sidney lifted his foot and freed Ben's fingers and Ben grabbed and cradled the mangled boat and Sara ran across the room. Scooping up Sidney, she hugged him. "You made him talk!" she cried. "You made him talk!" Ben was howling "Gimme sailboat, moron," and at last Sara hugged him too and kissed his throbbing fingers.

* * *

Shortly afterwards Sara felt able to move with the two small boys to Brooklyn, where her husband's brothers owned a mirror business and had offered her a job. She had delayed the move, ashamed of Ben, but now she was no longer ashamed. Little by little he had begun to make sense and by the time they moved and he met his uncles, Sidney had taught him to shake hands and say, "Gimourning."

Soon after they moved, Sidney started school. Ben stayed at home with a housekeeper and waited impatiently all day for three o'clock when he and the woman could go to the schoolyard to pick up Sidney. He would hold the housekeeper's hand tightly until he saw Sidney's class come into the yard in size place order and then he would run with flailing arms and tripping feet to greet his brother, shouting "Gimourning! Gimourning!" But Sidney, fourteenth in line, with knickered boys in front and in back of him, would say loudly, "Jerk" and "Shithead" and "Gedoudahere," and after a while Ben knew those words too, and by the time he was ready for kindergarten he spoke quite well, albeit at first with a bothersome, rattling stutter.

Still, it didn't prevent him from tagging behind after Sidney and his friends in the empty lots and alleys in which they played stickball and ring-a-levio, although it sometimes prevented him from explaining to Sara at night his frequent torn pants and cut knees and bruised arms. Or something did. He feared the loss of Sidney's company more than he feared scrapes and cuts and punches and the stinging flesh-reddening searing that Sidney called an Indian burn.

But Sidney was not always cruel to him. His cruelty was chiefly a public display, name-calling and tricks and physical abuse whenever Ben followed behind in the pack of boys.

When they were alone, Sidney was different. When they were alone, he would let Ben listen to his radio or play with the doctor kit Sara bought him on his eighth birthday, or the chemistry set he was given at nine. Ben would be Sidney's patient, forever getting his temperature taken and his heart listened to and his back thumped hard and his mouth stuffed to overflowing with delicious candy pills. And Ben would be Sidney's taster, sniffing, then gulping, the foul drinks Sidney concocted. Holding his nose, Ben would bravely swear the marvelous oaths by which Sidney bound him, the secret curses prompted by scatology and the movies. "I'll be fucked to shit if I ever fail you," "I'll be your faithful servant forevermore."

Later there were rituals inspired by Sidney's extensive reading: the hand in the gas flame, the hairs pulled out close to the temples, the bloody signatures on folded scraps of paper. Ben never tired of time spent with Sidney, even when Sidney abused him. Sara said Sidney was a genius and that genius had its own ways. And Ben was inclined to agree with her, although he didn't know what genius was. Still, he knew that Sidney was endowed with a unique gift.

He called it imagination, a quality he found grievously lacking in himself. He felt uninventive, dull, shallow. Sidney was exciting, unpredictable, full of undercurrents. What was a kick in the shins compared to experiencing the world through Sidney's eyes?

Ben submerged himself in Sidney's depths and felt, drowning, that he had landed somewhere.

He had slept. When he drifted to consciousness, he saw that it was after six. The office was silent. Cora and the other two nurses had undoubtedly gone home long ago. He sat up, astonished, startled that he had fallen asleep at his desk without any preparation for sleep. He had taken no pills since the night before. Then he remembered Annette Kinney and her baby and dissatisfaction replaced his contentment. Quickly he stood up and drew on his overcoat. He had yet to take his promised second look at the mother and child.

Annette was tearful when he saw her. "You said I'd have the baby by afternoon," she said accusingly.

"I said maybe by afternoon," he reminded her gently. She turned her head away and began to sob.

"I don't blame you for being angry with me," he offered, then wished he hadn't. But it was all right. She wasn't listening to him, but was crying loudly now.

"Please stop," he cajoled. "The more you cry, the worse you'll feel." He made himself smile briskly and add in a stern voice, "If you go on crying, we'll have to give you tranquilizers and that won't be good for your milk."

Her tears subsided and he went on. "I think you'd better begin using a breast pump. Just to keep yourself ready. I'm going to tell the nurses to get you started."

"You are? You really think the baby's going to be all right?"

"Of course I do. I'm sure of it."

He had almost convinced himself until he stopped in the nursery and saw the baby's pale grayish color. Diehl was there too, agitated and ashen faced himself. "I'm sorry," Ben said to him.

The obstetrical resident didn't reply.

"Any improvement?" Ben asked.

"Not yet," Diehl finally muttered.

Ben looked down at the baby in its glass nest.

"I called you in time," the younger man said then, speaking up.

"Sure you did."

"I thought you were going to say I called you late," Diehl went on nervously. "It's been known to happen. I have a friend who got kicked out of Midstate because an attending lied about when my friend called him."

"You don't have much confidence in me, do you?" Ben frowned.

"It isn't you. It's this place. The buck-passing." Behind Diehl's bravado, Ben could hear how worried he was.

"You don't need to worry," Ben said. "I'm not like that."

The resident looked up, suddenly grateful. "*I'm* sorry," he said, and Ben realized how young he was. No more than twenty-seven, he thought. "You should get some sleep," he advised him paternally.

"I can't. Who can sleep around here? I'd give my right arm for two full nights of sleep."

Ben lingered awhile, feeling close to Diehl, understanding the depths of his exhaustion and anxiety. But there was nothing else he could think of saying to the younger man and, finally, taking a last look at the baby, he excused himself and hurried out of the nursery. Sidney would be back from Washington by now and would be coming to the hospital to do his rounds. He didn't want to run into Sidney. Not now. Not yet. Tomorrow, when the baby pulled through, then he could talk to Sidney about it.

He raced for the back elevator but to his dismay when it stopped for him he saw Sidney, looking elegant in a new blue cashmere coat and carrying a bulging briefcase, pushing out from behind a crowd of strangers. And immediately after Sidney emerged, so too did Thomas Alithorn, the chief of ob-gyn. Ben backtracked, turning toward the direction from which he had come, but Sidney saw him and called out, "Hey, Ben. Wait up a minute."

Ben walked reluctantly back. Sidney and Alithorn were deep in conversation. "Fascinating," Alithorn was saying. "Absolutely fascinating." Alithorn's aging face was well tanned, the result of daily tennis. When he saw Ben, he nodded, but his eyes seemed to stare right through him. Looking at Sidney again he said, "Come on over to my office and let's talk about it further."

Ben was used to being ignored by Alithorn. A political man, Alithorn picked his friends carefully, concentrating on the powerful old-timers or the up-and-coming stars. Still, he ran the department efficiently and was well thought of by the administration because he brought in a lot of money in the form of bequests and endowments. "I'll need to hear more," he was saying to Sidney, "but sure, it sounds possible. We'd like to help out."

Sidney set his briefcase down between his legs and pulled out a reprint, handing it to Alithorn. "I'm afraid I'm going to be tied up for a while. But here. Read this, and maybe we can talk about it Saturday."

"Fine. See you Saturday at eight." Alithorn, taking the reprint, hurried down the corridor.

As soon as he was gone, Ben said, "I've got to

go, too," and pressed the elevator button again, but Sidney asked, "What's your hurry?"

"I thought you were in a hurry," Ben said nervously, still not wanting to talk with Sidney.

"Why? Oh, you mean what I said to Alithorn?" Sidney glanced at the chief's retreating back. "That was just politicking. Never seem eager when someone wants to do you a favor." He gave Ben a paternal smile. Then he bent down and closed his briefcase. "Alithorn may let me take over some more lab space. And use some of the residents. A couple of them are very keen to do research. Matthews, Diehl. Diehl called me this morning and asked to work with me."

"Diehl?" Ben said edgily.

"Yeah. By the way, he said you'd had a bad baby last night." Pulling off a paisley silk scarf, Sidney asked, "Still bad?"

"Yeah," Ben nodded disconsolately.

"Well, don't worry about it. You win some, you lose some. Anyway, Kinney's not exactly what you could call unlucky. Doesn't she have two kids already?"

"The baby's not lost yet," Ben said, disheartened by Sidney's casualness. "It may pull through."

"Yes, but if it does, it'll probably be a vegetable." Sidney shrugged again. He prided himself on always taking a realistic approach to problems and saw pessimism as realism.

"Not necessarily."

"Well, I hope you're right, old buddy. I'll keep my fingers crossed." Sidney picked up his brief-case, stooping a little from the weight. Then suddenly he set it down again and said, "What went wrong with the delivery?"

"I was late. I had the baby delayed."

Sidney leaned closer to Ben. "Sleeping?"

"Yeah."

"If I were you, I wouldn't tell anyone about that." Sidney had lowered his voice. "Let them think Diehl called you late."

"I can't do that."

"Why not? Don't be a schmuck." Sidney rubbed a still-gloved hand across his forehead. "There's liable to be a malpractice suit," he whispered. "There'll be one for sure if the baby dies. But even if it lives, if it's retarded, there could be one. And how do you think that'll look for our practice?"

"I'm sorry," Ben said. "I wasn't thinking about that."

"Damn right you weren't." Sidney was struggling to keep his voice low. "Well, forget it. Just let me take care of it. Diehl's very anxious to get into research."

"I can't let him take the blame."

"I'm not asking you. I'm telling you."

"But I already told Diehl it was my fault and that I'd stick by him."

"Well, you're not going to." Suddenly Sidney pulled off his gloves and stretched out a hand to-ward Ben's jacket. "For Diehl, it'll all blow over in a while," he said. "It wouldn't for you." Sidney's fingers groped, then closed around the plastic container in Ben's pocket. "You have too much to hide," Sidney whispered. "So don't act like a damn fool."

A moment later, Sidney was gone and Ben was standing alone in the corridor, ashamed. He hated Sidney's advice and himself for having provoked it. He wanted to kick something. Anything.

Alone, he left the hospital and began to wander, first to the icy river, then across town and into the park, a snowy polar terrain. There was nothing new in Sidney's urging him to compromise himself, he thought as he walked, feeling like a lonely arctic explorer left behind by hardier comrades.

It had happened so many times before. He remembered the time he had written on limnology for his high school biology course. Visiting the Museum of Natural History, he had become fascinated by the museum's replicas and diagrams of freshwater ponds, the mysterious balance between the big fish and the small, the way the waters teemed with life. And so he had decided to write his term report on the subject, the very decision giving him a sense of purpose and accomplishment. And the research went so well that gradually he began to change his mind about science. He had disliked it at the start of high school, and had done mediocre work in chemistry. But he felt enthusiastic about biology.

Sidney was off at Cornell taking pre-med, and

one day Ben wrote to him and told him that perhaps he too would, after all, plan on a career in science, perhaps become a biologist or even a doctor. Sidney had written back, "Fantastic! Who knows? If you become a doctor, maybe we could share a practice someday."

But he had warned Ben that he'd better get a top grade in biology. "You got a B in chemistry. You'll have to pull an A in biology or else you won't get into a college with a good science program. And if you don't do that, you won't stand a chance of getting into a good med school."

Ben increased his efforts on the term paper and when Sidney was home at Easter vacation, showed it to him. But Sidney hated it. "Why'd you choose limnology?" he had asked. "You should have picked the cell. Or the circulatory system. Something important." Ben had explained limply, "I liked it." Sidney had shrugged and said, "Tell you what. I'll write a paper for you while I'm home." Ben demurred, but Sidney was insistent. "You picked the wrong topic, old buddy," he said. "You'll never get as good a grade with this as you'd get if you did the cell." Ben had finally acquiesced, and he got an A in biology, although he was never quite certain what grade he would have gotten if he had used his own paper.

In college—unlike Sidney he went to City and lived at home to save Sara money—he and Sidney had similar altercations. To Sidney, anything short of glowing success was failure, and he was always predicting failure for Ben and trying to get him to forestall it through deceit, urging him to cheat on exams, hire a fellow student to go over his papers for him, even to subscribe to a thesis-writing service he had read about somewhere.

Sidney never practiced deceit to advance his own career. He didn't have to. But when it came to Ben's career, he believed it was essential.

It wasn't that Ben was doing badly in college. He was as smart as the next fellow, if not as brilliant as Sidney. But, knowing Ben's early slowness, Sidney never quite trusted his advances during adolescence and young manhood. It was as if the past had greater reality than the present. When Ben found the work in medical school extremely difficult, Sidney said, "There's only one way a guy like you can make it through. You're going to have to start studying all night."

Ben promised to try. But he couldn't do it. To help him, Sidney, already an intern, produced amphetamines to keep him awake for hours on end, and barbiturates, to permit him brief restorative naps. "No harm in these," Sidney said. "No harm in anything but failure."

Following Sidney's advice, Ben had made it through medical school, and later through a grueling internship and residency, and at last he had become, like Sidney himself, a specialist in obstetrics and gynecology. Yet he always felt himself to be an inferior doctor. Years later, thoroughly disillusioned with himself, he returned to the barbiturates he had first come to enjoy during medical school. He monitored his habit, tried to keep it from overwhelming his life. But he never tried to give it up. It made failure tolerable.

Wandering through the park, his legs finally grew so weary that he felt grateful. He would be able to sleep now. Able to sleep even without the pills. He didn't want to have to take them. Not tonight, when at any minute the Kinney baby might die and he would have to break the news to Annette. Stamping through the snow onto an unfamiliar windy corner, he hailed a cab and rode to his apartment.

But he couldn't sleep. Lying exhausted on the living room couch, he kept thinking that if the Kinney baby died, he would blame himself fiercely for its brief labored life. And even if it lived, if it was in any way damaged, he would still blame himself, no matter whom Sidney blamed officially. And he would blame himself for whatever happened to Diehl, would have Diehl on his conscience too.

But he had no choice. As Sidney had said, he had too much to hide to risk a malpractice suit. Such a suit might dredge up his addiction and possibly result in suspension from the hospital. As long as he was taking his pills, he'd have to do what Sidney advised. And he couldn't give them up. They were the jewels with which he courted his beloved sleep.

Lying on his back, he withdrew the container from his pocket and spread a few yellow capsules on his palm. Golden and shiny in their clear jell covers, they seemed to him jewels indeed, and he held them gently and then at last got up and went into the kitchen to fill a glass of water. There was no point in fooling himself; he needed the pills.

Far below, outside the kitchen window, was a wide landscaped courtyard and, as he ran the water in the sink, he could hear sounds carried upward through the yard, music, a child crying, a door slamming, other people's lives being lived. He lifted the pills toward his mouth but suddenly his eyes narrowed and his fist tightened around them. Holding them hidden, he thought of the story Sara still told about her childhood in Russia, about how on a moonlit snowy night she had tossed a necklace of pearly white beads out of the window, expecting, or so she told it, that when the spring sun shone and melted the snow, the beads too would disintegrate into pale gray rivulets. Instead, she had found the necklace in the spring, the chain on which the beads were strung rusted and green, but the beads themselves still a pearly vivid white against the new grass.

Raising the courtyard window, he abruptly scattered his fistful of pills out into the snow. Then he dug in his pocket, took out the container, unscrewed it and shook out the rest of the smooth, golden capsules, watching them scatter into the wind.

* * *

That morning at seven-thirty the pediatric resident called him from the hospital. "You know the Kinney baby?" Ben held his breath. "It's off the oxygen. And it looks as if there's nothing else wrong. For now, at least."

"Does Mrs. Kinney know?" His misery of the night before was evaporating.

"Not yet. We thought you'd want to know before we told her."

"Great," Ben said. "Good work. I'm coming over right now. Don't tell her. I'd like to tell her myself."

He felt, as he walked swiftly to the hospital, that once again he was in his flying dream, his body weightless and perfect. He felt it still when he swirled open the curtains around Annette Kinney's bed.

She was sitting up, using the breast pump, and he was glad that he had thought of that distraction for her. But she was drawn-faced and there were tear streaks on her cheeks. "Now why are you crying?" he asked, scarcely able to contain his excitement. "Didn't I tell you not to let yourself get all upset?"

"I'm just so terribly worried," Annette said. "So scared." She set down the little rubber pump and covered herself with the rough sheet, wiping her eyes with a corner of it.

"Well, you don't need to be," he beamed. "And

you'd better pull yourself together right away. You've got this happy, healthy baby out there that needs you."

Annette stared at him, her eyes going wide with disbelief.

"They'll be bringing the baby to you for the eleven o'clock feeding," Ben went on. "You haven't missed a beat."

Comprehension and relief began to spread across Annette's face.

"Shall we walk over and see him together? Or do you want to call Frank first and tell him?"

Annette had her feet over the side of the bed already. "After," she said, stumbling into her slippers.

He gathered up her orlon robe and helped her into it, standing formal and dignified behind her as if he were wrapping her in an evening coat.

"Let's go see the baby first," she said, and took his arm.

They promenaded together down the corridor. "I told you it would be just a matter of a day or so," he said. He loved the almost palpable happiness that seemed to suffuse her, making her skin bright, and refrained from telling her how worried he still was. Only time would reveal whether the baby had received any permanent damage as a result of its oxygen deprivation.

"What do you suppose happened?" Annette asked happily.

"Who knows?" he hedged. "There are so many

mysteries about birth. There's so much we don't know."

The baby was in a nurse's arms, being diapered. Ben hardly recognized it except for its dark thatch of hair. It was red-cheeked and howling and unblemished. Annette dropped Ben's arm and pressed close to the glass. She had forgotten about Ben.

He couldn't forget about her. The incident haunted him. Although he had been taking barbiturates regularly for several years now, he had never before slept through a call to the hospital or endangered the health of a patient or a patient's baby. He had thought himself immune to such possibilities because he had monitored his habit carefully. He had never, until the night he had learned of Claudia's pregnancy, taken more than the tolerance-producing dose of six hundred milligrams a day. Never allowed himself the street addict's ignorant climb to ever higher and higher amounts. But despite the educated way he had handled his habit, it had put someone in peril. He made up his mind to stay off the drugs.

It was difficult, more difficult than the abrupt withdrawal itself. That was accomplished after three days of stomach cramps, nausea and weakness. He told Cora he had the flu, had her cancel all his appointments and stayed at home, shivering. In a corner of his bedroom was an overstuffed armchair from which one night, he didn't remember which or at what hour it had been, he had crazily ripped each cloth-covered button and held them in a sweating palm and at last put a few in his yearning mouth and swallowed, gagging before he vomited them onto the carpet.

But he hadn't fainted, hadn't had convulsions. Indeed, he hadn't experienced any of the more extreme effects that sudden withdrawal could produce in those who took higher doses of the drug. His real difficulties set in later, once the physical dependence was conquered. He was anxious, tremulous, and totally incapable of sleeping. His insomnia was a mutiny against his body, a nightly tossing and twisting of his limbs that left him feeling whipped and beaten toward morning and always, in those silent hours just before dawn, utterly abandoned and alone. He came to long for the very thing he had once most hated, the 4 or 5 A.M. call to hurry to the hospital for a delivery.

But no matter how acute his insomnia and loneliness became, he didn't let them drive him to writing himself a new barbiturate prescription. Every dawn, awake and brooding, he kept picturing Annette Kinney's tear-streaked face and hearing Diehl's agitated voice. He remembered his own residency and didn't agree with Sidney that no harm would befall the young man if he were blamed for the delay in the baby's birth. At the very least, his reputation would be stained, so that he would be starting his career with a serious mark against him.

Shouldering the blame himself would also stain a reputation, Ben thought. His own. But his career, such as it was, was already established. He had sufficient patients, and had colleagues who would continue to recommend others to him, no matter whether he won or lost a malpractice suit. As for his addiction, he doubted he could be suspended for it, once it was in the past. And so he lay awake at night, waiting for his insomnia to fade, as he imagined it would in time.

The loneliness was another matter. It was loneliness that had first caused his love affair with sleep. And unless he conquered it now, he would once again be seduced. But he couldn't look to Sidney for help in this. If anything, Sidney would want to see less of him, not more, once the baby was born. He would have to manage on his own. Would have to develop other distractions. One morning, lying in a tangle of sheets and watching a rainswept dawn that was nearly as dismal and dark as the night that had preceded it, he decided that he was going to marry Naomi.

CHAPTER THREE

MARCH

Emily Harper set down her grocery bags, turned the key in the lock and undid her bra even before picking up the bags again and entering her apartment. Her breasts hurt. Alternately plaguing and awe-provoking, they no longer seemed a part of herself but something separate, purposeful. Slamming the door, she thrust the bags into the kitchen and went into the bedroom where she slipped off her sweater and the irritating bra and donned one of Philip's loose workshirts. Then she returned to the kitchen, lit the oven and began putting away the groceries, all the while peering down at herself to marvel at her new majestic size.

The oven heating, she set the table, gathering plates and glasses into her arms and thinking as she arranged them that most likely she would nurse. Just last night she had read another book which argued that breast-fed babies were psychologically healthier than their bottle-fed peers. Sliding straw table mats into place, she made a mental note to ask Dr. Zauber what he thought of *Nurse Me! I'm Yours!*

She was forever storing up questions about her reading or anecdotes about her job at the neighborhood center to tell him and when she saw her friends she talked about him all the time. On her second visit to him, she had decided he was every bit as understanding as her old doctor, Mulenberg, and actually a good bit more intriguing, indeed, a fascinating man. Philip, who had read a lot of Freud, didn't see it. He said her absorption in the obstetrician was just another facet of the self-preoccupation of pregnancy. The obstetrician was a concretization of narcissism. But she told Philip he was just being jealous.

Finished with the table, Emily seasoned the chicken, shoved it into a roasting pan, and was just bending to slide the pan into the oven when she felt a familiar stickiness between her legs. She slammed the oven door on the chicken and still half-standing, half-squatting, pulled up her skirt and looked at her panties. There was a bright red stain on the white nylon. She swayed and nearly sat down right on the linoleum floor. And then she vaulted for the telephone.

It was five-thirty. She called Dr. Zauber at his office, trying to stay calm. But her usual self-possession was deserting her. Her fingers slipped and she dialed the wrong number, reaching a laundry instead of her obstetrician.

She sat down on the edge of the bed before she dialed again and this time pressed her finger hard into the plastic dial, making sure she didn't make another mistake. At last she was rewarded with the doctor's reassuring voice saying, "Hello. This is Dr. Zauber."

"Oh. I'm go glad I got you," she cried. "I was afraid you'd be gone already." But his voice went on in tandem with her own. "I am sorry I cannot speak with you right now, but if you will leave your name and number I will get back to you."

Embarrassed at having been so nervous as to mistake his tape recording for the doctor himself, she rattled her name and number into the machine and then, hanging up, unexpectedly began to cry.

The tears, burning and copious, astonished her even more than the bleeding had. She blotted them with the bottom of Philip's shirt, yet they continued to flow, until finally she had to acknowledge to herself what she had never before acknowledged, had to admit that although the baby had been Philip's idea, it had now become as important to her as ever it had been to him. The thought of losing it was suddenly unbearable and, lying back against the pillows, she began to sob uncontrollably. She wanted nothing but to keep the baby inside her. Crying, she wrapped her arms around her chest and clenched her legs together, wondering wildly whether this would help.

She was still crying when the phone rang fifteen minutes later and Dr. Zauber, in his soothing, quiet voice, asked her why she had called. She told him and was terribly ashamed of herself for crying, particularly when he assured her, "It's probably nothing. Twenty percent of all pregnant women have these bleeding episodes and fewer than half of them miscarry. Their bleeding just stops and that's all there is to it."

Still, it took her a while to calm down. "Shouldn't you examine me?" she worried.

"No. Not just now, though I will later tonight if the bleeding gets worse. Call me if it does. Otherwise, we can wait until tomorrow morning. In fact, I'd like you to come in then whether it's remained the same or it's stopped. And try not to worry too much. Chances are it will stop."

"But isn't there anything you can do now?" she implored. "Can't you give me medicine? An injection?"

"No. You know that, Mrs. Harper. If there's anything seriously wrong, it's just as well we find it out now."

"There must be something," she pleaded.

"Yes," he said finally, responding to her insistence. "There's something *you* can do." She heard him pause. "You can lie down. You can try to relax. Get your husband to watch TV with you. Or read to you. That's always nice."

Grateful, she wiped away the last of her tears, and as soon as he had hung up, obeyed his instructions, stretching out on the bed and pressing the remote control for the television. She didn't stir. And she tried very hard not to start crying again, even when she remembered that Philip had told her he was taking a group of his Social Studies pupils on a tour of City Hall this afternoon and wouldn't be home until late. Still, she was basically a self-controlled woman, one who despised tears and tantrums and the tendency of many others she knew to panic under stress, to mishear instructions on exams, misread job applications, mistrust or misconstrue the remarks of lovers and husbands. Willing herself to think positively, to concentrate on the fact that Zauber had said there was, at least, a 50 percent chance she wouldn't miscarry, she at last began to regain her composure.

It was fortunate, because when Philip walked in and saw her lying in bed, he paled, and although he tried to sound optimistic and casual after she had told him what had happened, she could see he was terribly alarmed.

She stayed in bed, getting up only to tuck a sanitary napkin into her panties. Philip rescued the chicken from the oven and ate some of it on the night table next to the bed. Then they watched a TV movie and afterward they took turns at reading the new Agatha Christie aloud. But Emily couldn't concentrate. She was watching the clock so that every hour precisely she could slip gingerly out of bed and go to the bedroom to check and change the napkin.

There wasn't much blood. Each time she looked there was just a small, scarlet pool in the center of the napkin. But she changed the napkin every hour anyway so that she could be a better judge of whether the staining was increasing or decreasing. And then, around one in the morning, there was no blood on the napkin at all.

She yelled the information out to Philip and ran to the bedroom and threw her arms around him. She wanted to jump, to leap, to fling her arms around and around. She had never felt happiness be so physical, so energizing. For Philip too, happiness became movement. Normally so sober and even pedantic, he clutched her and twirled her. They were waltzing around the bed. A moment later she grew prudent, afraid that in their jubilance they could make the bleeding start again, and she got back into bed and Philip lay down next to her, settling on top of the covers in order not to disturb her. He stroked her hair and at last she grew altogether relaxed, and now when she wanted to check the napkin she no longer got out of bed but just pulled the covers up over her head for privacy and in the half-light peered at the napkin and poked her head out of the blankets, grinning and joyous. The bleeding had not resumed. It had vanished, just as Dr. Zauber had said it might.

He seemed utterly miraculous to her then. Falling asleep at 3 A.M., Philip's arms entwined around her shoulders, she felt bound to Zauber with a new compelling gratitude.

"It was because of you," Mrs. Harper said to him in his office the next morning.

"What was?" Ben asked her, puzzled.

"That I stopped bleeding."

He smiled modestly. "I didn't do anything."

"Oh, you did. You calmed me down. Wouldn't the bleeding have gotten worse if I'd gotten all upset?"

"Not necessarily."

"Well, you got me to take it easy. To stay in bed. I figure it would surely have gotten worse except for that. So it was because of you."

The phrase stuck in his head. Daily, for over a week now, he had been planning to call Naomi but time after time, the phone receiver already off the cradle and in his hand, he had hesitated, worried about exposing his newly hatched dream of marrying to the tasks of reality. In order to marry, he would certainly have to make love successfully to Naomi, and he had been impotent for years. Of course, Masters and Johnson, whom he had heard speak at a gynecologists' convention, had claimed that virtually all impotence was curable, provided a man could find himself a willing partner. But would Naomi be willing? He remembered dis-

tinctly the hurt look on her face when he had said
goodbye to her in Sidney's examining room.

Then, listening to Mrs. Harper elaborately exaggerating his role in the cessation of her bleeding,
and feeling flattered despite himself, a clever plan
occurred to him. He would admit his addiction to
Naomi. And tell her that it was only because of
her that he had at last decided to go off the pills.
He would explain to her he had been eager to
come to her drug free and capable of starting a
serious relationship. It might move her. Certainly,
whether or not she fully believed him, it would
flatter her.

Mrs. Harper was staring at him with curiosity
and he snapped his attention back to her, saying,
"Don't exaggerate my role. I really didn't do anything. There's so much we don't know about first-
trimester bleeding—what makes it start, what
makes it stop . . ."

Mrs. Harper fidgeted with a blue cardigan
folded in her lap. "Then you told me to lie down
just to give me something to do?"

"More or less," he admitted.

She blushed. "I guess it was because I sounded
hysterical."

He saw the way the color flooded her cheeks,
saw how she crossed her black-booted legs and,
quite unconsciously, shifted her skirt so that it
rode upward on her thighs. She was flirting with
him.

It made him smile bitterly to himself. It was

ironic that he should be so admired by his patients
and yet feel himself to be so undesirable when it
came to the women he encountered outside the office. But he would have to take his chances with
Naomi. A time-consuming relationship was, he
was still certain of it, his only hedge against returning to the pills. And perhaps Masters and
Johnson had been wrong in one respect. Perhaps it
was not so much a willing partner that a man
needed, as the will to find himself a willing partner. He hadn't had that will before. He had it
now.

Mrs. Harper was saying, "Well, no matter what
you say, I'll always be grateful that you called me
back so promptly."

He sat back, lost in his own musings. The baby
had given him the will for courtship, he thought.
Mrs. Kinney's baby. Or was it Sidney's baby?

"I guess I'm keeping you," Mrs. Harper said
apologetically.

"What? Oh, no. No, I'm not so very busy this
morning, Mrs. Harper."

But she was standing up and draping her overlarge cardigan around her shoulders. "Emily," she
smiled.

"Emily," he said.

As soon as she was gone, he impulsively picked
up the phone and dialed Naomi.

He reached her at the magazine and knew at
once that he had been right to worry that she
might not be receptive to him. She sounded aloof

and told him outright, when he suggested their getting together, that she wasn't sure she wanted to see him.

"Why not?" He held the phone tightly, his knuckles paling, afraid that she was already involved with some other man. There had been no one special that day she had come to his office; he was sure of it; but that had been over a month ago.

"I find you confusing," she answered him in the direct fashion he had noticed on the day of her first visit to him. "I'm not sure I understand you."

He felt relieved. "You're hurt. I hurt you by not calling sooner."

"Yes. That's part of it. You did hurt me."

"Then that's okay."

"Okay? Okay for who?" she quipped.

"For both of us. You see, I can explain. There were reasons for why I acted as I did. And for my not calling sooner. Please just give me a chance to explain."

She resisted but he knew he had piqued her curiosity. "What about tonight?" he asked, pressing his advantage.

"Tonight? I'm afraid I'm promised to Petey."

"Petey?" He felt a loss of hope until she went on, "My son. He's spending the afternoon at a schoolmate's house and I'm supposed to pick the two boys up and take them to a movie."

"What about afterward?"

"No. I'm awfully beat today."

He almost gave up right then and there, but he knew that if he did, it would be weeks before he would feel ready to risk another rejection. He couldn't afford those weeks. Every night that he went home alone to his small, silent apartment, he had to wrestle with the urge to go down and purchase more pills for himself. "Please, Naomi," he said, his voice growing embarrassingly urgent. "I've got to see you. It's terribly important."

"It can't wait?" she hesitated, and he noted that it was his very desperation that seemed to be influencing her to consider his plea. He stored the information he had gained in a corner of his mind and said, "It shouldn't wait."

She was silent for a moment and then she acquiesced. "Okay. Tell you what. The movie's not till seven. I get out of work at five-thirty and if you're free then, we could have a quick drink. But it'll have to be at my place. I've got to go home and change my costume from girl reporter to Supermom."

Naomi's apartment was in the flower district above a plant store whose windows were lined three-deep with giant palms and rubber trees. Getting out of his cab and approaching the building, he imagined himself about to penetrate an exotic rain forest. But the entrance to the apartments above the store was behind a corroding metal door. He had to push on it mightily to get it to open. Then he rang Naomi's doorbell, and climbed steep flights of metal stairs to reach her.

He was perspiring heavily by the time he approached the fourth-floor landing and heard her voice above him calling, "Just one more to go." He took the rest of the steps two at a time, trying not to seem out of breath, and then he was standing close to her and she was leading him inside to her apartment, a loft really, a single, vast room dominated by an enormous skylight.

It was sparsely decorated. There were no soft armchairs, or end tables. There was only a large, flowered couch and a handsome colonial chest and bench—the spoils of separation, he thought, and wondered how long it would take Naomi, on her journalist's income, to make her loft look homelike and complete. Still, despite its size and emptiness, the room was attractive, hung with colorful Guatemalan appliqués and, beneath the skylight, a welter of rampaging ferns and ivy.

"I imagined you in a place like this," he said. "Something offbeat."

"Does that mean you like it?" She was closing the door and grinning at him and he realized that despite his having fixed on her to rescue him, he had forgotten her smile, forgotten the way it journeyed so widely across her cheeks and lingered and lazed before it faded.

"Yes, I like it," he said, meaning it. His own apartment was cramped and small. It had a luxury address but had been made by mitosis, the landlord's having split the building's large, old-

fashioned apartments into half their former sizes.
It was true he had two bedrooms and two bathrooms, but all the rooms were tiny and one of the
bathrooms was so small he thought it had been
created in the space once occupied by a deep hall
closet. When he moved in, it still had an outside
lock with a silvery closet key and room only for a
stall shower, not a tub. He resented his minimal
allotment of space and envied the vastness of
Naomi's.

"I like it a lot," he said, smiling back at her. She
was wearing a wraparound denim skirt and a T-
shirt. Her mother costume, he supposed. But her
chest was weighted down with Persian silver and
filigree. "It's different. It suits you."

"I didn't choose it just to be different, you
know," Naomi explained, draping his coat over
the spindly-legged bench. "I just couldn't afford
anything better when my husband and I split up."

"Where did you want to live?"

"Oh, someplace with a view. A grand view of
the river."

"And a terrace?"

"Yes. Exactly. A terrace."

She was still smiling and it occurred to him that
he ought now to embrace her. A caress might
arouse her, make her amenable to the plan he intended to propose to her. Or even better, it might
promote some stirring in his own body. In the
past, before he had started quieting himself with
the pills, he had felt desire, however minimal,

when he embraced women. That his desire fled
when he was called upon to act was another matter altogether.

Reaching out, he willed himself to kiss Naomi's
olive-toned cheek and, a moment later, to wander
her earlobe with a pilgrim finger. But before he
felt any hint of desire, she pulled away, saying, in
her husky voice, "You know, it's odd. The day we
talked in your office, I thought you were annoyed
with me. I thought you didn't even like me."

"Oh, I just had a lot of things on my mind," he
hedged.

"No. I felt you were suspicious of me. You were
saying, 'What does she want from me?'"

He looked away. "I wasn't very nice," he admitted, thinking he would have to proceed more carefully, would have to avoid embracing her again
until he felt he had impressed her more favorably.
"I wasn't quite myself that day," he added.
"That's what I wanted to tell you about."

"Why don't you, then?"

But he couldn't go on just yet. Not with her
thoughtful plum-colored eyes searching his. "Can
we have that drink?" he asked. "I think I need a
drink first."

"Sure. I'm sorry." Seeming distressed at being
considered inhospitable, Naomi began walking
rapidly through the large, open room toward a
corner that was outfitted with sink, stove, refrigerator and unfinished wooden counters. He followed her, tense.

"There's only Scotch," she said regretfully over her shoulder. "Hope that's okay."

Her back was turned. Impulsively, he decided not to wait for the drink, when her eyes would once again be upon him, but to plunge into the worst of his confession at once. "I was taking barbiturates," he said quickly. "That time we saw each other, I was loaded up with Nembutal. I'd been taking it for years. And wishing I could stop just as long."

She was bending to pull the bottle of Scotch from a cupboard lined with canned goods. When she extricated it, two tins of tuna fish clattered down onto the floor, but she ignored them, turning to him with a face filled with uneasy surprise.

"Lots of doctors do, you know," he added, hoping to minimize her disapproval.

It didn't help. When she spoke, he heard disdain in her deep voice. "That's what you had to tell me? You had to see me tonight to tell me about something you've been doing for years?" She set the Scotch bottle down on the table next to where he stood and withdrew from him, busying herself with rinsing two thick-rimmed glasses at the sink.

He shook his head. "I wanted to tell you that I've stopped."

"Hurray for you."

"Naomi?" As she dried the glasses, he reached a hand out toward her. "I was taking them because I was looking for you." The well-rehearsed line crept to his lips. "And I stopped because I found you."

Naomi moved further away. "That's ridiculous. We hardly know each other."

"I'm in love with you. Really I am."

Naomi began to giggle. "Me? Why me?"

He had asked himself the same question repeatedly ever since the thought of marrying her had first occurred to him. And he had been unable to answer it. Except to tell himself that he had sensed that she was available. He hated that explanation. "Because you're adventurous and independent," he offered, hoping to persuade both her and himself that he had sound reasons for his courtship. "A risk taker," he added flatteringly.

Naomi was dubious. "You don't know me well enough to make such a statement." Turning away again, she opened the refrigerator to wrestle out an ice tray. "I could be anyone. Anyone at all." She sounded indignant and, when she snapped the tray open, ice cubes skidded along the kitchen counter and down onto the floor.

Embarrassed and feeling his cause hopeless, he hid the disappointment in his face by bending to pick up some of the scattered cubes. Then he decided to try his luck one more time. "I'm not always potent," he said softly, his eyes on the linoleum. "And I'm terribly lonely." Admitting to neediness was not a form of communication with which he felt comfortable. Sidney was always trying to provoke him into revealing vulnerability and afterwards he would mock him for it. But he had noticed that when he had spoken to Naomi on the telephone this afternoon, she, unlike Sidney, had seemed to respond favorably to his direct expression of need. "I'm afraid that if I don't have someone to be with, I'm not going to be able to fight the pills."

When he stood up, ice numbing his fingers, she said appreciatively, "Well, at least you sound honest now."

He felt encouraged. "I'm trying. It isn't easy." But dropping the cubes back into the tray, he still avoided her gaze.

"Why not? Who isn't lonely? I've been so lonely lately that I've been sleeping with my boss. Even though I know his wife."

A small surge of confidence arose in him and at last he faced her once again. "You can't feel good about yourself for that," he commented. "Do you see him often?"

"Matinees," she said belittlingly.

His spirits soared. "I'm glad. I was hoping you might have some time on your hands. You see, I need you to help me."

"Help you how?" She ran a worrying hand through her springy curls.

"Be with me. Spend time with me."

Naomi stared at him. "Getting involved with you seems crazy to me," she said, shaking her head. "After what you've told me about yourself." Then she remembered that she had still not poured their drinks and did so now, Scotch splashing over the rim of the glasses onto the table.

Half-standing, he forced himself to reach across the two feet of linoleum that separated them, and, grasping her arm, drew her to him, sinking into a chair and holding her firmly in front of him so that she could no longer avoid him with chores. "Why? What have I told you? That I was taking drugs? Look at it another way. I've told you that I've been strong enough to stop taking them and to start myself on a new path. And I can stay on it, if you'll help me."

Her legs began to tremble slightly against his bent knees and he lifted her skirt ever so slightly and caressed the backs of her thighs. "There are so many things you and I could do together. Do you like the theater? Restaurants?" She had, despite herself, nodded her head. "Traveling? There are medical conferences all over the world that I never attend because everyone else goes with his wife or his lover and I've never had anyone I wanted to take. But I'd take you. We could go to France, to Scandinavia, even to China, if you want. Listen to me, Naomi, it's not really so crazy and you know it."

He wasn't sure if it was his words or the insistence of his palms on her thighs that was reducing her resistance to him. Slipping his hands farther up her legs, he continued both efforts. His palms sliding under her nylon panties to squeeze her buttocks, he said, "Come away with me this weekend. We could go to Vermont. My nurse told me about a great place there, where she goes skiing all the time. And afterward, next weekend or whenever, we can plan on something better. Bermuda."

Naomi quivered under his hands. "Do you feel anything now?" she asked. "Anything sexual, I mean?"

"Not just yet. Sometimes it takes me time. That's why I want to go away with you. So we'll have time. You've read Masters and Johnson haven't you?"

She nodded, bending toward him slightly, her legs unsteady. "Were you always impotent?"

"No. Yes. Most of the time. Enough of the time so that when I started taking the pills it was a way of not having to worry about sex again. Among other things I didn't want to worry about."

"I don't know. I don't know," she said wistfully. "I feel sorry for you. And I like you. Despite myself, I like you. But you scare me too."

"Don't be scared." His hands continued to press her round buttocks. "I won't hurt you again." Then pressing his lips to her dark-toned belly he whispered, "You and I have a history. Not much of one, I'll admit. But somehow it makes it easier for me to talk to you. And I need someone to talk to or else I'll go back on the pills again. You can see that, can't you?"

She was no longer pulling away. He brushed his lips repeatedly across her belly, his hands preventing her skirt from falling. When he let go of her, she had agreed to go to Vermont with him.

He had learned something about Naomi, he thought. Behind her defensiveness, she was a woman who needed to be needed. It was a handy thing to know, but then perhaps he had known this about her all along. Perhaps it was her very desire to be needed that had made him think of her. Leaving her loft, his long legs hurtling down the stairs, he felt uncharacteristically optimistic and powerful.

The next day, he had to tell Sidney his plans. Sidney had taken the morning off in order to prepare a lecture he was delivering at the medical school later in the day and he had no patients. It was a better time than most to approach him with details. Knocking on his door, Ben slipped inside, hoping that he would be in an agreeable mood. But he couldn't tell. He was making notes in longhand on index cards and said, "What is it?" without looking up.

"It's about the weekend," Ben began uneasily, and wished that Sidney would look at him when he talked.

"Yeah?" Sidney's ballpoint made a scratching sound.

Trying to encourage himself, Ben reminded himself that Sidney owed him a wealth of weekends. He was forever covering the office while Sidney attended conventions and conferences or traveled to the Caribbean to supervise the research on his pill. He forced himself to go ahead. "I'd like the weekend off. I'm thinking of going skiing. In Vermont."

Sidney put down his pen. "Skiing? Since when do you ski?"

Having captured Sidney's attention, he grew more confident. "I thought I might take lessons."

Laughing, Sidney picked up his pen again. "There's no snow in Vermont this week."

"Well, it might snow."

Sidney shook his head from side to side as if he found Ben amusing. "That's funny. You're kidding aren't you?" When Ben too shook his head, Sidney grumbled, "You might have mentioned it sooner. Claudia and I were thinking of possibly flying up to Boston this weekend to see her mother."

Disappointed, Ben said, "Oh. I'm sorry. I was hoping you had no plans."

"They're not definite," Sidney admitted.

"Then couldn't you postpone? You see, I've already talked to a woman I know about going with me. If I'm going."

"No kidding? Who?" Sidney looked surprised and more than a little annoyed.

"Naomi Golden."

Sidney spoke condescendingly. "You're joking. What do you see in her?" Then he smiled. "I know what she sees in you. Dollar signs."

Ben felt his resolve begin to weaken. "You think so?" he asked hesitantly and thought of explaining to Sidney exactly why he badly needed companionship these days, no matter its source. But somehow he couldn't bring himself to do it. If he told Sidney now that he had given up the barbiturates, before he himself was certain his reformation would last, Sidney would be skeptical at best. But if he waited and surprised him with the information once his withdrawal was permanent and well established, Sidney would be impressed. "Well, maybe you're right about Naomi," he said. "But still, I'd like to go. I haven't had a weekend out of the city for ages."

"All right," Sidney said at last, begrudgingly. "But don't expect me to cover for you. Ask Burt Herron. Or Sam Schwartz. That way I can still get away myself if I want to."

Harry Mulenberg was sitting in his wheelchair in the front row of the amphitheater in which Sidney Zauber was lecturing. The room was packed, jammed principally with students but with a goodly scattering of attending doctors and hospital personnel as well. It was rare for the Wednesday guest lecture to draw such a crowd, Mulenberg thought, but then Sidney's research had been mentioned on television and in the newspapers and doctors were no different from everyone else in the way they responded to celebrity. Because Sidney was becoming famous, they wanted to be able to say they'd heard him speak, and most of them would approve his speech no matter what he said. It was what the psychiatrists at the hospital called the "Yea Phenomenon," Muelnberg mused; people tended to say yes, to nod and grant agreement to anyone who seemed already to have garnered public esteem.

He turned and looked around querulously at the audience. Sidney had read from notes, had rarely raised his head, had erased diagrams as fast as he had drawn them. Yet still the audience was listening approvingly, and many people were nodding admiringly. A moment later Sidney finished speaking and applause broke out. Before it subsided, a man from the hospital's public relations staff snapped pictures of Sidney and the enthusiastic audience both.

"Dr. Zauber will take questions now," the young resident who had introduced Sidney said as soon as the room was quiet again. He stepped to the podium and Sidney moved a few feet away from it.

A number of hands shot up and the resident began calling on people. Whenever he did, and a question was asked, Sidney would saunter to the podium to deliver his answer and afterward would modestly retreat to the side of the platform again, letting the young resident take charge.

"How many women did you say you had already studied?" one student asked. "How much longer will you be doing your follow-up studies before you publish?" asked another. So far the questions were simply requests for restatements of

information Sidney had already given. Mulenberg
raised his hand. He would give Sidney a hard one,
he thought. A question Sidney would have to pon-
der before answering.

There were other hands fluttering in the audience but he knew the resident would call upon
him next; it was customary to recognize elder
staff members before the younger doctors and
students. He waited, his arm in the air, framing
his question while Sidney gave a lengthy answer
to the previous query. But when Sidney had finished speaking, he didn't step away from the podium. He remained there and himself nodded to a
questioner at the side of the room, another student, and then to one in the back, an intern. Mulenberg kept his hand up during both answers.

The resident, his eyes on Mulenberg, whispered
something to Sidney. Sidney looked at his watch
and whispered something back. And then the resident said, his voice conciliatory, "I'm afraid Dr.
Zauber won't be able to take any further questions. He has an emergency consultation at Midstate at five."

There were groans of disappointment from the
audience, but Sidney hunched up his shoulders in
an apologetic shrug, and, arms raised, palms upward, said, "Well, maybe you can learn something
from this too. The fun and the glamour are in research. But patients always come first."

The students liked it. Again, there was applause
and immediately afterward a handful of young

men and women rose and moved eagerly toward Sidney, who was already packing up his notes.

Just then he seemed finally to see Mulenberg, although the students were closing ranks around him, buzzing with interest and admiration. He stepped outside their white-jacketed circle for a moment, and looking at Mulenberg with a smile, waved at him, a large, elongated opal gleaming on his right hand. "Harry! Nice to see you! Didn't know you were here!"

Mulenberg didn't wave back. Putting both hands on the wheels of his chair, he began maneuvering his way out through the crowded front aisle of the amphitheater. He was furious with Sidney for not acknowledging him, and as he pushed his way toward the elevator he had the nagging thought that his former protégé was trying to hide something. He couldn't think what it might be, but he made up his mind to try to find out. He knew one of Sidney's Caribbean researchers. Had heard some vague but negative gossip about the pill from him. Instead of taking the elevator down to the Founders' Lounge, where he was supposed to meet Thomas Alithorn for a drink after the lecture, he asked the operator to let him off on the fifth floor. Then, tediously, he made his way to his office.

It was dusty, he noted pettishly as he pushed through the door. Sidney Zauber looked through him as if age and illness had made him invisible as well as ineffectual, and even the maintenance staff seemed to believe he would never get back to work again. But he would show them. It was just a matter of time. Already, his leg was growing stronger. He could even, he noticed, place some weight on it now as he leaned down to open his bottom desk drawer and pull out his old Rolodex.

He found the name he was looking for and placed his call. But when the long distance operator connected him with Keith Neville's clinic, a nurse reported that Neville couldn't be reached today at all. "He gone to St. Lucy," the woman said in a lyrical West Indian accent. "He reach home tomorrow."

Disappointed, Mulenberg muttered, "Have him call me tomorrow," and gave the nurse his home number. After a whole afternoon at the hospital today, he'd have to rest up tomorrow before trying to come in again. Then, hanging up, he made his way back to the elevator and took it down to the lounge.

Alithorn was there already, he saw as he propelled himself awkwardly through the swinging leather-paneled doors. A waiter leaped to help him, but he brushed him aside and wheeled toward the fireside table his old friend had chosen.

"Hey! Harry! Great to see you," Alithorn called out, his suntanned face enthusiastic. Mulenberg reached out across white linen to shake his hand and for a moment forgot about Sidney Zauber. At least the chief of the department still considered him a friend, a person of value, despite his infirmities. Pulling his chair close to the side of the table, where he could be opposite Alithorn and yet still enjoy the pretty sight of the flames in the lounge's giant fireplace, he said buoyantly, "What're we drinking?"

It was Alithorn who brought his mind back to Sidney. As soon as they had ordered, he said, "Did you hear Sid? How was it? I meant to get over and hear him but I got tied up."

"He was all right," Mulenberg muttered and wondered whether he and Alithorn were still on good enough terms for him to criticize Sidney and be taken seriously.

"Only all right?" he was saying dubiously. "He's our house genius." Then Alithorn stuck his hand into his pocket, pulled out a small, carved ivory animal and began stroking it thoughtfully.

"Some genius," Mulenberg said, deciding to chance an attack on Sidney, but resolving not to make it sound personal. "I know a guy in the Caribbean who says Sidney's research protocol is wretchedly designed. He says they've spent all the money doing follow-up studies of women who stay on the pill, and none at all on women who go off it."

"You can't do everything. There's just so much money and you have to figure out how best to spend it," Alithorn said, his eyes on the carving. "Anyway, it's not my lookout, is it? It's the Deutsch Foundation that will have to worry about that. Now, if you told me he was screwing up around here, that might be another story."

Mulenberg swallowed the last of his bourbon and, feeling warm, dug out a cube of ice and chewed on it. "When a guy who can't bear to be questioned makes a mistake," he said sharply, "he starts not answering to anybody."

"What do you mean?" Alithorn raised his eyes inquisitively to Mulenberg's. But the incident in the lecture hall was too embarrassing to relate. Mulenberg retreated to generalities. "Sidney's been awfully arrogant lately."

"Well, why shouldn't he be?" Alithorn muttered, disappointed. "Weren't you, in your heyday?" He shook his head. "I'm surprised at you, Harry. There are a lot of guys around here who are jealous of Sidney Zauber, but they're the guys who never amounted to much themselves." Suddenly he handed his piece of ivory across the table to Mulenberg. "Maybe being in that chair is getting you down. You ought to have a hobby."

Glancing at the carving only briefly, Mulenberg tried to resume his discussion of Sidney. Perhaps he really ought to be more specific. "This fellow in the Caribbean I mentioned," he began, but Alithorn had lost interest in the topic. "Why don't you come with me to my netsuke dealer sometime?" he interrupted Mulenberg.

"I'm not the type for hobbies."

"You'd be smart to develop one. It'd help, now that you have so much time on your hands. Here, look at the ears on this tiger. Now the fellow who carved this was really what you could call a genius."

Mulenberg studied the tiny animal. "I suppose you're right," he murmured, feeling shunted aside once again. The heat from the fireplace began to oppress him and he pushed himself slightly back from the table, his eyelids drooping.

"What's the matter?" Alithorn asked. "You dizzy?"

"No," Mulenberg said. He straightened up in his chair and opened his eyes wide. But he had dropped the little carved tiger. It wasn't in his hand or even in his lap and Alithorn had to bend and retrieve it from under the table.

On Friday Ben hurried most of his patients. He had told Naomi he would finish up as early as he could, and would call her and pick her up at her office in sufficient time to avoid the rush hour traffic. But he was delayed by Claudia, his last patient for the day, who telephoned to say she would be a bit late for her two-thirty appointment. Waiting for her, Ben impatiently browsed for a second time through the file on her which Cora had set on his desk.

It had come from Sidney's file cabinet. Sidney had met Claudia in his professional capacity. She had first come to see him some six years ago at a time when Harry Mulenberg, her gynecologist, was out of town, and ever since then she had been

in Sidney's care. Even after they married. It was
unorthodox, but Sidney always said he saw no reason why so many doctors eschewed looking after
their own wives and children. Who else would
give them the most concerned care?

Of course, Sidney had also said that if Claudia
got pregnant or ill, he would pass her on to someone else; it was medical tradition. What puzzled
Ben, had puzzled him ever since the night he had
learned of her pregnancy, was why he'd decided
to pass Claudia on to him. He was sure that Sidney didn't think particularly highly of his professional capabilities. Yet he'd chosen him over
Stearns, over Alithorn. Why?

Curious, he studied Claudia's file, hoping to
find a clue. But he came across nothing—nothing
that aided him. Claudia had first visited Sidney
because of a mild case of vaginitis, he read. She
had regular and painless menstrual cycles. She
was in excellent health and had no drug allergies.
She did have cystic breasts, and a retracted nipple, and as a result Sidney had recommended she
use an IUD, rather than pills, for birth control.
She'd had no trouble with the IUD. She had no
trouble with anything, he thought. Her gynecological history was as exemplary as her social behavior.

He was still reading Sidney's scrawl when Cora
opened the door and let Claudia in. "Mrs. Doctor
Sidney Zauber," Cora said. The two women were
fond of each other and Cora loved to make Clau-

dia laugh by embroidering her name with Sidney's title.

Claudia smiled at Cora until she had closed the door and left. But as soon as they were alone he saw that she was upset. Her white skin seemed paler than usual. Her smile didn't fade. It vanished. "Is something wrong?" he asked her.

"It's Mulenberg," she said, her voice subdued. "Marilyn just called me. That's why I'm so late. He's had another stroke, he's in the hospital again."

He leaned forward, concerned. "I'm so sorry. Is it serious?"

"It was on the left side of the brain. He can't speak. It'll take months before he's better. If he gets better."

"I'm sure he will. He'll be getting the best of care."

"I hope you're right." She shifted in her chair and then stood up, squaring her shoulders, commanding herself to stop brooding. Her arms, in beige cashmere, were long, the palms turned forward, like a dancer's.

"Shall we get started?" he asked.

"Yes. Yes, sure." But when he walked toward the examining room she didn't follow him. Instead, she dawdled, digging into her pocketbook for a handkerchief, blowing her nose, putting away the handkerchief and taking out a pocket mirror, with which she studied her eyes.

"Claudia?" he said, reminding her he was waiting.

At last she began moving, catching up to him, her silk skirt rustling. She was incredibly graceful, he thought, and reached his arm out to open the door for her. And then suddenly he remembered Naomi's awkwardness. Her habit of always augmenting her speech with gestures. Her tendency to drop things. To spill and scatter them. It was the last thought he wanted to entertain this afternoon when he was on his way to meet her. He turned his head away from Claudia, holding the door wide, keeping his eyes averted.

In the examining room, as she sat on the edge of the table waiting for Cora to take her blood pressure, there was no way to escape admiring her. No way to escape seeing the regal way she held her neck. No way to avoid looking lingeringly at her eyes, her neck, her hair. Indeed, he had to, for these were the areas he always examined first, the places where he looked for gross metabolic changes. But her eyes were vivid and unclouded, her neck was smooth and straight, her hair was thick and glistening. He could see at once that pregnancy was agreeing with her, could tell that she was doing well, and all without touching her.

Nor was he eager to touch her. Sitting there, her body statue-still, she was somehow forbidding, alarming to him.

"Slip your robe down," Cora was instructing her. "So Ben can check your breasts."

She did, but still he didn't want to touch her. Her breasts were white, translucent, their surface ornamented by a tracing of tiny, vivid blue veins. The areolas were large and brown, the nipples a healthy pink. But one was fierce, an erect little turret, while the other was collapsed, bent inward. Oddly, the irregularity delighted him. She was not perfect after all. He put his hands forward and began palpating her breasts, and then at last she was no longer Sidney's wife but his patient.

It made him sensitive to her in a way he had never been.

"That nipple's always been like that," she said. "Ever since I was a girl."

"I know. It was in your file." He touched the flattened nipple and tried to push it upward to see if it would emulate its mate but it remained inverted.

"It's ugly, isn't it?"

"Not at all."

"I always thought it was. When I was a girl, it embarrassed me dreadfully."

"Poor Claudia."

"Sometimes it still does. It makes me feel ugly."

"You've got the pregnancy blues," he commented, wanting to be supportive.

"You think so?"

"Sure. I'll have to tell Sidney to be nicer to you."

"No. Please don't." Her voice was surprisingly strained and she half sat up on the table.

"I was kidding," he said, experiencing a sudden surge of alarm. "I was only kidding."

He patted her on the shoulder and she lay back down again and he signaled to Cora that he was ready to do the internal examination. Cora adjusted Claudia's legs into the stirrups and pushed back the sheet that had been covering the lower part of her body. And then she stepped away and he put his fingers into Claudia's vagina, trying to measure the size and placement of the fetus. "Everything's fine," he said as he probed. "One hundred percent fine."

It was only then, just as he was withdrawing his hand, that he noticed that her thigh was bruised. There were several black-and-blue marks, a few quite purplish and vivid, a few others faded and ash-gray, on the outside of her thigh. "What happened?" he asked her, touching them. "Those look quite nasty."

She winced and said, "I fell."

He frowned.

"It was on my way to work a couple of weeks ago. Right in front of the museum."

"A couple of weeks ago and then a couple of days ago too?"

"Yes," she said quickly. "It's terribly icy there, right across from the park."

Suddenly his mind was flooded with memories of Sidney's impulsiveness and violence toward him when they were young, the pinches and kicks and punches he had endured, the lies he had invented to prevent Sara from knowing her elder son's cruelty, her younger son's submission.

"Can I get up now?" Claudia was asking.

He heard her as if she were a voice in a dream. There seemed no point in answering.

"You're finished, aren't you, Dr. Zauber?" This time it was Cora questioning him.

He forced his mind back from the distance it had taken him. "Oh, yes. Oh, sure."

Claudia slipped energetically from the table, but when she stood, the paper gown falling around her thighs and shielding her, he couldn't stop thinking about the bruises. He wasn't sure that Sidney had beaten Claudia, and yet some instinct told him it must be so. Certainly it would at last explain why Sidney had wanted her in his care, and not in that of some gossiping stranger.

Ben went into his office while Claudia dressed and, preoccupied with his new theory, wondered why the notion of Sidney's indulging in sadistic sexual play with Claudia had never before occurred to him. Then he remembered that it was shortly after Sidney had started seeing Claudia that he had started taking the barbiturates daily, quieting himself, dimming his perceptions. His mind was no longer so dulled. He sat at his desk and determined to question Claudia about her relationship with Sidney. But she came in, armored in silk and cashmere, her face a mask, and immediately began asking him about the results of the examination.

"How's Sidney taking your pregnancy?" he said, trying at least to introduce the subject of Sidney. She answered him quite smoothly, with her usual well-mannered restraint. "Quite well, thank you."

Suddenly he felt sexually aroused. Although he found the notion of Sidney's beating Claudia repellent, it also excited him. With whom was it he identified, he wondered. With Claudia, the victim? Or with Sidney, the aggressor? "I usually ask my patients about their emotional states," he said, trying to sound casual. "Oh, whether they're looking forward to the baby . . . Whether their husbands are . . . Whether the pregnancy affects their sexual closeness . . ." Claudia was looking at him coolly. "That sort of thing," he wound down.

"Everything's fine," Claudia said. "Just fine."

Her answer made him feel ashamed of having wanted to probe and as suddenly as it had come, his feeling of arousal vanished. He still wasn't sure whether his notion that Sidney had injured Claudia was correct, but he knew with perfect surety that Claudia didn't want him to pursue the subject.

He could appreciate that. When he was young it had always seemed to him shameful that he tolerated Sidney's tantrums and abuse, but the thought of others knowing that he did had always seemed more painful than pain itself. So he said nothing further to her about the bruises after all, but simply answered her questions and let her leave, her self-respect intact.

His was another matter. Locking his desk and preparing to call Naomi to tell her he was on his way, he realized that she had faded in significance, had become vague and unreal to him. It made him angry with himself. He had done precisely what he oughtn't to do if he was to carve out a life for himself that was independent of Sidney. He had allowed himself to get so wrapped up in Sidney's affairs that his own had grown shadowy, trivial. Dismayed, he tried to remember Naomi's face, and failed. When he dialed her, he felt he was calling a stranger. But then she was on the phone, her disembodied voice ebullient. "Will you be here soon?" she was asking. "Shall I meet you at the front or the side?"

"Talk to me a minute," he said.

"About what?"

"About anything. What you're doing. What you're wearing."

"I'm reading next week's issue in galleys and wondering when you're going to get here. And I'm wearing a turtleneck and a llama-hair skirt. Why?"

"No reason. I just wanted to know."

"Is that okay? Do you want to know what's underneath? Do you only weekend with women who wear garter belts?"

He laughed. Her bantering had made her real

to him again. She was clumsy, but she was amusing, approachable. "I'll be at the side entrance," he said. "In half an hour."

Repeatedly, he kept losing his sense of her and having to find her again. When he pulled up across the street from her building, there was a crowd of people emerging through revolving doors beneath a cantilevered roof and at first he couldn't tell if Naomi was among them. Then he thought he saw her, her face partially concealed by the hood of an embroidered sheepskin coat. Then he thought that no, Naomi was the more heavyset woman walking just to the left of the one in the sheepskin and wearing a purple fun fur. It was only when the woman in the sheepskin hood spotted him and waved that he recognized Naomi completely.

She came hurriedly across the street, her eyes busily judging the traffic and peering at the Buick he had rented. Then she climbed inside and kissed him on the cheek, lighthearted, pleased to be getting out of the city. "I didn't figure you for the Buick type," she commented, reaching for the seat belt.

"I'm not. It's not mine. I rented it."

"You mean you don't own a car?" She sounded incredulous.

He took her remark as criticism rather than a mere question and answered stiffly, "I rarely have need of one."

"Oh? I thought all doctors owned at least two, whether they needed them or not. A Porsche and a Cadillac."

"Whatever gave you that idea?"

"Actually, it's three," Naomi went on, elaborating her notion. "The third one's a Mercedes. And they trade them in every year."

"Not all doctors."

"No, not all. Some of them are too busy making money to get down to the car dealer's."

It was a while before he recalled that it was Naomi's style to be playful and that she had been teasing him. Then he chided himself for having forgotten so much about her and to bring himself into emotional touch with her, tried touching her literally, putting his hand on her skirted thigh. She placed one of her own over his, and little by little he became more comfortable.

"Are you a good skier?" he ventured, turning and studying her face in an effort to memorize it. "I never asked you."

"I'm good but not great."

"Do you think we'll have snow?"

"Sure I do. But then, I'm an optimist."

He squeezed her thigh and then, having to extricate himself from a tangle of cars trying to enter the highway, let go of her. But he was no longer feeling quite so estranged. She amused him, he thought, as they drove bumper to bumper through the northern suburbs. And, with her dark skin and eyes, she was attractive enough, if not a beauty like Claudia.

She did most of the talking. "What do you think of Bergman? Truffaut? V. S. Naipaul?" Most of the names she mentioned meant nothing to him. "Doris Lessing? Have you noticed that nowadays women writers only write about women, and men writers only write about men? We don't have fiction anymore. We have purdah."

"Tell me about yourself," he countered. "I—I'm not a man of wide interests."

"You could be," she said softly. "I'm sure you could be."

Pleased, he nevertheless tried to keep the conversation directed toward personal rather than intellectual subjects. "Who left whom?" he asked. "Did you leave your husband or did he leave you?"

"I left him. But he had it coming." She frowned. "Of course, now he has an excuse to be mad at me, and so most of the time he doesn't send the child support."

"It must be terribly hard for you to make ends meet."

"Terribly. But as I told you, I'm an optimist. I always figure there'll be good luck just around the corner. I'll write a book that will sell. Or some rich relative I never met will die and name me as his heir. Or I'll learn to have less expensive tastes."

He patted her hand. "You're so different from

me. I'm so cautious. So worried. So negative. I hope I don't drag your spirits down."

"No," she said generously. "And who knows? Maybe I'll lift yours up."

He really did enjoy her, he decided, and speeding ahead through gold-domed Connecticut towns he put his arm around her and kept it there except when fog drifted across the road.

Still, it was difficult to translate enjoyment into passion. Alone with Naomi in a tiny attic room in the inn Cora had recommended, he grew nervous and argumentative. The room itself irritated him. It was lit by dim, yellowish lightbulbs and there was nothing in it but a lumpy double bed and a scarred dresser, as if guests who came to the inn had few needs beyond those that could be met in bed.

"Isn't there even a chair to put that on?" he said crossly to Naomi, who had begun to unpack her suitcase on the bed.

"No. So much for your nurse's taste in accommodations."

He heard her with annoyance and wanted to suggest they leave and drive farther. Drive anywhere. But before he could speak, Naomi had begun to remove her skirt and sweater. Next she removed her underwear and sat down on the edge of the bed, her legs dangling.

He stood still. But it might as well be now or

never, he thought. Moving slowly toward her, he
pulled her to her feet and pressed his lips to her
curly hair. There was no point in delaying their
encounter any longer. His body would either fail
him or rally to his support. Whatever happened,
afterward he would know once and for all
whether or not it was going to be possible for him,
now that he had the will for it, to establish a binding relationship.

"Aren't you going to undress?" Naomi asked,
shivering slightly.

"Later," he murmured, pushing her to arm's
length and regarding her breasts. "Later. I want
to look at you."

"Please," Naomi repeated. "I feel funny with
me undressed and you dressed. As if I were one of
your patients."

"Oh. I'm sorry. It didn't occur to me." He stood
and began wrestling with his jacket and shirt.

"Hold me," she said, as soon as he was naked.
"Hold me, I'm freezing." He embraced her again
and they slid under the bed quilts.

In bed he tried everything that had ever
worked for him in the past when he had had successful sex. He caressed her belly, ran his fingers
down the insides of her thighs, turned them to
brushing against her nipples. But he felt as he always did in bed. As if he was turning pages. Was
acting by rote. Was outside himself and looking
on. He didn't want her to know and he increased

his activity, rubbing at her clitoris first lightly then strenuously. She grew excited, and put her hand out toward his penis, stroking him. But he remained soft. He decided to try licking her, hoping that setting off an alarm of passion in her would produce an echo in himself, and he slid down along her body, his tongue tentative at first, then insistent, tapping, a tool. But his mind was elsewhere, dryly reviewing the day, the long drive, the disappointment over the room.

Naomi, shifting her body, suggested he let her mouth him for a while, and he did, but it was all to no avail.

"Let's stop for a while," she said at last, raising her head and moving away from him. "Maybe you'll be more in the mood later. You're tired from the drive, I imagine." She sat up, moved to the head of the bed, and pushed a pillow behind her back. But her willingness to give up after all the planning and effort he had expended infuriated him. He pulled her back down, so that she was lying flat on the bed, and then twisted his body so that he could lie over her with his mouth once again on her clitoris and his penis up against her lips.

"Please, let's stop," Naomi pleaded, her voice muffled. "Maybe you'll be less tired in the morning."

But he was feeling a compelling, driving desperation. "It will work. I know it will." Lying over her, he held her so tightly that she began to try to squirm free. "Don't give up now," he ordered, and sucked at her even harder than he had before.

But she was pulling away. "We're not machines," she said, her voice more mournful than angry. "And I don't know about you, but I'm exhausted right now. It must be nearly one."

"I'm not tired," he said bitterly.

"Sure you are," she insisted. Then she yawned elaborately. "Let's try again in the morning."

Disappointed and angered, he got out of the bed and walked to the window under the eaves, his thin body taut, the shoulders tightly hunched.

"Okay?" Naomi asked cajolingly. But he stared out the window and didn't answer her. The sky was dark, moonless.

"I hate high drama in the middle of the night," Naomi pronounced. "I can face anything, so long as it's after the sun comes up." She fluffed up another pillow and took it in her arms, and then lay down alongside it. "You sulk if you want. I'm going to sleep."

He felt enraged at her and furious with himself for having imagined she could help him. She was too ordinary, too lacking in glamour, to excite him. He would wait until she was asleep and then head back to New York. He would leave her in Vermont, stranded. It would serve her right. Or, better still, he wouldn't sneak from the room. He would tell her how she had disappointed him. How her awkwardness put him off, her uncultivated accent grated on his ears, and her very style, her flamboyant costumes and elaborate jewelry, made him wince.

He turned, ready to injure her in any way that he could, and began walking toward the bed. And then he saw that she was already asleep. Her breath was coming in long, drawn-out sighs and her arms were curled forlornly around the pillow. Shaking with anger, he looked down at her, only to realize that whatever else he was feeling, and had been feeling all evening, it wasn't loneliness. He was bitterly disappointed, furiously despairing, but he wasn't isolated, cut off, bored, estranged from emotion.

Stooping, he sat on the edge of the bed. Perhaps he *should* rest for a while. Perhaps he should wait and tell her in the morning how angry she had made him. Perhaps, and his hand stole gently to her curls, he might, after all, feel aroused in the morning. It had been years since he had spent an entire night with a woman, years since he had awoken from his sleep beside one, years since he hadn't failed to leave at once or to send the woman home in a taxi after his impotence had been displayed.

Disentangling the quilt from Naomi's shoulders, he lifted it a little and climbed underneath it. She mumbled something in her sleep, clutching at the pillow in her arms, and he looked at her with amusement. Then, pulling the quilt so that it covered both of them, he wrapped his arms about Naomi and the pillow both.

Of course, he was wide awake for hours, saw white, then stone-gray clouds drift past the window, heard pattering on the attic roof and, later, torrents of pounding rain. He hated being awake, resented the night noises in the old building. Below him, a bed squeaked. Across the hall someone was snoring, someone less deserving of rest than he. But he lay next to Naomi and eventually fell asleep with his arm caught under her breasts.

Toward dawn he imagined he heard a bell ringing insistently, and he awakened with a throbbing need to urinate. His penis was enormous, engorged. He slipped out of bed, shivered his way into the icy bathroom, then flung himself back under the quilt. His penis had withered but when he pressed against Naomi's side for warmth it began to grow again.

She rolled onto her back with a startled groan of awakening and he climbed on top of her. He felt himself shrinking but then she was reaching for him and pushing him inside her and, her eyes closed, was grabbing at his shoulders as during the night she had clutched the pillow. He began to move up and down on top of her and underneath him she was arching toward him. And suddenly his penis was throbbing, lurching, arrowing into her, and he had come, too soon for her but hardly soon enough for him.

"I figured it might happen this way," she said, her voice bland, matter-of-fact.

"Did you?" He himself was astonished, shaken.

"Sure," she smiled. "I know as much about sex therapy as you. Morning erections."

He chuckled, beginning to feel quite pleased with himself, and put his head down into the crook of her neck. "You might have indicated last night that that's what you had in mind, instead of just acting so bored," he murmured.

"No. If I had, you'd have found a way of making it not work."

"You think I make trouble for myself?"

"God, do you ever." Her arms, still encircling him, were hoops, binding him to her.

"But you like me, don't you?"

"When you're not being so compulsive." She shifted and slid out from under him. "You know why I put up with you last night? I knew it wasn't going to work and yet I kept thinking of an article I once read about infants who wouldn't cry, or even eat, unless someone handled them, touched them, fondled them."

"Nurse Naomi," he joked, and reaching out put a hand between her legs. "The further adventures of."

"You even have a sense of humor," she laughed. "At least I think there's one hidden in there." She touched his forehead, then took her fingers and moved his hand away. "But I don't like to come in the morning."

"Well, you just might have to, if I'm no good at night."

"You might get better."

"But then again, I might not." He began to fondle her again and this time she didn't resist him. Soon she was moaning under his fingers. But although his penis failed him once again, refusing to erect in response to her pleasure, he was far less worried than he had been the night before. Even though he had no choice but to play observer as she began to quiver into orgasm, he didn't feel detached. He was a spectator, but not a removed one. Flaccid, he could nevertheless feel in himself a tension and breathlessness that echoed her own.

They missed breakfast. They heard the knocking on the door, grasped the innkeeper's assertive, "It's now or never," but Ben looked out the window and saw pelting rain and gathered the quilt around their heads again and they went back to sleep. That afternoon he took Naomi to an antique shop and when she admired a particular pair of dangling gold earrings, decided to buy them for her. While she dawdled at the back of the shop, he approached the cash register counter, set the earrings down on it and hurriedly counted out bills from his wallet, signaling to the shopkeeper to get up from his stool at the door and take his money. Just then Naomi ambled up to the counter and, seeing him with the bills in his fist, looked at him inquisitively. Then her eyes wandered to the thick wallet he still held in his other hand.

For a moment, he stood motionless.

"Yes?" the shopkeeper, an elderly, wizened man, said.

Ben stared over his head, remembering with a start what Sidney had said about Naomi's being interested in him only for his money. Certainly all weekend she had been making jokes or casual remarks about money. Certainly, too, she had very little of it, while he had a great deal. Between his savings and his investments, he was worth close to a quarter of a million dollars. It wasn't a remarkable amount. No more than any unmarried, child-untrammeled Park Avenue doctor might be worth after ten years of practice. But to Naomi, on her Newspaper Guild salary, he must seem rich indeed.

"You want those?" the shopkeeper was saying in a nasal drawl.

"I—I'm not sure the lady really likes them," Ben said, turning suspiciously to Naomi.

"These?" Naomi had noticed the earrings on the counter now and her dark eyes were glistening. "They're wonderful!"

Suddenly he laid the money on the counter and handed the earrings to her. What difference did it make why she wanted him? What difference did it make how he got her, as long as he got her. She was his chance to change, to come awake and stay awake.

She had slipped one of the earrings onto an earlobe.

"You look beautiful," he whispered, and put an

arm around her shoulders, his finger teasing the
gleaming pendant.

It rained on Sunday too and they ended up
spending the afternoon antiquing again. In a
dusty garage Naomi came across a worn carton
filled with African wood sculpture and she began
pensively to sort through the pieces. "Why not
buy one of these for your office?" she said, holding up an ebony animal with long, curved horns.
"These are very good, and very old, I think, and
the prices are ridiculously low."

"What's wrong with my office the way it is?"
he asked.

"It's too bare," she said bluntly. "Devoid of personality."

Insulted, he took the wooden antelope from her
hand and set it back in the box. And then he softened, admitting to himself that she was right. He
had never thought he had the taste or imagination
to decorate his office, and so he had left it barren
of ornamentation. Besides, he wanted to please
her. They had tried to make love twice again, and
although he had been potent only one of the two
times, that success, and the one of the morning before, had made him feel exquisitely encouraged
about himself and enormously grateful to Naomi.
Even her taste for exotica seemed to him charming and singular today. Reaching back into the
box, he pulled out a different carving, the figure

of a woman with elongated neck, great, rounded breasts and a large, smooth stomach.

Naomi nodded. "It's lovely. And it would even make some sort of a statement."

He bought both carvings and, on the way back to New York, kept the newspaper-wrapped packages on the seat beside him, brushing against them from time to time. All the while he drove south, he kept wishing they were going north again and kept dreaming of what it would be like never to have to return to New York, never to have, again, to work, to see patients, to see Sidney. In his mind's eye he imagined driving with Naomi up into Canada, of reaching snows that would never melt and mountains that would take their breath away, and it was with the greatest of reluctance that he approached the bridge that led to the looming city beyond. "We got here so fast," he said sadly to Naomi.

"And a lucky thing too," she commented. "I've still got to go and pick up Petey at his friend's."

Still, he drove more slowly as he crossed the bridge, afraid that his tenuous attachment to Naomi would not survive the strains of the city.

But it did. Although, sexually, their relationship continued to be stressful, he and Naomi saw a great deal of each other in the next few weeks. They went to the theater, dined grandly at Lutèce and informally at La Petite Ferme, and sometimes just ate hamburgers and watched television in Ben's apartment.

He liked that best, liked walking into the kitchen to fix drinks and returning to see her cross-legged on his couch or sprawled on the floor, her chin in her hands. It was as if each time he left her side, he expected to find her gone when he returned, and it was with a jolt of absurd delight that he would realize that indeed she was there, really there, just where he had left her.

CHAPTER FOUR

APRIL

"Listen, old buddy," Sidney said, barging into Ben's office one evening late in April. "Can you come over for dinner tonight? I need to talk with you." He was meticulously dressed in a blue knit blazer and white shirt and on his cuffs gleamed gold links in the shape of Asclepius's staff. But his face looked drawn, as if he had been losing weight.

"What's up?" Ben hedged, rising from his chair and busying himself by searching for his raincoat in the closet. He was meeting Naomi for dinner in half an hour, but was reluctant to say so. Knowing that Sidney had a way of making him doubt himself and waver from whatever goals he set, he had for several weeks now been maintaining a new emotional distance from him, avoiding confidences and limiting their conversations to discussions of patients and peers.

He had thought at first that such a distance would be difficult for him to accomplish, if only because Sidney might consider it a kind of defection and insist on an accounting. But to his surprise, Sidney had hardly seemed to notice any change in their relationship. Always self-absorbed, he had been unusually preoccupied all month and even now, looming in the doorway, he seemed unaware that Ben hadn't accepted his invitation to dinner. Walking to the desk, he reached for the telephone, and announced, "I'll tell Claudia to set an extra place."

"I can't make it tonight," Ben said softly.

Sidney let the phone receiver careen noisily into its cradle and stared at him. Above his eyes, deep creases appeared, so precise they seemed carved with a knife.

"I've got an appointment," Ben went on cautiously and, finding his raincoat, draped it over his arm.

"Can't you break it? There's something very important I've got to discuss with you."

"What is it?"

"I need you to do something for me. To go down to the Caribbean and check something out for me." Preempting Ben's empty chair, Sidney swung his legs up on the desk. "I've got a guy heading up one of my clinics down there who keeps insisting that before we start testing the pill in the States this summer, we ought to do another major study down in the islands. He claims there's been an increase in birth defects in his area and that the defects could be related to the Zauber pill."

Puzzled, Ben sat down opposite Sidney, taking the patients' chair. "Birth defects? But the pill is one hundred percent effective in preventing conception."

Sidney nodded, his fingertips massaging the lines above his eyes. "Yes. We haven't had a single case of pregnancy in any of the women who've stayed on the pill. It's the ones who've gone off it this guy wants to study. Apparently some of their babies have shown defects and he claims my pill is involved."

"Do you believe it?" Ben frowned.

"Not really. There are plenty of other more likely factors. But this guy's been making noise for some time now and I'd like him checked out. How legitimate is he? How good are his records?"

"Don't you think you should go down yourself?"

Sidney shook his head slowly. "No. My going down would suggest I was taking the guy more seriously than I'm prepared to do just yet. Besides, I've got to be at the hormone meeting in Chicago on Saturday."

"Really? I didn't think you were going. I'd thought I might—"

"Yes?"

"Oh, nothing." He had been hoping to have a long, work-free weekend with Naomi, but he could see that, one way or another, he was going to have to serve Sidney this weekend. "Okay," he acquiesced. "I'll check this guy out for you. What exactly is it you want me to do?"

"Just talk with him. And look over his research. His name's Keith Neville. Is he sound? Or is he just one of those black ideologues who thinks all birth control is racial genocide?" Rising, Sidney began walking to the door and added, "Come on. I'll tell you the rest over dinner."

Ben looked up, startled. "I can't go to dinner. I just told you that."

Turning, Sidney shook his head and brushed his hand across his eyes. "Right. You did. I forgot." Then, angered, he shot out, "What's with you anyway? We hardly see you anymore."

Ben shrugged, still trying to keep his own counsel.

"Well, say hello to your girlfriend," Sidney snapped. "Or whoever it is who's been keeping you busy." Reaching for the doorknob, he added mockingly, "Maybe it's a boyfriend."

Annoyed at the taunt, Ben blurted out, "It's Naomi Golden," and a moment later was furious with himself.

"Naomi Golden." Sidney's frown deepened. "Of course."

"Well, what difference does it make? What do you have against her?" Ben asked, troubled despite himself by Sidney's negativism toward Naomi.

"I told you once. I think she's after you for your money."

He found the courage to reply, "You're wrong. In fact, Naomi's not even sure she wants me. In any sort of permanent way, that is. Lots of women feel there's something wrong with men who get to be forty without ever having married or even lived with someone."

"The rules are different when it comes to doctors," Sidney intoned. "You have a lucrative practice. A safe future. If Naomi isn't after your money, I don't know my own name. But that's not all I have against her. I think she's not good enough for you." Coming back from the door, he moved close to Ben and put a paternal arm around his shoulders. "She's not classy enough."

"She's okay," Ben defended his choice, Sidney's arm heavy on his shoulders. "She's witty. Easy to be with."

"What's that got to do with class?"

Ben shrugged. He didn't like discussing Naomi with Sidney, or Sidney with Naomi for that matter. Their antipathy to each other was boundless. He extricated himself from Sidney's embrace and pulled on his raincoat. "I'm late. I'd better go."

"Sure," Sidney said and preceded him out the door. "But let's have dinner tomorrow night, so I can fill you in."

* * *

Later that evening, waiting for Naomi at the bar of a crowded French restaurant, he kept reviewing what Sidney had said about her. He wasn't especially troubled by Sidney's view of her as a gold digger. He had already resolved his feelings about being wealthier than she, and made up his mind that he wanted her, whatever her reasons for wanting him were. But he couldn't help beginning to ask himself why he wanted her and whether it was sensible to want her and whether, after all, he might do better than Naomi. By the time she arrived, late and flustered, he had worked himself into a state of deep disappointment in her.

Her curls were too disheveled, he thought; windblown and in need of a cut, they seemed less attractive to him than they had only the evening before. And her voice, when she greeted him, was too loud. Worse, when the maître d' showed them to their table, he noticed with dismay how she gazed with barely concealed curiosity at the food on other diners' tables, and when the waiter offered to hang up the raincoat she was sliding from her shoulders onto the back of her chair, he saw that she was wearing underneath it an outfit he particularly detested, a violet silk shirt tucked into a flimsy, multicolored peasant skirt.

At last, when she began to tell him an office scandal, embroidering her story with gestures and comic faces, he ceased listening to her words but concentrated with extreme annoyance on her facial and bodily movements. Yesterday he had thought them expressive; tonight he condemned them as excessive.

He continued to sit in judgment on her throughout the appetizers they were served. Then, just after they were brought their main course, he was called to the hospital to deliver a baby. He spoke brusquely into the telephone the waiter placed at his elbow, took three hasty bites of peppery duck and rose to say goodbye to Naomi. He had decided not to suggest to her, as he usually did when he was called away in the middle of dinner or a show, that she go back to his place and wait for him.

She too stood, reaching on tiptoe to kiss him goodbye. Her breasts arched, her nipples paraded against the violet silk of her shirt. Suddenly he thought with a start that he had been seeing her through Sidney's eyes all night. At the same moment it occurred to him with unusual clarity that Sidney would begrudge him any woman toward whom he developed an attachment. Sidney would always prefer to keep him alone, uninvolved, at his beck and call. Astonished at the realization, he returned Naomi's kiss, handed her the keys to his apartment, and whispered, "Wait for me at my place when you're finished. I'll get back as quickly as I can."

It had begun to rain right after he left the hospital and, walking, he had gotten drenched. His shoes made dirty, wet prints on the carpet in the foyer and as he walked into his living room he felt chilled and disconsolate. But seeing Naomi with a book in her hands and a cup of coffee at her elbow, his spirits lifted. Whatever Sidney said about her, she was making him happy. It made him recall his ambition to marry and later, when they were in bed, listening to the rain beat furiously against the windowpanes, he brought the subject up, asking her whether she was still so down on the idea of marriage as she had been the day she had first come to his office.

"I try not to think about it," Naomi said, but she cradled into his arms.

"If you have to try, then it means it must cross your mind sometimes." He stroked her hair, his fingers knotting in the intemperate curls.

"Those ideas always cross people's minds when they're having affairs," Naomi said. "It's the Victorian holdover. The notion that you can't have sex without its leading to marriage."

"I don't care how you rationalize it," he responded, pleased. "You've thought of it. You've considered it."

"In a way," she admitted. "But it isn't thinking, really. It's more like just daydreaming."

"What would make you think of it," he persisted, holding her more tightly. "Really think and not just daydream?" When she didn't answer, he prodded her by asking, "What would help? What can I do?"

"I don't know," she said thoughtfully. And then, brightening, "Maybe it would help if you'd take more of an interest in Petey. A lot of the time I feel you keep forgetting I have a child. You never ask me about him."

"I'm sorry." He remembered the evening he had first met the boy, a sturdy seven-year-old with Naomi's dark, appealing eyes but a sober, even sullen mouth. He had gone downtown to Naomi's loft that night, picking her up there because they were going to an off-Broadway show, but she was still dressing when he arrived and had called out from the bathroom that he should talk with her son awhile. He had tried, asking the boy what he wanted to be when he grew up. But Petey had shrugged his shoulders and looked bored with the question. It had discouraged him. He had unfolded the newspaper he had bought on his way downtown and opened it noisily, absorbing himself in the headlines. Petey had turned on the TV.

"Petey's part of me," Naomi was saying. "When you don't ask me about him, I feel you don't really know who I am or what I'm about."

"Look," he said impulsively, "I have to go down to the Caribbean for Sidney on Friday. Why don't you and Petey come with me? I'd be working a lot of the time, but still, we'd have the evenings together. The three of us. It'd be a chance to see how we all get on together."

"Are you sure you want to get on with Petey?"

"I suggested it, didn't I?"

She nodded happily, agreeing to his suggestion, and he pulled the blankets up around her shoulders.

Everything seemed so simple to him that night. Listening to the rain beating against the windows, he was lulled into an optimism more restful than sleep itself. If all that stood in the way of his marrying Naomi was her son, surely he would find a way of coping with the boy. Then he and Naomi could give up their respective apartments and find a home for the three of them, perhaps a house up in Westchester, or a co-op in the city with a big terrace for Petey to play on. And more than two bedrooms. Three.

His breath caught with excitement. They could have a baby, he and Naomi. A cousin for Sidney and Claudia's child. It wouldn't have to be very much younger, really. They could start on it even before they got married. How surprised everyone he knew would be when he announced that he was going to be a father! And how pleased his mother would be. The last time he had seen her at the nursing home—was it already a year ago?—she had complained fretfully throughout his visit about his still being a bachelor and thereby frustrating her yearnings after immortality. Perhaps he ought to visit her this weekend. Tell her about Naomi, if not yet about the grandchild. Perhaps he could get a flight to the Caribbean that made a stopover in Miami. Closing his eyes he pictured

Sara's delight at learning he was at least planning to get married.

"They're bringing your mother down right away," a suntanned nurse assured him when he arrived at the sprawling, expensive nursing home he and Sidney had selected a year and a half ago after Sara had broken her hip. He had telephoned from the airport to say he was on his way, hoping to find her downstairs waiting for him, but the nurse explained, "She's still in her room. Putting on the finishing touches."

"Makeup?" he asked. "Does she still like makeup?"

"Oh, certainly. And that's a good sign, don't you know?"

He nodded. "It won't be very long, will it? I've got to be back at the airport at noon."

"No. She's been a little under the weather lately. A little slowed down. But they're helping her. She'll be right along."

Impatient, he paced the lobby of the nursing home and then made his way out into its open Spanish courtyard, sitting for a moment on the edge of a plastic lounge chair beneath a stand of tall palms. Several elderly, white-haired men and a gray-headed woman, reclining in similar chairs, looked up at him expectantly and then returned to gazing at the sun through the trees.

He saw his mother long before she spotted him. Actually, he recognized her by the ruffled blue

blouse he had sent her for a birthday present last
year, because except for the blouse, the woman in
the wheelchair looked nothing like Sara, who had
always been robust, neatly coiffed and well
groomed. This woman was bone-thin, had white,
matted strands of hair that jutted out from her
head like the rays on a child-drawn sun, and was
wearing worn blue slacks stained with food. Her
lips were inverted and in her lap she was carrying
a set of false teeth.

"Hello, Mama," he said and stooped down to
kiss her. But at the last moment he averted his
lips. Her lipstick, vividly violet, was smeared un-
evenly beyond the corners of her loose lips and he
felt repelled by the sight. Drawing back, he
thought how much he used to love to kiss her in
the days when she wore French cologne and deli-
cately applied lipstick.

Sara looked at him uncomprehendingly at first
and then began to nod her head, saying, "My little
boy. I knew you'd come to me."

"I didn't know you'd gotten so thin."

"I wrote you, darling."

But he had had no letter from her in three
months, only doctors' reports.

"Aren't you eating? Don't you like the food?"
Her loss of weight startled him.

"They've started to poison the food," she answered, her eyes tearing. "They put prussic acid
in it. I wrote you about it. You've got to speak to
them, Sidney!"

"I'm Ben," he said, puzzled at her mistake.

"How's Ben?" she asked.

"I'm Ben." He shifted his position so that he stood between her and the powerful sun.

"You're Sidney. There's no mistaking the two of you. Ben looks like your father's side."

"Mama, I'm Ben." He was growing annoyed with her. He tried to muster pity for her senility and her flagging memory, but all he felt was irritability. She saw it and sighed, "What is it? What's the matter?"

"You look terrible!" he answered loudly, paying back her oversight of him by harsh appraisal of her. But when large tears appeared in the corners of her already-watery eyes, he added more gently, "It would help if you put your teeth in."

"Uh-uh." Despite the tears, she shook her head stubbornly. "They don't put poison in the liquids, only the solids. So if you don't have your teeth in, they can't get you. Upstairs just now, they tried to make me do it, but I wouldn't. Not even for you, darling."

The group of old people under the palms were staring at them. "Okay, okay," he murmured, not wanting to make a scene.

She beamed, her toothless smile broad. "You always were a good boy, Sidney. I knew you'd understand."

Sighing, he nodded his head and repeated, "Okay, okay," trying to convince himself that it really made no difference to him whether or not she thought he was Sidney. But it did, and he couldn't avoid thinking bitterly that it had always been Sidney on whom her heart was fixed, always Sidney for whom she watched and waited, always Sidney for whom her once satin-skinned arms made room, while he got a pat or a peck on the cheeks. He had been superfluous to her as a child and now, in her senility, she had just about forgotten him altogether.

"How are you?" she was asking, her tears gone, her mouth relaxed. "How's your wife?"

"I don't have a wife," he reminded her, "I came down here to tell you I'm thinking of getting married."

Bewildered, she stared at him. "You divorced the shiksa?" Her hand went to her matted hair and she rocked her head worriedly from side to side.

He shivered slightly in the sunlight, frightened by the hold her daydream had over her. And then he said, his voice quivering, "I was only kidding, Mama. Just kidding. Of course Claudia and I are still married."

"Oh. Thank God." She clutched at his sleeve. "You got me so woried." And then, turning her head and glancing at a spot directly to the left of him, she said as if to a third person, "He got me so worried. He's such a joker. All the time a joker." Her neck was stretched forward and her head was tilted as if she was struggling to hear what the person she was now addressing had to say, and then at last he heard her use his own name, or at least one of his childhood appellations. "You don't think so Benjy? You don't think he's funny?"

He cast his eyes toward the empty spot she was concentrating on. The intensity of her vision was so compelling that she was like an actress and he the audience, all disbelief suspended, and for a moment he almost expected to see his boyhood self materialize there, where she stared. And then he shook his head, shaking off the spell she had cast, and said, "Look, Mama, I've got to go now."

"Not yet!" Her watery eyes reddened and again she reached out to clutch at the sleeve of his jacket. "Don't go. I've been waiting so long for you and you got here so late."

"I have to, Mama." He pried her hand loose, and, lifting it, set it gently down on the arm of the wheelchair.

"You have work to do?" she asked, subsiding. "Patients?"

"Yes."

"I guess it's all right then." She closed her lips, but her throat emitted a sighing sound anyway. "I always tell everyone that a doctor's mother has to be more patient than a patient."

Extricating himself, he moved swiftly past her and past the lounging white-haired men and the gray-headed lady, certain that he could not endure another moment of her company. She had made him feel, more acutely than usual, that he

was a man without identity, a shadow, a mere
tracing of humanity.

In the airport, where Naomi and Petey were
awaiting him in front of the Air West Indies ticket
counter, he attempted to slough off the bleak
mood his visit to his mother had produced in him.
He had work to do, he reminded himself, spotting
Naomi from a distance, her head bent in animated
conversation with her son. He had to show her he
could relate to the child.

On the flight down the he hadn't really tried at
all. He had been preoccupied with thoughts about
his mother and had noticed that anyway Petey
seemed to prefer to talk to Naomi. Whenever he
mentioned Ben, he referred to him in the third
person. "How come he's here?" and "Is he going
to be with us the whole time?" Ben had decided to
let the boy grow used to him gradually. Now,
seeing him standing with Naomi, he thought of
buying him a chocolate bar and stopped at a
newsstand. But perhaps Naomi didn't like him to
have sweets. He turned from the candy display and
purchased a Miami newspaper.

At lunch, a hasty affair in the airport coffee
shop, the boy continued to ignore him. Throughout their hamburgers, he chattered endlessly, but
still only to his mother. "Remember the time
Daddy took me to Disney World? Remember the
time we all went to Great Adventure and the mon-

keys got on the car? Remember the ride where I was scared when the little cars started flying?"

"Watch out, Petey!" Naomi was trying to prevent Petey from continuing his memories in a standing position. "Stop. Sit down," she commanded. But Petey was evading her grasp and was standing, was whirling his arms about. A moment later he had overturned Ben's water glass, drenching his trousers.

"God, Petey!" Naomi fussed. "Petey, tell Ben you're sorry!" But the boy, sullen, simply squirreled back down into his seat.

"It's not you," Naomi whispered to Ben. "He misses his father." But he couldn't help taking the child's rejection of him personally and his mood grew even darker. Drying himself, he retreated into his newspaper and let Petey have Naomi all to himself. It occurred to him that he oughtn't to be so passive, that he ought to try to court the boy, try to find some common meeting ground. But he felt so colorless and inept after his visit to his mother that the effort seemed utterly beyond him. On the plane, strapped into his seat, he read *Newsweek* while Naomi and Petey played Ghost and tic-tac-toe.

Neville's clinic was in the hills, up a winding, dangerous country road. Driving to it in the unfamiliar car he had rented at the airport, Ben had to swerve several times to avoid not only stray goats but stray children and even adult men who stood forgetfully or defiantly in the middle of the road, conversing with one another. Naomi had suggested that since it was already late in the day, he postpone his first meeting with Neville until tomorrow. But he had felt duty-bound to put in an appearance at the clinic, even if it was just to announce his presence on the island, and dropping Naomi and Petey off at the hotel, he had driven directly inland.

In front of him now, high up toward his left, he saw what must be the clinic, a large, rambling wooden house with wide verandas and a graceful peaked roof. An almost illegible sign on the main road said, "Howeville Clinic. Government Property," and he swerved to the left to follow the tiny dirt road it indicated. There were soda cans and deep ruts marring the path; clearly the clinic was often visted on foot.

The small road went straight up a mountain and for a while he lost sight of the clinic building, then caught a view of it again when he came out, sun blinded, from under a tunnel of lianas. It seemed, from the distance, breathtakingly beautiful, the realized dream of Eden engineered by some long vanished planter. He suspected that although there were miles of rain forest and banana plantations between the house and the sea, the turquoise waters would be visible from the estate's lawns.

Parking under a clump of flowering trees, with the house still high up and to his right, he remembered to leave the windows open. It was late afternoon and the heat was pasting his white shirt against his skin. Now he could see that the verandas were lined with clusters of women and children. They were sitting squat-legged on the porches, some of them chatting, some of them dozing, some of them eating from nested tin casseroles.

To enter the building, he threaded his way through the crowd. Most of the women and children moved to make room for him to pass but one of the women sat motionless, her back against a porch pillar and her legs directly extended across his path. He looked down at her, annoyed at her rudeness, and waited for her to curl in her legs, only to realize she was not looking at him but at the brown, perspiring baby at her breast. There was something odd about the woman, about her concentration. Or was it the baby? Stepping across the woman's still-extended legs, he glanced back and watched the child suckling. It was naked, he noticed, and skinny. And the hand with which it clutched its mother's breast had only two stubby fingers. In between, there was a knot of twisted flesh. When the woman noticed his eyes on the baby's hand, she moved at last, pulled her legs under her, and draped a shawl over herself and the child.

A hand clapped his shoulder and he turned to see a slight white-coated man before him. "Dr. Zauber?" the man said. "I'm Dr. Neville." He was short, his skin black but his eyes narrow and Oriental, and although his hair was gray, there were few wrinkles on his face.

"I'm afraid I've come at a bad time," Ben apologized, glancing back at the patient-crowded veranda.

"It's always a bad time," Neville said.

Indoors, his eyes adjusted slowly to the absence of sunlight. Neville was walking swiftly and he hurried to keep up with him. They entered a large, rectangular room, once the planter's parlor, he surmised, but now furnished spartanly with Neville's wooden desk and a few straightbacked chairs. "Dr. Zauber," Neville was saying. "But not *the* Dr. Zauber."

"I'm sorry," Ben responded, automatic in his apology. "But you know how busy Sidney is."

"Of course." Neville's voice was cold.

"He was sorry he couldn't come himself."

"I'm sure." Neville sat down. "Well, what is it you want to do? Start looking over my material now?" He gestured impatiently to a stack of shabby, speckled notebooks and manila folders heaped on a corner of his desk.

"I thought I'd just introduce myself today, since it's already so late," Ben said. "And then come back tomorrow to look over the material."

Neville's voice grew less harsh. "Good. I was afraid you were going to try to rush through it all tonight. There's quite a bit, you know."

"What exactly have you got?"

"Your brother didn't tell you?" Neville shook his head. "I've got detailed follow-ups on eighty women who were part of the Zauber pill study here at various times during the past three years and who later went on to become pregnant. They're women who dropped out of our program either because they changed their minds about having children or because they accidentally forgot to keep taking the pill."

"How many of the offspring are defective?" Ben asked.

"Eight," Neville announced, his tone once again unfriendly.

"How many would you expect to find in this population? What's typical?"

"Considerably fewer. A good two hundred percent fewer."

"It could be a matter of chance," Ben suggested.

"It could be. Sure. It could be. But I don't think it is."

Ben shrugged. "The pill's been tested on six islands. The study's been going on for three years. No one at any of the other clinics involved has reported anything like this."

Neville, his voice cool and matter-of-fact, said, "Maybe no one else was looking."

Ben looked at him and saw unblinking eyes and a firm immobile mouth, and thought irrelevantly that Neville reminded him of someone. Tiny but intransigent-looking, he radiated extraordinary self-confidence. "If the implications of my study are correct, the Zauber pill could be thoroughly discredited."

Ben continued to stare at him. Then, suddenly, he felt an odd nervousness, almost an excitement, surge through his body. His hands felt sweaty and his breath short. But he swept his nervousness aside. It was foolish to be nervous about the Zauber pill. Sidney never made mistakes. Whatever he turned his mind to, he accomplished with dazzling success. Only a year ago, Ben recalled, Alithorn had jokingly said that he wished Sidney would make a few more misdiagnoses, or even lose a patient, if just to make him less susceptible to going to pieces the first time he did.

"Well, I'll certainly be glad to look over your material," he said to Neville. "Though I doubt you've got anything going for you but chance."

"That's fine," Neville said, rising from behind his desk. "All I want is a fair reading."

"I can certainly promise you that."

"Good." Neville reached for his hand and shook it. "Till tomorrow, then. Tomorrow will be excellent. It'll give me the time to get my material a bit better organized."

It was still light when Ben reached the hotel although already he could hear the tinkling sounds of a steel band and see suntanned guests gathering for cocktails in the thatch-roofed lounge opposite the lobby. Heading for the seaside cottages in which the hotel accommodated its guests, he skirted the lounge and made his way along the deserted beach. Over his head, palm trees rustled and beneath his feet surreptitious sand crabs delved. He paused for a moment to stare at the sun, hovering low and dominant on the horizon. Then suddenly the sun, a celestial swimmer, dived into the sea and it was night. Streamers of orange, pink and purple still emanated from the place where the sun had been, but they began to melt into each other, to drift and disintegrate, and at last they were gone altogether, vanished without a trace.

He stood at the water's edge and, watching the sunset, felt the excitement he had experienced earlier in the day increase, grow intense in the enveloping blackness. He was happy, he realized with a start. He had completely gotten over the numbness of body and spirit his visit to his mother had produced, and he was feeling vital and energetic. Running, he began heading up the beach, seeking the cottage he, Naomi and Petey had been assigned.

Namoi wore a backless yellow dress to dinner and they danced to the steel band and watched a floor show of agile limbo dancers who undulated and slithered and finally seemed almost to liquefy as their bodies slipped beneath ever-lowering rungs of flame. His hand on Naomi's smooth back, his eyes on the velvety stomachs of the limbo dancers, Ben enjoyed himself so enormously that even Petey seemed less of an encumbrance than he had earlier in the day. The boy was asking Naomi about the exotic fruits and vegetables laid out on a flower-decorated buffet table behind them, and Ben took a stab at interesting him by telling him the story of how Captain Bligh, before his men had mutinied, had brought breadfruit to the islands. To his surprise, the story captured the boy's attention and he listened to it without fidgeting.

Later, when Naomi went back to the cottage for a few moments to get herself a shawl, Petey reciprocated by telling Ben a story of his own. "I caught a crab down on the beach this afternoon," he said. "A real big one. And you know what? The lifeguard took it and said if I'd let them, the hotel could use it tonight for crab races."

"No kidding! That's wonderful. We'll have to bet on it!"

Petey grimaced. "The races are late. After the dancing. My mother said I'd have to go to bed."

"That's terrible," Ben said, and saw the boy warm to his sympathy. "Tell you what. I'll fix it so you can stay up."

"You will?" Petey's dark eyes widened.

"Sure I will."

When Naomi returned and Ben led her back onto the open-air dance floor, he told her what he had promised Petey. "I don't mean to interfere," he said. "I suppose you don't want to let him get in the habit of staying up late. But after all, this is special. He caught the crab."

Naomi, swaying rhythmically, said, "Are you sure it's all right? I didn't want him staying up late because I was afraid you'd feel he was in the way."

"Oh! But I don't feel that way. I thought I would, but somehow I don't."

"I'm glad," Naomi sighed. "I was upset this afternoon when I saw you two weren't getting on."

Petey was slumped in his chair, his eyes half-closed, when at last the band stopped playing and the crab races were announced. A tuxedoed master of ceremonies intoned the name and color of each crab and pointed out that the one with the orange stripe on its back had been caught by one of the guests. "The young man over there," the MC said, gesturing at Petey, who shivered with delight and sprang to his feet.

Ben could feel his expectancy. It was almost tangible, a current forcing the thin body to bob up and down and the feet in blue sneakers to shuffle and leap, all lethargy gone. Pushing back his chair, he grabbed Petey's hand and they maneuvered their way through the throng gathered around the MC, Ben weaving in and out and Petey treading on his heels. Then he shoved Petey forward, giving him two five-dollar bills, and said, "Quick now. Give the MC a five for you and a five for me."

By the time the bell was rung and the glass

bowl was lifted so that the creatures could begin
their sluggish exodus up and over one another toward the perimeter of the racing circle, Petey
could no longer stand still. Around and around the
circle he tore, rushing from Ben to whichever side
of the ring his orange-striped crab approached,
giggling and veering sharply whenever the crab
changed directions. Finally his crab was out and
away from the others and from far across the circle Ben could hear him shouting encouragement
to it. Leaving the spot where he stood, he hurried
around the circle and came up behind Petey just as
the boy, arms flailing, shouted, "We did it! We
did it!" Ben knew he meant himself and the crab,
but he hugged the boy tightly and, echoing his
sentiments, said with him, "We did it! We did it!"

After they had collected their winnings, he and
Petey, hand in hand, headed back to Naomi who
hugged them both. "Let's swim before we go to
bed," he said to Naomi. "Let's skinny-dip down at
the end of the beach. I want to do all the corny
things."

"Me too," she whispered. "As soon as Petey's
asleep."

They put Petey to bed, walked hand in hand on
the deserted beach, tried acrobatically to make
love in the still-warm water but were defeated by
the lapping waves which kept forcing them apart.
At last they gave up and lay on an enormous
beach towel on the sand. Twice Naomi asked him

how things had gone at the clinic but both times he said, "Sssh" and put his fingers to his lips and after, his lips to hers. To talk about Sidney and his pill and the clinic, even to think about them, might rob him of the exquisite happiness he was feeling. "Let's swim again," he suggested after a while, deflecting conversation. But Naomi was chilled and tired.

He wasn't. He left her sitting on the beach towel and probed his way energetically into the shallows, then let his feet relinquish security and began kicking boldly. There was no moon and the stars were hidden behind clouds. But he felt no fear in the water, only a delicious exhilaration.

That night, in bed with Naomi, she seemed to him a magnet that was drawing him to her. He didn't have to plan his caresses or his thrusts, didn't, even for a moment, have to urge his body to follow the dictates of will. He made love to her twice and afterward he still wanted her a third time. "You're manic," she said. "We've been screwing for hours."

"I have so much time to make up for."

But he could see that she was tired and he let her rest. They still had tomorrow. And who knew? Tomorrow might possibly be even better than today.

He rose early the next morning, eager to get through Neville's records and have some time in the afternoon with Naomi and Petey, who were still asleep. He had coffee at the terrace dining room and took off for the clinic at once. But when he arrived, Neville was nowhere in sight. "It's his abortion morning," a nurse in a miniskirt explained to Ben as he climbed up the steps to the clinic's veranda.

"Will he be long?"

"I don't know, but he left word for you to join him."

He nodded and followed behind her to the back of the sprawling wooden house where she paused, opened a door and started down a cinder-block corridor that had been added onto the house. At its far end, he saw swinging doors and, beyond, a small, quite modern operating suite.

"There's a labor and a recovery room too," the nurse said proudly. "Dr. Neville started his clinic here, right in the house, before independence, and then afterward, the government gave him the money to modernize."

Neville, wearing surgical dress, nodded good morning as Ben entered. "You're just in time. I was waiting for you. I have a patient here who was one of the test women." There was a young, vaguely familiar woman stretched out on the operating table, her body covered by a large, multi-patched sheet. Turning away from her, Neville said in a low voice, "She gave up the Zauber pill about six months ago, got pregnant soon afterward, then came in here asking for an abortion a few days ago. I tried to discourage her. I hate doing these late ones, don't you?"

Ben nodded and Neville went on, "But she insisted. Said she'd heard the baby was going to turn out bad. I asked her who'd told her such a thing and she said she'd been to the obeah-woman." He laughed. "The fortune-teller! Still, it's her own choice to make."

The woman on the table was eyeing Ben and Neville nervously. Now Neville turned back to her and peeled off the sheet. Ben, looking at her, realized the woman was a housekeeper he had seen at the hotel.

"All the others this morning are early ones. Easy ones," Neville said, reaching for a sponge. With it, he began to color the woman's belly with red antiseptic, then he covered the painted area with a sterile sheet with an opening in its middle. The woman bit her lower lip and Neville said, "It's nothing. Not nearly so bad as a cactus prick." He had soothed her and now he inserted a tiny syringe into the midline of her belly, just below the graceful, mounded curve. On the woman's skin a small, white, foaming bubble erupted and she clenched her teeth.

"That's it. It's over," Neville said, patting her arm. "There's no more pain at all. Just some cramps later when you expel the fetus."

He moved quickly afterward, inserting a longer syringe straight into her stomach. The needle point disappeared and he pushed down on the syringe saying, "There. It's home." The housekeeper, already anesthetized, was gazing at the ceiling. But Ben was staring at her belly. For a moment, his eyes intent, he thought he saw it shudder as if to expel the needle. Yet the woman's eyes were still placidly examining the ceiling. Now the needle heaved from side to side as if pushed by an unseen hand. He looked away. He had seen it all innumerable times before but he had never grown used to it, never stopped marveling at that one strange moment when, always, despite all rationality, it occurred to him that the fetus knew of and was struggling against its imminent death.

Neville now attached a thin, plastic tube to the syringe and began feeding through it the small drops of fluid that would, many hours later, force the fetus to emerge. "That's it," he said to the woman, patting her again.

She was lying back, her eyes closed.

Neville did sixteen other abortions that morning but they went quickly. They were early ones, done by suction, and none of them involved women who had been using Sidney's pill. Sixteen fetuses were suctioned out into several huge glass jars, Neville listening intently as he finished with each woman for what some French doctor had named, inadvisably Ben thought, the cry of the uterus. The dry sound of an emptied womb. For the first time, it occurred to him that, given his dislike of abortions, he ought himself one day to work on birth control techniques. What would Sidney say? Would he laugh if he told him that he was no longer content with being a clinician alone, but wanted to do research.

Afterward, the two doctors went into Neville's office and Neville handed Ben his folders and notebooks, plus a stack of X rays and a box of transparencies. "How much time were you planning on spending?" he asked.

"Four or five hours. How long do you think it'll take to go through all this?"

Neville didn't answer him directly. Instead, he said, "Suppose I asked you to stay into the evening? Could you do it?"

"I could, but I was hoping to get done early. Go snorkeling. Or sailing."

"Please," Neville said, suddenly insistent. "I'd like you to be here when she's ready." He gestured upward with his chin toward the floor above where the housekeeper had been put to bed to wait out the effects of the prostaglandin with which she had been injected. "After all, she'll be Case Number 81. You can examine the fetus afterward, if you wish."

"All right," he agreed, sorry to give up his recreational plans but flattered by Neville's wish to involve him in his research. "Okay. I'll just call down to the hotel and let them know I may not be there 'til late."

Naomi was uncomplaining. "Fine. Maybe I'll take Petey into town. Show him the way the rest of the world down here lives. Not just the tourist scene."

After Ben hung up, Neville's nurse brought him a tray of deviled land crab and some unfamiliar, profoundly sweet fruits. Nibbling, he settled himself as comfortably as he could in the straight-backed wooden desk chair, reached for Neville's notes and began reading.

The material surprised him by its thoroughness. Neville had kept remarkable records, managing to follow his sample of eighty women even though some of them had moved to different parts of the mountainous island and, in several instances, even to other islands in the region. He had tracked down each of the women, had examined their infants and the women themselves, had gotten detailed information on the women's medical histories and the course of their pregnancies, and, notoriously difficult in the islands, located and taken family histories from the fathers of a majority of the defective children. When the subjects of his study would not or could not come to him, he had himself traveled, and at his own expense, to examine and question them in their home villages.

Neville's records were painstaking, the work of a man devoted to research. Like Sidney himself, Ben thought, and imagined for a moment that Sidney would be pleased to learn he had hired, in

Neville, a scientist with standards as rigorous as his own. Then he read on, although after a while his eyes and even his forehead began to ache. The birth defects Neville had found had occurred, for the most part, in the hearts, tracheae and esophagi of the infants he had examined. But there were also two cases of limblessness. Reading, he rubbed at his temples. They were throbbing. Still, he went on and, concentrating, paid careful attention to the questions Neville had asked in his lengthy interviews.

His argument against the pill rested on the fact that the defective children had consistently been born into families with normal parents and siblings and that, in every case, the mothers of the afflicted infants had reported that they had taken no other drug but Sidney's prior to their pregnancies. At least superficially, Ben thought, it looked as if Neville's suspicion of the Zauber pill was based on sound theory. But he was sure he would find a question Neville hadn't asked, a line of reasoning he hadn't pursued. He didn't believe it was possible that the Zauber pill could in actual fact be harmful. Neville simply didn't know Sidney and his renowned infallibility.

Reading, he began to take copious notes, and all the while he wondered to himself at the audacity of a provincial doctor like Neville trying to play David to Sidney's Goliath.

* * *

It had grown dark by the time Neville swung open the door to the big, steamy office and shouted, "Come on. She's started!" Ben, poring over his notes, sprang upright and ran after Neville, who was himself racing up the central staircase behind the miniskirted nurse. "I was just about to invite you for some dinner," Neville called out. "I was afraid it might be several hours more."

"I *was* just getting hungry," Ben admitted, his long legs carrying him rapidly up the stairs so that he was right behind Neville. The nurse, already inside, held the door open for them and Neville spoke soothingly to the hotel housekeeper, whose face was strained now, her hands on her belly. And then, so quickly it was almost instantaneous, the fetus slipped from between her quivering legs into Neville's palms.

It was a tiny, kitten-sized creature that cried as soon as Neville caught it. Ben averted his eyes. He disliked prostaglandin abortions with their all-too-frequent record of producing live fetuses incapable of sustaining life. Too bad he couldn't shield his ears. Neville had placed the fetus on a wheeled instrument cart the nurse had rolled to the side of the bed and from its direction he could hear it as it continued to moan, its cry a shallow, muted, barely human lament.

It would die within minutes, he knew, and waited, still not looking at it, concentrating instead on Neville's swift movements as he delivered the placenta. Then at last, the fetus ceased crying and Ben turned to look at it.

Its chest was heaving mercilessly, its skinny legs were raised skyward, and it had no arms. Beneath miniature, beautifully formed shoulders jutted knobs of bulging, twisted flesh. He reached out a hand to explore them but as he did, a revulsion he thought he had conquered years ago in medical school swept over him, making him gag. By the time he had gained control over himself, the fetus had given one last, tortured pant and, legs no longer twitching, was lying absolutely still.

"Take it to the lab," Ben heard himself commanding the nurse. "Don't let the mother see it!"

Later that night, after examining the fetus with Neville, he got into his car and drove thoughtfully back down the twisting mountain road. He had been deeply affected by the sight of the armless fetus and in view of it, and in view of Neville's undeniably excellent research, it seemed to him now that there was indeed a strong likelihood that the Zauber pill was fallible. Of course, whether it was or wasn't, only further study would tell. But in the meantime Sidney ought to cancel all further testing of the pill until the dropouts from the other island clinics could be located and questioned. Of course, he'd be devastated. Poor Sidney. For a moment he experienced the unfamiliar emotion, a feeling of pity for Sidney. But to go ahead with further testing of the pill was out of the question. Driving through a field of tall trees whose bulbous roots stood sculpturelike above the earth, he stepped on the gas pedal and began to speed.

It was after midnight when he reached the hotel and Naomi, sun reddened, let him quietly into their cottage. He embraced her and then moved immediately to the telephone. He'd best call Sidney at once. Most likely he would be asleep, worn out from his hectic one-day excursion to Chicago and an afternoon of exhausting meetings and panels. The phone would wake him, scattering his dreams, shattering them. Dialing the hotel operator and asking her to connect him with Sidney's number in New York, he resolved to break his news as gently as possible.

Naomi, hovering over him, asked him what happened and while he waited to be connected he told her a little of the day's revelations. "That goddamn Sidney," Naomi exclaimed, outraged by his brief account. He looked at her reprovingly and said, "Ssh." The phone was already ringing on the other end of the wire and Sidney was picking it up.

"Ben? Yeah. G'head."

Sidney answered so promptly that Ben realized he hadn't been asleep at all, but must have been sitting right beside the phone, awake and anxious. "G'head. What'd you find?" Despite its staccato, Sidney's voice sounded tired, slurred, and once again Ben resolved to be as considerate as he could.

"Well, Neville's an interesting fellow," he began. "Runs the only women's clinic this side of the island. Works incredibly hard."

"I know all about his clinic," Sidney broke in. "What about his stuff?" Ben could hear impatience make Sidney begin to speak more loudly.

"He runs the clinic with government money. I guess that's common down here."

"For Christ's sake, Ben," Sidney exploded. "Just tell me whether the pill is sour or not."

He hesitated a moment longer and then he said, "Yeah. It's sour. Really sour."

Sidney was silent. Alarmed, Ben nevertheless launched into a summary of Neville's findings, mentioning that Neville had until tonight spotted only eight problematic births, but that the figure had just gone up to nine. Still, Sidney kept quiet. Ben talked on, and was about to tell Sidney that in his considered opinion it was essential that further research on the pill be suspended until the dropouts on all the islands could be investigated, when he suddenly realized that he had been talking into a dead phone. Sidney had hung up so silently that he hadn't even heard the click.

CHAPTER FIVE

MAY

Emily, struggling back into glen-plaid maternity slacks after her monthly examination by Ben Zauber, looked into the dressing-cubicle mirror, pulled the drawstring of the baggy pants disdainfully, and decided that she would, after all, use the rest of her time off from work this morning to buy herself a few maternity clothes of her own. The slacks had been given to her by her cousin Dorothy, along with a bulging cartonful of ill-fitting polyester blouses and skirts that Dorothy had worn while carrying her own child several years before. Emily had accepted the hand-me-downs eagerly, telling Philip she really didn't want to buy her own things because she didn't think it wise to spend money on so transitory a need as maternity clothes.

But there was more to her refusal to go shopping than mere thriftiness. She had been feeling unattractive lately, feeling so heavy and unfashionable in figure that she had hated the prospect of seeing herself in the impertinent lights and revealing three-way mirrors of department stores. But she had discussed her feelings with Dr. Zauber during her checkup and, as always, he had made her feel better about herself.

"I don't find you unattractive," he had said. And then he had mused, "There's no intrinsic reason to associate pregnancy with loss of sexual appeal. There are lots of cultures that idealize the pregnant woman." He had gestured to an African wood carving that had newly appeared on his wall and added, "You have to fight the culture."

"How?" she had asked. "I don't think you can." Their conversations these days always excited her, made her remember how she had felt in college when her professors spurred her to be thoughtful and to question.

"*Act* as if you feel attractive," he had said. "Sometimes acting as if we feel something *makes* us feel it."

Emily had been cheered by his challenge, even though she didn't quite believe she could effect the change in herself he was urging on her. But she had promised to try to listen to him and to come in for her next appointment looking more attractive even if she didn't quite feel it. Remembering, she slipped Dorothy's blouse over her hair,

which had long since outgrown the chic trim her
hairdresser had given her in February, stepped
into her flat-heeled shoes, and started down the
corridor to the receptionist's desk to make her
next appointment. If she skipped lunch, she'd
have plenty of time for a long look in Bloomingdale's before she was due at the neighborhood
center.

She was almost at the receptionist's desk when
she heard loud voices behind her in the corridor.
A woman's voice was pleading, "Sign! Please, just
sign! All I need is your signature." And a man's
voice was shouting, "Get out of here! Get out now.
Right now." Turning, Emily saw a tall, white-
coated man she thought must be Ben Zauber's
brother, the doctor who shared the office suite
with him, and an elderly heavyset woman in an un-
stylish pillbox hat. The woman was waving a sheaf
of papers at the man, whose craggy face was
glowering with anger. "Sign!" the woman pleaded
again, thrusting the papers at the man's chest.

"Get out or I'll call the police," the man
boomed back.

"You'll call the police!" The woman was indignant. She stepped closer to the man. Her pillbox
hat came as high as his neck. "*I'll* call the police.
The DA."

"I'm a surgeon, not a bookkeeper," the man intoned.

"The nurse said I had to see you," the woman
shrilled.

The man clenched both his hands into fists and Emily saw his entire body shudder in a paroxysm of fury. Then he slowly raised one of his fists. The woman didn't see it. She was glaring up at him. Emily froze, sure that the man was about to smash his fist into the woman's upturned mouth, and too terrified to intervene. Just then the red-faced nurse who sometimes sat at the reception desk darted down the corridor past Emily and, racing up to the embroiled couple, grabbed the woman, spinning her out of the man's reach. His arm sank heavily to his side and a moment later he disappeared down the corridor and out across the waiting room. In the distance a door slammed shatteringly.

"Who was that? What was that all about?" Emily said, approaching the nurse. The heavyset woman was still holding her papers clutched in one hand, although now she was crying and blotting her eyes with the other.

The nurse didn't answer but turned her full attention to the sobbing woman, saying, "Ssh. Calm down, calm down now."

"But I don't know what to do anymore," the woman moaned. "I've written to him. I've called him. I thought if I came down personally, it would work."

"I know. I'm sorry." The nurse purposely ignored Emily. The older woman was too upset to pay attention to her.

"I'm going to call the county medical society," the woman wept. "I am. This time I really am."

"Oh, I wouldn't do that, honey. Really I wouldn't. He'll come 'round. Just give him time."

"Am I the only one?" the woman asked suspiciously.

"The only one who what?" Emily asked.

The nurse responded to Emily at last, turning from the older woman to give Emily a professional smile and saying, "Mrs. Harper, I know you want to make your next appointment and I'll be with you in a moment if you'll wait outside in the front."

Emily stood her ground. "You might give me the courtesy of an answer."

Emily's obstinate insistence made the nurse more reasonable, "I'm sorry," she said quickly. "It was just, well, a private matter between this woman and her doctor. We're all entitled to privacy, aren't we?"

It mollified Emily. She confided, "I thought the doctor was about to hit her."

"You're imagining things," the nurse said, her wide-pored cheeks flooding with color. "What an idea! That was Dr. Sidney Zauber. You've heard of him, haven't you?"

Emily nodded. "Dr. Ben Zauber's brother. He was in the newspapers."

"Well, there you are," the nurse said, as if she had settled the whole matter.

"You're sure it was nothing serious?" Emily asked hesitantly.

"Yes. Of course."

At last Emily nodded again, thinking that perhaps she had mistaken the craggy-faced doctor's intentions. Perhaps she had simply interpreted intense argument as intended assault. She didn't want to be considered a troublemaker. Still, she lingered a moment longer, wondering if the elderly woman would ask for her support. But although the woman had stopped crying, she still took no interest in Emily. Instead, she began leafing through her papers, checking each one anxiously and looking up at the nurse occasionally as she did so. "Could you try it for me?" she said to the nurse when she had finished her perusal. "Maybe that would work."

The nurse sighed, then nodded, and said, "Okay. I'll try. Do you want to come back for the form or have me mail it on to you?"

"I'll come back." The woman handed the sheaf of papers to the nurse.

Embarrassed, Emily moved away. Clearly she was making a nuisance of herself. The other woman didn't need her assistance. Convinced that she had misperceived the situation, Emily headed for the waiting room and as she walked away the nurse called out quite sweetly, "If you'll just give me a moment to finish up here, I'll be out at the desk right away and we'll make your next appointment pronto."

Emily shrugged and decided not to wait. She'd already wasted ten minutes of her shopping time and made a fool of herself to boot. "That's okay," she apologized to the nurse. "Take your time. I'm sorry I interrupted. I'll call in for my appointment this afternoon."

In the waiting room, she retrieved her raincoat from the pink-striped loveseat where she had draped it and hurried off to Bloomingdale's. The nurse was still talking in the corridor with the elderly woman.

Ben waited out the commotion in the corridor, loath to tangle with Sidney when he was in the middle of a tantrum. But he knew he ought to say something. Sidney had never taken placidly to filling out or signing medical insurance forms but lately, what had once been a mere dislike had blossomed into sheer hatred. When patients mailed the forms to him, he tossed them into his wastebasket. When they telephoned to inquire about why they hadn't received them back yet, he claimed the forms had never reached him. And when they brought them down to the office personally, he raged at them and withdrew.

It was as if Sidney had become phobic about signing his name, Ben thought, sitting worriedly at his desk. All month he had not only declined to fill out a single insurance form, but he had even refused to sign any letters or checks. Cora had complained to him that Sidney, who normally oversaw the financial end of the practice and paid all the suppliers' bills, had not once this month agreed to sit down and go over monetary matters with her. Nor would he let her take charge and replicate his signature. Her sense of order and efficiency offended, she had urged Ben to have a talk with Sidney about delegating some of the office responsibilities.

He had put it off. To his extreme shock and annoyance, he was already engaged in a constant dispute with Sidney about his research. In this, Sidney had been as inactive as he had been about financial concerns. He had refused to cancel the Caribbean project or even to consider altering its direction to study the dropouts. Nor had he communicated with Neville, although Neville had left messages for him several times, and had even taken to calling Ben, too.

The noise in the corridor had at last subsided. Ben rose. Sidney's outburst was over. He might as well have another go at the matter of the research. And while he was at it he could mention to Sidney that signing the damn insurance forms would cause less hassle and time loss than refusing to sign them was doing.

Sidney was on the phone. He signaled to Ben to take a seat and he started for the chair alongside the desk, only to notice that it was piled high with unopened bills. He sat down on the leather couch opposite the desk instead. But even here there was an immense scattering of wrapped journals and unopened letters and manila envelopes. As he sat, the pile shifted, some of the mail slipping down behind the couch cushions. He pulled it out and saw in his hand a thick envelope from Keith Neville. He knew what it contained. Neville had told him on the phone several days before that he had almost completed an article on his findings about the Zauber pill and was about to offer it to one of the most prestigious medical journals. A publication where he had a good contact on the board of editors. He had promised Ben he would send a copy of the manuscript to Sidney.

Ben was dismayed to see that Sidney hadn't even opened it. Thinking of Neville, he remembered anew the armless fetus and the suckling baby with a knot of flesh for fingers. It was essential that, until his pill was cleared of suspicion, Sidney stop testing it. And it was essential that he inform the Deutsch Foundation of Neville's theory. Fingering the envelope from Neville, he changed his mind about discussing Sidney's irritating new disruptiveness in the office. There was no point in attacking him on all fronts. It would be best to concentrate his efforts on the more important one. As soon as Sidney was off the phone, he leaned forward and shoved the envelope from Neville on top of Sidney's desk.

Sidney frowned, ripped it in half, and tossed it into his wastepaper basket.

Ben was appalled. He stood up, gesturing at the

wastebasket with a jutting chin. "That's going to be published, Sid."

"Fat chance." Sidney picked up his phone and started to dial another call.

"Listen, Sid," he found himself pleading. "This is not something you can afford to kid around about. Neville's going to get the damn thing published."

"So what? No one'll take him seriously."

"I think a lot of people are going to take him seriously."

"Let's wait and see."

"You can't afford to just wait and see. It's in your own best interests to report his findings, at least to the Deutsch people, before he does. If you don't, they're bound to be angry and who knows, they might withdraw their support from you altogether."

Sidney had been calm, if unresponsive. But now suddenly he too stood, and, the phone receiver still in his hand, hurled his voice across the desk at Ben. "Don't tell me what my own best interests are! I ought to know what my own best interests are!"

Ben felt a nervous cramp in the pit of his stomach, as if he had to move his bowels. When they were little, Sidney's tantrums had always affected his stomach, adding to his fear of his brother's explosiveness a terror of his own potential loss of control. "All right, all right, calm down," he said ingratiatingly, trying to ignore the tremulousness in his gut. "Just promise me you'll read what Neville has to say." His deferential manner filled him with self-loathing, but he knew from long experience that it could soothe Sidney. "I know you're busy, but try to make time for it," he murmured.

His tactic worked. Sidney's voice quieted and he grumbled, "Okay. I'll read it. Maybe tomorrow."

Ben retrieved the segmented article, each half still in half a manila envelope, from the wastebasket and put it back on Sidney's desk. "Thanks," he remarked enthusiastically. "That's all I'm asking of you."

In Bloomingdale's maternity department, Emily sorted through the racks of tent-shaped dresses, fingering the spring silks and summer cottons. Preoccupied with her own needs and longings, she quickly forgot about the unpleasant incident in the Zaubers' office. There were a myriad of pastel blue jumpers; she had never known pastel blue to have so many gradations. She wanted an unusual dress, a striking, colorful, dramatic dress. Even a sexy dress, she thought, smiling to herself at the notion.

It was odd the way her mind turned constantly to thoughts of sex these days, even though she considered her new capacious body dumpy and undesirable. She was forever aware of a pressure in her loins, a tension that made her ready to make love with Philip every night whereas always before he had had to pursue and persuade her if he desired her more than three or four times a week.

Dr. Zauber said her new interest in sex was caused by hormones, and she should be glad about it. But it made her anxious. Philip was marvelous about satisfying her increased demands for love-making, but she couldn't help wondering whether he really enjoyed their times in bed. Was he just humoring her? Was he secretly yearning for some flat-bellied svelte creature? Would it really be possible for her to do as Dr. Zauber had suggested and, by fighting the cultural stereotype about pregnancy, cease to feel so unappealing?

Catching a glimpse of herself in a mirrored pillar, she doubted that mind could conquer *her* matter, and she couldn't help scolding her body. Why couldn't it have felt so desirous when it had looked desirable, and sexless now that it was bloated? Well, there was no help for it, she decided, at last selecting a few dresses from the rack. It was just another of the ways in which nature showed its cruelty, its fondness for practical jokes.

"Can I help you?" a young, redheaded salesclerk asked, coming up to Emily and gesturing at the clothes over her arm.

Emily relinquished them and followed the salesclerk into a dressing booth. Then she drew the curtains and once again removed Dorothy's slacks and blouse. But all the dresses disappointed her. They looked dreadfully unflattering. Their skirts seemed to be made of acres of fabric. She tried on a dark-flowered print, the best of the lot, a second time. Slipping it over her head she struck a fashion model's pose, one arm on her hip, one leg thrust angularly forward. "Come here, darling, I want you," she pouted to her reflection, laughing at herself and swirling yards of fabric across her stomach. "Do you hear me, Philip darling?" she said, enjoying her game.

Suddenly she blushed with feverish embarrassment. The salesclerk had pulled aside the curtain to the dressing room and was saying, "How're you doing?"

"Not so well," Emily confessed, wondering how much of her playacting the salesclerk had seen. "I—I wanted something sexy," she explained.

The salesclerk giggled. "You're not the only one. A lot of women who come in here want bright colors and vivid patterns or even black lace and beige crochet."

"Why don't you sell it then?"

"It's the manufacturers," the salesclerk said. "They don't make if for Maternity."

Emily thought about cultural stereotypes and how hard they were to change. She would have to mention this to Dr. Zauber the next time she saw him. Already, although it was another full month before she would see him again, she was storing up material for their conversations. He was always so shy, and yet so interesting to talk with, so thoughtful. She smoothed out the folds of the dress she was wearing, wondering if he would like it and whether Philip would, and finally took it off and asked the salesclerk to write up the bill for it.

"Sometimes I think the manufacturers think pregnancy has nothing to do with sex," the salesclerk murmured as she wrote.

Emily began to laugh, thinking of her nightly adventures with Philip. "If they only knew," she said to the clerk.

The young woman seemed to understand what she was talking about. She winked one jade-green eye and her shoulders began to shake. "If they only knew," she sputtered, her long red curls dancing. And then the two of them were giggling helplessly, noisy, convivial conspirators.

Emily was still smiling to herself when, on the way to the elevator, with her new dress wrapped and boxed, she saw a woman she thought she recognized standing at the negligee counter. The woman was tall and pale, with shiny blond hair, and Emily remembered having seen her at the Zaubers' office several times. Her large leather handbag was placed carelessly open on the counter, and she was holding a white silk negligee up to the light.

She must be rich, Emily thought. She must be rolling in money. Anyone who bothered with pregnancy nightclothes had to rolling in money. She herself had had to make do by borrowing a few gowns and a robe from her mother, who wore a size sixteen. Emily passed Claudia and eyed her jealously.

Claudia waited up for Sidney, resting on the chaise longue in the bedroom, wearing the new silk negligee she had bought, and wondering what kind of mood her husband would be in when he returned from the hospital. A bad one, she surmised, at least if the phone call she'd had from Cora right after she'd gotten home from work could be taken as any indication of what she might expect.

Cora had been indignant. She'd said Sidney had threatened to fire her. All because she'd spoken up for some woman who'd wanted his signature on her medical insurance form. Sidney's moods were getting her all mixed up, Cora had complained. They'd always been bad, ever since she'd first come to work for the Zaubers eight years before, but in the past month they were really getting impossible. She couldn't talk to him, couldn't reason with him. She had asked Claudia to use her influence with Sidney to make him relent, both about herself and about the woman's form.

Claudia hadn't been very encouraging. Once Sidney made up his mind about something, his opinion could only be altered by a change that came from deep within him, never by the reasoning of others. No one really had influence over Sidney, Claudia thought.

It was one of the things that she had once found so fascinating about him. She had been his patient before she had been his wife, referred to him by Mulenberg's office. Sidney had spent a half hour with her before he examined her and asked her a host of questions about herself. She had been surprised. Mulenberg had never probed into her personal history. But Sidney had seemed intensely interested in minutiae and that, too, had seemed fascinating to her. Of course, answering his questions had been difficult for a woman as reserved as herself, but because he was a doctor, and because he seemed to need, not merely want, her answers, she had spoken up as forthrightly as she could.

He asked her about her age at the time of first intercourse, and whether she had ever been pregnant, and whether she had pain during intercourse when she didn't have the infection, and posed dozens of questions about the birth control pills she had newly persuaded Mulenberg to let her take. She had told him everything he wanted to know and even told him about her father, a lawyer and a poet and a drunk, who had died in an auto crash when she was fifteen, and about her mother, who had left him once, the winter Claudia was thirteen, returning too late to have prevented Ezra Harding's series of Scotch-gaudy nights in bed with his tremulous daughter.

Claudia had spoken of it only once before, not to her mother and never while her father lived. She had told the story to Harry Mulenberg after she had been his patient for three years. She had gone to Mulenberg during her first Thanksgiving vacation from Radcliffe at the urging of a boyfriend who wanted her to get a diaphragm. She had never used the diaphragm but had broken up with the boyfriend instead. In those days sex had seemed ugly, a bother, only a means to an end to her. She had stopped seeing the young man who had given her Mulenberg's name, and many another young man too, always after only a month or two of intimacy. But she went on seeing Mulenberg for Pap smears and breast examinations. And one day, about to graduate from college and jealous of the many friends she had who had formed more lasting relationships than she had been able to, she had blurted out her experience with her father to Mulenberg.

He had seemed the perfect person to whom to unburden herself. Kindly and casual, even flippant about sex, he made her feel that somehow he could lessen her fears of sexuality, put them into perspective.

She needed perspective. For years after the brief incestuous encounter with her father, she had been sure that in some way, although she had been the victim of lust, she had also been the instigator. She remembered well that at thirteen she had been involved in a fierce adolescent battle with her mother, and had used flirtation with her father, the more powerful parent, to win occasional victories over maternal rules and regulations. But when her father, drunk, had taken her to bed, she had felt degraded, rather than victorious. And despicable. As if she herself had planned the seduction. It was only after Harry Mulenberg, growing angry and red in the face as she told her tale, said, "Jesus Christ! You call that a father! What a son of a bitch," that she felt the first stirrings of absolution from her guilt.

Afterward, her love life began to improve. By the time she first met Sidney, five years after her confession to Mulenberg, she had put the experience with her father behind her, had a half-dozen full-blown, long-lived romances and affairs, and learned to feel better about her body. But she never told any of the young men she slept with about the incest. When she told Sidney, she did so because he seemed to her merely an extension of Mulenberg, a professional persona and not an individual personality.

Sidney's response to her story had been cool, clinically nonjudgmental. After examining her, he had given her a prescription for antibiotics and she had gone home and thought no more about him.

Four months later, he had called her at work and invited her to the theater. She had been distressed, recalling at once all she had revealed about herself, and had almost refused him. But it was Christmas week. And she had just broken up with the young Columbia law student she had been seeing for six months. And she was terribly lonely. She went out with Sidney and he didn't refer to what she had said in the office but talked to her about the theater, medicine and her new job at the photography museum. When, several dates later, she herself brought up the uneasy matter of her revelations, he had said, "I never let my professional knowledge of someone affect my personal knowledge of them. You and I are starting out from scratch. You can tell me anything you want, or you can keep quiet about yourself altogether. As far as I'm concerned, I've forgotten everything you told me in the office."

At the time, his words had seemed generous to her. She had confessed what troubled her most, and Sidney had not only accepted it and her along with it, but had been willing to go past the past, to wipe it all out of his memory. It made her feel free. She was twenty-five and he was almost forty.

Months later, by the time he asked her to marry him, she knew that it was an impossibility to shut out of the memory anything one has learned, and that Sidney had sensed something about her during their first encounter which had made him keen to draw her to him. Knowing this had made her feel less free. Indeed, there were times with Sidney when she felt trapped, imprisoned. But Sidney was already an eminent doctor and researcher, and she had always been drawn to power. Sidney intrigued her. He had a blustery egotism and self-assurance that made him totally unlike the people she had grown up with. He was brilliant, and knew it, and successful, and knew it, and as a result he was totally uncompromising. He rarely ingratiated himself with anyone, whereas being submissive and pleasing had been so ingrained in Claudia that she thought it a breach of manners to have a strong opinion.

Sidney's manners were terrible. He was rude, self-centered, even explosive whenever he cared to be. His respect for other men in his field was nonexistent. She found herself admiring his disregard for everything she had been raised to consider socially essential. While she herself continued to be impeccably polite, she secretly reveled in Sidney's rudeness.

When he proposed to her, her best friend and roommate Bootie Talcott warned her that men like Sidney were wonderful to visit, but disaster to live with. But Claudia ignored Bootie's advice and accepted Sidney.

He'd rarely made love to her before they were married, but the few times he did she remembered vividly. He had never been tender, but he had been intense, and she had had with him the first orgasms she had ever had during intercourse. But his work was so demanding, so time-consuming, that often, even during their courtship, he claimed to be too tired for sex. Courtship was exhausting for everyone, he always said, but especially for doctors who, more than other men, needed the tranquility of a permanent liaison, the stability of marriage.

Lying yearningly in his arms, Claudia had decided he was right. And then on their honeymoon, she had had to beg him to make love to her. And only when she had begged and wheedled for several days, did he agree. She had found it insulting but it had excited him.

In the remaining days of their honeymoon—they had gone to Geneva where Sidney delivered a paper on birth control at an international conference—he continued to make sex a reward she had to strive to obtain. He insisted on sexual games that unnerved and dismayed her. He would make love to her only if she would first tell him her sexual fantasies, or read to him from pornographic novels, or masturbate him lengthily while he lay on the bed reading medical journals with which he had overstuffed their suitcases, or let him fondle her clitoris while she sat spread-legged on the toilet.

She found most of his requests humiliating, not in and of themselves but because she had hoped that once they were finally living together and there were no longer the strains of late-night meetings, he would be excited by her body alone. Throughout her high school and college years her cool, distant, long-limbed beauty had provoked instant passion in a myriad of men and boys. But Sidney wanted her to work at arousing him. Or needed her to work at it.

She assumed it had something to do with his practice and an overexposure to women's bodies and genitals. But although she was bitterly disappointed, she did his bidding, the very fact of his resistance making her keen to accommodate him. By holding himself back from her sexually, whether willfully or undesignedly, he made himself a prize which she had perpetually to win again through feats of compliance.

At home, in the Fifth Avenue co-op her mother gave them as a wedding gift, these feats were mostly in the bedroom. He liked her to beg him to make love to her, to stand before him naked and masturbating and pleading with him to enter her, or to beat her across the buttocks or the thighs and have her playact the part of a bad little girl, begging him for forgiveness for some invented wrong. But even in the rest of their apartment, she found herself humbling herself to him. In the kitchen he was fault-finding, demanding perfection in the offerings she made for their guests. And unless she made herself obsequious and deferred to his attitudes and opinions in the living room, he would refuse to have sex with her altogether.

Nothing disturbed her as much as that refusal because it was only after sex that Sidney would let her have access to what she wanted far more than his body. It was only after she had served and pleased and stimulated him sufficiently for him to let down his guard with her and ejaculate and relax that he would open up to her at all, letting her be privy—sometimes—to his thoughts, his dreams, his soul. She craved these. She considered him the most brilliant man she had ever known, and certainly the most renowned.

Sidney's career had flourished during their marriage. He was made a full professor at the medical school, was courted by innumerable research foundations and was rumored to be next in line for a top advisory position with the World Health Organization. The more successful Sidney became, the more she took pride in being married to him, trying to forget that when they were alone, he allowed her little pride.

Sitting on the chaise, she finally heard him at the door and felt the surge of excitement she always experienced when he returned home at night. But she didn't get up to greet him. She knew how methodical he was, how he needed, when he first arrived, to pour himself a drink, to look through his mail, and to wash away the hospital, scrubbing and running the hall bathroom sink endlessly. She sat with her toes curled under the cool silk and waited.

At last he came into the bedroom and, seeing her, gave her a slight half-bow. "That's nice," he said, nodding approvingly at her nightgown. "You look glamorous. Almost like your old self." He lay down on the bed opposite her, his shoes on the coverlet, his arms behind his head, asking, "What did you do today?"

"Nothing much. I went shopping. And then to my job."

"You didn't have lunch with anyone?"

He sounded so suspicious that she looked over at him sharply. "No. Why?"

"Just wondered." He kicked off his shoes, removing them with his feet alone.

"Cora called me."

"Really?" He sounded annoyed.

"She said you'd said you were going to fire her."

"That's true."

"Whatever for, Sidney? She's been with you and Ben so long."

"She doesn't follow instructions."

"But you always said—"

He cut her off. "It's none of your business."

"It was something to do with insurance forms," she persisted.

"You want to get laid?" Sidney said harshly. "Then don't start fights just before bedtime."

She pursed her lips. She did want to make love.

He got up off the bed and bent over her on the chaise, putting his lips to her hair. "Take off your nightgown," he suggested. "And lie down on the floor."

"The floor?" She didn't like making love on the floor. It always seemed so barbarous to her. But she went along with the suggestion, stripping off the negligee and sliding down on the carpet. If she argued with him he might retreat from her. Then once again they would sleep on opposite sides of the bed. She would have to masturbate in the morning after he left for the office, and feel the terrible emptiness that masturbation always brought with it. No matter how it physically satisfied her.

Of course, even if they did start to make love, she had no assurance he would come inside her and make her come that way too. So often lately he didn't. Instead he would deny her his penis, preferring to make her bring herself off just the way she did when she was alone. Except that when she was alone she could lie in bed under the concealing covers. When she did it for him, he made her stand in front of him while he sat and watched her with cool, abstracted eyes.

"Kiss me," he was saying. He was squatting over her on the floor, his fingers fondling her clitoris and plunging in and out of her vagina. He looked massive, leaning over her, but so did the bed, the chaise, the bureau. With her back pressed down against the bedroom rug, she felt dwarfed. "Kiss me," he repeated, but he didn't bend toward her at all.

She tried to raise the top of her body up toward his face so that she could oblige him but he moved his head away just as hers came up. He laughed then and lowered it toward her, but every time she tried to kiss his mouth, he turned his head and she brushed his ears or his hair or his nostrils but never his lips.

"If you kiss me, I'll come inside you tonight, baby. I really will."

She kept trying to catch his mouth with hers.

"Beg me," he said. "I like when you beg me."

"I can't," she groaned. Nothing embarrassed her so much as his demanding that she beg him for sex, tell him she was hungry for it, greedy for it.

"Then I won't go on." He sat up on his haunches.

"Please," she said, swallowing her pride. "Oh, please. I need it. I need it so badly." She spoke by rote. He had given her the words with which to beg him years ago, along with all the other rituals and incantations that excited him. But at the time the words had had no meaning for her. They did now. She really did want him. "Please," she went on. "Please, oh please."

"Okay," he said. "Sure, baby. Sure."

She felt encouraged, glad that she had played her role, however humiliating it had been. And then he turned her over and entered her rectum and pushed into her so hard she felt a cramp high up in her stomach, and after he had come she lay there, still hurting a little and wondering anxiously whether having sex that way was bad for the baby.

"You okay?" Sidney said. "You okay, sweetheart?"

She kept silent.

He kissed the back of her neck. "Don't be mad. I did it for your own good. You'll stay turned on till tomorrow and it'll give you something to look forward to." When she didn't reply he touched her earlobe with his lips and whispered, "It's good to need things. It makes life worth living, because you just might get what you want the next day."

She lay under him, pondering his words. He had a way of stoppering her anger by suggesting that whenever he had most deprived her or most insulted her, he had done it for her own good. It was part of his cleverness, part of what she so admired about him. She could never be certain of his motives in being cruel to her.

"Okay. Get mad at me," he said as she continued to brood. He rolled off her and helped her sit up. "Come on. Get mad. It'd be good for you." But once he demanded her anger, she couldn't give it. He reached for her nightgown and began helping her into it, manipulating her arms as if she were a small child. "Poor baby, poor Claudia," he said as he helped her get dressed. "I make you so mad and you don't let it out." He put his arm up to her mouth. "Here. Bite me. Go ahead."

Although he was teasing her, he was gentler now than he had been before they had had sex. She decided to let her anger go. It was easier for her to quash it than express it. Self-control had been her birthright. "I was just worried about the baby," she said at last in a bland voice. "Whether that kind of fucking's still okay now that I'm pregnant."

"Let me be the judge of that," Sidney said. "Don't you trust me? Don't you know I love you and I wouldn't ever really hurt you?"

She wasn't sure, but she wanted to trust and believe him. Thinking to herself that at least he had come inside her and hadn't rejected her altogether, she finally let him cajole her into getting up and keeping him company while he had a drink. He hadn't had any dinner, he told her. But he wasn't hungry. He just wanted a drink. She walked in front of him into the kitchen, glad they hadn't quarreled, either before sex or after. At least now he might talk to her, confide in her, share some of his thoughts and adventures with her.

In the kitchen he sat at the glass table and she poured him a bourbon and handed him a glass of ice water. He got out his sleeping pills and took two, as he always did before bedtime, and sipped the bourbon slowly. "Actually, I'd love to get drunk tonight," he said. "I've been jumpy all day. Edgy."

"I heard."

He smiled. "You mean Cora? That was nothing. I nearly struck a woman. One of my former patients."

"Why?"

"She got me furious. Following me around with her insurance forms. Checking up on me. You know I can't bear to be checked up on. It drives me up the wall." He smiled at her again. "But you wouldn't understand. Rage isn't an emotion you know anything about. It's banned in New England."

"I've felt it," she said, eager to show him that she understood.

"Have you? God knows I've been trying to teach it to you." He drank his bourbon and reached out his glass and she got up and poured him another drink, leaving the bottle on the counter alongside the sink.

When she sat down again she said, "But why have you been so upset? What's wrong?"

He shut his eyes for a moment and then opened them wide, studying her face as if he had noticed but not yet been introduced to her and was wondering what language she spoke. "I told you," he said. "I told you about Neville's allegations."

"Oh that," she responded, relieved. She was afraid it had to do with her. "But he's wrong. I'm sure he's wrong. You told me so yourself."

Sidney shook his head, then smiled in a quizzical way. "You really do believe in me, don't you?"

"Of course I do."

"Because you want to?"

"Of course."

He frowned and polished off most of his bourbon. "Because you have to," he said. Then he took out another of his pills and swallowed it with the last of the amber whiskey.

"You shouldn't do that," she said. "Not when you've had all that bourbon."

"Why not?"

"You know why."

"You know I never take too much."

"I know you never have."

"Don't tell me how to live my life," Sidney suddenly shouted, rising out of his chair. "I'm sick and tired of having people tell me how to live my life. If it isn't Ben, it's you. If it isn't you, it's Cora. For Christ's sake, just get off my back."

"I'm sorry." She pursed her mouth and got up and went into the bedroom. His moods were growing worse, just as Cora had said. She sat in front of her dressing table and brushed her hair and cried a little and then after a while forced herself to wipe her eyes and go outside and say goodnight to him. She was always the peacemaker, the apologizer. Someone had to be.

He was sprawled on the living room couch. She thought he was asleep at first. But his hazel eyes were open, the pupils wide and glittering. "Would you really care if I took too many pills?" he asked her as soon as she came up to him, as if he had been lying there in the dim lamplight, waiting for her to appear and continue their earlier conversation.

"Of course I would."

"I wonder."

She wanted to insist that certainly surely absolutely she would care but she couldn't get the words out of her mouth. She stood close-lipped and watched him as he shut his eyes. He fell asleep right in front of her, seeming to experience no passage at all between awareness and unconsciousness. She tiptoed out of the living room quietly, unsure for the first time since she had known him whether she was sorry or glad that he had gone to sleep and left her all alone.

Ben too began to notice the change in Sidney. In the office he was perpetually irritable and even at the hospital, according to the gossip Ben overheard at the nurses' station, he was edgy and querulous. Worse, he had even begun making errors, minor things, tiny miscalculations and minuscule misdiagnoses of the sort that other physicians and surgeons made all the time. But they were unusual for Sidney.

"Sidney's not himself lately," he observed worriedly to Naomi one night over dinner in a restaurant in Chinatown.

"That's nice," Naomi commented, deftly maneuvering her chopsticks.

"No, no. Be serious." Whenever he mentioned Sidney to her, she made sarcastic remarks about him.

"Okay. What do you need him for?" she said. "There, is that serious enough?"

Disconcerted, he dropped a piece of lobster from his chopsticks midway between the serving dish and his plate and as he tried to retrieve it, Naomi went on, "Why don't you practice on your own? Get your own office. You're just as good as—no, better—than he is."

He shook his head. She could never understand

how counterfeit such statements always sounded to him. "Sidney's a genius," he said.

"Not in my book. In my book, he's poison." It made Ben uneasy about saying anything more about Sidney's disturbing new moodiness and carelessness. Naomi would only use whatever he said to push her argument about Sidney's not being worthy of his adulation. She would take off on the topic, insisting that in her opinion, he could manage perfectly well without him. He kept silent, concentrating on his food, and when Naomi asked, "Anyway, what did you mean about his not being himself?" he answered, "Oh, nothing," and changed the subject. "Remember that doctors' tour of China I once mentioned? I think it's in September. Do you want me to look into it?"

"God, that would be exciting!"

The waiter removed the lobster and produced their next dish, tiny birds served with their heads and beaks still attached. Naomi, her dark eyes bright, said, "Just being here makes me feel stimulated. Imagine what it would be like to actually be in China!" and throughout the rest of the meal they talked enthusiastically about the trip. But the next day Ben began looking in on Sidney in the operating and delivery rooms whenever he could spare the time.

He was uncertain of what it was he hoped to see or why it was he was so curious about the change that was coming over Sidney. But he *was* curious. That much he knew. Putting on a lab coat, cap and mask, he would casually enter the rooms in which Sidney was at work as if while on his way to do his rounds he had remembered something he had to discuss with him. Then he would pose a few questions and Sidney would answer and he would linger awhile, as if fascinated by watching his brother in action.

Sidney didn't object or even find his presence odd. He hated being checked up on, as he announced with great frequency, but his dislike of scrutiny didn't apply to being watched at surgery or obstetrics. At these, he felt powerfully secure. Often he had a coterie of invited observers standing behind him, medical students or residents or younger doctors or even, occasionally, a nonhospital acquaintance discreetly disguised in appropriate costume. The hospital had a number of surgeons like Sidney, men who thrived on being observed at the operating table. They considered themselves artists and, like all artists, craved an audience.

On the first few occasions that Ben watched his brother at work, he saw nothing to justify his concern. With a forceps or scalpel in his hand and residents at his elbow, Sidney, for all his irritability, was authoritative and in full command of himself. But one morning as he stood just behind Sidney, Ben saw him do something quite uncharacteristic.

Sidney had raised his scalpel, ready to cut an episiotomy between the legs of a woman straining to deliver an overly large baby, but instead of making his usual cautious, angled incision, he cut straight down, a clean-edged hurried red line dangerously close to the woman's rectum. The woman strained again, the baby's head appeared, and a split second later Ben heard a sharp popping sound.

"I went through," Sidney said matter-of-factly, pulling out the baby. Ben had often seen other obstetricians make such fourth-degree lacerations, had even made one once himself, but had never known Sidney to do so.

"She'll be all right," Sidney said. "Good as new in a week."

Listening, Ben at first experienced a deep, unbidden feeling of satisfaction. He was pleased at catching Sidney at being less than perfect. But a moment later, his satisfaction vanished. Sidney was preparing to sew up the long cut and was reaching for a needle laid out on the sterile tray behind him. He dropped it as soon as he got it between his gloved fingers. He grabbed another and at last began sewing. But as he tied each of his swift knots, his hands shook.

Ben stared at his unsteady fingers and a feeling of dread swept over him. "I've never known you to go through like that," he commented.

Sidney said, "I never did before. But everyone else does it all the time."

Sidney was right, Ben thought. But he'd also seemed unaware of the fact that his scalpel hadn't merely slipped but had been quivering in an unsteady grip. "We'll put her on a soft diet," he went on, hardly contrite or concerned, or even aware that Ben was staring at his hands. "She'll end up good as new," he repeated.

The patient had been given her newborn to hold on her stomach and, the lower part of her body numbed, was smiling beatifically at the baby. She was unaware of the torn, ragged flesh between her vagina and her rectum, but the nurse who was assisting Sidney, the lower part of her face masked, had narrowed accusatory eyes.

A few moments later Ben told Sidney he had to leave. He couldn't remain. He had seen something which he found enormously alarming. Sidney's hands had been as shaky as ever his own had been when he was taking drugs. Worse, Sidney's thinking had been quite peculiar. His response to his error had been shallow, and he hadn't even worried that his shakiness might be observed.

Could Sidney have been high, he wondered as he left the delivery room. But a second later, discarding his cap and mask in the giant wastebasket outside the swinging doors, he scoffed at the idea. He had always suspected Sidney of occasionally taking small quantities of amphetamines or barbiturates. And he had himself first learned to use them during his medical school crises as a result of Sidney's suggestion them. But his brother had always been highly critical of any doctor who relied on stimulants or sedatives to excess.

Still, Sidney *had* seemed drugged and not just

mildly so, he had to admit to himself as he entered the changing room. He had seemed exceedingly cut off both from what he was doing and from what others might be thinking. It was a phenomenon he remembered well. Sitting down on the edge of a cot, he reviewed Sidney's disconnectedness in the delivery room and, simultaneously, his erratic behavior in the office over the past few weeks. The more he thought, the more he favored his theory.

It made considerable sense. Distressed over the imminent exposure of his research, Sidney was behaving exactly as he himself had behaved when confronted with feelings of failure. He was drugging himself. But was it really possible? Perhaps he ought to try the theory out on someone else.

It would have to be someone he could trust. Someone who wouldn't, if he turned out to be wrong, say anything against him to Sidney. Abruptly, he got to his feet and left the changing room, hurrying toward the covered ramp that connected the main building of the hospital with the Alanson Wing, the neurological annex in which Mulenberg was still confined.

"Hi there. How's it going?" A nurse was standing in the corner of Mulenberg's big room, arranging one of the dozens of bouquets of flowers that arrived from former patients and professional acquaintances daily. Ben nodded to her and sat down in the visitor's chair alongside the bed.

The old man's face looked as white as the crumpled pillow beneath his head. His condition had not improved since his last stroke, although the hospital had done all it could for him. Now there was nothing further to be done and plans were being made to send him to a nursing home unless his wife, from whom he had separated the previous winter, agreed to care for him.

The care would be strictly custodial. He would either recover his speech or he would not; he would either be subject to another massive stroke or he would not. Those who visited him, including Ben who had come on several occasions, always left his room shaking their heads. But in Mulenberg's presence they pretended to a brisk cheerfulness. Ben attempted it.

Waiting for the nurse to finish her flower arrangement, he began telling Mulenberg hospital gossip. Herron was leaving to affiliate exclusively with Midstate next year; Arnie Diehl was getting married; Alithorn was trying to talk his new wife into quitting medical school. Whenever he finished communicating a tidbit of information, Mulenberg raised his eyebrows and blinked his eyes several times, suggesting that he had understood.

The nurse, her arms stuffed with green tissue paper, let herself quietly out of the door.

As soon as it closed, Ben looked cautiously at Mulenberg's locked, slightly scowling lips and said, "Sidney's pill is no good. He's suspected it for a while, but now he's sure of it."

Mulenberg's lips remained fixed but his eyelashes danced.

"It's worrying him badly," Ben went on, lowering his voice a fraction. "I think he's on drugs. Barbiturates. He hasn't said anything, of course. But it looks to me as if he's got all the signs. Trembling. Excitability. Paranoia. Loss of judgment."

Mulenberg made a harsh gutteral sound in his throat and for a moment Ben thought nervously that perhaps he shouldn't go on. But when the old man's lips remained as frozen as they had been before, he decided to continue. Mulenberg certainly couldn't, at least at present, repeat confidences. Perhaps he would never be able to. Besides, his eyelids were opening and closing repetitively as if to encourage greater communication. Ben began talking again, words coming more easily now, sentences forming on his lips before he even had time to consider them fully.

"I really love Sidney, you know," he began. "He's a remarkable person. And he's more than a brother to me. Our father died when I was very young and in a way Sidney's been the only father I've ever known. A mentor. A role model. I respect him tremendously. But at the same time, he can be a stubborn son of a bitch."

Pausing for breath, he was aware that he had never before allowed himself to speak disloyally of Sidney or to reflect aloud on any of his failings. Even as a child he had kept silent. Staring at Mulenberg, he remembered a game of Monopoly he and Sidney had once played with two older boys who had lived across the street from them when they were children. An hour into the game, Sidney, the banker, had pilfered a handful of peanut-butter-colored hundred dollar notes and slipped them under Ben's cushion, smiling slyly. A moment later he had shouted, "Someone here is cheating. Admit it! Admit it!" Ben had shivered and one of the boys from across the street had grabbed and searched both him and his chair until the notes cascaded down and then the three of them had held him and, tickling and pinching, begun to pummel him. He had cried and they had laughed. And Sidney had laughed the hardest. But he had never once defended himself sure that if he did, Sidney would invoke the punishment Ben had always found the worst, the refusal to speak to him for an entire day and night.

Suddenly, he leaned forward and spoke more loudly. "Sidney's so fucking sure of himself all the time."

He was rambling, but he drew comfort from the fact that Mulenberg still seemed to be agreeing with him, his eyelids as expressive as a nodding head. He looked down at him fondly and hoped that the nurse would stay away a long time. He felt he had a hundred things to say, and with a luxurious sigh he began unburdening himself further, continuing to speak rapidly and without any of his usual guardedness. "I had a drug problem myself for a while," he confessed. "But I was careful. I never went above tolerance. I think Sidney's taking a lot. And if he is, it isn't going to be easy to get him to stop. He's so pig-headed." Crossing his legs, he sat up straight, thoroughly enjoying himself. But just as he opened his mouth to speak again, he heard a door opening. Startled, he turned and saw the nurse he had seen before, her arms filled with flowers.

He was bitterly-disappointed and his shoulders slumped into their usual stoop. He had only just begun to express himself, only just begun to find the thoughts he wanted to explore. But he couldn't talk in front of the nurse. Standing up, he glanced again at Mulenberg, and thought that he too looked disappointed. "Well, most likely what I told you about Sid isn't even true. Most likely it's just my imagination." Mulenberg's eyelashes continued to signal to him as if he understood not only his monologue but his reasons for curtailing it.

The nurse came up to the bed and began straightening the coverlet on which Mulenberg's paralyzed hands lay immobile. "Isn't it incredible the way he understands everything?" she said. "I mean *everything.*"

Ben nodded and, leaning over, patted one of Mulenberg's short-circuited hands. "We'll talk more," he said appreciatively. "I'll come back and speak with you if I find anything out for sure."

*　*　*

Mulenberg died two days later, before Ben had a chance to confirm or discard his suspicions about Sidney, and he felt surprisingly desolate. He had hoped to have another opportunity to talk with Mulenberg about his brother. When Marilyn Mulenberg called to inform him of the funeral arrangements, he promised at once to attend.

"Wonderful. See you there," Marilyn said cheerfully, as if she had just obtained his agreement to attend a party.

Listening to her, he puzzled over her attitude. She had cursed Mulenberg when, shortly after his first stroke, he had separated from her. She had called his departure an aberration, a madness, the late-life psychological crisis of a man who, experiencing his first intensely personal brush with sickness and mortality, had romantically believed he could still seize the day and live out youthful fantasies of solitude and lack of attachment. Later, once her anger had worn thin, she had become depressed and refused to go out of her house or communicate with any of the friends who had once been hers and Harry's in common. But now that Harry was dead, she was suddenly sociable. "It's going to be a huge affair," she was saying. "So be on time if you don't want to stand."

On the day of the funeral, Naomi, looking trim in a navy blue suit, was waiting for Ben in-front of the funeral parlor when his taxi pulled up. Although she had never met Mulenberg, Ben had asked her to come to his services anyway. More and more, he had been trying to include her in his life, and while he had never risked having her to dinner at Sidney and Claudia's, knowing that Naomi and Sidney were mutually hostile, he had taken Naomi to one of Herron's cocktail parties where he had introduced her to several of his colleagues and once he had even gone to dinner with her at Sam Schwartz's house. The funeral had seemed to him a particularly good event at which to include Naomi. All his associates would be there, and they would see that at last he had learned to live as they did, in pairs, and could no longer be considered an isolate.

"Nearly everyone's gone in already," Naomi complained as he hurriedly paid his fare.

"Jesus!" he exclaimed. "I knew I was late but not this late." He had been delayed by Sidney, who had decided that he wouldn't attend the funeral only moments before Ben stopped by his office to pick him up. He had spent ten minutes trying to persuade Sidney to change his mind, but it had been to no avail.

"I never got on with Mulenberg when he was alive," Sidney had declared sharply. "So I've decided not to go. Why should I pretend to have been his friend? Why does death have to make everyone so sentimental?"

He had found Sidney harsh and yet, as always, been impressed by his resolute lack of concern for convention. If Sidney was taking barbiturates,

they certainly weren't altering the independence
and nonconformity that had always marked his attitudes.

He mentioned none of this to Naomi, but simply grabbed her arm and hurried inside to take
the elevator to the chapel floor. Something kept
preventing him from telling Naomi his suspicions
about Sidney. It was the fact that she was already
so unqualifiedly negative about him, he thought
as they boarded the elevator. She was still angry
with Sidney for the way he had spoken to her the
day she had come for the IUD, and she was outraged by the fact that he hadn't yet done anything
about the potential dangers of his pill. If now Ben
were to tell her that he believed Sidney was dead-
ening his judgment with barbiturates, she would
simply use the information as further ammunition
in her nagging efforts to persuade him to pull
away from Sidney. To set up a practice of his
own.

Upstairs, the chapel doors were still open; the
service had not yet begun. He was relieved to see
that there were quite a few latecomers like himself
still crowding the entranceway to the chapel and
trying to make their way inside. He slowed his
pace and waited for Naomi, who was trailing a
few steps behind him, attempting to remove her
suit jacket while still in motion. She had gotten
her arm caught in the lining. He paused to help
her free it. Then he looked at her, dismayed. Un-

derneath her jacket she was wearing her violet silk shirt.

"Couldn't you have worn something more subdued?" he grumbled disagreeably.

"Oh, I'm sorry," Naomi said, chagrined. "I was late for work this morning and I had to get dressed so fast it slipped my mind that we were going to the funeral." She looked up at him worriedly. "Is it terrible? Here, let me put my jacket back on."

"No," he said, affected by the rush of her apology. "No. You'll be too warm. Forget it. It's okay." But when he led her into the chapel, he walked ever so slightly in front of her.

It was jammed. Most of the seats in the blond wood pews were filled and there was a great crowd standing in the back of the heavily curtained room. He saw Claudia among the standees, talking quietly with Alithorn and his newest wife, a statuesque young woman. Claudia looked exquisite.

She had gained very little weight. Her pregnancy was cunningly disguised, apparent chiefly in the attractive swell of her breasts against the soft, dark crepe of the loose dress she was wearing. It had always been one of his favorites. Sidney had gotten it for her at Halston's for her thirtieth birthday. He wished again that Naomi had dressed more appropriately, if not more fashionably, and then led her over to meet his sister-in-law. He had mentioned each woman to the other, and both had been saying for weeks how much they wanted to meet.

"You must be Naomi," Claudia said, even before he'd introduced them. Her face was paler than usual and although her blue eyes were clear, the lids were puffy. Nevertheless, she rallied to the social necessity of greeting her brother-in-law's girlfriend. "I've heard a lot about you," she said in a quiet voice. "I'm so glad we're meeting at last, even if it did have to be at a time like this."

Naomi's manner was equally gracious, he noted with pleasure. For all her occasional awkwardnesses and lapses of style or forethought, she could always be counted upon for warmth and empathy. "Yes," she was saying to Claudia. "I feel so bad for you. I understand Dr. Mulenberg was a good friend of yours."

"Of so many people," Alithorn interrupted, looking over Naomi's head. "Did you ever see a crowd like this one?" he added, speaking to no one in particular but shaking his head proudly as if taking personal satisfaction in his old friend Mulenberg's popularity. Then, "I see some seats!" he announced and waved to a man in one of the front pews who was standing and beckoning at him.

"Better get them," his wife worried.

"Right!" Turning toward Claudia he said, "We'll save you and Sidney some space," and moved briskly toward the front of the chapel.

Naomi glared at his retreating back. "What a rude man," she exclaimed to Claudia. "Just offering to save seats for you and Sidney. Not for Ben and me."

"I'm sure he didn't mean to exclude you and Ben," Claudia tried to soothe Naomi. "Come on, let's all go and join him." But Ben shook his head. "No, he meant it all right. He doesn't socialize much with his staff but Sidney's always been his fair-haired boy."

"Where *is* Sidney?" Claudia interrupted, suddenly realizing how late it was getting. "He said he was coming with you."

"We had an emergency in the office," he lied, embarrassed to tell Claudia the truth of why Sidney hadn't come. If Sidney wanted to tell her the truth, that was his business. And most likely he would tell her. But looking at her swollen eyelids, and remembering how long she had known Mulenberg, he was sure that if he were Sidney, he'd never do it.

Claudia nodded, accepting his explanation, and turned toward Naomi. "Did you see the body?" she asked.

"No. We didn't have time. We only just got here."

"She had him laid out in his pajamas." Claudia's voice, as always, was well modulated and controlled, but Ben thought she looked indignant. She gestured with her chin toward the front of the chapel where Marilyn stood in a tight huddle with her two daughters, their heads bent in intense conversation.

"Marilyn said that Harry was the kind of man who had hated pretension and convention when he was alive," Claudia went on, "and that he'd have wanted none of it in death. She said he'd have wanted to be laid out just the way he looked when he died."

"Well, I suppose there's something to that," Naomi said. "From what Ben's told me, he was an unpretentious sort of man."

"Yes," Claudia said. "But I find it a little strange."

Naomi wrinkled her forehead and Ben watched the two of them. He couldn't help comparing them and noticing that although Naomi was a very good-looking woman, she did seem a little used-up, a little shopworn, when standing next to his youthful, glamorous sister-in-law.

Claudia saved him from his disconcerting thoughts by saying, "Harry looks pathetic. And just a little bit ridiculous. I had the craziest notion when I looked at him. I thought that Marilyn wanted him to look that way. That she was taking her revenge. Do you know what I mean, Ben?"

His eyes narrowed. In Sidney's presence, Claudia rarely revealed her perceptions. Just then a hush began to fall over the chapel. One of Mulenberg's daughters had stepped to the front of the room and was signaling for quiet. Claudia slipped away and went to join the Alithorns, sliding noiselessly into the aisle seat of their pew, and Ben and

Naomi remained among the now even more swollen ranks of standees.

"My mother and my sister and I are all very grateful to you for coming," the young woman said, her arms swinging shyly at her sides. "You all knew and loved my father and you know deep in your hearts what a special person he was. He was an informal man who hated pomp and circumstance, a man who loved life and hated death, which he fought with a passion in others and in himself." Ben leaned forward, listening with absorption, trying to catch the young woman's soft-spoken words. Then her voice quivered for a moment and she glanced at her mother who was sitting, blue-gray head bowed, in the front pew.

"Well," the young woman resumed in an even quieter tone, "Mother and Dad talked often about how he wanted to pass from this world. He wanted no words said over him. No religious ceremony. No fuss. I know that a number of those of you present wanted an opportunity to say a few words about Dad, and talk about his accomplishments and your memories of him. But it isn't what he would have wanted. My mother is absolutely certain of this. And so, that's all. This is what he would have wanted. Just to have you gather and remember him silently for a moment and then get on with your lives."

There was a stunned silence in the chapel. No one moved, not realizing at first that this was all there was to be of the funeral service. Mulenberg's daughter, glancing at her mother and at her elder sister who was already helping Marilyn into her raincoat, had to call out, "Thank you again. Thank you for coming. The interment will be for the family only." Only then did people understand that she meant them to rise and start filing out through the doors they had just entered. "We do appreciate your having come," the young woman added flatly.

Ben was dazed and upset. He had wanted to participate in mourning Mulenberg, in hearing him eulogized and praised, in contemplating his virtues and accomplishments. To have been denied that formality made him feel cheated, and he was certain now that Claudia was right about Marilyn. She *had* wanted to cheat his friends, and even the dead man himself. It was a demonstration of hatred. Although most likely Marilyn herself was unaware of it. Most likely she'd thought she was just being fashionably unconventional. And certainly she'd fooled most of the people in the chapel. Behind him Ben heard a woman speaking, her voice low. "Well, it was unorthodox. But she had a point. He was that sort of guy. Always telling dirty jokes." A man answered the woman, saying, "Yes, I guess so. I guess it suited him."

Suddenly he searched for Claudia in the crowd filing out of the pews. She was, he thought, so much more sensitive, so much more interesting than he had ever given her credit for being before.

She had understood and guided him to understanding Marilyn's deviousness, the insidious way in which she had manifested her hatred. Naomi saw only the surface of things. Her world was black and white. She loved or she hated; there was no middle ground for her. Claudia was different. More complex. More subtle. He couldn't help feeling that she and he had a great deal in common.

Most of the funeral guests in the pews had now left the chapel and were crowding out onto the landing, waiting for the elevators. He helped Naomi back into her jacket, watching the offending violet blouse disappear into navy sobriety. "I have to get back to work immediately," she said, fastening the buttons. "I've got that appointment I told you about and I have to leave work a little early."

"What appointment?" He had been so absorbed in his own thoughts that he couldn't make the transition back to her concerns, though he could tell from the sound of her words that it was a matter they had already discussed.

"With my ex-analyst," she prompted him. "Remember?"

He nodded. "Yes. Of course." She had mentioned it to him several times. In fact, he was paying for the appointment. Of late, whenever he had prodded Naomi about marriage she had said wistfully that she wished she could discuss it with her ex-analyst, who might help her overcome her anxieties in this area, but that she couldn't afford to go. He had promised her the money. "God," he said, remembering. "I'm glad you're finally going."

"Stupid to do it on the day of a funeral," she murmured.

"Don't be silly. Life goes on."

"I could stay a while longer, I guess. I mean, if you want me to. If you're feeling blue."

"No. I didn't really know Harry that well. And I should be getting back to work right away too."

They left the chapel. He had lost sight of Claudia but when they emerged from the elevator into the lobby, he spotted her again. The Alithorns had departed but she was talking now to a few other of Sidney's colleagues. They all treated her so appreciatively, he noticed, watching them stand in a semicircle with Claudia at its center. Was it because she was Sidney's wife or because she was so beautiful?

"Ben?" she said in a low voice before he could be certain, and broke away from her admirers. He stopped walking although Naomi was propelled forward by the crowd. "Are you going back to work right away?" Claudia asked.

The whiteness of her beauty seemed dazzling and for a moment he felt he could barely answer her. "No. No, I'm just seeing Naomi to a cab," he managed after a long pause.

"Come back for me, okay? There's something I'd like to talk to you about."

"Sure. Sure."

He was astonished, as if a wish he had made had been granted.

"It's about Sidney," Claudia said when he returned to her, her voice so muted it was more a breeze than a sound. So she too had noticed. He felt inordinately glad. Her words meant that he and she could, together, work out a plan of action. The idea delighted him. Claudia was glancing around at the crowd still lingering in the lobby. "Let's go outside. Can you walk me to work? The museum's only a few blocks away."

He nodded eagerly and they slipped through the revolving doors onto the street and began walking east in silence. He looked forward, seeing in the distance the tall treetops of the park and above them an expanse of azure sky. But Claudia kept looking back, glancing over her shoulder until at last they had left all the funeral guests far behind them. Then she said in an uneasy voice, "Sidney's taking drugs. Barbiturates. Not just at night but in the daytime too."

"I know," he said at once, wanting to help her by agreeing with her without delay.

But his agreement only seemed to upset her further. "But how could you have known? Sidney told me about it last night, but he said no one knew. He said he'd been very careful and that no one could possibly suspect."

"I figured it out," he answered vaguely.

"That's disturbing," Claudia said. "I didn't know until he told me, and I live with him. Oh, I always knew he took a few Nembutals at night when he couldn't get to sleep. But I never dreamed he could be taking the stuff in the daytime. What made you think of it?"

"I just did. Why does it worry you so much?"

"It's very simple," she said. "If you figured it out, then others will too."

"Not necessarily," he reassured her. "Or at least not right away."

"God, I hope you're right."

"What worries me," he confessed, plunging into an anxiety he had touched on with Mulenberg, "is not that people will find out, but that even once they do, it may not matter to Sidney. He might not care what people say. He might ignore them. I don't think it's going to be easy to get him to stop."

Claudia leaped at his words, her voice becoming more emphatic. "I'm sure you'll find a way. That's why I decided to tell you, even though Sidney made me swear I wouldn't. I can't reason with him, but I expect you can."

He didn't feel nearly as confident about his ability to affect Sidney's thinking as she seemed to, yet he wanted to encourage her trust. "I see. Yes," he said slowly.

"You've got to help him, Ben."

"Yes, of course. How could you imagine otherwise?"

She was pleased. "You'll work on him? Reason with him?"

"Certainly. I'll get after him this afternoon." But Sidney would be disagreeable and argumentative when he confronted him with knowledge of his addiction. "Or first thing tomorrow morning at the latest," he added.

"Thank you, Ben. I'm counting on you."

"You can," he promised. Then he said, "Tell me what else Sidney told you. Did he tell you how much he was taking?"

She shrugged. "No. He wouldn't say." Her eyes swept past his face to a brownstone across the street and she added, "We mustn't tell anyone else. It's too horrible."

He shook his head from side to side and sighed. "It *is* horrible. But in a way I can understand it. He's probably going to lose his grant, you know."

Claudia stopped walking and stared at him. Suddenly, she began to twist the strap of her large leather handbag around her wrist. He had never before noticed that she had a single nervous habit.

"What is it?" he asked. "What's wrong? Didn't you know his research was in trouble?"

Her eyes began to fill with tears. "He said something about it a while ago. I didn't believe him." She continued to play with her handbag strap. "He said one night that I couldn't afford to believe him."

"Well, it doesn't matter. He'll come out of it all right, and out of this pill business too."

"I wonder."

"Sure he will."

Claudia pursed her lips, and then she murmured, "I suppose. Yes, I suppose you're right."

She didn't want to discuss Sidney anymore, she told him as they reached the park and turned up the wide street that bordered it. It was making her too upset. Harry's death had really disturbed her, and now all this worry about Sidney was getting her down even more. Could they just be quiet for a while? She wanted to clear her mind, wanted to think about the things she had to do when she got to work. "Okay," he said. "Sure. Whatever you say."

He was enjoying being with her. She was still as graceful as ever and he was aware as they walked uptown that women as well as men turned and appraised her admiringly. She moved like a dancer and was clearly sturdy and strong, but her pale skin and reserved manner gave her a quality of noticeable and haunting vulnerability. He liked wondering if the people who looked at her thought she belonged to him.

And then, all too soon, they were across the street from the photography museum, waiting to cross. The branches of a tree overhead fluttered and cast delicate shadows across Claudia's cheeks. He saw them as tiny scratches marring her beauty and grew excited at the notion. He wanted to touch the marks, to trace them with his fingers. He understood for a moment why Sidney tyrannized her. She looked vulnerable, yet she was impervious. One could never really hurt her because one could never really get inside her.

Then the traffic light changed and Claudia took his arm. Her thigh brushed against his and she gave him a sidelong glance. A moment later, in the middle of the crossing, she did it again, and this time she hesitated for a moment so that he had to grasp her arm more tightly if they were to get to the other side of the street before the cars started moving again. When he touched her, his penis came erect.

"I excited you, didn't I?" Claudia said as they stepped onto the sidewalk in front of the museum. Her eyes moved down to his groin. "Just like that?" she added, in a cool, distant voice.

He thought of denying it, but it would have been like denying his own name. "Yes," he confessed. "I'm sorry. I was thinking about how beautiful you are."

Claudia laughed. "Don't be sorry. It's flattering. I'm glad to know that men still find me desirable."

He smiled and for a moment she seemed to sway toward him. Then she pulled away and darted up the marble steps of the small mansion in which the museum was housed.

Naomi was already at his apartment when he returned home from the office that evening. He had long ago given her her own set of keys to his place as, ever since he had offered to help her out with babysitters' fees, she spent almost as many nights in the week with him as she did at home with her son. He went into the living room and saw her curled up in her usual position on his couch, a book in her hand and a gin and tonic in a tall glass on the cocktail table beside her. But for the first time since he had started sleeping with her, it did not delight him to come home and find her waiting for him. Still, he bent over her and kissed her and remembered to ask her how her consultation with the analyst had gone.

"It was marvelous to see him again," Naomi said. "I wish you knew him. You'd like each other. I told *him* that, too. In fact, I told him all about you."

Her final remark made him acutely nervous. Although he had encouraged her appointment, he didn't much like the idea of a stranger's passing judgments on him. He supposed that was why he had offered to pay. Naomi might have scraped together the money for the consultation sooner or later; his paying for it, which surely she would have mentioned to the analyst, might have given the man a favorable outlook toward him. But he couldn't be sure. There was so much about himself that he disliked that the fact of being evaluated by others alarmed him.

As if reading his mind, Naomi said, "He said you sounded very good for me."

Relieved, he sat down opposite her. "What else did he say?"

"He thought your willingness to have me see him was a particularly good sign. Hal used to try to discourage me from going and refuse to pay the bills." Naomi sighed in remembrance and then went on. "Anyway, my shrink thinks that I really ought to give our relationship a chance by considering marrying again, since marrying seems to be what you want. He said that just because people have had one bad experience in marriage, it doesn't mean they need to fear they're going to make the same mistake next time."

He smiled and in response she stood up and came over to his chair, settling down on the floor, her cheek against his knees. "He said that a good man is hard to find."

He stroked her hair.

"And you are a good man," Naomi continued. "I used to think you were too reserved, too distant for me. But you've been getting so much better lately. You've really been trying hard. And you've been wonderful about Petey." She looked up at him, her expressive face appreciative. She was perspiring. The humidity in the air had brought beads of perspiration to her olive-toned forehead and was making her hair more curly and frizzy than usual. "I guess I could sublet my loft when the school term ends and we could try living together for the summer and then, assuming it works out, we could get married in the fall."

Out of force of habit, he embraced her, pulling her up toward him and pressing his lips to her warm, moist forehead, but all the while he was thinking of Claudia's cool, mysterious pallor.

"When is the end of the school term?" he asked at last.

"The end of June. I could sublet my place as of July first."

"Okay."

"Is that all?"

"I mean wonderful. Fantastic."

"That's better."

CHAPTER SIX

JUNE

The following morning, true to his promise to Claudia, Ben tersely instructed the nurse who had replaced Cora to tell Sidney that he wanted to see him. The nurse was young and plump and pretty, with a freckled face and a full-lipped, pouting mouth. Sidney had hired her, saying she had excellent recommendations, but Ben missed the less attractive, more mature Cora, whose efficiency and maternal ways had been comforting to him. "Let me know as soon as my brother's free, Miss Palchek. I'd like to speak with him," he said.

"Call me Palsy," the new nurse pouted. "Okay?"

He nodded, annoyed at her penchant for nicknames, and she went on, "He's not here yet, Dr. Z. He called a while ago to say he'd be a little late."

"Okay, Palsy. Just let me know when he arrives." He started down the corridor but Miss Palchek half-stood behind her desk, whispering loudly, "Doctor? Could I ask you something?"

He turned back and faced her. She looked up at him with wide childish eyes. "I was expecting the other Dr. Z. at nine o'clock. And it's nearly ten. I don't know what to tell the people who are waiting to see him." She gestured at the waiting room, which was starting to fill up.

"Tell them he'll be along soon." He felt troubled by her need for direction in so simple a matter. "He must have gotten held up at the hospital."

Miss Palchek shook her head. "But that's just it. The hospital's been trying to reach him too. He isn't there."

"Try him at home."

Miss Palchek pouted again. "I did. There was no answer."

"Well, he could be at any number of places. Maybe he had to go over to Midstate. Didn't you ask him for a calling number when you spoke to him?"

"Of course. But he said he couldn't be reached."

He shrugged. "Well, he must be on his way over, then. Just hold his calls and tell his patients he's on his way. And let me know as soon as he arrives."

Miss Palchek thanked him effusively. He dodged past her into his own office. When Miss

Palchek finally buzzed him to say Sidney was in, it was past eleven.

By then the waiting room was dense with patients, some waiting for him, more of them waiting for Sidney. He hurried toward Sidney's office and, coming up to the door, almost forgot to knock on it. But at the last moment he remembered how much Sidney hated to be disturbed without prelude and with the door already partly opened, tapped on its frame loudly to announce himself.

Sidney was standing at his big window, his back turned.

"You wanted to see me?" he asked, looking over his shoulder for just a second to make sure it was Ben who had knocked, and then resuming his stance at the window. He stood quite motionless there, as if he were absorbed by something he was watching, and didn't turn again. His unresponsiveness made it difficult for Ben to launch into the subject he had come to discuss and at first he answered, feeling foolish, "Yes. It's about . . . about your health. I'm worried about you."

"My health?" Sidney still didn't move. "What do you mean?"

"The barbiturates you're taking," Ben said, speaking directly at last, and waiting for Sidney to whirl around and deny his accusation. Standing straight, his back muscles tense, he was primed for a denial, prepared to argue with Sidney just to get an admission of his habit from him, let alone a plan for curtailing it. But to his astonishment, Sidney made no denial. Staring out the window, he said flatly, "So you know about it."

Ben quickly cleared a space for himself on the chair alongside Sidney's desk, scooping off the mail and setting it on the floor. "Yes. And I'd like to talk to you."

"Sure. Say anything you like." Sidney sounded exceptionally tranquil. "Claudia told you?" he asked, his back still turned, in the tone of a man asking a rhetorical question.

"No. Yes. Well, she said something about pills, but I had pretty well figured it out by then."

"Do you suppose anyone else has?" Sidney asked. But he didn't sound worried, only mildly curious. At last he left the window and ambled slowly over to the desk, sitting down facing Ben.

Once they were face to face, Ben was startled. Sidney didn't look well. Ben had thought back in the early spring that his brother had lost some weight, but now his diminishment was undeniable and disturbing. His cheeks were cavernous and his hazel eyes appeared larger and deeper-set than usual. Worse, they were dulled and expressionless. He was heavily sedated, Ben thought. His mind wasn't tranquil but tranquilized. "No. No, I don't think anyone else has figured it out yet," he said sternly. "But it's only a matter of time. You've got to give up the pills."

Sidney half-smiled, his mouth opening, but his lips not curling. "Look who's talking."

"I don't take them anymore," Ben announced slowly. "Not at all. I gave them up last winter." It was the confession he had postponed for months. "I didn't want to say anything and then have to feel ashamed if I couldn't stick to the decision."

Sidney leaned forward, his forehead furrowing. "Was it difficult?" He sounded almost jealous and for a moment Ben felt gratified and generous.

"Not so very," he lied, recalling the torment of his first sleepless nights and jumpy days, but hoping to encourage Sidney to do as he had done. "I did it cold turkey. But there are better ways. You ought to put yourself into a psychiatric clinic. Let them withdraw you. Or you could do it slowly yourself. Ten percent less a day."

Sidney said edgily, "I know."

"You just have to make up your mind to it."

Sidney leaned his chin on his elbow and offered thoughtfully, "I'll do it if it ever gets to the point where my competence is endangered."

"But it is," Ben argued passionately. "Look what happened the other day. That episiotomy you did."

Sidney tilted back in his high leather desk chair. "That was nothing. I told you that was nothing." He arched his neck, his head pushing against the headrest of the tall, thronelike chair, his eyes on the ceiling. "Look, Ben, I've been under terrible pressure lately. I need to relax. I need all the relaxation I can get." His head lolled forward and he shut his eyes for a moment. A murmuring, exhausted breath pushed its way up from his chest.

It frightened Ben, making him remember a time when they were children and he had awakened in the middle of the night to hear Sidney groaning and gasping for breath in the bed across from his. They were living in Brooklyn then and Sara had gone to play mah-jongg with some of her new friends. Ben had known that Sidney was sick and that he ought to locate their mother and get her to come home at once. But it was always Sidney who knew to which neighbor's apartment Sara had gone and Ben couldn't, no matter how hard he tried, rouse Sidney from his feverish nightmare. He was six. He had thought of leaving the bedroom and going down the dark corridor that led to the front hall and letting himself out of the apartment and ringing someone's bell, but he was terrified of the dark corridor with its pull-light he couldn't reach. And he had slumped down on the floor alongside Sidney's bed and begun to cry and in the end simply climbed into the bed alongside him. When Sara had come home she had found them both soaked with perspiration but asleep and in the morning Sidney had had to go to the hospital but Ben's diphtheria was milder and he was treated at home.

"Sid?" he said loudly now. "Sidney?" He leaned across the desk and grasped Sidney's white-coated arm.

"Don't worry, I'm awake. I hear you. I was just think—thinking." Sidney's words were slurring.

"The lethargy is nice, isn't it? The problem is that I can't hold onto it. It wears off so fast."

"And then you take more?"

"Yeah."

"That's why you have to give them up."

"I will. Don't worry. I will."

"In England they've been discovering that people on high doses of certain sedatives get even tenser on them than without them."

"I know about it."

"It's the same with barbiturates. They're paradoxical."

"Are you lecturing me?" Suddenly Sidney's calm gave way to anger. "Because if you are, you'd better stop! I know more about it than you'll ever know. I know what I'm doing. And I'll know when to quit."

"Suppose Alithorn finds out," Ben persisted.

"Suppose he does. What's he going to do? He'll tell me to take a vacation, that's all." Sidney seemed determined to deny that his addiction could result in complications for his career.

"Well, at least cut down. You could hurt someone. It's been known to happen."

"Rarely. Anyway, don't worry. I'm careful. And even with the stuff inside me, I'm still better than nine-tenths of the competition." Sitting forward, Sidney reached into the pocket of his white coat, and, withdrawing a small vial of pills, shook out two yellow capsules and swallowed them without water.

It occurred to Ben that he ought to say something, but afraid to challenge Sidney further, he remained silent. Sidney put the vial away and leaned his head back against the top of the chair once again, swiveling slightly so that he could put his feet up on the desk. "Don't worry," he repeated. He sounded calm again.

His drugged serenity wouldn't last long, Ben thought. When the pills began to wear off he would start feeling agitated. Or perhaps it would happen while the drug was still in his system, its chemical interacting erratically with the brain's own, as the English study was showing. Then Sidney would want more of the drug. And he would take it. Despair and self-doubt had never been part of his emotional makeup. As a result, he would be unable to tolerate the way they inevitably followed in the wake of the drug's initial soothing effects. It would make him strive perpetually to attain additional surcease from anxiety.

Such grasping had never been part of his own addiction. He had been cautious, never having considered himself sufficiently worthwhile to deserve even drug-induced happiness. Sidney, on the other hand, had always considered himself deserving of everything. It was ironic, Ben reflected, but in some mysterious fashion the very weakness of his ego had served to protect him while the grandeur of Sidney's was conspiring to betray him.

"You've got to cut down," he said firmly, suspecting the futility of his argument but hoping, still, that he might prove effective. "Take the Deutsch Foundation. What are you doing about Neville? His paper'll be out in August and you haven't even gotten in touch with the Deutsch people about it yet."

"I will. I will. Stop worrying all the time. Stop being such an old maid." Sidney swung his feet off the desk and leaned toward Ben, punching him playfully on the upper arm.

Ben stood up, annoyed. He was getting nowhere.

Sidney rose too and began to walk Ben to the door, his arm around his shoulders. "I appreciate your concern. And in case I forgot to mention it, I'm proud of you. Proud you got off the pills. I'll do it too, as soon as I'm ready. But in the meantime, not to worry. I'm not likely to do anything disastrous."

Ben twitched his shoulders, trying to dislodge Sidney's arm. He always found that embrace of Sidney's patronizing, confining. But he realized, as soon as Sidney released him, that Sidney's arm had felt considerably lighter than usual.

"Something splendid?" Philip asked dreamily. Emily's head lay cushioned on his stomach as the two of them sprawled on the rich park grass under a spectacle of cherry blossoms. "Like Constantine or Leopold or Maximilian?" he suggested.

"Eugenie," Emily said. "But pretty is better than splendid for a girl."

"Bella, Bellissima, Beldam," Philip chanted.

"That means an old witch."

"Oh, I'm sorry. But anyway, what about something flowery, to remind us always of today?" He curled a lock of her hair around his fingers.

"Like Blossom?" Emily asked.

"Yes, or Rose or Lily or Daisy. Or not a flower. Just something natural. Fern, Heather, Brooke."

"Rivulet," Emily invented, and thought how playful Philip was these days. He had always been fun to be with, although the amusement he provided tended to be informational, instructional. But lately he had put his pedantry aside, as if her pregnancy had given him the confidence to take life more lightheartedly.

"Sweet little, dear little Rivulet." Philip halfsitting, reached out, and patted Emily's stomach.

"No! Too French," Emily said, feeling giddy and pushing Philip back down. "And *too* long."

"You're right," Philip said. "Ada, then, if it's a girl. Or Abe, if it isn't. Those are definites, you hear?"

"Aba, Agha, Ama, Ana, Asa, Ava," Emily singsonged.

"Eben, Ibn, Ian," Philip countered.

Emily shook her head and said soberly, "The name isn't everything, you know."

"But it's half of everything," Philip said. "I mean, if we want him-her to go into journalism, we're going to have to do a last name first. Make it Trussel Harper or Ketcham Harper. And if he-she is going to make us proud by being in the arts, we ought to do something a little foreign—but not French, of course. Pablo Harper or Nokomis Harper or Kikuyu Harper."

"Kiki, Gigi, Fifi, Mimi, Lili," Emily rattled off.

"Lilly, Willie, Millie, Tillie, Billy," Philip intoned.

"Phily!" Emily said. "Oh, Philip, I'm happy. I really am, these days. Even though the world doesn't need any more children. And even though I'm scared."

"Still scared of having it?" Philip asked, brushing the hair out of her eyes.

"Not anymore. Of other things. Suppose it grows up hating me?"

"I won't let it."

"I positively loathed my parents till I was eighteen."

"But they didn't loathe you."

She listened to him and nodded. "That was so wise, darling. I see what the whole point is now."

He tickled her ear with a strand of grass and said, "Stop making fun of me."

"No, I meant it. It's not my being loved that counts in this, but my being able to love."

Philip hadn't followed her but suddenly she didn't want to talk. She had felt a tickle in her stomach, a strange gliding sensation just below the surface of her flesh. Her hand flew to the spot. But the sensation had ceased. Sitting up, she

waited for it to return, her forehead wrinkling
with concentration.

Philip sat up too. "You felt it again?" he asked
dubiously.

She nodded and a moment later reached out for
Philip's hand, pressing it triumphantly against her
stomach.

Ben was in the park that Sunday morning too.
Naomi and Petey were visiting the zoo and he had
promised to join them there before noon if he
didn't get tied up at the hospital. Naomi was
bringing sandwiches and after seeing the animals,
she and Petey were going to picnic under some
big, leafy tree in the meadow.

He hadn't been near the park since the day he
had walked alongside it with Claudia after Mulenberg's funeral. The spring had come and flourished and he had been indoors most of the time,
preoccupied with his practice and patients and
the increasingly disturbing condition of his
brother. But the past week had been particularly
beautiful, the sky cloudless, the winds gentle, the
air soft, and it had filled him with the classic longings and dissatisfactions of spring fever.

He had wanted to get out of the city and drive
to the country or to a beach, but unfortunately he
had committed himself weeks before to cover for
Herron on the weekend. As a pallid substitute,
Naomi had suggested the picnic and the park,
from which, by virtue of his intercom, he would

be as accessible as he would be at home or in the office. But now, just after he had negotiated the milling crowds around the seal pond and was about to mount the stairs in front of the cafeteria, he found himself turning and walking stealthily away from the zoo.

The park belonged to him and Claudia. He didn't want the vividness of his vision of her under the trees destroyed, and it would be if he sullied his memory by spending time with Naomi in the same setting.

He left the zoo and started out of the park, intending to go home and rest. Naomi would assume that he hadn't been able to break free in time and would call him after the picnic. Perhaps then she and Petey would come over to his place and watch the ball game on TV. It was not that he didn't want to see Naomi anymore. No, he still wanted her. Still needed her. Still found her terribly useful in fending off his feelings of difference and isolation. It was just that these days there were some places in which he did not want to see her.

He had meant to go home and await her call, but on Fifth Avenue he began walking uptown instead of east toward his apartment. The street was festive with balloon vendors and girls in pastel dresses. He walked slowly, enjoying the atmosphere, and only after ten minutes of strolling realized he had come to the corner on which Sidney and Claudia lived. He glanced across the avenue, surprised to discover he was opposite their building.

Certainly he hadn't planned to walk in their direction. He had no expectations of seeing them. They were away for the weekend, visiting Claudia's mother outside Boston. Yet he knew at once why he had come to their corner. He stood there a few moments indulging himself in fantasies about Claudia, envisioning her leaning out of one of the tenth-floor windows of their vast, sprawling apartment to ascertain what kind of weather it was, imagining her emerging through the brass-trimmed doors of the building in a flimsy linen dress and waving a polite goodbye to George, the sallow-faced elevator man who lazed now under the canopy, sneaking a cigarette. But the windows of Sidney and Claudia's apartment were closed, the blinds drawn, and no one emerged from the building. The elevator man tossed away the butt of his cigarette and lit another.

Annoyed at how puerile the spring day had made him, Ben forced himself to turn away from the building and start downtown again. If he haunted Claudia's habitat, like some romantic adolescent, he would miss Naomi's call.

He walked half a block and then paused for a moment for a farewell glance at the deserted-looking tenth-floor apartment. Just then he saw Sidney on the far side of the avenue. Tall, expensively suited. He and Claudia must have changed their plans. Decided to stay in town. "Hey!" Ben called above the traffic. "Hey, Sid!" He flung his voice out over the fast-moving cars and buses. But Sidney didn't turn around.

Darting forward, he tried to cross and catch up with his brother. But the traffic was too heavy, and he had to step back toward the curb and wait for the light to change. As soon as it did, he ran across the street, but Sidney was no longer in sight. He had gone into his apartment building. George had gone inside, too.

He followed them, hurrying to the back of the lobby, hoping to catch up to Sidney in the elevator. But the elevator doors were closing even as he scuttled through the lobby. He pressed the buzzer firmly to make sure George came down again immediately, and a moment later George was sliding open the mahogany doors.

"Dr. Zauber," George said, recognizing him. "Nice to see you. Nice day, isn't it?"

"Sure is." Impatient, Ben stepped inside the elevator and waited for George to close the doors and push down on the old-fashioned lever that ran the elevator. But George, his hand on the lever, didn't move. "No one's home," he grunted.

"Of course someone's home. I just saw my brother go up."

George looked away, his eyes cast down at the lever. "Can't be," he said, shaking his head. "He and Mrs. Zauber are away for the weekend."

"I just saw him," Ben insisted. "You just took him up."

Again, George stubbornly shook his head.

Ben tried to catch his eyes but George wouldn't look at him. His sallow, skinny face was tilted down toward the elevator lever. Ben looked there too, and saw, peeking between George's thumb and his fisted fingers, a crumpled five dollar bill.

On Monday morning Ben confronted Sidney about the incident, hurrying across the waiting room as soon as Miss Palchek notified him that his brother had arrived. There was only a handful of patients sitting on the waiting room couches and loveseats, and all of them were Ben's. Sidney did his elective surgery on Monday mornings and rarely got into the office until early afternoon. He must have had some cancellations, Ben thought as he tapped on his door; it was only eleven-thirty.

Although there was no sound from within, he pushed open the door anyway. Sidney was standing just inside. He was still wearing his street clothes, although his white lab coat was across his arm, and Ben saw at once that Sidney's expensive blue wool suit was the same one he had been wearing on Sunday. It was crumpled and stained now, as if Sidney had spent the night in it. "Were you in town yesterday?" he asked Sidney outright, as Sidney struggled out of his jacket.

"Yes." Sidney tossed the creased jacket onto his

couch, on top of the mail, but he didn't put on the lab coat.

"You didn't go up to Boston with Claudia?"

"No. She went alone. She's still there."

"I thought I saw you. In fact, I was sure I saw you. I was across the street from your building. I called out to you. And later I phoned you half a dozen times."

Sidney, still holding the lab coat, sat down heavily in his desk chair. "I know."

"Then why didn't you turn around when I called you?" Ben expostulated. "And why did you tell George to say you weren't home? And why the hell didn't you answer the phone?"

"I needed to be alone," Sidney's voice was hoarse and his face so haggard that for a moment Ben was sorry for his outburst. But he couldn't control himself.

"Why? What got into you?"

"I lost my grant. Layton called me Friday evening."

Ben looked at Sidney in confusion. One part of him wanted to say, "I told you so," and another counseled him not to be so small-minded, so petty, when obviously Sidney was in need of commiseration, not rebuke. For a moment he couldn't speak at all. Then at last he managed, "Oh, Christ, I'm sorry. How did it happen? What'd they say?"

"That the pill was going to be too controversial. That if I'd let them know earlier they might have advised a different way of handling Neville. That I ought to work up something else."

Once again Ben resisted the temptation to admonish Sidney and said, "Well, that's good, isn't it? I mean, they didn't cut you off completely, right? They suggested you come back to them with a different formula?"

"Yeah." Sidney sounded desolate.

"Well, you will!" For a moment Ben wished that Sidney were standing. If he were, he might clap him on the back in the hearty, brotherly fashion Sidney himself always relied upon to suggest support or concern. But Sidney was slouched in his desk chair, his head bent over his fingertips. "No," he was saying. "I spent a lifetime developing that pill."

"You're exaggerating. Anyway, maybe the same formula in slightly lower dosage would be just as effective. And less risky."

Sidney shook his head, moving it so slightly that Ben almost missed the gesture. "No. Deutsch doesn't want it. They want something new. I'd have to go to a different foundation."

"Then you will. It'll be no problem. They'll all want you again once the noise dies down."

"I was going to be so famous," Sidney said self-deprecatingly. "Remember when we were young? How we used to talk about my winning the Noble Prize."

Ben was discomfited by his brother's maudlin tone. He kept silent.

Sidney said, "What a joke," and dug a hand into the pocket of his trousers, removing his vial of pills. Staring, Ben thought of taking the vial out of his hands. But what would be the point? Sidney would just write himself out another prescription and fill it at one of the nearby drugstores as soon as Ben was gone. He watched Sidney as he swallowed two pills and then said quietly, feeling staid and infinitely older than his brother, "That's not going to make you feel better, you know. Not for long."

"Sure it will. It'll make me not feel at all."

Just then a strident ringing of the phone and a flashing yellow light distracted Ben from pursuing his argument. "Shall I get it?" he asked Sidney, who had slumped further down into his chair.

"No. I don't want to speak to anyone. I don't care who the hell it is." Shutting his eyes, Sidney added, "I don't feel like talking. I don't even feel like moving. I didn't even go to the hospital this morning."

"Who operated for you?"

"I canceled. It was all elective stuff. I rescheduled everybody."

Ben was dumfounded. Although he had foreseen the possibility of Sidney's collapse into irresponsibility, he had not expected it to manifest itself so soon. Yet the phone was still ringing and now Sidney lurched forward, grabbed the instrument between clenched fingers and hurled it off his desk, flinging it as far as its curled tether would allow. Then he stood up and shouted, "I'm not here! I'm not here! I'm not here!"

"I'll tell Miss Palchek," Ben said swiftly. "In fact, why don't you just go home? If there's anything urgent, I'll see to it." The light on the phone had stopped flashing.

"I don't want to go home. I want to stay here. I just don't want to speak to anyone or see anyone."

"Okay," Ben pacified him. "I'll make it clear to Miss Palchek. We'll see to it you're not disturbed."

Sidney slumped down into his chair. "Thanks, old buddy. I'll be all right in a while." He put his arms on his desk and his head sunk down on top of them.

Ben retrieved the phone, untangling its wire, and set it gently back on Sidney's desk. Then he hurried outside and explained to Miss Palchek that Sidney *really* didn't want to be disturbed, not for anything, and that she simply had to learn how to deflect his calls.

"But what about the emergencies?" she asked helplessly.

Ben sighed. "Pass them on to me."

Fortunately there were no real emergencies that morning, just two husbands irate that their wives had not been operated on as scheduled and demanding that Sidney explain to them why he had changed his mind. Ben was excessively polite with the first man, saying that Sidney had been called upon to operate on a woman with a Fallopian tube pregnancy. "She was in considerable pain," he apologized. "And danger. I imagine my brother didn't want to lose a moment. I'm sure he'll call you as soon as he's able." But with the second man who phoned, he was less ingratiating.

"I want to speak to Dr. Sidney Zauber," the man began shouting as soon as Ben explained who he was. "I don't care who the hell you are."

"He's not available," Ben said coldly, annoyed at the man's explosiveness.

"Well he damn well better get available. This is the second time he's postponed my wife's surgery, and he didn't explain himself the first time, either."

"He must have had his reasons."

The man didn't calm down but went on talking angrily about his wife's condition and the fact that he had already missed two days' work to be with her when she came out of anesthesia. "I want Sidney Zauber to call me and explain what's going on," the husband fumed. "Right away!"

"As I told you, he's unavailable," Ben repeated, and then an amusing notion popped into his head and he finished his statement by saying, "But I think he'll be here in just a few minutes. What was your name again? I'll have him call you first thing."

Five minutes later he telephoned the man and, making his voice deeper and as much like Sidney's as he could, said, "Mr. Burton? Sidney Zauber here." At once the man began shouting, but Ben spoke over his words, "Mr. Burton, I'm afraid I've got some rather unpleasant news for you. Your wife's condition is not as simple as we thought."

Immediately, there was silence on the other end of the phone.

"We're going to need some more tests before we go in."

"More tests?" Mr. Burton sounded suddenly panic-stricken.

He was really being taken for Sidney, Ben thought. It was the second time this year that it had happened to him. The first time, with his mother, it had unnerved him, but this time he was finding it quite entertaining. Making his voice even gruffer, he began to doubletalk about blood and tissue tests.

Would Sidney mind, he wondered idly as he talked. But no, how could he mind? Didn't he always say he hated to be checked up on? He was merely doing what Sidney himself would have done if he had found himself being excoriated by so irascible a man as Mr. Burton. "Could be complications unless we get the tests," he muttered. "Immense complications."

"Yes, of course." Mr. Burton was altogether subdued.

"You ought to thank your lucky stars I delayed," Ben concluded, imitating Sidney at his harshest. Then he hung up abruptly and, smiling, made a note to remind Sidney to order some spe-

cial tests for Mrs. Burton if he recovered himself
sufficiently to call the hospital this afternoon.

By two o'clock, just as Ben was on his way over
to the hospital to do his rounds, Sidney did appear
to have recovered. He knocked on the door of
Ben's office and, entering, sat down in the patients' chair alongside Ben's desk and thanked him
profusely for his understanding in the morning
and for handling his calls. "I'm okay now. I really
am," he said in a convincingly brisk voice. "I'm
going to start seeing my afternoon people now,
and I'll get over to the hospital around four."

"You're sure you're up to seeing patients?"

"Quite sure. I wouldn't risk it otherwise."

Ben appraised Sidney thoughtfully. He was
wearing his starched white lab coat and his face
appeared more rested, his eyes less dull. Yes, Sidney was all right now. But how long would he stay
that way? "How's Claudia?" Ben asked irrelevantly. "When's she coming back from Boston?"

"Why? Is she due to see you?"

"No. Not until the end of the month. I was just
wondering."

"Yeah. Well, her mother's been a little depressed. She's going to stay up there another day
or two, to see what she can do to help."

"I see," Ben nodded. But he suspected that Sidney was more in need of Claudia's presence than
her mother was. He thought of calling Claudia at
her mother's house and saying something to her

about returning as swiftly as she could. But why
make her rush home to face Sidney's disturbing
condition? At least at her mother's house she
could enjoy the sea air, nourish her senses, go for
walks, sleep soundly at night. She would be sleeping in the turreted bedroom she had occupied as a
child, he mused, remembering the time he had
visited her mother's seaside home and Sidney had
taken him on the tour. She would be sleeping in
her girlhood bed. She would be sleeping alone.

"I told her to stay with her mother and get a
good rest," Sidney commented. "She'd never have
gone if I hadn't urged her."

"I know," Ben said. "I'm sure."

In the next few weeks Sidney came late to the office every morning and sometimes, right after he
had arrived, he would abruptly change his mind
about seeing the women who sat eagerly waiting
for him and would direct Miss Palchek to cancel
his appointments and send all his patients home.
"I just can't see anyone today," he would say, offering no explanation for his decision.

Miss Palchek quit one morning, agreeing to hire
her own replacement if Sidney would accept her
resignation as of the end of the week. He did, and
two days later another new nurse, an elderly
woman named Miss Viviani, was sitting at Cora's
old desk making Sidney's excuses for keeping patients waiting for hours on end or for dismissing
them altogether. But even when Sidney did get

around to seeing his patients, Miss Viviani had her hands full. Sidney was perpetually antagonizing patients and Miss Viviani was perpetually having to assuage them.

Hardly a day went by when Ben, passing through the waiting room, didn't hear Sidney's voice raised in intense argument, and sometimes he could even hear it when he was in his own office, far across the corridors from Sidney's. One day, he overheard Sidney telling a pregnant woman that she was not following his dietary instructions. "You look disgusting," his voice carried out into the waiting room. "Like an animal!"

The woman, emerging into the corridor a moment later, stumbled past Ben in tears.

He went into Sidney's office and tried to reason with him. "You'll be losing patients if you carry on like this all the time."

Sidney shrugged. "When a woman eats the way that one's doing, she's making misery for me and for herself, too. Complicating the delivery."

"Still, you didn't have to be so insulting."

"It's the best way to get through. To get her to change."

Ben retreated. Sidney seemed to have a reasonable explanation for his tirade.

But he began to hear Sidney more and more often. Sometimes, his voice overbearing and indignant, he was chastising women who were trying to become pregnant, shouting at them that they had been passive about following his timetables for sexual intercourse. Sometimes it was women who wanted abortions at whom he railed, loudly accusing them of having been careless at using their birth control methods. And sometimes he mercilessly excoriated women who had come in for breast examinations on dates long past the ones they had been asked to observe.

These women seemed particularly irresponsible to him. When, on several occasions, he detected in one or another of them potentially cancerous masses, he would be callously blunt about his suspicions.

One morning the hapless patient was a youthful, pony-tailed woman with sad, deeply ringed eyes. Sidney buzzed Ben and asked him to come around at once; he had found a knoblike lump in the woman's left breast. Ben entered Sidney's examining room nervously, passed his fingers over the woman's breast, probed the lump, and thought it was indeed like a knob, that it would turn the woman off, but kept silent as Sidney began demanding excitedly, "Well? Well? It's C.A., right? No question about it."

Ben went on palpating the woman's breast with one hand and at the same time shook his head vigorously, trying to get Sidney to keep still. The woman looked as if life had already dealt her a number of harsh and unexpected blows.

"Not cancer?" Sidney said.

The young woman struggled upward, her neck arching.

"We'll want you to have a mammography," Ben said soothingly, easing the woman back down again. "And of course, it's early. It's a good thing you noticed it so early and came in right away."

"Bullshit," Sidney shouted at Ben, and then he said to the woman, "You must have had this lump for weeks. Months. But when I operate and there's cancer in the nodes, you'll tell me I spread it there."

The woman sat up again, her face ashen. "It's always the surgeon's fault," Sidney said. "Show me a woman who takes responsibility for her own deterioration and I'll show you a goddess."

Amazed, Ben once again shook his head, this time glaring at Sidney, but Sidney ignored him. "Show me a woman who takes responsibility for her own body . . ." he began, but before he could continue his sentence, the woman swayed dizzily and fainted.

Ben made her lie down again until her vertigo passed. Then he talked to her consolingly and had the slow-moving Miss Viviani make a mammography appointment for her. He was calm and deliberate. But as soon as the woman was gone, he snapped at Sidney, "Why did you break the news to her so bluntly? Why did you have to be so harsh?"

"Because I'm sick of having to coddle people who expect me to do the impossible."

"But you terrified that woman."

"She terrified me. I'm terrified of these surefire

disasters. Every surgeon we know is, but they all pretend it's nothing."

"Well, you certainly can stop being terrified now. That woman will never come back."

"Wanna bet?"

"She'll go to another surgeon."

"Who cares? Let her. Let her blame *him* for mutilating her."

Ben was appalled at Sidney's cruelty, and yet he felt it was understandable. His tongue loosened by barbiturates, Sidney had simply expressed something that many doctors thought but kept to themselves. He had been brutal, but behind the brutality there had been logic.

It was only after the incident that Ben decided that the drugs were striking at the keenness of Sidney's mind, obscuring his logic and magnifying his brutality. As he continued to increase his barbiturate dosage, ignoring all of Ben's repeated pleas to stop, his tirades began to make less and less sense. Ben heard him cursing for the sake of cursing, insulting for the sake of insulting, screaming for the sake of screaming. One afternoon he listened to him expelling a woman from his office for questioning him too closely about the side effects of various birth control methods. "Every interference has its risks," he was shouting. "In medicine. In life too. Goddamn it, in life too!"

Ben shuddered. The degree of Sidney's fury had virtually no relevance to the specific situation. As soon as the woman who had triggered the attack had fled, he hurried into Sidney's office and said, "You've got to grab hold of yourself, Sid. The barbiturates aren't calming you. They're making you more and more agitated."

"That's my business," Sidney answered him sharply.

"Surely it's mine too. If you keep this up, you won't have any patients left. And I can't afford the office on my own."

Sidney simply shrugged. "I don't think it matters to my patients how I treat them, as long as I treat them."

Ben left, discouraged, for the truth of the matter was that while a few patients had begun dropping Sidney now that he was so ill-tempered, many others were continuing to demand appointments with him. He wondered if any of them suspected that their physician was a drug addict, but concluded that none of them did. It was a thought too far beyond their imaginations.

The nurses were another story. There were three of them including Miss Viviani, the newest, and he was sure that, given their pooled experience and wisdom, they knew Sidney was on something. Yet although they were alarmed by Sidney, they covered up for him, explaining his actions to patients as well as they could, making excuses for him, softening his words whenever possible. They were, Ben supposed, as protective of the medical profession as he was, as interested in keeping it from scandal or condemnation.

Of course, they gossiped about Sidney among themselves. He had overheard them. But they spoke of him as being explosive or agitated or paranoid, naming his symptoms but not his ailment. Nor did they ever ask direct questions about his condition. Perhaps they hoped that by not giving it a name, they could avoid responsibility for his actions.

It was the same with the interns and residents at the hospital. And even with Sidney's peers, the other attendings and medical school professors. Martin Stearns had stopped him in the hospital corridors one afternoon and said, "I hear Sidney isn't feeling well. Is that true?" When he had nodded, "Yes," Stearns had said sympathetically, "Tell Sid I hope he's feeling better soon," but oddly enough he'd showed no curiosity about the nature of Sidney's illness.

Alithorn was equally uninquisitive, at least at first. But late in June Ben saw him talking to Sidney outside his office, his handsome, suntanned face looking unusually tired and troubled. Several days later he asked Ben to stop by and see him.

"Your brother's always been known as a moody guy, right?" he began, as Ben nodded nervously in the chair alongside his mammoth roll-top desk, an antique Alithorn had insisted be installed in his office. His was the only antiques-furnished office in the glass-walled modern building. He had chosen the antiques, he would explain to anyone who asked, because he believed they inspired trust and confidence in patients. He was fond of saying that medicine, like religion, had only started to invite disaffection once it espoused modern architecture. "Sidney had a reputation for temper tantrums long before I ever knew him, right?" he prodded Ben, looking over his head toward the door in his familiar distracted fashion.

Ben nodded again. Alithorn put his chin on his hands and, for the first time, gave him his full attention. "But his personality's been getting out of hand," he said. "He's been screaming at nurses, cancelling operations, terrorizing the interns. He needs a psychiatrist. You know what I mean?"

Ben said at once, "Yes, I believe so." Alithorn's expression was stern. Ben wondered how much he actually knew about what was causing Sidney's explosions.

"Good," Alithorn continued, "Now, I'm not asking any questions, and I don't intend to ask any. I've told Sidney this and I think he understood me. What psychiatric clinic he goes to is entirely up to him. It needn't be ours at all. But he obviously needs some treatment, and I'm more than willing to grant him a medical leave for as long as it takes. I'm counting on you to see to it that he goes."

Ben felt dismayed. "I've told him that myself," he blurted out. "So has his wife. Isn't there anything else you can suggest? Is there any way *you* can make sure he goes?"

Alithorn scratched at his chin. Then he looked away from Ben and pulled one of his small net-suke animals from his jacket pocket and began stroking it. "You've told him and he doesn't care?" he asked.

"Yes."

Stroking the figurine, Alithorn slowly shook his head and when he spoke, sounded discouraged. "What can I do?" he said. "Medical leaves are strictly voluntary. Of course, there's such a thing as suspension. Removing a man's operating privileges. But it's hardly Number One on the Hit Parade."

Ben stared at him, puzzled.

"Hardly the court of first resort. There have been some hellish lawsuits over removing a doctor's privileges. It's an ugly business. It can be as bad for the hospital as it is for the man himself. Unless, of course, the doctor in question has seriously broken hospital rules. Not shown up at staff meetings. Not kept legitimate records." He paused and looked at Ben unhappily. "Or wantonly harmed a patient."

Ben sat forward attentively, relieved that at last Alithorn had raised a matter that worried him more than any other, the possibility that Sidney might injure a patient.

"It takes a screw-up or two," Alithorn muttered sadly. "After that, it's a different story. If we've suggested to a man that he get help, and he hasn't paid attention to us, and he's had a screw-up or two, then we can begin to find a way of dealing with the situation." He emitted a long, drawn-out sigh from between slightly parted lips.

"I think I see what you mean," Ben said.

"We wouldn't want any screw-ups," Alithorn commented.

"Yes. I see that. But I'm not sure under the circumstances that they can be prevented."

Alithorn stood up, as if ready to dismiss Ben. "Well, I wouldn't be so skeptical," he said, smiling now. "Psychiatric clinics can do wonders these days, don't you think? With these personality problems, I mean."

"If a person checks into one of them."

"Well sure. Of course," Alithorn smiled. "That's up to you, isn't it? You and Mrs. Zauber. The people who are close to Sidney. Who can influence him." He put his carving back into his pocket and extended a hand. "He's a great doctor, your brother," he said, grasping Ben's fingers and shaking them hard. "A credit to the profession."

A half-hour later, walking through the hospital lobby on his way back to his office, Ben decided that although he had promised Claudia on the day of Mulenberg's funeral that he would himself take over the onerous job of talking Sidney out of the barbiturates, he would have to renege on that promise and demand her assistance. She had given him almost none, he had to admit. In fact, she had acted distinctly uninvolved in Sidney's condition once she had assigned the task to him.

She had stayed up in Boston for an entire week after Sidney had lost his grant. Then she had returned to the city briefly, only to set off for St. Louis to visit an old friend. She had called Ben several times from St. Louis to ask about Sidney, but seemed reluctant to come home even when he told her that he thought her absence was contributing to Sidney's accelerating deterioration.

He had assumed that she found Sidney difficult to be around just now. God knows, he did too. But she never said this. Instead, she excused her absence in terms of other people's needs: her mother's depression, her friend Bootie's problems with her difficult five-year-old. Well, he would have to get her to come back. Alithorn had as much as said that the responsibility for Sidney lay with both of them. And he couldn't work on Sidney all on his own any longer. For one thing, he couldn't supervise him adequately. More and more he could see that someone ought to be with Sidney at all times. Someone ought to determine whether or not he could be believed when he said he felt steady enough to go over to the hospital, calm enough to operate. He could do this himself during the daytime hours, and would do it, but there were the middle of the night emergencies and the early morning summonses and the sudden after-dinner calls. Claudia would simply have to come back.

Backtracking, he entered a phone booth in the

hospital lobby. But when he telephoned the number in St. Louis Claudia had given him, Bootie told him casually that Claudia had left several days ago.

"Are you sure?" He found the information incredible.

"Sure I'm sure. She's in New York."

"She hasn't called me," he murmured.

"I didn't know she was in the habit of calling you," Bootie said.

He was disconcerted by her tone and got off the phone a moment later, barely saying goodbye. Then he dialed Claudia at home, but there was no answer.

He tried her again from a luncheonette on Third Avenue, and a third time when he reached Park Avenue, stopping at an open phone booth. For some reason, he didn't want to go into his office and make the call from his desk telephone. But again he got no answer. Then it occurred to him that of course Claudia wouldn't be at home. It was after two, and she always worked at the museum in the afternoons. He dialed her there and asked the switchboard operator to put him through to her. But when he finally got Claudia's extension an unfamiliar woman's voice said, "Mrs. Zauber? Oh. Well, I'm afraid you can't reach her here. She's no longer working at the museum."

He was shocked. He'd had no idea that Claudia was planning to quit her job, let alone that she had done so. She'd worked at the museum for

years. Been a junior curator there even before
she'd met Sidney. He'd assumed she would stay at
the museum forever. How annoying that he'd
failed to take an interest in her plans. And how
annoying that she herself had been so close-
mouthed about them. He'd have to ask Sidney
about her decision to quit as soon as he got to the
office.

Unfortunately, however, Sidney was over at the
hospital, Miss Viviani reported to him as soon as
he walked in and picked up his phone messages
from her. "He didn't want to go," she gossiped,
shaking her head from side to side. "You should
have heard the argument he got into."

"With whom?" Ben asked, although he knew he
was being nosy.

"Some woman whose boy he delivered two days
ago," the aging, heavy-bodied Miss Viviani replied easily. "She suddenly took it into her head to
leave the hospital early, and she wanted the baby
circumcised immediately."

"I see." He was disappointed. For a moment he
had imagined that Alithorn, after reconsidering
their conversation, had changed his mind about
merely delegating responsibility for Sidney and
had called him up to take a firm, aggressive stand.

Ben saw his patients and then, finishing up
swiftly, decided to go back to the hospital. He
hadn't planned on returning there until it was
time for his evening rounds, but Sidney hadn't
come back to the office and he did want to catch

him and speak with him about Claudia. Anyway, it was just as well that he went over early. He and Naomi were planning on having a fast dinner at her loft tonight, then going to Petey's school to see his class perform *The Pied Piper of Hamelin*. He could get his rounds out of the way and not have to worry about being late.

He walked expeditiously back to the hospital and took the back elevator up to the maternity floor. Would Sidney still be there? Stepping off the elevator, he started hurriedly down the corridor. But before he'd gone more than a few yards a gray-haired nurse came bursting through swinging doors at the far end. Her crown of braids was slipping out from under her cap and her chest was heaving. He stopped to stare at her as she ran past him and to his astonishment she changed the direction of her flight and scurried back. "Dr. Zauber! Thank God you're here!" she cried and clutched his arm.

"What's the matter?" He pulled back. She had dug her nails into his arm so hard he had felt them through his suit jacket.

"It's your brother! He's in the circumcision room."

And then they were both running in the direction from which she had come. Ben was ahead of the nurse but he called out over his shoulder, "Who's with him?"

"Miss Field. She sent me for help."

A moment later he pushed breathlessly through

the swinging doors and into the circumcision cubicle off the nurses' station. He saw Sidney and the head nurse first, their white uniforms and Sidney's right hand smeared with blood. Miss Field was holding Sidney's scalpel behind her back and she was struggling to keep it there, as Sidney wrenched and wrenched at her arm.

Ben threw himself between them at the same moment that he saw the baby. It was lying in its rounded, scalelike bassinet, its tiny wrists bound to the side of the scooped-out basket by little cords. Its waist and plump thighs were slippery and smeared with blood. But it was howling, emitting a shriek that burst from its lungs with the urgency of a siren.

The howl was a good sign, Ben had time to think, before he tightened his fist, jerked back his arm and, with Miss Field behind him and only inches between himself and Sidney, pushed his fist into Sidney's stomach. Sidney doubled over and Ben caught him, so that he wouldn't stumble forward.

Miss Field ran out of the cubicle and slammed the scalpel into a desk drawer, just outside. Then she was back, helping the gray-haired nurse untie the baby from its surgical bassinet. A few seconds later the two nurses had extricated the infant and were running down the corridor with it toward the pediatric wing.

Ben let Sidney slump onto the floor. He looked dazed, his eyes still uncomprehending, his lungs gasping for breath. Waiting for him to stop his heavy breathing, Ben marveled at how easy it had been to immobilize him. It had never been easy in the past when, as adolescents, he and Sidney had tangled physically. In fact, it had always been Sidney who had bested him. He couldn't recall a single time when he had won one of their youthful battles. The more he had tried, the harder Sidney had always fought, striking out with ever-increasing vigor. He had learned something just now, he thought. Sidney had lost so much weight that their strengths were almost equal. Surprised, he bent over Sidney and helped him to his feet. Miss Field was returning, accompanied by a youthful mustachioed resident. "Stand up," he whispered to Sidney.

"The baby's all right," Miss Field said, slamming the door behind herself and the resident. "The blood was Dr. Zauber's blood, from the cut on his hand." Examining her unsightly uniform, she added, "I've put the child back in the nursery, but what are we to tell the mother?"

Before Ben could speak, the pediatric resident interrupted, "I don't see that we have to mention the incident to the mother at all, except to say that Dr. Zauber was called away for an emergency. If she really wants to leave tonight, I'll do the procedure." He turned respectfully to Sidney who had begun to look more alert although he still seemed unsteady on his feet. "Are *you* all right, Dr. Zauber?"

"I'm all right," Sidney muttered. "I'll be all right in a minute or two." He too looked down at his stained white coat and abstractedly started to unbutton and then rebutton it. Then his eyes began to focus on the people around him and, shifting his glance from face to face, he at last concentrated his gaze on Miss Field. "The floor in here was slippery," he said to her, his voice turning belligerent. "When I picked up the scalpel I slipped. It twisted in my hand."

Miss Field responded with astonishment. "You took it up by the blade. Mrs. Olding saw you do it. And you were staggering."

"You and Mrs. Olding interfered between me and my patient." Sidney's voice was controlled and icy.

"You were practically bouncing off the walls. You didn't know what you were doing! You cut your own hand! God knows what you might have done to the baby if we hadn't interfered."

Sidney gave Miss Field a scathing contemptuous look. Ben was awed. Sidney's belief in himself, his conviction that in all circumstances he himself was right and others wrong, was still utterly intact, whatever else about him was disintergrating. "That floor should have been dry," he went on. "Jesus Christ. What are you running in here? A city pool?" He gestured at the floor and the resident smiled ingratiatingly.

Ben looked where Sidney pointed. Indeed, there were drops of water just below the baby's surgical bassinet. Would Miss Field have to accept responsibility for the accident? He wanted to say something to her, to hint to her that with the amount of drugs he was taking, Sidney might have slipped in a desert. But he didn't dare speak. Not in front of Sidney. In any event, Miss Field seemed able to take care of herself. Scowling, she withdrew into her professional persona and said coldly, "You'd better go down to Emergency and have that hand looked at."

"She's right, Dr. Zauber," the resident fawned.

"I'm going," Sidney flung out. "Come on, Ben. Let's go."

He followed Sidney.

Outside, Sidney paused for a moment at a supply cupboard, looking for gauze with which to wrap his hand. "Help me with this, will you?" he said. Unexpectedly Ben surprised himself by answering, "Wait a minute. I want to ask Miss Field something." She'd been amazingly unflustered by Sidney's attack on her, he thought. He had to know why. Sidney looked at him angrily as he turned back toward the circumcision cubicle, but he ignored his irate glance and pushed open the door.

The resident was already gone and Miss Field was alone, staring down at the floor under the bassinet table and shaking her head. "Was Mrs. Olding with Dr. Zauber the whole time?" Ben asked her.

"Yes. That is, until she ran for me."

"Is that customary? I've rarely had a nurse in attendance during a circumcision."

"Dr. Alithorn left instructions this morning for a nurse to be with Dr. Zauber on all occasions," Miss Field said. "And for us to let him know if anything unorthodox occurs."

"I see." Suddenly he felt cheered. At least Alithorn was doing *something*. "Thank you," he said warmly to Miss Field.

Sidney's hand required several stitches and while Ben waited for the emergency doctor to finish with his brother, he went into the staff room and called Naomi, telling her not to expect him in time for Petey's play tonight. He had a woman in labor, he lied, and it looked as if it was going to be complicated and time-consuming. He would call Naomi later and tell her whether he could meet her at all that night.

"Poor Petey," Naomi said. "He'll be *so* disappointed."

Her words struck him as bizarre. Here his brother could have castrated an infant and Naomi was complaining about how upset Petey would be over Ben's missing him in *The Pied Piper*. For the first time since he had conceived his plan for marrying Naomi he found her ridiculously trivial. "Petey was really counting on your seeing him," she was still going on.

"I'm sorry," he answered coolly. "Some things

are more important than a seven-year-old's disappointments."

"Ouch," Naomi said. "You're certainly fierce tonight. Maybe Petey's lucky you're not going to see him."

It did occur to him then that, to be absolutely fair, he was himself the person responsible for Naomi's talking so trivially at so serious a moment as this one. If she failed to comprehend the darkness of his mood, it was because he had kept her uninformed about what was happening to Sidney, had continuously hidden from her scrutiny this disturbing aspect of his life. He would have to tell her about Sidney soon, if just to keep himself from feeling utterly isolated from her. But it was going to be difficult. She would be wounded at having been kept in the dark so long.

He couldn't face launching into the stressful subject now. Promising again to call her later, he hung up and tried Claudia at home once more. But still there was no answer.

In the cab going uptown, his hand neatly bandaged, Sidney was silent, subdued, not needing to pretend with Ben, as he had with Miss Field and the pediatric resident, that he was in total control of himself. After a while, he even let his head slump sideways into the corner of the cab. "I guess I'll come upstairs with you," Ben offered, thinking of Claudia and more anxious than ever to speak with her. Perhaps he could get a minute alone with her to tell her what had happened, before Sidney launched into some inaccurate defensive version of the event.

"Thanks," Sidney said, sounding surprisingly grateful for his offer. "I'm not quite as steady as I could be." He half-smiled in his peculiar slack way, his mouth open but his lips straight.

Ben kept silent. The cab careened up Third Avenue, making all the lights, until at last it was forced to a screeching halt by traffic heading west on Sixty-fifth Street. Then, in the sudden absence of motion, Sidney said, "Well, what the hell. I have no future anyway."

Ben found his brother's new self-pitying tone even less appealing than his earlier self-righteous one. He twisted forward in his seat, concentrating on the terrible driver they had chosen, surprised at how little sympathy for Sidney he was able to summon up. He was looking after him, looking out for his interests. But he felt little of the awe or even respect Sidney had always drawn from him in the past. "There's something I should tell you before you come up with me," Sidney said, scattering his thoughts. "Claudia and I have separated."

The cab jolted forward and Ben's head whipped around. "When? What happened?"

"When I lost my grant," Sidney said bitterly. "She cleared out like a bat out of hell. The way everyone else is going to, once they know." He shut his eyes. "Maybe you will too, old buddy."

Ben clutched the leather strap of the speeding cab.

"I always figured her for a starfucker," Sidney said, his eyes still closed. "I don't give a shit. I really don't."

Ben clung to the strap and kept his eyes forward. He was more unsettled by Sidney's information about Claudia than by the disconcerting events of the day. "You didn't tell me," he whispered, although he almost said, "She didn't tell me."

"I didn't want to talk about it."

Sidney opened his eyes, sat forward, and began fiddling with his pants pocket, trying to extricate his wallet with his good hand.

"Where is she living?" Ben asked.

"I don't know. She calls once in a while, but she won't tell me where she's staying. She quit her job so I wouldn't be able to track her down. As if I would. Who needs her?"

Ben turned and looked closely at Sidney who had not yet succeeded in drawing the wallet out of his back pocket. "I'll pay," he said, and quickly produced his own wallet.

"Maybe I ought to stay with you for a while," Sidney murmured, interrupting Ben's activity.

Ben concentrated on drawing change out of his jacket pocket.

"I'm worried about being alone." Sidney reached across with his good hand and tried to stop Ben's motion. "OD-ing," he whispered.

"Right," Ben said rapidly. "Of course. I hadn't thought of that."

"Or maybe you ought to stay with me. Though I'd rather we stayed at your place. The co-op's *hers*. I never really felt it was mine." Still trying to reach Ben's hand, Sidney added in his self-pitying tone, "I never really felt that she was mine."

"All right," Ben said brusquely. "Stay with me. You can sleep in the spare room."

He didn't like the idea of living with Sidney very much. But it had certain advantages he saw. He would be able to supervise him more adequately. And when Claudia called him, perhaps he would get a chance to speak with her too. Perhaps he could even convince her to call more frequently. If she didn't want to have daily contact with Sidney just now, she could call him. He would remind her that separated or not she was still Sidney's wife and ought at least to have the decency to stay in regular touch with the person upon whom she had shifted the burden of his care. Not that he blamed her. Looking at Sidney, fumbling and maudlin alongside him, he envied Claudia her freedom.

Upstairs, the once-meticulous apartment was a mess. There were heaps of dirty dishes on the living-room cocktail tables, stacks of mail and newspapers on virtually every chair and footstool and, in the kitchen, overflowing garbage bags on the counters, more dirty dishes in the sink, and small, disregarded mounds of broken crockery swept helter-skelter into the corners. All the rooms smelled foul and, waiting for Sidney to finish his packing, Ben opened windows. Then he cleared a space for himself on a chair at the hall phone and, calling Naomi, who had not yet left for Petey's play, told her about Sidney and the barbiturates.

It was easy for him now. His hopes for establishing regular communication with Claudia helped him overcome the reticence he had experienced just an hour ago. He was as thorough in his details as he could be and apologized many times over to Naomi for not having confided in her sooner. And then he told her that Claudia had left Sidney, and that consequently he would have to let Sidney stay with him for a while.

It wouldn't be for terribly long, he said. Still, Naomi and Petey mightn't be able to move in with him at the end of the month, as they had all anticipated. But they would do it soon, he promised.

Naomi was furious. "Goddamn it, Ben, I've already sublet the loft."

"See if you can postpone your tenant for a while," he said calmly. "I'm sure I'll have Sidney straightened out in a month or two."

Naomi sulked. She was furious with Sidney. "Damn Sidney," she railed. "That fucking Sidney."

"I know exactly how you feel. Poor baby. Poor sweetheart."

CHAPTER SEVEN

JULY

Claudia was firm about her decision in the daytime, but at night misgivings would invade her. What would become of her if she stayed away from Sidney permanently? What would become of the baby? Would it grow up resenting her for having deprived it of a father? Bootie had said, "All a kid needs is a mother," but Bootie's own child, a daughter the bohemian Bootie had had with a St. Louis sculptor she had never planned to marry and no longer saw at all, was whiny and secretive and hardly a good advertisement for single parenthood. Or so it seemed to Claudia.

At night in the brightly lit suite at the Mayfair House she had taken just after her return from St. Louis, she would cry for hours or hold imaginary conversations with her unborn child, begging its forgiveness for having run away from its father.

It had been easier in the beginning, when she had first left Sidney. She had felt, the night she had run coatless out of her apartment with her husband scrambling in pursuit behind her, that she had had no choice. If she had stayed even a second longer, he might have beaten her, not in play, as he did to become aroused, but in deadly disordered madness.

She and Sidney had been talking in the living room of their apartment and he had been drinking heavily, despite the fact that earlier, at dinner, he had swallowed two glistening capsules of Nembutal right in front of her eyes. The phone had rung and she had dutifully gotten up and answered it on the kitchen extension and then returned to the living room to tell Sidney it was Borkin Layton of the Deutsch Foundation. Sidney had poured himself another bourbon before going into the kitchen, and she had waited gingerly outside, nervous because of what her brother-in-law had said about Sidney's grant being in trouble and knowing it was unusual for Layton to call on a weekend.

Eavesdropping, she had heard Sidney's voice grow louder and more explosive as his conversation with Layton progressed. He was mad at Layton, she thought as she listened, or at Keith Neville, whose name she heard him shout several times during the conversation. Then she heard the

phone receiver slam down and waited for Sidney to
come out of the kitchen. But he didn't come, and
instead she began to hear toppling noises.

First, she heard a few glasses shattering, then a
tentative fall of pottery, and last a reverberating
riotous crash of china. She raced into the kitchen
and saw Sidney sweeping the pantry shelves with
an outstretched whirling arm, glasses and cups
and plates spinning and colliding and smashing
beneath his feet.

"Stop it! What's got into you?" she cried. His
face was purpling and his arms were quivering
with intense spasms. And then he lunged at her.

She started running. Sidney was mad at Layton
and Neville, but she was the only person present.
She knew in that moment the difference between
fear and terror. Sidney had always frightened her,
but until recently the tremulousness his loud voice
and arbitrary assertiveness had aroused in her had
usually had a pleasing component, an ingredient
of sexual and intellectual thrill. She had perceived
Sidney as a man in such full control of himself
and his environment that she had imagined that
he *used* fear, that he instilled it in others out of
some plan or intent, some thought-out goal and
this had made his mannerisms seem stimulating
rather than alarming.

It was only lately that she had begun to suspect that her vision of Sidney had been inaccurate. Or had become inaccurate. He wasn't in control. He was floundering. And now, as he came

stumbling out of the kitchen after her, she saw at last that he was out of control, and it terrified her.

She ran down the long foyer, tripping once over the edge of the patterned rug, but managing, despite her panic, to scoop up her large leather handbag from the front hall table. Sidney ran after her.

Trembling, she flung open the side door that led to the steps and slammed it. Scurrying down the steep metal stairs, she heard Sidney open the door and call to her, "You bitch, you fucking bitch." She hoped for his own sake he wouldn't try to run after her on his drug-enfeebled legs. But she didn't wait to find out if he would. She was on Fifth Avenue and in a cab before she had time to envision what would happen if he stumbled on the stairs.

And then she didn't know where to tell the driver to take her. She had no close friends of her own in the city anymore. She and Sidney had socialized chiefly with Sidney's associates and colleagues. They all liked her, but if she went to one of them, she couldn't trust herself not to blurt out what she had just been through, and within hours everyone at the hospital would know Sidney's shame. Her shame. Everyone would know the maniacal condition of her once-imposing husband.

There was Ben, of course. But he would just tell her to go back to the apartment and make sure Sidney was all right. He adored Sidney, worshiped him, perpetually did his bidding, no matter what was asked of him. Of course, Ben would offer to come with her, once she told him how terrifyingly Sidney had acted, but she couldn't go back upstairs, not even with Ben, not now, not after having seen Sidney in such disarray.

She told the driver to take her to La Guardia. Her mother was expecting both Sidney and herself tomorrow for a weekend visit. She would tell her mother she had come a day early, and by herself, because Sidney had unexpectedly been called out of town to chair a meeting. She caught the last shuttle flight to Boston.

It was only once she was home in her childhood room that she called Sidney, although throughout the flight she had had intervals of panic in which she had envisioned his having tripped on the steep, unused stairs of the apartment building, his having hit his already dazed head on stone and steel, his having lain undiscovered for hours. But her own need to escape his reach had been uppermost in her mind.

In Boston, she felt safe enough to call, and even, hideous as the thought seemed to her, prepared to notify the police if Sidney didn't answer the phone. But he did, and although his words were slurred and his statements almost incomprehensible at moments, she gathered he had had a sufficient remnant of self-composure not to have attempted the stairs once she fled. He even apologized for his rage. "Wassn' you. Wassn' you I wanted to hurt."

She had begun to cry and he had said, " 'S best you ran out. 'S best you don't come back until tomorrow."

Her tears had overflowed then. Hadn't he understood she wasn't in the city, and *couldn't* come back until tomorrow? Crying, she had said "Okay," hung up, and then lain awake for a long time, listening to the sea flagellating the rocks beneath her bedroom window.

The house had creaked all night, sea drafts stealing through a myriad of cracks and warped window fittings. Sidney was sick, she kept telling herself, as she huddled under her patchwork quilt. She ought to go back first thing in the morning. But she didn't want to, and as she relived her hasty flight from the apartment, she suddenly sat up in bed, fully aware now that something more than terror of Sidney's burst of irrational behavior was making her unwilling to return. Recalling his unsteady stance and spasmodic arms, she realized there had been a strong admixture of contempt in her terror of him. She had lost respect for him.

Damn the drugs, she thought. Had it not been for the drugs, he would not have been so wild, so unworthy of her admiration. Shivering in the cold room, she blamed the drugs for Sidney's loss of grandeur and did not believe, although he in one of his mocking moods had insisted she'd best believe, that it was because of his grandeur, because of grandeur evolved into grandiosity, that he had turned to drugs, sure he could control them, determine their effects, manipulate them, survive them.

If only he would stop taking them, she told herself, all would be as it had once been.

At last she lay back down, convinced that now, at least, she knew how to regain her respect for Sidney. If he gave up taking the sleeping pills, she would love him again. She would be able to go home.

But in the morning, when she delivered her ultimatum, Sidney rejected it. His voice was still slurry, but his words were thoughtful, almost clearheaded. "'M not sure. Don't think I can give them up. 'M think—thinking I don't really want to."

She felt lost, filled with doubts about her ability to live apart from him.

"Please," she said.

"We'll see. Meanwhile, c'mon back. I need you here."

She might have returned, his command triggering in her a wealth of memories of obedience, except that a moment later he added, "'M scared, 'M scared. I need you back here."

She had known then that she couldn't go back, not to this man who was slurring his words and begging her for what she ordinarily gave without hesitating. "Give up the pills," she had repeated, trying to make her voice authoritative.

"'S no way to guarantee it, suhweehaar." The

drugs made him shorten his words. It was his slur that put her off. "You're a fuckinbish, suhweehaar. I'll stay high all weekend if you don't come back, suhweehaar."

"And if I do?"

He didn't answer her.

"I'll call you tomorrow," she had said hollowly. But when she called on Sunday he didn't answer the phone and she imagined that, as he had said he would, he had gotten high and forgotten even his need for her.

From Bootie's, where she went after her stay in Boston, stopping in the city only to collect a few items of clothing, she and Sidney had similar conversations. "Come back," he would say, and she would waver and want to return, but she would force herself to say, "I will if you'll give up the pills," and he would say, "I can't promise. I will when I'm ready to." Then always, after he had stated his position, he would turn either to pleading for her return or to demanding it in a tone that lacked the strength she used to hear in his voice. He would say, "Come back. I'm frightened," or else grow wildly angry with her, screaming, "Get your ass back here, you fucking bitch."

She began to dread their conversations. This man she spoke with daily was not only not the man she had married but every time she spoke with him she felt he was eradicating her memories of that man. Talking to him, she lost her history.

After a while, she didn't even want to call him and, even more strongly, didn't want to see him. Not in decline.

When she returned from St. Louis she refused to tell him where she was staying, in case he took it into his head to seek her out, and she arranged a leave of absence from her job so that he wouldn't try to visit her at the museum. Yet at night, entering the lobby of the Mayfair House, she would grow irritated despite herself by the hotel's prosaic imitations of the hand-painted French ceilings she and Sidney had admired together on a trip to the Loire Valley, and her eyes would fill with tears. And in her suite, surrounded by unfamiliar and conventional objects, she would weep loudly.

She was homesick, pastsick. But worse still was facing the loss of a future. Until she had left Sidney, she had been able to project before she fell asleep each night not only the content of the next day, its rituals of tidying and shopping and preparing food, but the content of the next week, the next month, the next year.

Married, she was a citizen of a familiar country. Alone, she was like an immigrant; her past was in a foreign tongue that was already growing rusty, while her future lay in a language she could barely pronounce. And might never master.

Daily she resolved not to telephone Sidney and yet most nights she found herself dialing him once again.

One frightening night, although she rang him until four in the morning, he didn't answer. She set her clock for five, and again for six, and then seven, repeating her efforts hourly, although there was still no answer. And then, at nine, she finally reached Ben in the office.

"Sidney's staying with me," he comforted her, pleased at hearing her cool, well-modulated voice again.

"Oh. Thank God!"

"Were you worried?" Despite himself, a tinge of annoyance had crept into his own voice. "One would never have known it, from the way you've managed to make yourself so scarce. I was wondering whether you'd even notice that he wasn't staying in the apartment."

"I can't help myself, Ben. It's not that I'm not worried about Sidney." She sounded embarrassed.

"What is it then?"

She was quiet for a moment and he anticipated that, as usual, she would hide her thoughts from him. But something had made her less reticent than she customarily was. Perhaps it was being on her own. "I just can't bear to speak with him," she said. "He's different. Not the same man."

He listened to her carefully. "It upsets me to speak to him," she went on, qualifying. "But I do. Not every day, I admit. But I do call."

"Why do you?" He spoke slowly, struggling to keep his irritation with her under control.

She paused. He heard what sounded like sniffling, and then a tear-ridden murmur. "Because I feel so rootless. So alone. So cut off."

"Call me, then," he said swiftly. "I'll keep you in touch. Call me here in the office, anytime you like. Or at night, if that's when the loneliness hits you." He remembered so well that it had been for him chiefly in the dark, while others slept together, that he had felt his own desperate rootlessness. "I have a private number on the phone next to my bed. It's different from the one on my other phones."

"You don't think I'm hardhearted? Not wanting to speak to him?"

"No. I know what you're feeling."

"I miss him. The man he was." She was still crying.

"I understand. Call me."

She began phoning Ben several times a week.

It was the one bright occurrence in his life with Sidney. Sidney had seemed needy and frightened the night he had asked to stay with him. But once he knew he had a caretaker, a guardian against his fear that he might accidentally consume too many pills and fall into a coma that would, if unattended, rob his body of oxygen and leave him dead or brain-damaged, he was confident and arrogant once again. He was willful about going into the office or hospital, no matter how dazed or dulled his state, and he was impossibly demanding to live with. Ben had forgotten how much his brother liked to be waited upon.

Sidney would do nothing around the apartment. Ben took care of their clothing needs, making frequent trips to the laundry and the cleaner's, and he shopped for the two of them and prepared dinner, or at least set the table and laid out the ready-to-eat food he had purchased—oranges and bananas and cheese from the local Gristede's, fried shrimp and potatoes or barbecued chickens from Luby's Delicatessen.

Sidney ate very little of the food Ben set before him and never offered to clean up afterward. Sometimes Ben would ask for his help but although Sidney often said, "Sure, sure I'll do it," he never did, and when Ben would return to the kitchen, the waxy sandwich papers and dirty dishes would still lie scattered on the table. Ben himself would have to start brushing the garbage into a bag and washing the dishes, and after a while he gave up asking Sidney for assistance.

"Let's get a cleaning lady," he called out to Sidney one night. He was scraping greasy, food-laden dinner plates into the kitchen garbage pail and Sidney was lying on a couch in the living room, reading a newspaper.

"And have someone prowling around here whenever she wants and poking into our private papers?" Sidney got up from the couch and stood in the archway of the kitchen watching Ben. The pupils of his hazel eyes were large and dark. "Not on your life!" he added.

"What private papers?" Ben asked.

"My research notes."

"They're in the office."

"Well, it's the principle of the thing. I hate having my privacy interrupted. Besides, you're looking after everything perfectly."

Sidney sat down at the kitchen table to finish reading his newspaper and Ben washed the dishes, but he was enraged. Sidney was trying to turn him into a slave. "I don't like looking after you," he said sharply, shutting off the faucets.

"You don't?" Sidney smiled in his slack, half-hearted way. "You do it so well, I thought it was second nature for you. I always thought you'd make someone an excellent wife."

He put up with Sidney's taunts, and when Claudia telephoned him he would talk to her happily, trying to keep her on the phone for a long time. She always began her conversations by asking how Sidney was and he always told her the truth—"The same," or "Worse." Sidney was cautious about filling prescriptions for himself; he wrote them out under false names and never filled them at the same drugstore twice; but his habit was growing so demanding that sometimes he had to spend an hour a day traveling to ever more distant drugstores.

"You're not getting anywhere with him? With talking him into stopping?"

"Not really."

"Oh, Ben. Please keep trying."

After a few minutes of answering Claudia's questions about Sidney, he would try to get her talking about herself and the baby. Was she resting sufficiently? Exercising? Drinking plenty of milk? Or had her new obstetrician instructed her to be careful about milk in order to keep her weight down?

No matter what she told him, invariably he found fault with the way she was looking after herself and blamed the influence of the new doctor. She had switched to him right after leaving Sidney, and although she had explained to Ben that it had nothing to do with being dissatisfied with him, that it had to do only with her fears of running into Sidney if she came down to the office, he had been deeply hurt by her decision. Hadn't Claudia realized that just as pregnant women become profoundly involved with their obstetricians, so, too, did the obstetricians become involved with them? He still felt responsible for her well-being and inordinately wrapped up in the health of the baby.

"This Dr. Hecksher of yours sounds too casual to me," he would often tell her. Or he would say disparagingly, "Sounds like a faddist to me. Be careful."

Claudia didn't mind. She liked to be scolded, he noticed, or told what to look out for in new situations. She liked to receive advice. One night she said that she had begun to think that perhaps after the baby was born she shouldn't, after all, go back to her museum job. Perhaps she should do something different. Go to law school, maybe.

At first he didn't want to comment; he had never been able to form a firm opinion of Claudia's intellectual abilities. But she prodded him into discussing the subject of law school with her and listened very seriously when he outlined the steps she should take before making a decision, the people she ought to see, the law school admission tests she ought to examine. She even made notes.

Another night she asked him what she should wear to the party Bootie was planning in August when her paintings went on exhibit in a prestigious St. Louis gallery. "Should I wear something bohemian? Bootie surely will. Or should I wear something elegant? The Halston, if it still fits?"

Always when they spoke he felt sexually aroused.

He was alone with Sidney so much of the time that he was perpetually tense. But whenever Claudia called, the frustrations that Sidney provoked in him resolved themselves into sexual tension and this, at least, he could relieve. Lying stretched out on the bed, a pillow behind his head and Claudia's voice in his ear, he would know that he could soon attain peace, however momentarily.

Always, when she hung up, he masturbated.

Once, he managed to get Claudia talking about her relationship with Sidney. "Did he ever beat you?" he asked her shyly. "You know, that first time I examined you, I thought he might have."

She didn't answer at first. He imagined her drifting into diffidence, her face a mask, imagined her changing the subject as she had in his office the day he had noticed the bruises on her thighs. But at last she confessed, "Yes. Sometimes. A little."

"You liked it?"

"Oh no. No, I didn't."

"But you let him."

"He was so insistent. And I wanted to please him."

"But you must have liked it," he persisted.

"No. Well, maybe I did. I suppose it must look that way to outside eyes. I thought I was just doing it to hold on to him."

"What was it about him that you wanted so to hold on to?"

"He made me feel important. The rest of the time."

"Because of his fame?"

"Yes."

"Just that? Or other things?"

"Well, his personality, too. His intelligence. His authority. His imagination."

His hand had gone to his penis. He couldn't help it. Always her cool, unemotional voice excited him.

When they had finished talking, he hung up and made himself come right afterward.

Sidney didn't know that Claudia called and Ben didn't tell him. He seemed to assume Claudia had just decided to forget their relationship. He was angry, he told Ben, but not surprised. Claudia had always been heartless. Ben thought Sidney was hurt, but Sidney wouldn't admit it. "I never loved her anyway," he would insist. But Ben was sure that Sidney still longed for her, wondered about her.

"I'm puzzled about Claudia's not having moved back into the co-op," Sidney said one day.

"How do you know she hasn't?" Ben asked.

"I walked over there last week. Spoke to George. He said a new cleaning woman was coming in once a week and picking up Claudia's mail. I gave him ten bucks to tell me where Claudia was staying, but he told me to keep it. Said he really didn't know."

"I imagine you'll find out eventually," Ben reassured Sidney.

"Yeah. I suppose," Sidney said morosely. "Not that it matters. I suppose I'll be hearing from a lawyer."

* * *

"I hardly see you anymore," Naomi said to Ben. They were sitting in the kitchen of her loft and Naomi had put up water for tea. But instead of setting out cups and getting down a tin of tea, she paced around the small area, occasionally kicking a sandalled foot against the packing crates stacked in the corner.

"I've told you before," Ben said patiently, "I can't leave Sidney alone very often. And I can't have you up there when he's there."

"Why the hell not?"

"It would disturb him. He's terribly upset about Claudia's leaving him, and seeing me with you would just rub things in."

"Maybe he needs to have things rubbed in," Naomi commented. "Why must everyone pussy-foot around him all the time?"

"Please calm yourself," he begged her.

"And be a patsy like you?"

It was not the first time they had fought over Sidney, and usually he attempted to soothe her with promises that Sidney would soon be gone, or with encouraging, anger-dissolving embraces. But tonight, he felt he wanted to win her silence without compromise, wanted to work at obtaining the goal. He said nothing, and made no move toward her, remaining with his elbows set firmly down on the table while she stormed about among the boxes.

"Here Petey and I were supposed to move in

with you at the end of last month," she said, kicking hard at one of the crates, "and Sidney just snaps his fingers and you go running to him, not caring who you hurt in the process."

"That's not quite fair," he replied quietly. "Or even accurate."

"Sure it is. 'Sidney needs me. Sidney can't be left alone.'" She mimicked him, her eyes blazing. "But what are you doing for him? What's anyone doing? What's the hospital doing? If it weren't for the fact that I love you, I'd get my editor to assign a story on that fucking hospital. That fucking Sidney."

"But you do love me, don't you?" He felt utterly confident of her answer.

"Yes." She sat down heavily. "I do right now. But love isn't something that just stands still. That never changes. What you do affects my love."

"And what you do affects mine," he answered coldly. "It's hard to love someone who complains all the time. So no more complaining, all right? Let's just go to bed."

She looked away from him, frustration making her shoulders quiver.

"I hate making love here," she said. "There's no privacy here."

"It's your own fault. Taking a loft." He glanced around at the large, open space, only a set of carved Indian screens demarking the area where Petey was sleeping. "Let me ask you something," he went on, exceedingly calm and rational,

"Doesn't it say something about a woman's attitude toward sex when she leaves her husband and moves into a *loft?* With no doors?"

"It was all I could afford," Naomi countered. "And how dare you talk about my attitudes toward sex? What about yours when I first met you? I'm surprised I even bothered with you."

He stood up and reached for his raincoat. "I'm going," he announced. "You've been carping at me all night. I don't have to listen to this."

She stared at him, her mouth and eyes wide. "No. No, don't go. I'm sorry."

"I don't feel like making love tonight anyway. I'm not in the mood."

"Please don't go," she pleaded. "I'm sorry. I won't say another word about it."

He hesitated. "You promise?"

"Yes. Yes, I promise."

He stayed, knowing he had won. But he still didn't feel much like making love to Naomi. He wasn't sure whether it was because of her argumentativeness or because he had been satisfying himself so intensely in response to Claudia's disembodied voice. Still, he went to bed with Naomi, remembering, as he always did when they made love in her loft, to inhibit his usual grunts of passion in order not to awaken Petey.

"This place looks like a pigsty," Sidney said to him the next morning. Ben had made coffee, shaking the old grounds down the sink drain but scattering some of them onto the counter and the floor beneath the table as he did so. "Clean it up, will you?" Sidney asked irritably, sitting down at the table.

"Tonight," Ben said. "I've got to get out of here fast this morning. I have a consult."

He unplugged the coffee pot, poured two mugs of coffee, and set one down in front of Sidney. He drank his own standing, while rummaging in the refrigerator.

"It can wait," Sidney said. "This place looks foul."

"No, it can't." Turning toward Sidney, he gulped coffee.

Sidney's hand was clenched around his coffee mug and he too began to drink, raising the mug carefully to his lips. But his fingers were shaking. They kept tightening and loosening around the smooth ceramic sides. A second later, his fingers uncurled and he let go of the mug. It fell, shattering on the linoleum, and the steaming coffee splattered around his feet. Sidney didn't move them out of the way but sat, looking puzzled, at his empty hand.

Turning back to the sink, Ben got a sponge and began wiping the floor around Sidney's feet. They were dirty, he saw, and the toenails were starting to curve under, like talons. He stood, wrung out the sponge and, bending down again, wiped Sidney's feet.

* * *

Ben cleaned up the office, too, although there the messes were of a different order. Sidney not only continued to arrive late for his appointments, or to cancel an entire waiting room full of patients without explanation, but sometimes he would start to examine a patient and then stalk out of his examining room. Disappearing for fifteen or twenty minutes or sometimes not returning at all, he would leave the office to make one of his excursions to a drugstore. The abandoned patients called the nurses and the nurses called Ben.

"Dr. Zauber's had to leave. He's terribly sorry," Ben would mutter, embarrassed.

"He didn't say anything. He just walked out," the patients would complain indignantly.

"Young girl with cancer," he would say. "Terrible business." Or even, on occasion, "His wife. She's pregnant, you know. But she's been hospitalized for toxemia and it's preying on his mind." Usually the patients would soon begin to nod forgivingly. Once he got over feeling extremely shocked at his ability to lie so convincingly, he was amused to realize that he had, after all his years of feeling unimaginative, at last learned the joys of invention.

But many patients were starting to realize that something was seriously wrong with Sidney. Although they didn't suspect what it was, a few began switching to other doctors. By the middle of July, Sidney had confused or alienated so many women that his appointments chart showed numerous gaps and empty hours.

It was just as well, Ben thought. When Sidney did see patients, when he didn't cancel them or disappear, he was so aggressive that Ben's own patients would overhear his voice and act edgy and ill-at-ease. Some even canceled their visits with Ben.

Sidney was under better control of himself at the hospital, as if there some inner monitor still protected him from self-destruction. The consequences of a tantrum or a disappearance at the office were minimal; at the hospital they would have been disastrous. He was like a heavy drinker, Ben thought, a man who stumbles when he leaves a party but manages, once caution is utterly essential, to snap himself into alertness when he gets behind the wheel of his car. Sidney had managed to keep himself relatively free of harm at the hospital. He'd had no accidents after the incident in the circumcision room.

Of course, Alithorn had alerted everyone on the gynecological and maternity floor to keep an eye out for him. They stayed close when he delivered babies, closer still when he operated. When his mind seemed to waver, a nurse would immediately call his attention back into focus; when his hands trembled, a senior resident would offer to complete his cutting or sewing.

Still, Sidney might one day escape the protective net the hospital had cast about him, Ben worried. He might tremble so violently or move his scalpel so erratically that an injury would occur to a patient or a baby before there was time for intercession. He was right to worry. Only *he* saw Sidney at his worst. Saw him at home where he felt no need to maintain controls. Saw him swallowing his pills, staggering, muttering incoherently to himself.

He tried desperately to keep Sidney from going to the hospital when he was in these states, generously offering to take over for him. But invariably Sidney refused. He would turn livid, curse, scream paranoiacally that Ben was trying to interfere in his affairs, and even act physically threatening. He was forever clenching a fist or shaking an upraised arm.

He would back down and let Sidney go off to the hospital, but the whole time he was gone he would pace in panic up and down in his office, or in the living room of the apartment, or, on the days he was most worried, just outside the operating suite. For all his resentment of Sidney, he didn't want to see him injure anyone or bring disaster shattering down around his head. Yet he felt totally ineffectual when it came to keeping those possibilities at bay.

One night Sidney took so many pills that he was completely unintelligible at dinner and shortly afterward began to urinate right at the kitchen table. Ben helped him out of the kitchen and into the tiny bathroom and then, waiting outside the partly closed door, heard the telephone ring. He answered it on the hall extension.

The call was for Sidney. One of his pregnant patients had arrived at the hospital and would, the resident who called predicted, be ready to deliver in about an hour.

Glancing at the bathroom door, Ben decided not to tell Sidney about the call but to go to the hospital himself and deliver the patient without Sidney's agreement. He went into his own bathroom to shave and put on his suit jacket.

Before he finished, Sidney appeared in the doorway, his own jacket donned, although it hung unbuttoned and loose across his ever-diminishing chest. "Where do you think you're going?" Sidney said. "That call was for me, wasn't it?"

Ben answered truthfully, "Yes," and started to explain that he would go in Sidney's stead. Sidney turned und pushed out of the bathroom doorway, stumbling.

"Don't go," Ben called out. "Don't! Look at you!"

Sidney, his face unshaven, was still wearing the trousers he had dampened. He ignored Ben and slammed out of the apartment.

Ben finished dressing and raced to the hospital after him. Forty minutes later, while he was pacing up and down outside the delivery room, Sidney emerged in a scrub suit and mask and said sarcastically, "I did fine. And I looked fine too."

A nurse was wheeling Sidney's patient out

through the corridor and the woman, awake and cheerful, called out to Sidney, "Thank you, Dr. Zauber. Thank you for my lovely little girl."

Ben went home, but even though the delivery had gone well, that night he couldn't cease his pacing. Long after Sidney had come in and gone to bed, he continued to walk up and down in the living room, his feet aching.

"You've got to get Sidney to move out," Naomi lashed out at Ben in bed in her loft the next night. "It's not doing him any good, being with you. And it's having a rotten effect on you."

"I can't let him live alone," he answered her. "And Claudia won't have anything to do with him."

"Maybe if you didn't coddle him he'd get frightened and sign himself into a detoxification clinic and get help."

"Not Sidney."

"How can you be so sure?"

He shrugged and his gesture made Naomi even angrier. "I can't stand not knowing if I'm supposed to be moving in with you next month or not," she complained. "Can't stand not seeing you except for the hour or two you steal from Sidney in order to come down here and fuck me. Yes, that's all it is. All you want to do is fuck me. We haven't been anywhere together all month. Haven't seen anyone. Haven't even gone out to dinner. One of these days I'm going to get the idea that

what you want, what you really want, is to have
me leave you."

As soon as she said it, he began wondering if it
was true. Perhaps he no longer needed her. Perhaps he had learned from her all the rudiments of
relationships she was equipped to teach, and was
ready now for more sophisticated instruction. But
he would never have suggested to her that they
break up. He felt terribly grateful to her. She'd
done so much for him. "Sweetheart. Baby. What a
rotten thing to say," he chided her and ran his fingertips along the curve of her breast. Then denying her charge that his having less time for her
had anything at all to do with wanting to stop
seeing her, he said, "Let's have dinner out on Saturday. I guess I could leave Sidney alone for three
or four hours. Read him the riot act. Make him
swear he'd check with me first if he got a call to
go to the hospital. Do you think he'd listen?"

Naomi pulled away from him and sat up, her
curls shaking. "Sidney, Sidney, Sidney," she
fumed.

"I thought you just said you wanted to go out to
dinner."

"Yes. Yes, I do. But not just when Sidney gives
you permission to take me."

"It's not a matter of permission from Sidney.
It's a matter of my deciding he can be left alone."

He couldn't get her to see his side of the situation. After a while he gave up trying and made
love to her distractedly.

* * *

On Saturday night he knew as soon as he entered the restaurant she had picked that the food
would be bad. It was a little Italian place in the
Village he had never heard of before and although
there was a handful of men drinking at the bar,
none of the tables in the dining area was filled.
Still, he tried to look forward to the meal. Naomi
was wearing her backless yellow sundress and it
made him think nostalgically of the Caribbean. He
ordered a rum and tonic. She asked for a martini.

"What'll we eat?" he questioned her. "What are
they famous for here?"

Naomi sipped her martini and kept ominously
quiet.

"What made you pick this place?" he persisted.
"What's their specialty?"

Naomi tilted her martini glass to her lips and
drank so hurriedly that he realized even before
she answered him that trouble was brewing. "I
have something to tell you," she whispered as
soon as her drink was half-consumed. "That's why
I picked this place. I knew it would be quiet."

"Oh?" He waited while the waiter handed them
food-specked menus.

"I've been having second thoughts about us,"
she said as soon as the waiter was gone. "I wanted
to discuss them in some neutral sort of place."

He closed his menu and shoved it against the
wall. "I've had them too," he said quietly. "But I
wasn't planning to act on them."

"That's the difference between you and me," Naomi said, finishing the rest of her martini and warming to the subject. "That's what's causing the trouble. You're so passive."

He looked away, hurt. He had never insulted her by naming her deficiencies. She said quickly, "Oh, I don't mean sexually. That's fine now. I mean about Sidney. The way you let him dictate to you. Run your life. Run me out of your life." She brushed a hand across her forehead, pushing back her hair. "You do everything for him and nothing for yourself."

He didn't think it was true. "He's not running my life. In a way, I'm running his."

"You're not," Naomi insisted. "Take *us*. You were happy with me. You wanted me and Petey to move in with you. But just because Sidney barges in and takes over your place, you let him destroy your relationship with me."

"Destroy? I don't see that at all. We'll be living together soon. You just have to be patient for a while."

Naomi shook her head stubbornly, the gin making her at once courageous and flushed. "But that's just it. He is destroying things. He's destroying my feelings for you. I can't feel the same pride I felt about you when I feel you have no pride. That you're his lackey."

He looked away from her again, his thoughts in turmoil, and this time caught the waiter's eyes and signaled him to bring Naomi a refill. He didn't be-

lieve he was Sidney's lackey anymore; he was
looking after him, but he was no longer in thrall to
him. He acted like a servant, but he didn't feel
like one. Ironically, Naomi herself had been a fac-
tor in helping him achieve this new emotional
freedom from Sidney. He was in her debt. He'd
always be grateful to her. But watching her gulp
down her second martini, seeing how the gin
made her dark skin flush and her curls slip rakishly
out of place, he knew that although he could live
with her and make love with her, he could never
love her.

"Look, Ben," she was saying. Her voice had
grown huskier with emotion. "I didn't decide this
overnight. I've been thinking about it hard.
You've got to get Sidney to move out."

He acted distressed. He shook his head in despair. Then he said very sadly, "I can't do it, Naomi. I would if I could. But I can't do it. Sidney
needs me."

It infuriated her, as he had known it would.

"He doesn't need you. He doesn't need anyone.
He's incapable of need. He's just using you."

He shook his head again. "I love Sidney. He's
my brother. I've got to rescue him."

"It isn't love when you want to rescue someone.
It's self-aggrandizement."

"Call it what you want. But in any case, I can't
abandon him. Sidney's part of me."

"Then I'm not going to see you anymore," she
announced impulsively. "I can't stand the feeling

of being in love with a man who lets someone else
push him around, dictate to him all the time. Make
Sidney move out and I'll come back."

"I can't."

Her eyes filled with tears but she had gone too
far to retreat. "You poor bastard," she said.

He felt sorry for her, but he took refuge in the
fact that she, not he, was causing their breakup. It
was her doing. He had done nothing. "I still want
you," he said. "It's not that I don't want you. I'm
horny all the time." Reaching out for one of her
hands, he kidnapped it below the table to press it
against his unruly penis.

His expression of desire for her at so emotional
a moment simply offended her further. "I don't
care," she said, snatching her hand away. She
looked at him as if she no longer recognized him,
her eyes distant, and then she slid out of her chair
in a sudden swirl of movement. She dropped her
pocketbook, bent for it, scooped it up, dropped
her sunglasses, bent for and retrieved them and
was gone from the table a moment later, scurrying
through the bar, blurring.

Just as she neared the door he had a moment's
change of heart and thought of running after her,
taking her arm, turning her around and talking
her into one last-farewell time in bed. But what
was the point? He would just have to part from
her sooner or later, and this way he had allowed
her the dignity of feeling it was her own decision.
Of course, it might have been more amusing to

have demolished her dignity . . . deliberately.
The thought surprised him. He had never allowed
himself to think a thing like that, much less do anything so frankly cruel. He was interested. And, a
moment later, horrified. He called the waiter,
asked for another rum and tonic, and ordered
roast veal. But by the time the food arrived he had
no appetite. Pushing the plate aside, he told the
waiter to wrap the meat up in tinfoil for him and,
leaving, took it home, where he offered to share it
with Sidney.

He was with Sidney constantly after his parting
from Naomi, with him in the office, in the hospital, at home. Most of the time they were alone. He
had always, before Naomi, been an isolate and
Sidney had had not friends but admirers, colleagues and sycophantic junior staff members
who put up with his brusqueness because of his
reputation. But as he continued to deteriorate,
many people began to ignore him. He had always
been arrogant, self-absorbed and mocking. But he
had had power and prestige. Now that he was losing these, his personal traits, which had once impressed people as interesting, struck them as irritating.

One morning Ben was walking into the hospital
with Sidney when he saw James Herron coming
toward them. Herron had for years been trying to
woo Sidney to his house for one of his cocktail
parties, but Sidney had always claimed to be too

busy to attend. Now Herron turned on his heels as
soon as he saw the two brothers approaching and
headed in the direction from which he had come.

A few of the junior men, slower to recognize a
fall from authority, still tried, occasionally, to stay
in touch. Diehl left several messages for Sidney,
inviting him to come to his apartment to toast his
fiancée, and one ambitious young intern stopped
him on has way out of the OR several afternoons
in a row and proposed they have a drink together.
But Sidney wasn't drinking. In his only effort to
reduce the ever-present danger of his overdosing
and falling into a brain-destroying coma, he had
asked Ben to clear out his liquor cabinet. He rejected the offers of companionship that the
young men made by telling them gruffly that he
no longer drank.

Ultimately Ben and Sidney saw no one socially
but each other.

Toward the end of July, Miss Viviani quit. She
lumbered into Ben's office, her obese body moving more swiftly than he had believed possible,
and told him in a voice simmering with indigna-
tion that Sidney had just thrown a bottle of alcohol at her. "I can't stay here," she sputtered. "Not
a day longer. Not with him."

Ben had been sitting at his desk, a set of X rays
balanced on his lap, another propped up in front
of him against his books. He slid from his chair,
the X rays on his lap slipping onto the floor, and

hurried to Miss Viviani, putting his arm around her shoulders. The front of her uniform was soaked. "Please. I need you. I'm sure you realize that my brother is not always fully aware of what he's doing. He's not well."

"You said it," she barked. "He shouldn't be allowed to practice."

He patted her arm. "That isn't up to you or me. There are department chiefs and administrators who decide these things." He stroked the cloth on her sleeve. "Please stay. I need you."

"It isn't you," she said. "You're a dream to work for. But I can't stay here. Not with him the way he is."

"Please," he pleaded, humbling himself. "The patients need you." He couldn't face the trauma of hiring yet another new receptionist. "Please just stay on for a month or two. You can do that, can't you?"

She softened a little, leaning heavily into his arm. "Well, okay. I'll stay a little longer. Maybe they'll take away his license next Tuesday anyway."

His arm dropped to his side. "What do you mean? What are you talking about?"

"The Department of Professional Conduct," Miss Viviani said. "They've been writing him letters. About his not signing health insurance forms. And the last one said that if he didn't come to a hearing they're holding next Tuesday, they'd start an action to take away his license."

For a moment, he almost laughed. Here he had been guarding his brother against disaster at the hospital and yet disaster was looming from a direction he hadn't even thought to consider. Miss Viviani's information struck him as stunningly incongruous. But a second later he realized the seriousness of the situation and said tersely, "Let me see the letters."

Miss Viviani padded out and returned with a slim manila file. He told her to delay sending in his next patient and quickly perused the file. It was filled with letters requesting Sidney's appearance, then demanding it, then hinting at legal action if he didn't comply. The letters reminded him of the progressively threatening form letters relied upon by bill collectors. The last one stated assertively that Sidney would be subpoenaed to explain himself unless he voluntarily came down to a hearing on Tuesday.

Grabbing the file, he charged down the corridor and across the waiting room and burst into Sidney's office. He didn't knock, even though Sidney had a patient with him.

"I've got to speak with you at once," Ben said, ignoring the curious glance of the patient.

"I'm busy," Sidney intoned coldly.

"Busy or not." Turning to Sidney's patient, he added, "Excuse me, but you'll have to leave for a moment."

The woman obediently stood up.

Sidney raised a hand as if to signal her to sit

down again. "What the hell's going on?" he said. But Ben had already eased the woman through the door and shut it behind her.

"That's what I want to know," Ben fumed as soon as the door was closed. "That's what I want you to tell me!" He slammed the file down on Sidney's desk. "What are you doing about this?"

Sidney's voice was expressionless. "Oh. Those jokers." He swept the file to a corner of his desk with an impatient gesture.

"You've got to go down there on Tuesday," Ben said, lowering his voice in case Sidney's patient was waiting just outside the door.

Sidney swiveled his desk chair so that his back was turned. "I'm not going. You know how I feel about those fucking forms."

"Sid, be reasonable. They'll drive you out of practice if you don't show up."

"I'm a surgeon, not a computer," Sidney roared, and swung his chair noisily around so that he was facing Ben. His face looked so gaunt and his eyes so huge that for a moment Ben didn't recognize him. He seemed almost as emaciated as the concentration camp victims from whose photographs he had always turned away his eyes. Looking at him, he couldn't proceed with his argument. At last he focused his eyes downward, concentrating on his brother's refusal and not his appearance, and was able to say, "You won't have to sign the forms. You just have to put in an appearance. Just make up some bullshit story about why you haven't signed them in the past, say you're sorry, and promise that from now on you will. It'll be months before they get after you again."

"I'm not going," Sidney declared suddenly, his will not in the least diminished. "I didn't become a doctor in order to do paperwork. I don't have to explain myself to *anyone*."

"You've got to go," Ben expostulated, his eyes still cast down. "It's either that or plan on shutting down your practice. They're going to subpoena you."

Sidney leaned back in his chair and shoved his feet up on the desk in his favorite posture of resistance. Why did he so often assume this position? Spasmodic trembling often afflicted street addicts. Did his legs tremble less when he propped them against some firm surface? But he didn't have time to pursue his thoughts. Sidney was saying, "You go for me. You go down and say you're me."

Startled, he had to look at Sidney's face again. It was unshaven and the hair on his cheeks was growing in gray and wiry. Beneath the stubble, his skin was pimply and rashed. As Ben stared at it, Sidney seemed to become conscious of a tickling sensation, and he began to scratch himself. "I don't know any of these jokers," he said, and dug his nails into the stubble. "And they don't know me. They don't know what the hell I look like. You go. Say you're me. Tell them anything you want. Just get them off my back for a while."

It was true, Ben thought, that the men at the hearing didn't know Sidney or what he looked like. And it was just as well that they didn't, although in a way he wished that they could see him as he looked right now, his nails digging compulsively at his sparse beard. But if the men from the Department of Professional Conduct did see Sidney, he realized, just the sight of him might make them keen to penalize him. It was best, for both their sakes, to avoid that. He decided he would agree to Sidney's request.

The hearing was in a building on lower Park Avenue, a cold-looking modern building made all the less appealing for being set down on a block still lined with ornate turn-of-the-century mansions. The building was an imposition on old ways of doing things, Ben thought as he approached it, just as the very fact of a Department of Professional Conduct was an imposition of doctors' old ways of doing things. Entering the lobby, his resolve to impersonate Sidney weakened. He shouldn't be doing this for Sidney. He should have found a way of forcing Sidney to come himself. For all he knew, if he got caught impersonating his brother, the department could start an action to revoke his own license too.

Inside the revolving doors, he peered at his reflection in a mirrored wall. His face was furrowed, nervous. His shoulders were hunched. He ought, he thought, to smile and stand straight, to stop stooping and emulate the self-confident stance that Sidney had always had, at least in the days before his addiction. Thrusting back his shoulders and relaxing his face, he tried to assume the air of an eminent researcher. But although he was wearing his best suit and had borrowed Sidney's gold snake and staff cufflinks and one of his monogrammed handkerchiefs, when he entered the elevator he still felt insecure about his appearance.

The hearing room had windows on three sides and bright sunlight flooded Ben's eyes as he walked in, so that at first he couldn't see who else was present. Then he made out a large, T-shaped conference table and five men, four seated together at the top, like judges, and one sitting solitary across from the door, along the table's length. The solitary man had a stack of documents at his elbow.

"Over hear, Dr. Zauber," one of the four men at the top of the table said, gesturing him to a chair opposite the man who sat alone. "I'm Dr. Martin," the man who had spoken went on, "and this is Dr. O'Connor, Dr. Kaplan, and Dr. Ferlinghetti." He waved a plump hand at his companions. "And this is Mr. Stoner, our counsel," he added, pointing at the solitary man.

Ben slipped tremulouly into the chair Martin had proposed, and knew he should introduce himself, but when he opened his lips, no sound came out. Crossing his arms, he laid them heavily on the table for support and at last was able to say, "I'm Dr. Zauber. Sidney Zauber."

"You didn't bring counsel?" the lawyer asked. He had a piercing voice and looked at Ben aggressively.

"N-no," Ben stammered. "I thought this was an informal hearing." The sound of words coming out of his mouth, like the sound of a scream after a moment of paralyzed terror, reassured him, and he managed to add, "I thought I only needed a lawyer if you decided to proceed against me."

"True enough," Dr. Martin said. "Although it's customary to bring a lawyer." He had a flat, upstate New York accent and Ben had to concentrate at first to understand his emphases. "Well, no matter," Martin went on. "We can manage well enough on our own."

Ben looked at him closely. His face was round, with gold-rimmed glasses that shielded his small eyes, and he was wearing a yellow and green plaid sports jacket.

Suddenly Ben was glad that Sidney hadn't come. Sidney had always characterized doctors who took assignments with administrative committees as specialists in red tape, dullards who couldn't make a proper living at the practice of medicine and so had to resort to extra-medical occupations. And certainly Martin looked the part, with his plump face, his dull eyes, and his ridiculously provincial jacket. Sidney would have felt immediately antagonistic to Martin, and would have made no effort to conceal his sense of superiority. For that matter, Ben thought, he would undoubtedly have considered himself superior to the other doctors as well. Two of them looked very young and inexperienced, and the third was elderly and wore a hearing aid.

"We were rather surprised you actually showed up this morning," the lawyer said coldly, interrupting Ben's thoughts. "Based on your responses to our letters. Or, should I say, your nonresponses."

Martin made a gesture with his plump hand, shoving at the air between himself and the lawyer. "It's all right, Mr. Stoner. I'll address Dr. Zauber. Since he hasn't brought his own counsel, I think it would be fairer if we medical men questioned him."

He began to feel more comfortable.

"We've had numerous complaints against you," Dr. Martin said, leaning forward. The three men alongside him also sat forward, the one with the hearing aid perching on the very edge of his chair. "A Mrs. Farber first contacted us last January, saying that despite repeated requests on her part, you had refused to fill out her insurance forms. Subsequently we have received complaints from several other women. A Mrs. Daniels. A Mrs. Smith. A Mrs. Evans. Are these patients of yours?"

Ben nodded a polite yes.

"And is it true that you have refused to fill out their health insurance forms?"

Again, he nodded. "Yes. It's true."

"But why?" Dr. Martin looked perplexed. "Don't you recognize that these patients expect to pay you for your services to them by being reimbursed by the health plans? That they have already, in effect, paid out money for your services by subscribing to a health plan?"

"Yes. Yes, I do," he said humbly. But he couldn't think of what to say next. How could he possibly explain to them, in any way that would seem sufficiently rational to them to prevent their moving to revoke Sidney's license, a behavior of Sidney's that he himself knew to be irrational. Could he tell them that Sidney was phobic about signing his name? Could he tell them that Sidney wasn't even sending out bills anymore? Could he tell them that not signing insurance forms, and not asking to be paid, were the least worrisome of Sidney's new habits? Could he tell them that his brother was a barbiturate addict whose professional life met almost no standards of professional conduct?

He shifted uneasily in his chair, and then at last ventured, his voice low, "I have a philosophical objection to the procedure, sir."

"A philosophical objection?" Behind his glasses, Martin's eyes blinked. "By the way, you don't have to call me 'sir.' We're all peers here."

Ben raised his voice slightly. "My objection to the procedure is that—well, it's always seemed just a little bit socialistic to me." The man with the hearing aid smiled.

"Filling out those forms smacks of Big Brotherism," Ben added.

"What's that?" Martin's plump face looked perplexed.

"Third-party payments make a mockery of the doctor-patient relationship. Right now it's insurance companies that are dictating to us, but the next thing we know, it'll be the government."

Martin began to nod and the two young doctors bobbed their chins up and down infinitesimally.

"We're told what to charge, what tests to perform, and we're even asked to put down questionable diagnoses, just to suit the forms. We're not our own men anymore," Ben said. He could see he had given the committee an argument it found not altogether unreasonable. Perhaps it had been made before by other recalcitrant medical men. Although he was certain that Sidney's refusal to sign the forms had nothing to do with philosophy, he went forward with the argument, his voice at last reaching its customary pitch. "Medicine used to be a matter of private practice. But these days we have no privacy. And neither do our patients, really. Do you realize what an invasion of privacy these insurance forms constitute?"

Even the lawyer was looking at him a little less hostilely than he had earlier. "We're being told how to practice medicine by insurance salesmen," Ben continued, turning slightly to include the law-

yer in his gaze. "Middle men. Economic vultures."
As he warmed to the argument, he raised his voice
even louder. There was no point in playing Sidney
as altogether humble. Surely some of his reputation for irascibility and arrogance had preceded
him here.

"But Dr. Zauber," Martin said cajolingly, "none
of us likes it. But we do it. We go along with it
because it's accepted practice."

"We can't take this kind of thing into our own
hands," the man with the hearing aid interrupted.
"Much as we might like to." He smiled again.

"You can't fight city hall," one of the young
doctors interposed. "Or the state capital, for that
matter. Not bare-handed."

Ben allowed himself to look thoughtful.

"And it's not as if your philosophical stance was
harmless," Martin said. "It's all well and good. We
understand how you feel. But you're hurting innocent parties—patients—when you undertake this
battle. After all, they've already paid the insurance companies. They expect reimbursement."

Ben thought of saying, as Sidney surely would
have, "Not if I don't bill them," but he knew that
would make the committee lose its feeling of iden-
tification with him. He looked down at his arms
on the table and then said slowly, "Well, yes. Yes,
I see."

"You would be better advised to take your
stance by writing for some of the professional
journals," Martin went on. "I mean, when you can

spare time from your other writing." He looked at Ben deferentially. "We're all familiar with your research, Dr. Zauber."

Ben allowed himself to accept the implicit compliment and to smile appreciatively at Martin. "Yes. Yes, I suppose you're right. I suppose battles like these are best fought in print, and not through direct action."

"Yes. That's just it," Martin said. "So if, in the future, you would just start filling in and signing the forms—"

"There'll be no further action against me?" Ben finished his sentence.

"That's right," Martin nodded.

"Thank you," Ben said swiftly. "Thank you."

"But we plan to monitor you," the long-silenced lawyer at last chimed in. "If this occurs again, you won't have the courtesy we afforded you this morning. We'll move against you, I can assure you."

"I understand," Ben murmured. "Of course."

He stood then and the four doctors stood too. Martin extended his hand. Ben walked to the head of the table and saying, "Thank you," once again, grasped Martin's fingers. Then he shook the hand of each of the other doctors. The man with the hearing aid had a weak, arthritic grip and after trying to convey his gratitude through a useless, unreciprocated handshake, Ben put his arm around the man's shoulders and clapped him on the back. Then he hurried out of the hearing room, suddenly in desperate need of the toilet.

In the men's room opposite the elevator, his intestinal pangs relieved, he stopped once more to look at himself. The mirror was cloudy and streaked but the face that looked out at him had clear, intelligent eyes and a smooth, no longer furrowed brow. He smiled at his reflection, and congratulated himself on the performance he had just given.

A half-hour later, still pleased, he entered Sidney's office. "How'd it go?" Sidney, his legs propped up on his desk, demanded imperiously.

The smile that had been playing on Ben's lips ever since he had left the hearing suddenly vanished. "Badly," he said impulsively, the word surprising him as much as it did Sidney. "They're going to take away your license."

Sidney swung his feet to the floor.

Enjoying his discomfiture, Ben frowned. Then a split second later, he let a smile return to his lips and said, "I was just kidding, old buddy. It was fine. Terrific."

Sidney's gaunt face was white. "Don't tease me, you son of a bitch," he roared.

It was difficult to know where his thin body manufactured the stamina for rage, Ben thought. But he quickly apologized. "I'm sorry. I don't know what got into me. Actually, I wanted to tell you how well it went. They believed me. They even almost apologized for harassing a man of my eminence over such trivia."

Sidney began to relax and he too smiled in his slack way. "No kidding. They did?"

"Yeah." Ben removed his jacket and undid the cufflinks he had borrowed from Sidney. "But they did say that it better not happen again. I think from now on you really are going to have to fill out insurance forms. Or let me do it for you. Otherwise they really might start an action against you."

"Have you sign my name?" Sidney muttered distractedly.

"Why not?"

Sidney pondered his question. "Yeah. Why not? Yeah, okay."

"I'll start now," Ben offered, setting the cufflinks down on the desk and scooping up a pile of unopened mail. "Give me something with your signature."

Sidney rummaged through his wallet and handed him his American Express card. He took it, shoved it into his back pocket, and started to leave. But at the door he paused. "I guess it would be best if no one knew I was doing this for you, don't you think?"

Sidney nodded. "Yes. I suppose so."

"I'll just tell Miss Viviani that you've finally decided to take care of your correspondence, but that since it's so backed up, you've asked me to help out for a while. I'll dictate letters, and diagnoses for the insurance forms, and then have her put the typed material on your desk. I'll sign in here."

"Okay," Sidney said. "Sure. Whatever you think best."

Ben went into his office and before he saw his first patient that afternoon, spent a half-hour practicing Sidney's bold, complex signature. What he was proposing to do for Sidney was probably illegal, he thought as he concentrated on the swirling "Z," so different from his own less dramatic one. But it wasn't a bad idea. He should have thought of it earlier.

That evening, over dinner in Ben's small kitchen, Sidney asked Ben to return his American Express card. Ben was just opening the refrigerator to take out the raspberries he had been fortunate enough to find at Gristede's for the night's dessert. His back to Sidney, he said, "Your American Express card? Oh, my God. I lost it."

He heard Sidney expel a loud, furious breath before he shouted, "You lost it! How the hell could you do a careless thing like that?" He turned around slowly, the bowl of raspberries in his hands, to see Sidney purpling with rage. "Do you realize how complicated it is to get another one? Jesus Christ!"

He studied Sidney's face. "Well, maybe I didn't lose it after all," he said deliberately. "Maybe I've got it after all."

"Where?" Sidney demanded.

"Here," he said and, shifting the bowl to one hand, delved in his back pocket with the other.

"Give it to me," Sidney ordered.

"Come and get it," he said, and waved the card in the air.

Sidney sprang to his feet. Although he was desperately thin, he still possessed remnants of the impulsive energy he had always displayed when he and Ben had fought as children. He lunged forward and for a moment Ben felt his old familiar fear of Sidney's temper afflict the pit of his stomach. But he stood his ground, shaking the card tantalizingly just out of Sidney's reach.

Sidney grabbed for his arm and he dropped the bowl of raspberries and moved backward, still dangling the card. Sidney changed his direction and, eyes narrowed, lunged once again. Ben stepped aside, agilely avoiding the raspberries that had scattered all around his feet. A moment later Sidney slipped and, hurtling to the ground, collapsed with a look of indignant surprise amidst the crushed raspberries.

Ben laughed. They had been tussling as if they were boys still, except that now, with Sidney's strength so depleted, they were better matched. Or actually, he had to admit a moment later, they were again badly matched; Sidney had had no real chance against him. "Just give me the card," he was saying, kneeling among the berries.

Momentarily ashamed, Ben bent over him and handed him the piece of plastic. Sidney grabbed it ungraciously and, standing up, sulked out of the kitchen.

In the living room that night, Ben continued to laugh over the incident. And then suddenly he got up from the couch and shut off the television set. He had discovered something, he thought. He had at last found a way of preventing Sidney from being harmful. It was all a matter of strength. Once the idea struck him, it seemed so obvious that he felt stupid for not having thought of it sooner. But instead of dwelling on his dullness he began to consider what he might do with the discovery, and soon he began to feel exhilarated, exultant. He continued to walk around the room but he was striding, not pacing, his legs moving in great bounding arcs. For the first time since Sidney had come to live with him, he knew that at last he had a plan for controlling him.

He waited before trying out his plan. There was no point in attempting to force Sidney to stay away from the hospital unless he was summoned at a time when he seemed truly dangerous, stupefied. Like the time he had pissed in his pants, he thought. He waited, but he knew the time would come.

When it did, it was on the night of a heat wave that gripped the city mercilessly. Coming home from the office, Ben turned up all the air conditioners to their maximum and yet still the apartment was intolerable. He stripped to his underwear, but Sidney seemed not to feel the heat.

At dinner Sidney huddled inside his dirty blue suit, the only one that fit him at all decently now that he was so emaciated, clutching the overlarge jacket tightly against his chest. He didn't eat a morsel and after dinner, in the living room, he acted even more unaffected by his surroundings. Ben had switched on the TV set to a Busby Berkeley musical. Sidney began to talk to himself, muttering and murmuring and gesticulating. Just then the telephone rang. Sidney tilted forward on the couch, swaying.

"I'll get it," Ben said and hurried to the hall phone.

The call was for Sidney. One of his obstetrical patients had arrived, been examined, and would, according to the resident on the other end of the phone, be ready to deliver shortly.

"He's not here," Ben murmured. "He can't make it. I'll come instead."

He hung up the phone just as Sidney appeared in the hallway, stumbling.

"Wassn' for me, was it?" Sidney asked. "Wassn' the hospital calling me?"

"Yeah, it was," Ben admitted.

Sidney tried to pull himself together, pushing back his shoulders. "Who was it? Wha's wrong?"

"I don't think you need to know," Ben said coldly. "I'm going for you."

Sidney listened expressionlessly as if he didn't quite understand. Then comprehension spread across his face. "The hell you are!" Scowling, he lunged at Ben, just as he had on the night they had fought over the American Express card.

This time Ben sidestepped immediately and Sidney crashed dizzily onto the floor of the hallway.

"You're not going for me," Sidney said, trying to stand. But he couldn't straighten up without a prop. He dragged himself toward Ben and grasped one of his legs.

"Oh, yes I am," Ben said and, kicking, freed his leg.

Sidney tumbled backward. Ben waited, watching him warily. And then suddenly Sidney sprang to his feet, rage making his strength return, and he leaned forward to punch Ben, his fists clenched in fury. Ben froze, maintaining his position, and just as Sidney's clenched fists came toward him, he sidestepped once again. Sidney's hands pounded against plaster.

"I'm going for you," Ben said calmly. "You can see that it's for your own good."

Sidney didn't turn around. He began pummeling the wall madly. Astonished, Ben stood predator-still. And then, alarmed that Sidney was hurting his hands, he grabbed him and wrestled his arms to his sides.

Sidney went limp, and at last Ben knew their struggle was over. It had, he thought, been even easier than he had first imagined it would be.

Holding Sidney, he began to half-drag, half-pull him to the spare room. This too was easier than he had expected it would be. Sidney's weight seemed almost half of what he remembered it to be. Pushing him through the door, he felt marvelously strong. He helped him onto the bed and said generously, "You try and sleep. I'll be back soon." Then he unfastened Sidney's belt, assisted him out of his trousers, and started to cover him with a blanket.

Sidney's legs began to tremble. "I need another pill," he whispered.

"No. You've had too many."

Sidney ignored him and reached for one of the jars on his night table, unsteadily extracting and swallowing two pills.

He sat down at the foot of the bed. Sidney's legs were still shaking uncontrollably. Unnerved, he put his arms around them, trying to provide the control that Sidney's nervous system seemed no longer to have. But the legs went on shaking. And they were filthy, he saw, sweat-stained and traversed by dark rivulets that ran from thighs to ankles. Sidney had neglected his whole body, his

once so strong and even elegant body. On his
stomach there was the start of a red, blistery barbiturate rash. He held tighter to Sidney's legs
which shook and shivered within his grasp,
twitching involuntarily. And then at last the
twitching subsided. Sidney had fallen asleep.

He left a moment later and handled the delivery for Sidney. He was ashamed of having re-
sorted to force to get Sidney to stay at home. But
he was also proud of himself and when he fondled
the fat, squalling boy he produced for Sidney's patient, he felt his brutality had been for a good
cause.

The next morning, Sidney was awake early. He
came into the kitchen only moments after Ben put
up the water for coffee, settling himself on a
chair, his head in his hands. Ben looked him over
carefully. Sidney had a hysterectomy scheduled
for eight, he knew, and he couldn't tell from his
silence and his exhausted slump whether or not he
was in condition to go to the hospital or needed to
be restrained again.

"I'm all right," Sidney muttered, seeing Ben
eyeing him. "I'm not even angry. I guess you felt
you had to do it. For my own good."

It made Ben feel much better, not only about
his treatment of Sidney the night before, but
about Sidney's condition this morning.

"You making coffee?" Sidney asked. "I could
use some."

"You could use a shower too," Ben said quietly. "You're starting to stink."

Sidney said nothing.

"If you're going over to the hospital, at least take a shower first. And don't wear that fucking blue suit you've been wearing all week. It smells."

Sidney looked at him unhappily and Ben walked over to his chair and kicked it resoundingly.

"Cut it out," Sidney groaned, his hand to his head.

"Then take a goddamn shower." When Sidney still didn't move from the chair, Ben kicked him hard in the ankle. Sidney cried out in pain and bent to rub his ankle. Then at last he rose and began walking unsteadily to the hall bathroom.

Ben followed him, thinking that if Sidney didn't obey him and get washed, he would himself enter the bathroom, turn on the shower and push him under the water. But as he stood outside in the hallway, he heard the water start.

He felt pleased, and yet still peculiarly irritable. He glanced down at the door, staring at the key that always reminded him that once, years ago, the room had been a closet, and thought hostilely of locking the bathroom with Sidney inside. That would teach him a lesson. But he knew he was allowing himself to become overly provoked by Sidney's eccentricities and, controlling the urge to taunt him further, went back into the kitchen.

Sidney emerged five minutes later, still dirt

streaked; he hadn't actually washed but had simply let the water pour down on him. Still, he looked considerably better than he had earlier. He'd been partially successful, at least, Ben thought. Satisfied, he went into his bedroom and brought Sidney one of his own suits, newly cleaned and wrapped in plastic. Perhaps a fresh suit would mask his odor, at least until they reached the hospital where it would blend into the miscellaneous smells of antiseptics and anesthetics, patients and personnel.

But in the elevator, leaving their apartment, he grew irritable again. "You still stink," he muttered.

Sidney closed his eyes and held tight to the railing. Ben moved away from him and, when they left the elevator and emerged onto the street, walked a little in front of him. But he had decided not to try to prevent Sidney from operating this morning. Sidney seemed rational enough. He had remembered what had occurred between them last night and had even understood why Ben had been so tyrannical. There was no point in making an issue over each and every operation and delivery.

At the hospital, Ben parted from Sidney on the ob-gyn floor, letting Sidney head toward the operating suite while he set out to do his rounds. But after they had said goodbye, Ben turned for a moment and looked over his shoulder. Sidney was standing absolutely still, his legs not moving, but his arms shaking and shivering.

"What is it? What's the matter?" Ben said, returning swiftly to Sidney's side.

Sidney continued to shake. "I need more," he whispered. "Right now. Or else I better reschedule."

"Rescheduling at the last minute is crazy. You want me to take over for you?"

"No. I want to do it. But I can't move without shaking," Sidney said worriedly. "Look." He pushed a leg forward and Ben saw it quiver.

"C'mere," Ben said, and grasping Sidney's arm propelled him into one of the public bathrooms opposite the elevator. Sidney began to fumble at once for his pills and Ben looked for a paper cup in the dispenser on the wall. Sidney got out two pills and Ben ran the cold water tap, filled the cup and handed it to Sidney.

Sidney swallowed, water cascading down the front of the borrowed suit jacket. Then he slumped down on one of the toilets.

Ben watched him, pacing up and down in the confined area. "How do you feel now?" he asked several times, but Sidney didn't answer. He leaned his head against the metal partition of the toilet. His arms continued to shake. Then at last, the movement of his arms stopped. "I'm all right," he mumbled. "I'm all right now."

"Let me see." Ben stopped his pacing. "Let me see if you can walk straight."

"Of course I can."

"Let's see."

Sidney got up from the toilet and began walking, concentrating on his steps, his eyes cast down.

"Yeah," Ben muttered. "You're okay. But you've got to stand straight."

Sidney was still peering at his feet. "Straighten up!" Ben ordered.

Sidney raised his eyes slowly, his shoulders still stooped. He looked birdlike, Ben thought. Ridiculous. Fisting a hand, he pummeled Sidney's stomach. Sidney doubled over, groaning in surprised pain. Ben grabbed him by the arm and, forcing him upright, slapped him hard across the face. He slapped him twice. Then he said, "Come on! Straighten up!" and Sidney did.

Emily sat restlessly in the Zaubers' waiting room and hoped she would be called into her doctor's inner office soon. There were fewer women ahead of her than there usually were, yet she could see from those who were there that it would be at least another half-hour before her own turn came.

Bored, she took a pencil and a small spiral notepad out of her handbag and began checking over the chores she and Philip still had to accomplish if they were to get the baby's room fully ready before her delivery date. They had ordered the linoleum for the floor, and she drew a line through that item on her list. They had selected the crib, a white one with a delicate tracing of flowers on its side, and had even, last Saturday, completed the painting of the walls, Philip boldly working the roller and she meticulously attending to the woodwork.

She drew two more lines, noticing as she wrote that there was still pale lemon paint under her fingernails. But the curtains still had to be decided upon, and the changing table, and the rocker. She knew exactly the one she wanted, a capacious rush-seated rocker with a high back that would cradle her as she cradled the baby and make her so cozy and snug that she could nurse without tension. Emily put an asterisk alongside the word *rocker* and, absorbed in her list, was surprised when at last the nurse called out, "Mrs. Harper, you can go inside now."

Dr. Zauber was on the telephone. She saw him pick it up just as she opened the door of his office and for a moment she hesitated in the doorway, unsure whether to remain standing or to proceed at once to the patients' chair next to the desk. Telephone etiquette was years behind the technology itself, she thought, and wished the doctor would indicate what she ought to do with a glance or a wave of his hand. But he had a look of such intense absorption on his face that he seemed virtually unaware of her presence. "Yes, go right ahead," he was saying. "Yes, I understand that the mother suggested you call me." Emily decided to remain standing.

"Hypotonic?" Zauber said into the phone, his forehead furrowing. "But isn't it a bit early to be sure?" He kept the mouthpiece close to his lips. "Ah, I see. Yes, of course. It's the diminished visual pursuit and the poor vocalization that are so pronounced." Zauber shut his eyes. When he opened them again he looked right at Emily but she felt he was looking through her. "Poor Mrs. Kinney," he said, sighing. "Yes, of course I remember the circumstances. No, there were absolutely no prenatal complications."

Growing tired, Emily shifted her weight and at last made up her mind to sit down whether Zauber signaled her to the chair or not. She moved forward. Then she heard a change in the doctor's tone that startled her. His voice had grown deeper, angry. "We did everything that could have been done. Started oxygen therapy immediately. Had to keep it up for thirty-six hours."

Zauber sounded so harsh that Emily retreated again. "Sure I have a theory about it. We had a screwball on duty that night. A kid named Diehl. He did the initial exam and forgot all about her. Didn't even inform me she was in the hospital until she was ready to deliver."

Now Zauber laughed, but his laugh was brittle. "Yeah, I guess you've had your problems with residents too. Well, thank you, Doctor. Let me know the results of the neurological workup."

When Zauber hung up the phone he had such a scowl on his face that for a moment she hardly recognized him. Nor did he seem to recognize her. "Mrs.—Mrs.?" he said, looking at her and then shuffling through the manila folders on his desk.

"Mrs. Harper," she said brightly, but she felt hurt.

"Oh, yes. Mrs. *Harper*." He emphasized her name, as if to imprint it. Then he half-smiled and said, "Emily. Of course. How goes it?" and she forgave him his momentary lapse of memory. But all through their talk at his desk, and even when he examined her, she felt his mind was elsewhere. Frequently when she asked him a question he failed to respond, or looked up at her, startled, as if he had forgotten she was still there. His inattention upset her, but she chided herself for being overly demanding. Clearly he had many important things to worry about.

CHAPTER EIGHT

AUGUST

In August, so subtly that he was barely aware of it at first, Ben lost interest in exercising restraints over Sidney. For several weeks the city had been sweltering under a thick, gray cloud that seemed never to shift but to sit ominously overhead, clamped tight like the lid of a stone-gray coffin. It was difficult to breathe, let alone to be constantly alert and supervisory. He began to monitor Sidney less closely, and imagined that this change in behavior was due to lasstitude. But gradually he recognized that he had been affected by more than summer doldrums.

For several weeks he had derived great pleasure from discovering that his physical power was greater than Sidney's. Using that discovery, he had prevented Sidney from performing surgery or

delivering babies when he was heavily sedated.
And he had seen to it that when he deemed him
lucid and permitted him to go to the hospital to
perform his medical duties, he showered, dressed
presentably, and walked with a minimum of shuffling and daydreaming. He'd even managed to
halt, if not reverse, his dangerous weight loss by
kicking and slapping him to get him to chew and
swallow at mealtimes.

But the thrill of pummeling Sidney into obedience was disappearing. What was the point? He
had, after all, proven to Sidney which of the two
of them was the more powerful. One evening late
in August, when the telephone rang and a breathless resident asked for Sidney because one of his
patients was getting close to delivery, he knew
even before he looked in on his brother that he
was going to allow him to handle the birth.

He told the resident to hang on and made his
way down the corridor to Sidney's room, shaking
his head as he did so. It was astonishing that Sidney still had patients. True, he hadn't many. Most
of them, especially the gynecological ones, had
been warned off by his peculiarities of appearance and behavior. But a tiny handful of women
still insisted on his services. They were chiefly
women who had been infertile before coming to
Sidney. Pregnant at last, they clung to him with
an almost superstitious loyalty. As if it were he,
and not his science, that had made implantation
possible.

Outside the door to Sidney's room he paused, his nose assaulted by the odors from within. Although Sidney hated to sit down for proper meals, and had to be forced to consume meat or vegetables, in his bedroom he often devoured fruit, candy bars and sweet drinks. He never cleaned up afterward. The floor of the room was piled high with old newspapers and magazines he didn't want to discard, and on top of these was a second edifice of sticky candy wrappers, toppled soda cans and rotting fruit peels. Worse, he had begun to urinate in his sleep, soiling both his bed and his deep armchair. Ben inhaled deeply through his mouth before turning the knob and entering.

Sidney was slumped in his armchair, staring quiescently at the ceiling despite the blaring TV. He was hugging his stained blue jacket tightly across his chest. He looked like a drunk. Or one of the ambulatory schizophrenics that roamed the poorer areas of the city. "Phone for you," Ben said. "About a Mrs. Stephens. I told the resident to hold on."

Sidney ran his hands across his chest, as if seeking assurance about his substantiality. "Do you think I ought to go?"

"Yeah, I guess so."

Sidney seemed pleased. He pulled himself up from the armchair and balanced himself cautiously, his feet spread wide apart, before starting to walk in an unsteady broad-based gait to the hall telephone.

"Should I shave?" he asked when he had hung up the phone.

Irritably, Ben shrugged. "Suit yourself."

"Is there any change?" Claudia's voice on the other end of the wire that night sounded blue although she was packing for the long-awaited visit to St. Louis for the opening of Bootie's art show. Ben supposed the trip was making her nostalgic. She had mentioned once that she and Sidney had gone to every one of Bootie's exhibits, even the first one, in a storefront.

"No. No change," he murmured.

"Does he ever ask about me?"

Annoyed, he answered her with a curt "No." She was really impossibly neurotic. She refused to see Sidney, but she also refused to stop romanticizing her past with him. The one refusal made the other possible.

"Oh, Ben. It's so disheartening." She was quiet for a while and then she added, "But you will keep working on him, won't you?"

"Of course, I will."

"Maybe after the baby is born he'll see things differently. See he has a future after all."

"Sure," Ben said. He spoke halfheartedly. He wished she'd be more realistic. Sidney was increasing his barbiturate consumption rather than curtailing it. Most likely he'd never be able to give up his habit. All they could really hope for was that he didn't take so much of the drug that he overdosed.

He longed to say this to Claudia. To make her comprehend exactly how deteriorated, how detestable Sidney was. But Claudia had become so friendly. She called so often. And once they'd even had dinner together. Her interest in him might vanish if she ceased believing that, adoring Sidney, he would somehow salvage him for her. "You'll get him to come 'round," she was whispering. "I haven't given up hope."

He said, "Me either." But afterward he added hesitantly, "Though if you'd seen him lately, you might not be so hopeful. Sometimes I think he looks almost like a derelict."

"You're exaggerating," Claudia protested at once. "Sidney could never! You're being cruel. It's not like you."

He pondered her remark. He no longer knew what was and wasn't like him.

"It was fine. I was fine," Sidney mumbled, returning home an hour later and standing in the doorway of Ben's room.

Ben's eyelids flickered. "No problem?"

"No. You were right about my being able to go tonight."

Ben didn't tell him that he had decided to let him go no matter what his condition. He couldn't even explain his new callousness to himself, let alone hope to make it comprehensible to Sidney.

* * *

Sidney accompanied Ben to the office the next morning although it was Saturday and his appointments calendar was blank. Walking alongside him, Ben felt embarrassed. Sidney shuffled and stumbled and occasionally stopped moving altogether to enter upon an intense, mumbled conversation with himself. But fortunately the neighborhood was deserted. Everyone who could afford the time and money to flee the polluting clouds and debilitating humidity seemed to have done so, leaving the usually bustling side streets abandoned and strangely quiet. Only the avenues were busy, laden with shoppers and traffic. Ben slowed down to keep pace with Sidney on the side streets but at each crossing he walked slightly ahead of him.

He missed Claudia's presence in the city. He found this surprising and tried to analyze why. After all, he saw so little of her, even when she was in town. Their relationship was chiefly electronic. She rarely wanted to see him face to face. Indeed, she rarely wanted to see any man. Although she was separated, she still seemed to be preserving herself for Sidney, and fantasizing their reunion. It was unlikely that she would seek any emotional or sexual liaison until she gave up her fantasies. Saw what Sidney looked like these days.

Suddenly he heard the screech of brakes behind him and his thoughts of Claudia vanished.

He was out in the middle of Park Avenue, and the light had turned red. He leaped nimbly onto the island in the middle of the street. But now there was a terrible blazoning of car horns. He turned and looked behind him and saw Sidney still striking out into the street. He was stumbling forward, swaying as he walked. A swirl of cars heading uptown on Park Avenue swerved to avoid hitting him, and still he moved forward, bemused.

Ben stood absolutely still, startled. A driver leaned out his window and shouted at Sidney, "What's the matter with you, you fucking drunk!" and a pedestrian, marooned on the island with Ben, screamed, "Stand still! Stand still!" Yet Sidney kept walking, oblivious, miraculously escaping death.

It was only when he reached the island and Ben grabbed him and pulled him to safety that he at last seemed to understand the danger he had been in. Leaning heavily on Ben's arm, he broke out into a drenching sweat.

"I'd really like you to come and see Sidney when you get back," Ben said to Claudia when she called from St. Louis that night. But she was dressing for Bootie's party—she was wearing the dress he had suggested, she said flirtatiously—and she didn't want to take the time to discuss anything serious. "I was just calling to check in. I'm terribly rushed. Besides, we've been over and over my feeling on that subject."

"Just say yes, then."

"Please, Ben. I don't want to do it."

"And I want you to. He's worse. He's really got me worried." He had made up his mind that this time he was going to persuade her, no matter how she resisted. Most likely in the long run it would make no difference. She would never turn to him. He wasn't her type. She obviously leaned toward more successful, imposing men than he. But he would never know unless he got her to see Sidney. If only she could smell him and visit his lair! If only she had seen him as he had stumbled blindly across Park Avenue this afternoon. "I won't take no for an answer," he warned.

She was silent. He perceived her stubbornness as a barrier he could surely topple, if only he was clever enough, and wondered that he had not really put his mind to it before.

"I'm not asking you, Claudia, I'm telling you," he announced, remembering how easily Sidney used to command her to do his bidding. But a moment later he lightened his tone, and added, "And who knows? It might be just the thing to help him. I thought that's what you wanted. To see him helped."

When at last Claudia said she might come over when she got back from St. Louis, he was unsure whether she had been responding to his harshness or to his last-minute suggestion that a visit from her would help Sidney. But it didn't matter. All he wanted was for her to have a good, long look at her husband.

Afterward, he lay on his bed, legs crossed, arms behind his head, and, feeling uncommonly pleased with himself, began to stroke his ardent penis. He was just about to come when his excitement was interrupted by the ringing of the other extension of his phone.

Grudgingly, he picked it up. A high-voiced, harried obstetrical resident was calling Sidney from the Emergency Room. "We've got one of his patients down here," he rattled. "She's bleeding quite a bit. Looks like placenta previa." He lowered his voice. "There's nothing to do yet except send her upstairs and watch her. But her husband's a real pain in the ass. He wants Dr. Zauber to come right over and look at her. I told him that Dr. Zauber was—was probably out of town." The young man's voice, whispering, was filled with innuendo. "I said at best you'd be coming in his stead. Then the asshole says it's Sidney Zauber they've been paying for and he doesn't want any substitutes." The resident's voice rose to a normal level. "But of course, if he's out of town—"

"That's okay," Ben said coolly, cutting him off. He had lost his erection. "He's here. I'll tell him. He'll be over as quickly as he can get there."

Sidney seemed to be drowning in sleep. He was having a nightmare and his arms and legs were thrashing. When Ben turned on the overhead light

and touched him on the shoulder, Sidney pulled
on him with all the desperate strength of a pan-
icked swimmer. He kept trying to drag Ben down
onto the bed alongside him. Ben gave him a shove,
and Sidney sprawled away, his eyes still closed,
but his mouth open, agape, as if the air were water forcing its way into his lungs.

"Wake up, wake up," Ben demanded. "Wake
up now. Get *up!*" At last Sidney rose to consciousness and came awake, shuddering. "There's a call
for you from Emergency. Do you want to go?"

Sidney grasped what Ben was saying only
slowly. First he rolled onto his side, shielding his
eyes from the light, then he nursed his forehead
with his hands, then at last he said, "Yeah, sure I
want to go."

"So go."

Sidney sat up and reached for his jacket from
the end of the bed and began pulling it over his
pajama top. Then he reached for his pills, knocking several vials off the night table before getting
one firmly in his hand.

Ben went back to his room.

It couldn't have been more than twenty-five
minutes later when the phone rang again. He had
just shut off his reading lamp, hoping to regain his
earlier feelings of delicious arousal. He picked up
the phone in the dark, but snapped on the light as
soon as he heard the voice on the other end of the
wire. It was the same high-voiced, harried resi-

dent he had spoken to earlier and he was rattling, "Doctor, can you get over here quickly? There's been some trouble."

He felt his breath seem to stop for a second. He had to wrestle to regain it before he could speak and for a moment he remembered his childhood panic at being asked to say words he couldn't force up from inside himself. But at last he had both breath and words. "What trouble? What's happened?" He waited, steady. Whatever it was, Sidney would have deserved it. He tried not to think about Sidney's patient.

"Your brother's been hurt," the resident said.

"My brother?" Astonished, he floundered for words again. He had been anticipating different information. "Sidney? You sure?"

"It's not too serious. That patient he came to see—her husband jumped Dr. Zauber in the corridor. Knocked him flat." The resident's speech was hurtling.

"Knocked him flat?"

"Socked him. But he's all right. Just a bit dazed. We didn't think he could make it home on his own, though. Thought you'd better come for him."

"Yes, of course." He was in full control now. "I'll be right over." He started to put down the phone but the harried resident was saying, "You can't really blame the husband. Your brother examined the woman and told the guy he could take her home, there was nothing wrong. But she was bleeding a lot. And Dr. Zauber was staggering. He practically sat down on the woman when he examined her."

"Thank you, Doctor," Ben said curtly. "I'll be right over."

"The guy began yelling that your brother was an incompetent drunk," the resident raced on. "And Dr. Zauber just walked right past him. Stumbled past him. You can't really blame the husband. His wife was hemorrhaging and Dr. Zauber was just telling him to take her home."

Ben hung up and dashed out the door of the apartment. Sidney was waiting for him in the doctors' lounge. His jacket was ripped, his nose was bleeding, and one of his eyes was shut tight, the skin above it just starting to purple.

Sidney's hospital privileges were revoked the next morning. Alithorn demanded to see both Ben and Sidney in his office at ten o'clock on Sunday morning and announced without ceremony, as soon as they were seated, "We can't keep carrying you anymore, Sid. I'm sorry. I did it as long as I could, out of respect for the man you used to be. But you're not the same man anymore."

Ben felt immensely relieved. He had taken great risks all month by ceasing to supervise Sidney. He had thought he might have to take still others before managing to get him suspended. But now the suspension was accomplished. And no one but Sidney had been hurt in any way. To himself, he whispered, "Thank God." He had not wanted to see any of Sidney's patients injured through his brother's incompetence. He had wanted only to achieve Sidney's suspension. To have Sidney receive this ultimate blow to his pride.

If Sidney had reacted to the loss of his research grant by nursing his disappointment in himself with increasingly high dosages of barbiturates, surely this second professional catastrophe would stimulate him to take even greater quantities. He would withdraw further and further into sedation. Become even more hermitlike and eccentric than he already was. Claudia would run from the sight of him, and even her fantasies would skitter and scramble away.

Already the news of his suspension was making Sidney behave more inappropriately than usual. Instead of apologizing for his condition last night, he was regarding Alithorn with a fierce, paranoid glare. At last he muttered, "But I didn't do anything wrong. I didn't hurt anyone. In fact, I'm the guy who got hurt."

Alithorn had kept his eyes averted, looking at neither Ben nor Sidney. Now he observed Sidney coldly and said, "You got-hurt by the wrong guy. The fellow who punched you is with the *News*. A reporter."

Sidney, not yet grasping the implication of Alithorn's information, continued argumentatively, "So what? He punched me. I haven't done anything wrong." Tilting his chin defiantly, he pointed to his bruised eye.

Alithorn bent and opened the file drawer of his desk. "But you have, Sid. Lots of things. Little things. I've got a whole list of them." Extracting a sheet of paper from the drawer, he glanced at it and said, "Staff conferences you failed to attend. Patient records you failed to write up. A circumcision you started but failed to complete. That sort of thing."

Sidney pulled himself to his feet, outraged. For a moment Ben felt almost sorry for him. His mind was so befuddled that he couldn't understand why he was being suspended. He had never accepted the idea that drugs could alter his competence and he still believed himself to be as good a doctor as he had ever been. From his point of view, the suspension was undeserved and Alithorn was betraying him. After all, he and Alithorn had frequently entertained each other at their homes. "You can't suspend a doctor unless he's incompetent," Sidney was shouting. But although his response made some kind of bizarre sense to Ben, he was sure that to Alithorn it must seem totally irrational.

"You are incompetent," Alithorn said, growing increasingly alienated as Sidney acted more and more uncontrolled.

"How? When? Where?" Sidney demanded. "Where's your proof? There's nothing you can use as proof against me."

"Not coming to meetings," Alithorn repeated dully. "Not keeping proper records."

"Technicalities," Sidney said.

"Telling that woman to go home last night."

"A matter of medical opinion," Sidney was on his feet, but he was swaying. "I'm calling my lawyer. I'll sue you, Tom."

Alithorn sighed and drew one of his netsuke figurines from the pocket of his sports jacket. He was clearly being made nervous by Sidney, Ben thought. Or else feeling guilty about him. He had stopped looking at Sidney altogether and was keeping his eyes on his tiny carving.

"I told you back in June I'd sue you if you made a move against me," Sidney shouted.

Alithorn, his head bent, said softly, "I believed you then. I don't believe you any longer. I don't think you're capable of organizing yourself enough to call your lawyer."

"We'll see about that," Sidney went on threateningly. "You won't like the publicity, Tom." But although his words were harsh, his voice was beginning to lose its conviction. It was dawning on him that Alithorn meant to screen him out of his vision, and thus his regard, utterly.

"I'm not worried about bad publicity anymore," Alithorn said, still looking down. "Not from you and your lawyer." But the carving wasn't giving him the distance from Sidney he wanted. For the first time since the meeting had begun he turned and looked at Ben. "The man who punched Sid has already convinced his editor to start a series on incompetent doctors. It's a subject the papers have been trying to get a lead on for years. There were two reporters over at the residents' apartment early this morning, asking questions about Sidney. You've got to keep him away from the hospital. You understand, don't you, Ben?"

"Yeah, sure." Ben said, and at last Sidney too seemed finally to understand. When Alithorn continued, "I don't want him anywhere near here," addressing his remarks to Ben as if Sidney himself could no longer be expected to make decisions, Sidney sat down heavily in his chair and bowed his head into his hands. "I don't care if you have to tie him down to make him stay home," Alithorn finished. "If he admits a patient, we'll put her out on the street."

Sidney, his words muffled behind his hands answered, "Don't worry. I'll stay away. I'll let you have your way."

Alithorn raised his shoulders and looked helplessly at Ben. "He thinks it's some kind of personal vendetta." Then, turning back to his figurine, he said softly, "It's funny. Harry Mulenberg once said to me that when a man who doesn't like to be asked questions starts screwing up, he won't answer to anybody. I didn't know what the hell Harry was talking about. But I do now. Sid, this isn't my fault! It's yours!"

Sidney shook his head stubbornly.

It made Alithorn begin to defend himself. "Jesus, Sid, you know how much I always respected you. Everyone did. Everyone around here." He shook his head, his eyes on his own hands. "That's how come I kept you on as long as I did. I figured—everyone figured—that you'd snap out of your—your personality problem. Get over your emotional difficulties. Give up—give up—" he hesitated and then at last said, his voice almost inaudible, "—the barbiturates."

Sidney murmured, "I told you back in June I wasn't taking barbiturates."

Alithorn said, "I know you did. But let's face it, Sid. You were. You are." For a coward, Ben thought, Alithorn was at last displaying some nerve.

Sidney shook his head, melancholy. "You can't prove it."

"I don't want to prove it. I don't need to prove it. I'm suspending you for missing meetings. But there's a chance, just a chance, mind you, that if you were clean, I could get you back on staff. When all of this dies down." Alithorn suddenly sounded cheerful, happier than he had been all through the discussion. He put the carving back into his pocket and moved from behind his desk to stand in front of Sidney. Then he laid a paternal hand on Sidney's shoulder.

"You think I like this? You think I like being dictated to by outside pressures? If you got clean, if you went over to Downstate and let them withdraw you, then I'd do whatever I could. I swear I would, Sid." Having made this offer, Alithorn smiled, pleased at his own generosity.

Sidney, shook his head. "That would be an admission. There'd be records," he said suspiciously.

Alithorn backed away, holding his hands out as if he were offering something tangible. "It's the only thing I can suggest, Sid. The suspension is definite. It's got to be."

Sidney stood up slowly. He looked like an old man. So thin that his flesh was turning transparent. So weak that he had to lean on the arm of the chair to lift himself. "Thanks, but no thanks."

Ben offered Sidney his arm. He took it gratefully and, head bowed, began shuffling toward the door.

Alithorn repeated, "Go to Downstate." But Sidney, head bent, shuffled right past him.

At home that afternoon, Sidney drugged himself heavily and went right to bed. It was just what Ben had expected him to do. He himself watched the Sunday ball game on TV, happy to be seeing it indoors in the luxury of air conditioning, and felt more relaxed and comfortable than he had in weeks. But when the game was over, Sidney was still in bed and he grew worried. Suppose he had overdosed?

He hurried to Sidney's room, suddenly anxious. The TV next to the bed was blaring as usual and he snapped it off. Bending over Sidney, he listened for his breath. Then at last he heard it and

stepped back, relieved. He didn't want any harm
to come to Sidney. No physical harm. He had no
intention of reneging on his promise to Sidney to
safeguard him from the dangers of overdosing. Indeed, he felt more than willing to watch over him
as long as he stayed drugged and defeated. In
fact, he rather liked being his brother's keeper.
Covering Sidney with a blanket, he went into the
kitchen to prepare himself something to eat for
dinner.

"Have an affair," Bootie was saying as she and
Claudia sat in the warm darkness alongside her
pool. Bootie had swum for over an hour, her sleek
body tireless, her long, black hair trailing like
seaweed behind her. Claudia had merely watched,
envious of Bootie's energy.

Ever since the party last night, her back had
been aching, and although she had remembered
that swimming was good for back pain, just the
effort of getting into a bathing suit had seemed
too great for her this evening. She listened to Bootie inattentively at first, preoccupied by her body.
Pregnancy had given it speech. It was so alive
with whispers, nuances and insistences that often
she could barely concentrate on what was being
said beyond the confines of her own flesh and
blood. But she knew that Bootie had been looking
forward to their time alone together. All day yesterday, before the party, they had been swamped
with chores, and today they had had to accom-

pany Bootie's daughter and her friends on a noisy picnic. Claudia tried to ignore her body and be a companionable guest.

"I'm eight months pregnant," she giggled. "Hardly the time to start an affair."

"It's been known to happen," Bootie argued earnestly. "There were two men at the party last night who kept talking about you obsessively. But you were so standoffish."

"I didn't like either of them," Claudia sighed.

"You don't like anyone," Bootie expostulated. "Even before you got so big you were standoffish. I introduced you to half a dozen men and you didn't make a move toward any of them."

"I couldn't help it. I'm just not interested in men these days." Nor was she interested in much of anything, she thought, except the constant secret communications deep within herself.

"Isn't there anyone you like?" Bootie was probing. "What about your brother-in-law?"

Claudia shifted on the plastic lounge chair, raising herself up onto an elbow to relieve the pressure on the small of her back. "My brother-in-law. You must be joking."

"You certainly spend a lot of time talking to him."

Claudia laughed again. "I like him, but not in the way you mean. He's the soul of kindness. But he's very boring."

"I met him at your wedding but I don't really remember him."

"He never makes a lasting impression. He's sweet, but terribly uptight and passive. I used to think he was impotent except that he managed to find himself a girlfriend this year. Oh, and one time, when he and I were alone together, I turned him on." Gossiping was helping her forget the ache in the small of her back. She leaned forward enthusiastically.

"What happened then?"

"Nothing. He got all flustered and looked as if he wanted to die of embarrassment."

"That's not for you," Bootie nodded. "What you need is somebody assertive. Somebody who's sure of himself."

"Somebody like Sidney," Claudia mused.

"God, no. Not a controlling son of a bitch. I'm talking about self-confidence, not solipsism."

Claudia frowned, displeased by Bootie's outburst. Sidney was the one subject she and her oldest friend could not discuss without growing short with one another. "Frankly, I've never understood what you saw in Sidney," Bootie went on, as if she hadn't already said it a dozen times previously.

"I loved him," Claudia said coolly. "Let's just leave it at that."

Bootie shivered and drew a thick towel from the foot of her lounge chair and draped it around her shoulders. "You didn't. You never did."

"Of course I did. I do still."

Bootie let an incredulous sound escape from her throat. Claudia felt out of patience. Her back pain had begun to impinge on her consciousness again and now on top of physical distress she had to cope with Bootie's being so provocative. She'd been challenging her about Sidney all weekend. And she had no right to do so. She'd never had a deep attachment in her life. Even her daughter seemed of only peripheral importance. All that mattered to her was her painting, and yet she perpetually expressed contempt for everyone else's relationships.

"You don't know what love is," Claudia couldn't help saying.

"That's true, but neither do you." Bootie sounded undisturbed by her criticism. She prided herself on her emotional detachment and often asserted that intimacy was the artist's greatest enemy. "You're right about me," she went on. "But I'm right about you too."

Claudia stopped listening to her. The ache in her back was sliding into her stomach. Sneaking into it. She felt a dull, surreptitious cramp in the pit of her belly and shut her lips, listening to her body's signals.

Bootie mistook her silence for encouragement. "If you loved Sidney—if you'd ever loved him—you wouldn't have avoided him all this time. You wouldn't be sitting here talking with me right now. You'd be with him, trying to get him into some drug rehabilitation clinic."

She couldn't reply. The cramp had deepened, twisting and tightening within her. She was frightened, and thought of telling Bootie what was happening, but Bootie had hurt her feelings. She had had no right. No right to judge. No right to hurt her so. To make her feel pain. Such pain. She clutched the arm of her chair in the darkness.

And then the pain was gone, as unexpectedly as it had come.

"I'm awfully tired tonight, Bootie," Claudia announced, as soon as she could speak, trying to mask both anger and physical anguish. "I think I'd like to go to bed."

"You're mad at me, aren't you?" Bootie asked. She shook her head. "Just tired. Beat."

"Okay," Bootie nodded, "as long as you're not mad."

She managed a relatively convincing smile of reassurance and started up toward the house. But suddenly, as she moved heavily up the lighted flagstone path toward the back entrance, the pain in her stomach came again and this time it was so strong that she nearly doubled over.

The pain was all over here. It was in her throat, her ribs, her very fingertips. She moaned.

Bootie was at her side in a second. "What is it, baby? Are you having contractions?"

She shuddered. "I don't know. How am I supposed to know?"

"Maybe I should drive you to the hospital."

"It's too early. Way too early." And then she moaned again and clutched at her belly.

"Oh, honey. Oh, baby," Bootie said. The towel

slipped from her shoulders and she wrapped her arms around Claudia. "I'm sorry for what I said before. About you and Sidney. I'm no model of mental health either."

"It's okay." Claudia's anger at Bootie dissipated. What did it matter now? And then she was groaning. She would have fallen except for Bootie's arms around her. Bootie held her tightly until she was quiet and then said, "Come on. Get in the car. You've got to get in the car."

His private number was ringing. Awakening, Ben looked drowsily at the lighted dial of his clock and saw that it was 2 A.M. Then he reached for the phone, alarmed. Hardly anyone ever called him on his private number except Claudia and he was sure that she would never have called him at that hour unless she was in trouble. "Claudia, what is it? What's wrong? Where are you?" he rattled.

"Nothing's wrong. I'm all right. We're all right." He heard her but her reply made no sense to him. Tensed for bad news, his brain charging his lips with expressions of anxiety, he stammered out, "It's so late. Where are you? What is it, darling?"

And then she was saying, "St. Louis General. Oh, Ben, I'm so happy. So lucky. So happy," and he knew from the exuberance in her voice that she had had the baby. "It's a boy," she trilled. "Ezra Samuel Zauber. Oh, Ben, he's beautiful."

Understanding at last, he was filled with even

greater alarm. "Premature," he murmured. "Oh, God, I should never have let you go to St. Louis!"

"My doctor said I could. It wasn't your responsibility. Anyway, no harm's done."

"How do you know? What's the baby's weight? Who delivered you? I want to speak to him."

"Oh, Ben, slow down. Talk to me first. Congratulate me. Oh, I was so scared. Tell me congratulations. Tell me it's wonderful."

"I don't know if it's wonderful. You can't take premature babies lightly," he scolded.

She began to giggle. And then he was laughing too and saying, "Forgive me. I didn't mean to sound so pompous. It was just that you got me so worried. Of course it's wonderful. Of course it is. Provided the child's all right."

"He is. He really is."

"Then tell me what happened. Tell me exactly what they've told you."

"They said they'd have to keep him in an incubator until he reached full weight, but that there was no reason he wouldn't reach it in a week or so. And that there's nothing wrong with him. They said I was lucky. Terribly lucky."

Her happiness was infectious. For a short while he put his professionalism aside and let himself respond fully to her joy, listening to her as she chattered to him in an excited voice he barely recognized as her own. She kept telling him over and over again about the baby's fair hair and minute but perfect body, and about how Bootie had driven her to the hospital while still in her wet bathing suit, and she kept interrupting herself to say, "It came so fast. So fast. You wouldn't believe how fast."

"Premature babies do," he smiled. "There's never much warning."

"I'm glad. Now it's over."

"I'm glad for you. I've—I've never felt so worried in my life as when I first heard your voice."

"Dear Ben," she said. "How kind you always are."

It was only after he had allowed her to talk to him luxuriously and at length that he asked her again for the name of the obstetrician who had delivered her.

"Dr. Peter Michaels. A resident," she said.

"A resident! My God! Forget about Ezra. You're lucky *you're* alive." As soon as he spoke, she began laughing again, giddy. He felt immeasurably close to her.

"Look, sweetheart," he said when her laughter had subsided. "I'll call Dr. Michaels tonight, and tomorrow I'll fly out, just to make sure everything's as okay as you say it is."

"Oh, no. You don't need to do that." Claudia stopped speaking and in the silence that followed he had a vision of her lying in her hospital bed, her gemlike blue eyes radiant and her pale skin flushed and vibrant. "Everything is all right," she assured him when she resumed speaking. "You'll see when you speak to Dr. Michaels. And I imagine Sidney needs you much more than I do."

"Sidney?" Suddenly he felt disappointment invade him. He had forgotten all about Sidney.

"Put him on," Claudia continued. "I—I guess I'd better tell him about Ezra now too."

"I'll tell him for you in the morning. He's asleep right now." He paused, annoyed. "It's hard to wake him when he's asleep."

"Please try."

Resisting, he said quizzically, "I thought you said you didn't want to speak to him. Not until he gave up the pills."

"I know, but I feel differently now. I've been thinking about it since I got to the hospital. I've been thinking how heartless I seem to everybody. To you. To Bootie. To Sidney."

"Not to me, Claudia. You don't. I swear it."

"But just yesterday you sounded as if you thought I was monstrous for not speaking to him." She sighed deeply and went on, "When you said that if only I would come and see him, it might help him."

Remembering, he clutched the phone in frustration, furious with himself for ever having suggested she talk to Sidney.

He had been feeling so intimate with Claudia just now, had been feeling that it was his own son who had just been born, his own wife who had just delivered. All his years of envying others their closeness at the moment of birth had been banished as she talked. But why not get Sidney for her if that was what she wanted? He still believed that once she perceived the full disorder of Sidney's condition, her fantasies about him would come to an end. And tonight was perfect. If ever Sidney had drugged himself into an impenetrable stupor, it was today, after his disturbing talk with Alithorn. "Hang on," he said amiably. "All right. It may take a while, but I'll get him for you. And afterward, I'll call Dr. Michaels."

It took him a full five minutes to rouse Sidney and make him understand that Claudia was on the phone with something urgent to tell him. And even once he was out of bed and moving toward the phone in Ben's room, he seemed more asleep than awake.

His body limp and his mind drifting, Sidney staggered down the hallway. As he walked, he kept repeating, "Who? Who's it? Wha's up?" so that by the time Ben sat him down on the bed and put the phone in his hand, he was no longer sorry in the least to be turning Claudia over to her true husband. He was sorry only that she couldn't see him. Sidney's arms and legs trembled with agitation, and his trousers, smelling of urine, were damp. But even his voice would be enough to put Claudia off for good. It was husky, hoarse and barely audible. "Suhweehar? Suhweehar?" he was mumbling.

Ben retreated from the room just as he saw

great, watery tears begin to spill down Sidney's
ravaged cheeks, and the whole time Sidney was on
the phone with Claudia, he himself used the hall
phone in Claudia's behalf. He spoke at length to
the resident who had delivered her, and afterward
questioned briefly but closely the pediatrician
who had first examined the baby. Satisfied that
Claudia's optimistic version of Ezra's present con-
diton and future potential was correct, he was just
hanging up when Sidney came into the hallway.
He passed Ben in silence, stumbling toward his
own room, his eyes blinded by tears.

On Monday morning Ben could think of nothing but Claudia and Ezra. It was all he could do
not to call Claudia the minute he awakened. But it
was very early, and it had been close to three in
the morning before she and Sidney had finished
speaking last night. He had best let her rest, and
phone her later, once he got to the office. He himself was exhausted from the emotional excitement
of the night, and he could easily imagine her fatigue. Controlling the urge to telephone her, he
dressed and shaved and went into the kitchen,
planning to make a huge pot of coffee to get himself going.

To his surprise, Sidney too was already awake,
and had actually started the coffee. Even more
startling, Sidney had shaved. But he had done
quite a sloppy job, nicking himself mercilessly.
There were tiny beads of blood burgeoning next

to his ears, around the cleft on his chin, and all down his scrawny neck. "What were you trying to do?" Ben addressed Sidney sarcastically. "Guillotine yourself?"

Sidney looked abashed. "I was turning over a new leaf," he said. "In honor of the baby."

"Baby?" Ben raised an eyebrow quizzically.

Sidney's eyes blinked rapidly and he frowned. "My son."

Ben stared at him, his head to one side.

"Claudia had the baby. She called." Sidney's lips trembled and then he looked down at the table. "Didn't she?"

Ben watched Sidney closely, enjoying his confusion, and waited several seconds before leaning across the table and pounding him on the back. "Of course she did. Congratulations."

Sidney smiled, relieved. "You had me worried, old buddy. For a moment I thought I'd made it all up."

"Of course you didn't. I spoke to Claudia too."

"I thought so. I thought she said she'd been talking to you."

"Yeah, well. Congratulations." Ashamed of having teased Sidney over the baby, he stood and moved to the stove, pouring two cups of coffee. "Let's drink to the kid." He set a cup in front of Sidney.

"I've had some," Sidney said, rejecting the coffee. "I've been up for hours. Thinking."

"What about?"

"About everything. About Alithorn. About Claudia. About the baby." He slumped in his chair. "What's its name? What'd she name it? I forgot."

"Ezra. After her father."

"About Ezra," Sidney went on. "I was thinking that for Ezra's sake I ought to make some changes."

Abruptly nervous, Ben got up from the table and busied himself at the refrigerator, searching for some bread to toast. "What kind of changes?" he asked, his back stooped.

Sidney answered him first with a long sigh. Then he said, "I ought to give up the pills."

Ben's tension grew acute. He kept his back turned, fearing his face would betray his feeling.

Sidney said in a loud, excited voice, "I'm going to stop taking the pills. I am."

Ben heard him get up from the table and walk to the kitchen sink. Then he heard him turn on the tap. He couldn't keep searching through the refrigerator any longer. Couldn't keep his face turned from Sidney's all through breakfast. Straightening up, he drew a loaf of white bread out of the refrigerator. But his edgy feeling continued. Trying to open the package, his fingers turned thumbs. He couldn't undo the paper-wrapped wire that held the bread closed.

Sidney was still running the faucet. Ben stole a glance at him and saw him fill a glass with water and dig down into his jacket pocket.

"I'm going to stop," Sidney said in the same excited voice he had used earlier. "I swear I am." Ben saw him take a vial of pills from his pocket, open it and swallow several capsules. "After lunch," Sidney said, gulping the water.

Ben's anxiety vanished as swiftly as it had come. He ripped open the package of bread, thrust two slices into the toaster, and plunged down the lever.

"Or maybe tomorrow," Sidney said, putting away his pills.

By the time the toast came jiggling up, Ben was laughing to himself.

"You don't believe me, do you?" Sidney asked, finally shutting off the water.

Ben shook his head.

"I don't blame you," Sidney said. "Why should you? I don't even believe myself." He sat down and put his head on his arms and his shoulders began to quiver.

Ben softened. For once, Sidney's sadness struck him as authentic, rather than maudlin and excessive. There was such a darkness in his mood, such a desperate admission of helplessness, that Ben could no longer generate any bitterness. He stood over Sidney and patted his shaking back.

Claudia too was sad when he spoke to her from his office later that morning. She said she supposed it was postpartum depression, but he suspected it was not because Ezra had been expelled

from within her that she was downcast, her exuberance of the night before vanished without a
trace. It was because she had at last begun to expel Sidney too. Disconsolate, she said, "Oh, Ben, it
was a terrible shock to speak with him. A shock
despite everything you'd told me. He sounded so
disconnected. So hopeless."

"I know, darling," he comforted her. "I'd been
trying to prepare you."

"He just kept muttering and mumbling. I could
hardly understand him, except that a few times he
swore that for the baby's sake, he was going to
withdraw."

"I wouldn't take that too seriously," Ben said
gently. "He said that to me too this morning."

"And you didn't think he meant it?"

"No," he said slowly. "I didn't. I don't think he
can pull himself together enough to try it. I really
don't."

At home that evening, when Sidney began talking about withdrawal once again, he paid hardly
any attention to him. He had bought himself a
roast chicken for dinner and was carving it when
Sidney appeared in the entrance to the kitchen
and announced loudly, "I've figured out how to
withdraw."

"What's to figure out?" he said, not even bother-
ing to look at him. "Alithorn already told you. And
I've told you a hundred times. Just check into

Downstate." He had sliced off both drumsticks and now he set them neatly down on a platter.

"I'll be damned if I'll do that and give Alithorn the proof he wants about me."

"There's no other way." Bored, Ben began to cut off the wings.

"Yes, there is." Sidney spoke excitedly, his words racing. "You could supervise my withdrawal. I'd stay in the hall bathroom. That's a good spot because it has an outside lock. You could open the door at intervals and give me the pills. A smaller amount each time. It would only take a couple of days."

Concentrating on the task at hand, Ben ignored Sidney and began arranging the wings alongside the drumsticks on the platter. Sidney's words struck him as bizarre, his scheme a perfect illustration of the bad judgment barbiturates notoriously produced. "Why not lock up the drugs?" he asked after a while, as he might ask a child.

"Because in the beginning I might not have the willpower to follow the schedule. I might try to go out and buy pills." Sidney continued to speak with pressured intensity. "But if I was in the bathroom, there'd be no problem. Even if I tried to push past you when you opened the door, you could easily force me back inside. You're so much stronger than I am now.

Still treating Sidney's words lightly, Ben tackled the white meat and said offhandedly, "Sounds risky to me. You could have convulsions."

"Not if we do it right," Sidney answered. "Not at ten percent less a day. And if I did have a convulsion, you could raise the barbiturate level intravenously and bring me out of it."

Despite his pressured speech, Sidney sounded so serious that at last, finished with carving the chicken, Ben turned to look at him. When he did, the carving utensils slipped from between his fingers. Sidney was wearing nothing but a hugh towel wrapped around his waist and legs. His chest was bare, the barbiturate rash glaringly red, and his hair was dripping wet.

He had showered. At first Ben couldn't believe it. It had been weeks since Sidney had washed himself without being prodded into it. But clearly he had cleansed himself this evening. As soon as Ben had grasped what had happened, a vein in his temple began to throb.

"It'd work. I'm sure it would," Sidney said. "Don't you think so?"

Ben's head began to nod. Sidney's plan could work. It was a wild, brazen scheme. A paranoid's scheme. Clearly Sidney had dreamed it up in order to withdraw without entering a clinic. He'd always had a passion for privacy but now that he'd been suspended from the hospital, that passion was accentuated. He feared letting Alithorn have proof of his addiction, and in a clinic there would be records. But at home all would be secret. It *could* work. The throbbing above Ben's eyes grew more agonizing. He had to sit down. Massaging his forehead, he slid heavily onto one of the kitchen chairs.

"Do you follow me?" Sidney asked. But he didn't answer. He was afraid to speak. He'd call Sidney names. Double-crosser. Spoiler. He'd shout that he had no right to change his mind. Not now, just when everything had been going so well. He sat mute, words swirling through his mind but imprisoned behind his tightly clenched lips.

Sidney took his silence as a lack of comprehension. "Don't you understand?" He sat down opposite Ben and reviewed his plan. "It'd really only be the first day or two that I might give you trouble. After that, I'd probably stop having to be restrained. I could stay in the bedroom, and you could just lock up the drugs."

He sat and listened to him stonily. Sidney grew more insistent. "Look, I know it'd mean your having to stick very close to home for a few days. You'd have to be here right on schedule. But only at first. And I'd try to be cooperative. I'd try not to make it difficult for you." Just as they had the night before, Sidney's eyes began to fill with tears. "I know how difficult I've been. I know all the sacrifices you've had to make for me. You gave up Naomi for me, didn't you? Gave up having any sort of a social life. Just to stay close to me. I appreciate it, Ben, I really do. But you can do this one last thing for me, can't you?" Tears cascaded down Sidney's nicked cheeks.

His brother was insane, he thought. No. They

were both insane. Sidney's mind, eaten away by drugs, had grown soft and sentimental. His own, consumed by ancient resentments, had turned bitter and hard. "I know this means putting you in the position of a jailer for a few days," Sidney continued. "I know it's not pleasant. But I'm begging you." His voice trailed off. "I can't do it alone. I don't have the will power."

Sidney's confession moved him, but still he didn't speak.

"Remember when we were kids?" Sidney asked cajolingly, the silence triggering his memories. "Remember when I taught you to talk?" He was speaking as if he wanted to cash in on a debt incurred long ago and never repaid. "Remember how everyone thought you'd never learn? That you were retarded? That there was a screw loose?"

Ben shivered.

"I didn't let you down, though, did I? No matter what." Sidney's eyes pleaded with him.

"Remember 'I'll be fucked to shit if ever I fail you'?" Sidney grinned. Ben closed his eyes. He couldn't bear to see Sidney imploring him.

"You've got to help me," Sidney finished. "There's no one else I can ask. And I've got to do it. For Ezra. For Claudia."

At the mention of Claudia, Ben saw her. With his eyes closed, he could picture her as vividly as if she were right next to him. His mouth went so dry that he could barely concentrate on Sidney's next words. "There's nothing to it, really. I've got it all worked out. And after it's over, I'll move out. You'll have your life to yourself again. Everything will be back to normal. Everything will be just the way it used to be."

The vision of Claudia went swirling out of his mind and his forehead throbbed more and more violently. In his mind's eye he saw Sidney, but not the emaciated figure who sat opposite him now. It was the Sidney of a year ago, tall, husky, imposing. He was barging into his office and barking commands at him. Then he was younger. But still husky. Hulking. He was slapping him. He was shoving him. For one vivid moment he saw himself writhing in terror inside his mother's dark, cavernous cedar closet. Sidney was outside, pushing the door shut. He was crying and Sidney was laughing. Why had Sidney been so cruel as a child? Nothing he had read had ever adequately explained to him the roots of sadism. The reasons why it sprang up not only in the children of abusive parents but in those of the adoring as well. Now he could see Sara too. Her arms were opening wide for Sidney. Dangling at her sides for him.

But the past had ceased to matter. He had vanquished the past. He had sat in Alithorn's office and received Alithorn's instructions, while Sidney sat excluded and ignored. He had safeguarded Sidney's patients and cajoled and quieted them, while Sidney had done everything in his power to alienate and injure them. He had beguiled the Department of Professional Conduct into thinking he was Sidney and done a better job at calming them than Sidney could ever have done.

A dumb animal rage began boiling up in the pit of his stomach. He had been a shadow and he had become a man of substance. He had been a fool and he had become a clever man. He couldn't, he wouldn't, go back.

"Please, Ben?" Sidney said again.

He felt suitable words stirring in him. They were gathering on his tongue, pushing through his lips, coming to his aid. They were giving him a chance at survival, just as years and years ago they had once come to his rescue, enabled him to hold his own against Sidney. "Okay. All right. Okay." At first his words were brief, miserly. "Okay, if you're sure it's what you want to do." Then they began flying from his lips. "Sure. Let's try it. But remember, it was your idea, not mine. If it doesn't work, it isn't my fault."

Sidney looked at him ecstatically. "Oh, it'll work. I'm sure of it."

"All right, then." His headache was gone. He felt marvelous. "When do you want to try it? I think the sooner the better."

"Me, too," Sidney beamed. "Absolutely." He stood and put his arms around Ben, clasping him tight. "And thanks, old buddy."

Together, they went through the shelves and cupboards in the hall bathroom, removing all the medicines and even the shampoos and colognes and shaving lotion. Sidney wanted the cabinets bare. "If you were delayed and had to get here late one time, who knows? I could swallow anything. It's been known to happen."

Ben concentrated on the task at hand. His mind felt empty but, his arms filled, he made his way out to the kitchen and deposited the toiletries he was carrying. Sidney followed him, his arms also laden. Then Sidney went into his bedroom and emerged carrying his barbiturate vials. In the kitchen he said, "Don't forget to give me food when you give me the pills. Otherwise my weight might go down again and ten percent less a day won't be quite as effective."

Back in the bathroom, which was still steamy from his shower, he instructed Ben, "I'm going to take enough pills in with me to see me through the night. You won't need to give me any more until morning. Then, around seven, start me out with four hundred milligrams, and give me the same dose every five hours until the following morning. Then you can start going down."

"You were taking two thousand milligrams a day?" Ben exclaimed. It was even more than he had calculated.

"Does that shock you? It shocked me a little when I got up so high and could still keep functioning."

"No." Ben tried to hide his surprise. "It was just

that I'd figured on even less. Figured it was less, I mean."

Sidney had dressed, discarding the bath towel for a pair of loose gray slacks, a white shirt, and his torn blue suit jacket and now he glanced at himself in the mirror and said distractedly, "Yeah, well, it doesn't make any difference. It'll just take a while longer to get completely clean." He studied his reflection, shuddered, and turned away from it. "God, I hardly know myself."

By the time it had grown fully dark outside, they had emptied out all the bathroom cupboards. Sidney sat down on the toilet seat and waved Ben away. "Let's get started."

For one instant, Ben hesitated. "Are you sure you know what you're doing?"

"Sure I'm sure."

Abruptly, Ben walked to the door and, his mind vacant of all further misgivings, went out and closed it quietly but securely.

"Lock it," Sidney called out, his voice muffled by the door. "You'd better keep it locked."

Ben turned the key.

"See you at seven," Sidney shouted.

"See you."

At a quarter of seven he was packing a flight bag with a few journals to read on the plane and an extra shirt in case the humidity made the one he was wearing look limp. His plane didn't leave until eleven, but he could go around to the office and start canceling his day's appointments.

His minimal packing accomplished, he went into Sidney's room and snapped on the TV. The neighbors were used to its sound. Sidney had been in the habit of playing it all day long, and always very loud. It would be a good idea to leave it on so that it could mask any sound that Sidney might make. For surely he would be noisy. Once he realized that he was alone, he would undoubtedly begin to shout and to tug and wrench at the door with his thin, ineffectual arms. And of course after the barbiturate hunger struck him, he would scream. But he was too weak to make too great a commotion. And most likely he would go into convulsions by nightfall, so that by the time most of their neighbors returned from work, he would be utterly silent.

Of course, he could be unlucky, Ben thought, listening to the impressive sounds of the TV. Sidney might be one among the small percentage of addicts who did not experience convulsions on abrupt withdrawal. But it was worth taking the gamble. The statistics were with him. Chances were Sidney would have severe seizures and, left unattended, die. Still, to be on the safe side, he ought to leave him unattended for as long as possible. Perhaps nightfall was really too much to hope for. He would have to take a plane back from St.

Louis, and yet make it look as if he had tried quite hard to catch an earlier one.

Turning away from the TV, he started the air conditioner. The room, as usual, smelled rancid and he hoped the air conditioning would make it less foul. Then he thought of opening the windows and really letting the room air out. But he decided against it. When he returned from St. Louis and called the police, they would wonder why a man with Sidney's medical knowledge would have been so foolhardy as to have attempted the notorious dangers of abrupt barbiturate withdrawal. They would have to be convinced of Sidney's lack of judgment these final weeks, and Ben's words would mean nothing. Even Alithorn's description of Sidney's irrationality in his office two days ago would be but a suggestion, an innuendo. But Sidney's garbage-strewn floor and the rank odors emanating from every corner of his room would shout out his judgmentless decay.

Shutting off the air conditioner, Ben started for the front hall door.

He tried to move quietly when he passed the bathroom, but Sidney must have been listening for him. He called out at once, "Thank God you're up. I don't think I could have waited a moment more."

"It's not seven yet," Ben answered him loudly. "It's just ten of."

"Well, start me out anyway," Sidney said. His voice sounded thin and tremulous.

"Ten more minutes."

"I need it now," Sidney called out. "I'm shaking."

"You told me not till seven."

"Don't be such a stickler," Sidney shouted. "My head is exploding. I feel sick. Really sick." Suddenly he began kicking on the bathroom door.

Ben lifted his foot high and kicked it from his side. "Cut it out! You'll wake this entire building!"

"Then give me the pills," Sidney pleaded.

"I will at seven. But only if you quiet down. If you make noise, I'll make you wait. I swear I will."

Behind the bathroom door, Sidney quieted down.

"Good," Ben said. "That's it." Then he walked noiselessly past the bathroom and let himself out of the apartment.

Claudia was astonished to see him. And happy, he thought. She was in a private room and when he knocked and entered, she slid from the bed and embraced him heartily before retreating to her usual more formal greeting, the familial brush of her lips against his cheek. He had a moment of holding her in his arms, her body sensuous in a white satin nightgown, her heart beating loudly against his. Then she stepped back and exclaimed, "Ben! I can't believe it! What are you *doing* here?"

"Are you sorry I've come? Shall I go?" he

teased her, glancing at the door as if ready to leave on command.

"Oh, no! I said you didn't *have* to come. That everything was all right. But as long as you're here—" She took his hand and held it tightly in both of her own.

"It was Sidney's idea. He's been terribly worried about you and Ezra."

"Really?" Claudia, releasing his hand, looked surprised and doubt flickered across her eyes. "On the phone I didn't have that impression. Not when I spoke to him the night before. In fact I wasn't even sure that he understood that Ezra was early. Or cared." She frowned and he could see that her heart had begun to harden toward Sidney.

"Well, perhaps he didn't at first," he said, apologizing for Sidney as he had learned to apologize for him in the office, his voice thoughtful and sincere. He felt immensely competent. More competent than he'd ever been before. More competent than he'd ever before imagined he could be. "You may be right about his early reaction. But when I got home from work last night he kept pumping me for all the details. He was very worried for you. And Ezra, of course. I kept telling him that I'd questioned both you and the pediatric resident quite closely, and that everything was fine. But Sidney was concerned that possibly you and the pediatrician were being less than straightforward."

Claudia sat down on the edge of her bed, her forehead furrowing. "What do you suppose made him so concerned all of a sudden?"

"Your call," he said with exhilaration. "Yesterday morning I thought he'd been unaffected by it. At least in any meaningful way. I told you that when we spoke, didn't I? But last night there was something altogether different about him. I noticed it as soon as I got home. He'd showered. I can't tell you when he did that last."

Claudia was looking at him dubiously, her eyebrows arched.

"I'm beginning to change my mind about him," he went on. "I think there's hope after all."

"That's a turnabout." Claudia had her head to one side, as if she were suspicious. Watching her, he realized what a good job he'd done only yesterday of persuading her how desperate Sidney's condition was. "The thing is," he continued, trying now to let his voice reveal awe, "that last night Sidney was full of plans. And not vague ones, either. He was specific, practical."

"Really? Like what?"

"He said he would check into Downstate's detoxification unit on Friday. He was that definite."

Claudia at last seemed impressed. "And you thought he meant it?"

He nodded. Soon he could relax. Soon her vanity would go to work to corroborate his story. "It was your call that did it." At once Claudia's white cheeks flushed with a pale, prideful pink. "If he does what he says he's going to do," he added exuberantly, "if he goes into the unit on Friday, he could well be out by the time you bring Ezra home."

A shadow drifted across Claudia's face then, and he wondered if she would admit to him that she was no longer certain she wanted Sidney back. But as usual, she hid her more troubling thoughts, and when she spoke she tried to explain away the change in her expression as concern for Sidney. "You don't think he'd try to withdraw on his own, do you?"

He sat forward, looking startled. "Why do you say that?"

"Oh, you know the way he is. How he always likes to be in charge."

"Do you suppose—" he started to say, his face wreathed with worry. And then he shook his head vigorously. "No. Sid's too smart for that. Much too smart."

"I guess so," Claudia nodded in agreement. "I guess you're right."

"I'm sure I am." He glanced at his watch then and sighed. "And now you'd better take me over to the nursery. I've got a lot of questions and I've only got an hour or so."

"Only an hour? You're not staying overnight? You could stay at Bootie's. I'll call her and—"

"I can't," he said regretfully. "I wish I could. But I don't like to leave Sidney overnight."

"Oh. Of course." Claudia stood up quickly,

bending to put on her slippers. "You're absolutely right. What time is your plane?"

"Four-thirty." Marveling at the curve of her buttocks beneath white satin, he nevertheless remembered to add, "That's the last direct flight. After that, it's milk train planes."

"You'd think there'd be more direct flights," she said wistfully. Then she straightened up. "Well, let's get going. I can't wait till you see Ezra."

He took only a quick look at Ezra, but spent a long time talking to Dr. Hess, the pediatrician in charge of the prematurity nursery. "My brother couldn't come himself," he explained. "But needless to say, he was very worried about the baby. He felt quite strongly that one of us should come and see you. There's just so much you can be sure of on the phone."

"He needn't have worried," the youthful Hess said. "The boy's coming along nicely. He's gained one-half ounce already. Still, I can understand your brother's wanting one of the two of you to come out and talk. I'd be concerned if my wife delivered in some unfamiliar hospital. They say many chefs won't eat in restaurants because they know what goes on in the kitchen."

Ben laughed and settled into his chair, letting his flight bag rest near the wall behind him. "That's it," he said. "That's it exactly."

He got on splendidly with the pediatrician, who

afterward offered to give him a tour of some of
the hospital's special facilities. But he didn't have
time, he demurred. If he missed his direct flight,
he'd have a lousy trip home. The pediatrician
sympathized and Ben said goodbye to him, had a
few farewell moments with Claudia and left the
hospital.

He managed to miss the plane quite nicely by
telling his cabdriver after they were already a
half-mile from the hospital that he had forgotten
his flight bag. The driver turned back. Ben raced
up to Claudia's room, searched uselessly for his
bag, ran with Claudia to Hess's office and found
the bag still in the corner where he had set it
down, kissed Claudia hurriedly and then, as soon
as she had left him at the elevator, returned slowly
to his waiting cab.

The driver was discouraged. "It's getting close
to rush hour," he complained.

"Well, try," Ben said. "That's all anyone can do,
right?"

In the end, he missed his plane by six minutes
and had to wait for the five-thirty. That one had a
stopover in Pittsburgh, so that he didn't arrive
back in New York until after ten-thirty. If Sidney
was going to have had fatal spasms, he thought as
he stepped off the plane, he would certainly have
had them by now. But just in case, he would give
him a few extra minutes. He went into the men's
room and used the urinal. Afterward he dawdled
in front of a newsstand, engaging the news dealer

in conversation about the muggy weather. Then he hailed a cab to take him home.

His ability to plan and execute his moves with obsessive calm deserted him as soon as he was in his apartment building. Waiting for the elevator, his heart began to pound and, getting into it, he nearly closed the door on his fingers. Outside his apartment he fumbled with his keys and dropped them. He had to force himself to control his unsteady hands in order to pick up the keys and unlock the front door.

Inside, the TV was still blaring. He heard it with a shudder of annoyance and ran to Sidney's room to turn it off even before he backtracked and approached the bathroom door. Then, in the intense silence, he hesitated, perspiration coating his forehead.

Agitated, he stared at the key to the bathroom door. If Sidney were alive, he would be in a terrible predicament. He would actually have to kill him, injecting him with an overdose. And afterward, even if he told the police he had been trying to bring him out of a convulsion and, distraught, hadn't realized how much intravenous barbiturate he was administering, they would be exceedingly suspicious. But he would have no choice. His hands shaking, he felt momentarily terrified of touching the key. And then he grasped it and began to turn it.

Those were the only really bad moments. As

soon as the door swung open, he went stonily tranquil again. Sidney was dead. He had swallowed his tongue and choked. He lay gray-faced on the bathroom floor, his arms and legs extended at asymmetrical angles, as if in the moment of his final convulsion, his limbs had danced. His long, skinny neck and arms were stiff, his legs not yet gone into rigor. He was so relieved that for a second he thought absurdly that he wished he could thank Sidney for making things easier for both of them. Then he smiled at the notion and grew serious, regarding Sidney's body with pride. Had he killed his brother? And done it so skillfully? It seemed so unlike him. So beyond his capabilities. And yet, although it was inexplicable and unaccountable, clearly it was true. He felt no remorse, only an enormous sense of accomplishment.

But there was still more that had to be accomplished, he reminded himself. And he hadn't much time. He ought to be calling the police within the next few minutes, and first he had to wipe off the silvery key and hide it someplace safe. Most likely the police wouldn't even think to ask whether the bathroom had an outside key, but in case they did, he wanted it secured in a spot where they would think it had long ago been tossed. Then he had to replace all the medicines and lotions he and Sidney had carried from the bathroom into the kitchen last night. And flush away the barbiturates Sidney had turned over to him. It had to appear as if Sidney, deeply anxious over the well-being of his

wife and son, had sent him to St. Louis in the
morning and only then decided, impulsively and
recklessly, to attempt an abrupt withdrawal.

Of course, he would have ranged free in the
apartment, he thought, taking a last look down at
Sidney's body. He wouldn't have isolated himself
in the hall bathroom. Still, it was logical that he
would have died in there. He might have entered
it after a last minute change of heart, a loss of
courage or will, or a premonition that he might be
about to have a convulsion. And then, alarmed
and hoping against hope, he might have searched
through the bathroom medicine cabinet for some
forgotten barbiturates. That there would be foot-
prints on the inside of the door, and possibly even
clawing fingerprints as well, made sense too. Sidney might very well have closed the unlocked
door accidentally and then, weak or dazed, been
unable to let himself out. He would have kicked
and clawed until his strength failed him.

Ben began on his chores, going about them me-
thodically. Stepping gingerly around Sidney's
body, he made rapid trips in and out of the bathroom, restocking the shelves of the cupboards and
cabinets. He didn't worry about his fingerprints.
Of course he would have handled all these objects.
They were his, the contents of his own bathroom.

The only things he took care to wipe off and
afterward handle with a towel were the key,
which he placed deep down in a box of curtain
rings, cup hooks and long-abandoned locks in the

kitchen tool closet, and the barbiturate vials Sidney had given him last night. These he touched most cautiously, spilling the contents away down the toilet and then leaving the empty vials helter skelter in the bathroom.

At last, with the towel, he opened the medicine cabinet over the sink, letting its mirrored door swing ajar. And then, proud of himself, his work finished, he called the police.

They said they would be right over and while he waited for them to arrive, he called Naomi. The police might question him about the degree of his attachment to his sister-in-law. But perhaps they would be less prone to suspiciousness if the first person he called in his moment of shock and loss was the woman he had been engaged to at the time Sidney had moved in with him.

Naomi, startled awake, sounded uncomprehending and even a little angry at first. But moments later her voice was, as he had counted upon its being, alive with sympathy and the urge to succor. "Poor Ben. Oh, my darling. Oh, God. How terrible for you. What can I do? Is there anything I can do?"

"Come be with me," he said. "I feel empty. Frightened. As if it were myself who had died."

Perhaps, he thought as he waited for her acquiescence, the police would ask Naomi what she knew of his relationship to Sidney. He smiled to himself. Surely she would tell them her perceptions, would harp on what she had always considered his neurotic devotion to Sidney.

"I know I've hurt you cruelly," he went on before she had a chance to speak. "But we'll talk about it later. Tomorrow. For now, please just come and be with me. I need you very badly."

She said she'd dress, ask one of her neighbors to stay with Petey in case he awakened, and be over as soon as she could.

Two policemen, dispatched by radio, were at his door only moments later. He spoke to them in a voice that sounded breathless with shock. "I just got home. I called out to my brother. He didn't answer. I looked for him in his room. Then I found him. In the bathroom. Here. Dead." Affecting a motionless paralysis, he pointed the way to the bathroom.

When the police went inside he waited outside in the hallway, as if to look once more upon his brother's body was too much of an anguish to be endured.

A few minutes later, the police emerged and one of them went downstairs to the car. The other spoke gently to Ben in the hallway. "Looks like suicide. All those empty pill bottles. We're going to have to call homicide. And have the ME take a look."

Ben nodded, unsurprised, but right afterward assumed an offended look and said, "Suicide? Not my brother."

"I'm afraid it could be," the policeman replied softly.

Ben shut his eyes and said nothing more, deciding to save his breath and wit for the homicide people.

They arrived all too soon, several men from the forensic unit starting to explore Sidney's body with thermometers and syringes, determining how long he had been dead and drawing blood samples for the medical examiner, while two detectives searched in his room for a suicide note. Finding none, a gray-haired detective with wiry steelwool eyebrows led Ben into the comparative calm of the living room and began questioning him. "You're a doctor, I understand. And your brother was one too?"

Ben felt wary. At first he answered the questions with mere nods or shakes of the head, as if too overcome with grief to reply more fully. But after a while he sensed he'd better elaborate. "My brother was a barbiturate addict," he confessed haltingly, letting shame mingle with the grief in his voice.

"What do you think he died of, Doctor?"

"Withdrawal."

"Not an OD?" The detective looked interested. "Couldn't he have been trying to take his life?"

Ben shook his head. "Not Sidney. No. He'd just gotten a new lease on life. His wife—well, they were separated but still very much involved with each other—his wife just gave birth to their first child." He let his voice trail off.

The detective looked even more intrigued. He had round, fat cheeks into one of which he now popped an exploring tongue, pausing before he asked, "Was there anything else unusual about the past few days? Anything else that might have made your brother want to give up his habit suddenly?"

"Just the baby," Ben said. Then he added, the words seeming to slip from his mouth, "And the suspension."

The detective sat forward. "Yes?"

For a moment Ben chewed his lower lip, as if wishing he could withdraw the words he had just spoken. He looked at the detective unhappily. And then he said in a very quiet voice, "My brother's hospital privileges were revoked on Sunday."

"I see. Because of his addiction?"

Ben nodded.

"Can you tell me about it?"

Slowly, he described Sidney's interview with Alithorn, and the detective drew out a notebook and pen. "I thought," he concluded his account, "that in a way it was all for the best. Because afterward Sidney began to talk about withdrawal. Alithorn suggested that if he went into a detoxification clinic, he might let him back on staff."

The detective, nodding again, asked for and made a note of Alithorn's full name.

"I never should have left him," he said as the detective wrote.

"Why did you, Doctor?" The detective's eyes, looking up abruptly, were an intense blue under steel-wool brows.

"His wife gave birth prematurely. In St. Louis. My brother couldn't travel in his condition. He begged me to go out for the day and make sure his wife and son were in good hands. He said that assuming they were all right, he'd check into Downstate on Friday."

"And you believed he wasn't contemplating withdrawal on his own?"

"Of course I believed that. He was taking over two thousand milligrams of barbiturates a day. Every medical man knows how dangerous barbiturate withdrawal can be."

The detective, his expression unreadable, said, "Who'd you see in St. Louis?" His tongue went probing into his cheeks as he waited for Ben's reply.

"My sister-in-law. The baby. And a Dr. Ernest Hess. Head of the prematurity nursery."

"Give me that name again," the detective said, and wrote it down. Then, "I understood you to say earlier that you kept a very close watch over your brother," he mused as he ceased writing. "That you never left him alone for more than a few hours at a stretch. How come you didn't get back here until close to midnight?"

Ben began telling him about how he had missed

the four-thirty flight and as he spoke, he let his voice quiver with self-reproach. "If I'd been on time. Oh, God. If I'd been on time. If I hadn't missed the plane, he might still have been alive."

His display of emotion seemed to affect the detective. He said considerately, "No. I don't think so. Did you examine the body?"

He shook his head.

"He seems to have been dead for quite a few hours."

Ben slumped down onto the couch cushions and grew silent, his face deeply pained.

His years of keeping his thoughts to himself served him well. The detective, having to fill the gap in their interview, offered, "I saw your brother's room. All that stuff on the floor. I guess he wasn't exactly in his right mind."

Ben began to feel more secure. But, he said, "Please," in a quiet, hurt voice. "Please. My brother was a very renowned physician. A credit to the profession."

The detective shrugged. "I'm sorry." Then he asked briskly, "What about the deceased's wife? Does she know of the death yet?"

He shook his head again. "I haven't called her yet. I couldn't bring myself to do it. She and Sidney were very much in love."

"Why'd they separate then?"

"He needed constant care. Constant supervision. It was too much to ask of any woman. Of anyone."

"You did it," the detective observed.

"That was different. He was my brother. No, more than a brother. More like a father." To his surprise, Ben almost felt like crying. "He taught me everything I knew." He supposed the thought of all he had learned from Sidney had somehow authentically saddened him. But how wonderful! Pulling a handkerchief from his pocket, he blew his nose loudly, while the detective looked away, embarrassed.

"Someone better notify the wife," the detective muttered.

"Yes, of course," Ben said, putting away his handkerchief. "My girlfriend will. I've asked her to come over." They were both relieved when just then the telephone began ringing. "You want to get that?" the detective asked. Ben stood up slowly, his shoulders stooped. "I guess I should." As he walked out of the living room he saw one of the uniformed policemen summon the detective into the kitchen. He tried not to think about the tool closet.

He took the call in his bedroom. It was his answering service. The brusque night operator said, "A Mrs. Emily Harper is trying to reach you. Says she's started having labor pains. I told her I wasn't sure you were back in town yet." Copying down the number the operator proffered, he kept listening to hear whether there were sounds of cupboards being opened and closed in the kitchen.

But he could hear nothing. Impatient, he dialed Emily.

The husband answered, "Dr. Zauber? How good of you to call right back. My wife's begun having pains. We've been timing them."

"How close are they?"

"They're coming every nine or ten minutes."

"Regularly?"

"Yes. For the past hour."

"Okay," Ben grunted. "Take her over to the hopsital." He started to hang up but the husband begged, "Hold on a moment. She wants to talk to you."

He held on, but the wait seemed interminable and he began to feel more and more uneasy. He didn't like leaving the detective out of his sight for so long. As soon as Emily got on the phone, he shot out, "Go over to the hospital. I'll join you there as soon as I can. I can't talk to you now." And then he started anxiously back toward the living room.

Before he was halfway down the corridor, the detective reappeared. "Who'd you call?" he asked, his tongue popping into his cheek.

"One of my patients. She's in labor." Did he have to ask the detective's permission to leave? Was he under suspicion? He couldn't tell.

"You going to deliver the baby? You up to it?"

He heard the detective with joy. Certainly if he'd been more distrustful of him, he would have detained him longer. "I think it might help," he said hesitantly. "Take my mind off things."

"Yeah. I suppose you could use that." The detective drew his notebook from his pocket once again. "Well, go ahead. We might ask you to come down to the homicide zone office tomorrow. After we see the ME's report. And after we've spoken to . . ." he flipped pages with his broad fingers, " . . . the deceased's wife, Dr. Alithorn, Dr. Hess. Once we've looked into things. But it looks pretty routine to me. Unless there's anything you've left out."

"Nothing. Nothing important."

"Yeah, well if there's anything else we need to ask you, we'll be in touch." The detective snapped his notebook shut and put it away. "By the way, your girlfriend's here. I've been talking to her."

"Where?" Ben peered toward the front hall door and then looked abruptly away. Two men were carrying Sidney's draped body from the bathroom.

"In the kitchen," the detective murmured. "She's been here awhile. Hope you didn't mind my not telling you sooner."

Ben made an uncomplaining gesture with his hand.

"Nice woman," the detective went on. "I was chatting with her while you were on the phone. Says you were supposed to get married except she couldn't take the way you were always spending so much time looking after your brother."

Ben bit his lip. "She was jealous, I guess."

The detective said, "They're always jealous about something. If it isn't your family, it's your work." He shrugged and asked, "You want to go see her?"

When Ben hurried into the kitchen, Naomi raced toward him. Her dark eyes were full of pain for him and she held him tightly, her arms binding him like hoops. How long would he have to go on seeing her before he could break up with her again? Not until Claudia too had been questioned about his devotion to Sidney. Not until Alithorn had described Sidney's irrational behavior in his office, and the doctor in St. Louis had reported Ben's concerned avuncular interview with him. Not until the ME had filed his report and the police had checked the St. Louis flights. But eventually, after a while, he would find some excuse to quarrel with her. Kissing her upturned face, he buried his lips in her raucous curls. No matter. Claudia would be in mourning for quite some time, her idealization of Sidney rekindled now that he was dead. It would be a while before she would be emotionally available, and even then, it would be a while before he could be sure that he was the type of man who could interest her. Though he had the imagination. He could see that clearly. And a prodigious, an imperial intellect.

"Aren't you keeping that baby waiting?" the detective was asking. He was watching Ben caress Naomi with a glint of vicarious enjoyment in his blue eyes.

"Right," Ben said, and drew his body away from hers. She was crying. "Poor Ben. Poor Sidney. Oh, what a fucking waste."

His feeling of success was overwhelming. He forced himself to stay stooped, to maintain his usual hesitant slouch as he left the room. But once he was on the way to the hospital he straightened up, his long legs striding free.

Emily had been shaved, given an enema, and put to bed in a tiny private labor room. A white-haired delivery nurse slathered her belly with a plastic gel and hooked her up to the fetal-heart monitor and the resident on duty, a young black woman, examined her. Later, Philip read aloud to her a crumpled copy of the *Daily News* he had found on her night table. But after a while, Emily couldn't concentrate.

She asked Philip to stop reading and in between contractions she held his hand and watched the contractions and the baby's heartbeat translated into wriggly hills and small, bumpy plains on the monitor. When the contractions came, she ceased caring about the machine, and pulled her hand out of Philip's, her fingernails digging into her palms. Then as soon as the immediate stress was over, she reported that the contractions had been more interesting than painful, and went back to holding Philip's hand and studying the geography of her ordeal.

It was Philip who began to look blanched.

Twice he called her "Champ," and repeated the old saw about how if men had to give birth, there would be an end to babies.

"It's nothing," Emily assured him, "nothing at all," and resolved that for Philip's sake she would leave her hand in his when the next contraction came. But she couldn't do it. The bite of her nails into the soft flesh of her palms somehow alleviated the sensation of being pulled and pushed apart deep inside herself, in a place she had never before known existed.

"I wish Zauber would get here," Philip complained.

"He will. He'll be here soon."

She loved Philip utterly at that moment, loved the worried pallor of his face, and the way he stroked her hand with his thumb whenever he was clasping her, as if trying to add to mere comforting pressure a hint of remembered sensuality. He was stroking her that way when she felt a great spurting of fluid between her legs, a sensation she had feared would dismay and embarrass her, but which instead made her feel deliciously free and exultant. On the fetal-heart monitor she saw right afterward a tall, jagged peak and she felt she was somewhere else, somewhere high in hot, wondrous mountains that sparkled with lakes and pools and rushing waterfalls. She closed her eyes and dozed for a few minutes.

When she awakened, Zauber was there. He was standing at the foot of the bed, conferring with

Philip, the resident and the nurse. He was all in white. Starched.

He looked like a god, she thought. Like a savior. Like the way Cortez must have looked to the Indians. And everyone in the room, except herself who was distant and dreamy and uninvolved, was watching him deferentially as he studied her chart and the tracings of the monitor. When he had finished his perusal of her records, the resident and the delivery nurse left the room discreetly and Zauber came to the head of the bed. "How are you doing?" he asked.

"Fine," she tried to smile. But there was another contraction on its way. She turned away from him, concentrating on the breathing exercises she had learned in her childbirth classes. When the contractions came, their urgency shattered her usual concern with sociability and propriety. And indeed she quite enjoyed the way they freed her of obligation and restraint. She was alone with her baby. They were in the mountains. They were climbing. She was out of breath. She was panting.

"She seems to be having quite a bit of pain," she heard Philip say to Zauber as she slid slowly down the slope she had been climbing.

"Well, what did you expect?" Zauber sounded so white and wintry that Emily half-sat to stare at him.

"Lie back down," he admonished her. "I'm going to examine you. Check up on that resident."

Philip laughed ingratiatingly and she wondered what had struck him as funny.

"Can you hold off for just a second?" she asked. "I feel—I think there's another—" Zauber didn't wait for her to finish her sentence. He was at the foot of the bed, forcing her thighs apart, so that when the contraction came she felt unable to ascend. She thrashed her legs, unable to climb free.

"Can't you stay still?" Zauber commented. His voice was icy.

"It hurts," she said, panting.

She saw him look up and give her an annoyed, even contemptuous glance, but then once again the baby began to push at her. Too soon. She hadn't rested yet. Zauber was probing inside her. "Wait. Wait," she cried out loud to the baby.

Zauber said, "I haven't got all night."

Philip had returned to the chair and was sitting on the edge of it, shaking his head. "The pain is really something," he said. "All the preparation doesn't really prepare you."

Zauber said, "Maybe you ought to go out for a while." He looked down at Emily's chart and spoke without lifting his eyes. "You know, maybe it would be better if you weren't here. I think she's playing up to you."

She heard him with anger. "You promised Philip could stay the whole time!"

"Give the poor man a rest," Zauber sighed. "Let him get a cup of coffee." It had begun to snow all around him and she couldn't quite make out his features. "Now be quiet and let me finish up." He pushed her legs apart again.

His fingers felt frigid. She shivered and saw him through the snow. Perhaps she could melt him a little. Melt him and make him warmer toward her. Perhaps he was still worried about that woman she had heard him talking about the day she had first noticed his cold streak.

She wanted to ask him but suddenly another contraction distracted her. She started to perspire, exuding moisture from every pore in her body. The baby was tearing at her. It was marching. Parading through her. Trampling her flesh. It was her enemy. In its quest for life, it would stop at nothing. It would rend her asunder.

She shrieked. The sound thrilled her. She was still alive. She had thought the creature in her belly had killed her but no, the sound that hurtled from her throat reassured her that she was unhurt. She began to relax, her palms opening onto the bedsheets.

"If you can't control yourself, Mrs. Harper, I'll have to send your husband away," Zauber said. "It isn't fair for him to have to listen to you carrying on like this."

"He doesn't mind," Emily said as soon as she could speak.

"I don't mind," Philip echoed loyally. He reached for a piece of gauze and began wiping her forehead. But then Zauber whispered something to him.

"If you think so," Philip answered. His voice betrayed relief.

"I really do. Go ahead. You take a break." Zauber clapped Philip around the shoulders and Philip stood and eagerly left the room.

Emily began to shiver again.

"Mrs. Harper," Zauber said, sitting down in the chair Philip had vacated. "I have a theory about birth. About labor that is."

For a moment he reminded her of his old self. He seemed to want to explore cultural phenomena with her, as he sometimes used to do in his office. She remembered how flattered she had always felt when he chatted with her. But she wasn't in the mood for intellectual conversation now. It was the wrong time. The wrong place.

"Excuse me," she murmured. "I can't concentrate." Her teeth were chattering and already her stomach was starting to cramp.

"My theory is that all pain can be suffered in silence if the sufferer wills it," he said, ignoring her plea.

She shook her head. She didn't agree. She had liked the primitive reassuring screams that had begun to issue from her throat. But she couldn't explain her point of view. She had to start panting again.

"I'm convinced of it." He crossed his legs and sat back. "I've become a great believer in willpower."

She wished he would stop speaking. His words

were squalling through her ears and his eyes were shiny and hard as icicles. She couldn't bear the way they pierced. But she couldn't say words at the moment. All she could do was groan. The baby was beating against her spine. She arched, her back surging with pain. It was splintering, she thought. Her spine was breaking into a thousand shreds and shards. "Oh God," she yelled. "Oh God. Oh help me."

Zauber was watching her, his features composed. "Mrs. Harper, I'm disappointed in you."

She shivered and pulled the blanket up around her neck.

"Actually all the literature indicates that much of the pain of childbirth—the expression of pain, that is, the screaming and shouting and carrying on that are so distracting for the people who have to work with women in labor—is mere hysteria. It's culturally determined. Not all women scream and carry on. Eskimo women don't do it much. Whereas Puerto Rican women are notorious for making unnecessary noise. Studies have shown—"

"Please," she managed at last. "Please don't talk to me now. I'm in pain. I didn't know it was going to hurt like this."

He closed his lips. They looked white, frosted over. "Who are you to ask for pleasure without pain?" he said, his lips barely parting.

What happened next was something that she was never able to make Philip believe. She felt, slowly at first and then with an increasing urgency, another contraction coming on, and she opened her mouth to scream, and her mouth was a vast wide open tunnel and there was another tunnel at the bottom of her and she was sure that if she could just get them to connect she could make the baby crawl out through the top of her. She tried to scream wider and then she felt a door lock across her mouth and a hand, his hand, clamp down across it, and she kicked and flailed and thrashed her legs and he said, "See? See what I mean? You don't *need* to make noise."

She lay back, limp, her eyes terrified. He was smiling at her, but his smile was twisted, askew. She began to whimper and he said, "I was trying to help you. To teach you something."

Her heart began to beat so wildly she thought it too was trying to burst out from within her. Zauber shrugged, looking at her with disdain. "You weren't listening to me, were you?" He stood and said coldly, "I'll call your husband back in."

She tried to tell Philip what had just occurred. She was drenched in sweat and her teeth were chattering. "Zauber's crazy," she said. "There's something wrong with him." But Philip was wiping her forehead and saying, "I think you're getting a little hysterical, Champ. Do you think you ought to ask for some Demerol?"

"No. It's bad for the baby. And I'm *not* hysterical. I'm perfectly rational." But it was difficult to convince Philip of her rationality when now, in each minute, she had only a few seconds of composure. The contractions were coming without any but the most minimal separations, and each time one enthralled her she could do nothing but groan and cry out, her thoughts scattering like seeds. Still, whenever the pain subsided even for a second, she tried again to tell Philip that there was something different about Zauber, something peculiarly arbitrary and detached about him, and that she wanted someone else to deliver their child. But she couldn't get Philip to understand.

She screamed, "He's crazy. Fucking crazy," but then she was shrieking, "Oh God, make this stop. Kill me. Kill the baby. I can't bear this. I'll go crazy." She knew it was no wonder that Philip didn't listen to her about Zauber. He was too alarmed by her shrieks whenever the contractions came. He called the delivery nurse and Emily heard him say, "I think she's delirious."

The nurse held a moist cloth to Emily's lips. "She's okay. She'll be ready to push soon. I've heard a lot worse than her." She winked at Philip. "Some of them even ask God to kill their husbands." Straightening up, she added, "But if you want, I'll ask Dr. Zauber to come have another look and see if he advises an injection."

Emily shrieked, "No. No," and the nurse said, "She doesn't want anything." She patted Emily's arm encouragingly. "Well, you're almost there, honey. A few more big ones and you'll be ready to push." She glanced at the monitor, her forehead wrinkling. "Just a little while longer."

"You sure you don't want any Demerol?" Philip asked again.

But Emily was in the midst of another contraction and she couldn't reply. And then the nurse was bending over and tearing back the sheet and listening to her belly with a curved stethoscope and staring at the fetal heart monitor and yelling something and there was a great scurrying and commotion in the tiny room and the resident was back and barking instructions to two white-jacketed men who were trying to lift Emily onto a gurney, rolling her sideways while at the same time someone else was digging an IV needle into her arm, and the resident was shouting, "Get Dr. Zauber. We've lost the heartbeat" and someone was clamping an oxygen mask over Emily's mouth just as she tried to ask, "What is it? What's happened. Tell *me*." And then they were wheeling her down the corridor to the delivery room and Philip was running alongside her saying, "Can you understand me? Can you hear me, darling? The baby's heartbeat stopped during the last few contractions. It's alive, but they've got to get it out fast."

"Not Zauber, not Zauber," she wanted to scream, but the mask was over her mouth.

She slept. She was up in the mountains again. Someone was calling her name. She awakened to its sound and saw Dr. Zauber holding a fat white snake in his hands. No. It was her baby. Her baby was part serpent. She began sobbing.

Zauber was gazing with curiosity at the snake that was her baby. It writhed, and he held it without moving, regarding its twisting head as if hypnotized.

"Dr. Zauber?" A nurse, capped and masked, thrust herself forward from behind Zauber. The snake hissed, gasped.

Zauber was motionless, abstracted. "Hadn't you better cut it?" the nurse whispered. Zauber raised his eyes to stare at her.

"You'd best do it now."

Zauber said, "Quiet! Sssh!" his voice a hiss like the sound coming from the snake.

Suddenly the nurse reached past him. In her fingers something steely flashed. Then at last Zauber began to move. "You're in my light, Nurse!" he snapped, and began wrestling with the wriggling creature in his hands.

Emily held her breath, listening for the sibilant sound, but it had stopped. The room was silent. She groaned and Zauber cut the snake that was wrapped around her baby. She slept again.

"It's dead," Zauber was saying. "It choked. Couldn't be helped." She was in a bed with white curtains all around it and Zauber was standing at the foot of the bed. He was shrugging. "You'll have another, I'm sure." And then he was gone.

* * *

Much later that night Philip was holding her in his arms. "Is our baby dead?" she asked.

He nodded. His lashes were glistening.

"What was it?"

"A boy."

She turned toward the curtains opposite him. "Zauber killed him."

"No. The cord was wrapped twice around his neck. He was born dead."

"He was alive. Zauber didn't cut the cord fast enough."

"No. He told me he cut it as quickly as he could."

"He didn't. He was distracted. Detached. Like when he was in the labor room with me."

"No. No, darling. You're just terribly upset right now."

"He said terrible things to me."

"You said terrible things." Philip tried to smile through tears. "I never knew you knew half the words you said, Champ."

"I hate Zauber."

"It wasn't his fault. These things happen."

"He wanted it to happen."

"Oh, Emily! Oh, darling!" Philip let go of her and pressed the buzzer for the nurse. Emily slipped down onto the mattress. A moment later she heard Philip whispering, "I think she needs a sedative."

"I don't. I'm all right."

"You're still confused. They doped you up."

The nurse stuck a needle in her arm and Philip sat down beside her again.

"If you don't believe what I'm telling you, I'll never be able to love you again."

"I believe you. Sssh. I believe you." Philip began patting her hand as if she were a child and the nurse tiptoed away.

Behind her eyes, Emily felt a smooth, creeping numbness. "There was a nurse there, I think."

"She's just gone away."

"In the delivery room, I mean."

"Of course. There were two."

"Talk to the nurse."

"I will. Sssh, darling. I will."

"You've got to believe me."

"I do. But sleep now. Sssh. Sleep." Philip's hand began to move up and down her arm. "Sleep. We'll have other children. Lots of them." He stroked her rhythmically. "We'll make love. We'll start another baby as soon as the doctor says it's okay. But for now, sleep. Oh, my darling, try to rest. Sssh. I believe you."

He didn't believe her. She let her eyes shut, trying not to blame him. He couldn't help it. But still her heart hardened against him. She would never ask him for anything again, she thought wildly. Never trust him. Not him or anyone.

She fell asleep thinking that she would never love or make love again.

AN OCCULT NOVEL OF UNSURPASSED TERROR

EFFIGIES

BY William K. Wells

Holland County was an oasis of peace and beauty . . .
   until beautiful Nicole Bannister got a horrible package that triggered a nightmare,
   until little Leslie Bannister's invisible playmate vanished and Elvida took her place,
   until Estelle Dixon's Ouija board spelled out the message: I AM COMING—SOON.

A menacing pall settled over the gracious houses and rank decay took hold of the lush woodlands. Hell had come to Holland County —to stay.

A Dell Book $2.95   (12245-7)

Dell Bestsellers